REPAIRING THE WRECKAGE

RUTHLESS & ROYAL
BOOK 2

AUTUMN JONES LAKE

COPYRIGHT

REPAIRING
THE
WRECKAGE

Ruthless & Royal Book #2
Copyright 2024 Autumn Jones Lake
All Rights Reserved
Cover Design: Shanoff Designs
Cover Photo: Wander Aguiar Photography
Cover Models: Connor R. And Morgan
Proof Reading: Julie Barney
Digital ISBN #: 978-1-961848-10-8
Model Paperback ISBN #: 978-1-961848-11-5
Alternative Paperback ISBN #: 978-1-961848-12-2
Alternative Hardcover ISBN #: 978-1-961848-13-9

DEDICATION

All the scars on my heart came from those who swore they loved me.

CHAPTER ONE

Molly

MY RAGE-FUELED ESCAPE-MY-LIFE PLAN FIZZLES AT THE Empire International Airport.

Thwarted by ticket prices.

What was I thinking? Airlines don't offer "broken heart" discounts.

A last-minute ticket for the places I'd want to go would drain almost everything I've managed to save in my bank account.

Defeated, I turn away from the ticket counter and shuffle toward a low, white bench by the floor-to-ceiling window looking out over the parking garage. Fatigue drags my butt down to the bench where I sit with my back to the window. I rest my elbows on my thighs and drop my head into my hands. Every nerve from my shoulders to my fingertips throbs, triggering a cascade of misery to rain over me.

The sound of shattering glass echoes in my mind.

I destroyed the car Griff gave me. The car we lovingly restored together.

No, no, no.

Every time I think I've pushed "the big bad thing" that made me take a bat to the car out of my head, images of Griff and Kiki in bed together replay.

The only man I thought I'd ever love betrayed me for all the world to see.

Running away won't solve this pain.

1

Forget my lack of escape funds, I have a job, and my internship this summer. Remy went out of his way to secure the internship for me. It's important for the career I want to have one day.

Why should I give up my future just because Griff decided to stick his dick where it didn't belong?

"You all right, miss?" a rough but kind voice says from above me.

I tip my head up. Awareness that twin hot, wet trails are running down my cheeks chases a response out of my mouth. Embarrassed, I quickly wipe the tears away.

"Huh?" I mumble stupidly, staring at the airport security guard standing a respectful distance away.

"You, um, look upset." Alert dark brown eyes bore into mine. "Do you need help?"

Help getting over my boyfriend. But I don't think this stranger can help me with that need. "No, no. I'm fine." I force a quick, fake smile. "Thank you."

He's young. Probably not much older than my brother. And apparently persistent. "Are you waiting for someone?" he asks.

Do I look suspicious or something?

"Not really." *Way to give a vague answer, genius. He's going to call for backup any second.*

"Here." He reaches into his pocket and pulls out a flat green-and-white card. "You look like you could use a hot chocolate. Starbucks is on the second floor." He tips his head toward the escalators.

Empire International is only "International" in name. The airport's small—I can see the green-and-white Starbucks awning from where I'm sitting. But I nod and reach for the card. "Thanks."

He studies me as I take the card from his hand. Our fingers briefly touch. His eyebrows pinch together.

Crackers. What if he's not worried I'm a safety risk? What if he watches *Supreme Underground Fighter*? What if he saw the episode last night and feels sorry for me because I'm a pathetic loser whose boyfriend couldn't wait to cheat on her?

I gotta get away from him before he asks more questions.

I stand and hike my small backpack over my shoulder.

"You have any luggage?" he asks. Okay, maybe he's still trying to decide if I'm a teenage terrorist and hasn't seen the show.

I hate this!

"Just one bag." I shrug, inching my backpack forward.

"Traveling light. Smart." One corner of his mouth curls up. He's cute. The short sleeves of his uniform shirt are stretched to their limits by his muscular arms. He's tall, towering over me without looming. Not as tall as Griff, though.

Good grief, am I going to compare every man I meet to Griff for the rest of my life?

"Thanks again." I wave the gift card through the air and turn toward the escalator.

Being at the airport but unable to fly anywhere seems masochistic. But I haven't decided where else to go. The Uber I took from Johnsonville cost more than I make at Miller's Farms in a week of afternoon shifts. Remy's going to go nuclear when he sees the charge on his credit card. *I'll pay him back.*

Upstairs, I step off the escalator and walk into the small cafe. The line's short. I've barely settled on my order when I'm motioned toward the register by a tired-looking cashier. "Iced blonde cherry mocha and a blueberry scone." I choke out the last word. I'll never be able to eat another muffin again without thinking of Griff, so scones it is from now on.

The cashier tilts her head and frowns at me. I force my second fake smile of the morning and hand over the gift card. "I'm not sure how much is on it."

She nods and takes the card. There's enough for my order and maybe another coffee later. I stuff the card in my pocket and pull out a crinkled dollar bill for the tip jar.

A few minutes later someone calls my name. I collect my order at the counter and turn around. Every seat in the tiny cafe is jammed full of travelers with their carry-on bags. To keep the green mist of jealousy at bay, I head downstairs and reclaim my bench by the window.

I don't want to go home. Obviously, I can't stay *here* forever, though. Not every security guard will be as friendly as gift card guy. I bite into my scone. Crumbs tumble down my chin, landing on my chest. I brush them off my sweatshirt and take a sip of my iced coffee.

The fake, cherry-chocolate sweetness floods my mouth and I almost gag. Why couldn't I order plain iced coffee like a normal person?

"Feeling better?"

This time I smile up at the security guard. I lift my drink. "Much. Thank you, again."

"No problem." He pats his pocket. "I'm one of the Airport Angels. We keep a stash of cards to hand out to weary-looking travelers."

"Wow. That's, uh, really nice of you."

He shrugs.

Unsure of what else to say, I sip my coffee again. This time, the unusual flavor isn't as shocking to my tongue.

"You need me to call anyone for you?" he asks.

"No." I pull my cell phone out of my sweatshirt pocket and check the battery life. Not wanting to deal with any "where are you" texts from Remy, I put it in airplane mode when the Uber dropped me off. Still have forty-five percent. Did I even grab my charger when I left the house?

"All good." No idea who I'll call when I finally decide what to do but I don't want to impose on this stranger any longer.

"My name's Nathan. If you need anything." He glances over his shoulder toward the ticket counter where a customer's raising his voice at the person in line behind him.

"Thanks, Nathan." I don't feel like giving him my name and he doesn't ask.

He wanders toward the grumpy travelers, stopping to speak into a radio clipped to his shoulder.

That's enough fun at the airport. It's time to figure out my next move before I get into trouble for loitering.

I'm not ready to throw myself into the unknown, yet. As much as I hate it, the pain in my heart can't be soothed by running away.

CHAPTER TWO
Griff

A CLOUD OF VANILLA MIST SURROUNDS ME. *MOLLY.* I breathe deeper and move closer to her warm body.

But she's not there.

I hug a cold pillow to my chest. The bitter scent of cheap detergent fills my nose—not vanilla.

Confused and groggy, I bolt upright.

Shadowy darkness surrounds me. The barest hint of the rising sun peeks around the heavy gray drapes. High in the corner of the room, the steady red, blinking light reminds me I'm being observed like a science project.

"Fuck," I groan. Still stuck in this fucking mansion having my every move filmed for the dumb reality show I signed up for.

I fall back against my pillows and stare at the ceiling. This isn't the first time I've had a dream about Molly, only to be shocked into the cold reality that I'm locked in this golden prison.

Embarrassed, I flick my gaze to the camera again. Pointed right at me. The soulless red light blinks, almost as if it's mocking my misery.

I hope to fuck I haven't been talking in my sleep. I turn my head and glance at the photo on my nightstand, touch my finger to the glass over Molly's face.

Miss you, Muffin.

God, I hope I win this thing and get home to my girl. Make up for all the time we're missing together.

Someone bangs on my bedroom door.

For fuck's sake. *What now?* We're not supposed to be downstairs until ten a.m.

"Stonewall!" *Bang, bang, bang.*

"What?" I shout.

"Office. Phone call."

Phone call? From who? What office?

I hurry out of bed and open the door. "A phone call for me? Who?"

Deadass—my fellow contestant and a certifiable dumbass—stares at me with a dopey expression and shrugs. "Cops? I didn't ask questions. Jordan asked me to come get you and here I am."

"All right. Give me a minute."

I should slam the door in his face but my mind's going over all the possibilities. Did something happen to Molly? Remy? We're not allowed any phone calls. Why'd they allow this one?

Stone-cold fear grips me.

It has to be my mother. Why else would the police be involved?

Dread settles in my stomach. The last time we spoke, I was an asshole to her. It's not like we've ever had normal mother-son conversations, though.

Five minutes later, one of the producers I recognize—Jordan—meets me.

"Follow me, Griff." His pinched, squinty expression seems extra annoyed this morning.

"What's going on?" I ask.

"Johnsonville Sheriff's Department needs to speak to you."

Home. Last I knew my mom was down in New Jersey. Maybe it's not about her. "What happened?"

"They wouldn't tell us. Need to speak to you." He stops in front of a shiny, dark wood door I've probably passed a dozen times but never bothered to open and see what's inside. "We can't monitor the call, but same rules apply. You can't discuss the show or—"

"Give me a fuckin' break. You think my local sheriff's office gives a fuck about the filming of some random reality show they've never heard of?"

An extra wrinkle forms on his forehead and he shifts his gaze. I'm too worried about what might be wrong at home to give a fuck about interpreting his expression.

He presses his palm to a flat square above the doorknob and the door clicks. "Yeah, well, I'm obligated to remind you about the rules any time there's outside contact."

"Bro, I'm worried my mom might be dead. Giving the secrets of the show away are the last fucking thing on my mind."

His eyes widen and he backs away. "Uh, shoot. Sorry. Yeah. Take your time." He pushes the door wider and lifts his chin. Inside the room, black filing cabinets line one wall. A simple, dark brown wooden desk with a leather chair sits to my left. The desk is empty except for an old, black corded phone.

"Line one," Jordan says. "When you're done just hang up and leave. Door will lock behind you. I'll be down in the editing room if you need me."

I give him a blank look. I have no idea where that is. I stick to a few main areas of the house. Haven't bothered exploring anywhere but the gym, common area, kitchen, my room, and wherever they tell us to show up to film.

"It's right off the poolside gym downstairs," he explains.

Ahh, the area where Deadass, Naptime, and the other tool bags hang out. No wonder I've never been there.

"All right." I stare at him until he finally walks past me, his slim figure receding down the long, white hallway. A flicker of caution keeps me rooted in place. I don't trust him not to double back and listen in on my conversation.

When I'm sure I'm alone, I hurry into the office and close the door behind me.

I snap the receiver off the phone and hit the blinking red button. "Hello?"

"Griff! That you? Thank God."

"Jerry?" I frown. My boss at the garage? Why'd he tell the show he was a cop? "What's wrong? Are you okay?" Shit, is he calling to fire me? He said he was fine with me taking the time off of work. Did that change?

"I'm fine. But I got a problem here at the garage," Jerry says. "I called Remy and he's on his way over, but the cops are here and need to talk to you."

Shit. "What's going on?"

"Give me a second, would ya?" Jerry shouts to someone.

Anxiety spikes my blood. "Jerry, what's wrong?"

The background noise eases and in a quieter voice, Jerry says, "The car you and Molly were restoring. It's wrecked, Griff. One of the other guys opened the shop today, saw the mess, and thought we had a break-in. They called the sheriff. I woulda called you first and not involved law—"

Wait. Someone wrecked Molly's car? "What are you talking about?"

"The damage is bad but fixable," Jerry explains. "Cops wanna get a statement from you and ask if you want to press charges—"

"Let me talk to him," Remy growls in the background.

Muffled voices go back and forth. "Stall them for me?" Remy asks.

A few seconds later, Remy's voice bursts over the line.

"You motherfucker," he seethes. "What did I tell you?"

"Remy?" Why is he mad at *me* because someone wrecked Molly's car? If Jerry won't let me repair the car at the garage, I'll do it at Remy's place. "I'll fix the car when I get home. It's not a big deal."

"What did I tell you when you said you wanted to date my sister?" he yells.

Remy's apparently lost his mind, so I play along. "Uh, don't get her pregnant?"

"Don't *hurt* her. I said don't fucking hurt her. You promised."

Does he think I somehow wrecked the car? "Remy, I'm not even there—"

"I'm aware. We're all aware of where you are."

"I'll fix the car—"

"I don't give a fuck about the fucking car."

Now he's starting to piss me off. "What the fuck's going on? Is Molly okay? I'm sorry the car got wrecked, but goddamn, I'm doing this stupid show *for* Molly."

He laughs. A cold, hollow sound that expresses exactly how

pissed he is. But why? Over a car? Some stupid kids probably vandalized it.

"Doing *what* for her?" Remy asks in a low, deadly calm voice. "Fucking skanks on television? Because I gotta say, she wasn't real impressed."

Numbness crawls through my insides. "What're you talking about?"

"Last night's episode, Griff."

Fuck. I lean sideways and peer at the closed office door. Could Jordan or someone else be out there listening? Jordan said they couldn't listen in on a call with law enforcement, but I don't exactly trust him. I need to be careful. I can't get cut off before I figure out what the fuck is going on.

I answer in a voice barely above a whisper. "The show hasn't even started airing yet."

He pauses and when he finally speaks, seems almost calmer. "Griff, the show's been airing for a month. We've been watching it every week."

"Shit, really?" No wonder the few minutes a week I'm allowed to talk to Molly have seemed so strained. The calls are monitored. Before we're allowed to speak, someone reminds her not to ask about or discuss the show. The one time I came close to the topic of my workouts, they cut our call short.

"Yeah, really," Remy continues. "The whole world knows you fucked Kiki. Including Molly."

He could've said I fucked a narwhal in the Arctic and I'd be less shocked. "*Kiki?* What the fuck? Why would you think that?"

"Are you seriously gonna play stupid?" he asks like he's speaking to a lowlife trying to weasel out of a bet at The Castle.

"Remy, I don't know what you're talking about. I didn't fuck anyone. Did someone on the show say I did?" It wouldn't surprise me one bit if Deadass and his crew use their confessional time to spread gossip.

Kiki said some stupid shit that seemed scripted, and she's followed me around the house. I assumed the show was putting her up to it for the drama factor. The cheesy host of the show, Matt, refers to me as the "bad boy with a good girl back home" or something stupid like that. Woolly warned me the show was probably trying to tempt me into cheating on my girl since it would be great for ratings.

"Said?" He sighs into the phone. "Griff, they *showed* the two of you in bed."

His words make no sense. "That's not possible. It never happened."

We're both silent for a few minutes and a sense of impending doom or time running out rushes over me. "Remy, tell me what happened. Please? I don't know how much time I have before someone cuts me off." Jordan said they wouldn't listen in while I was talking to the sheriff. But if they overhear me talking to my girlfriend's brother, it'll be game over.

He blows out a long, frustrated breath. "You haven't seen *any* of the episodes?"

"No. We never see the footage. They're filming 24/7. Like I said, I didn't know it started airing. I thought it still had to be edited and would run in the fall. The set's locked down tight. We're not allowed to watch *any* television. Can't read current magazines, go online, nothing." Venom jokes about our restrictions being worse than a jury sequestered for a high-profile murder trial.

"All right," Remy snaps. "From episode one, they've framed you as the bad-boy fighter with the good girl back home."

"Okay, that I knew. Matt's said it a few times."

"Right. Well, on the first episode, they showed a lot of clips of Molly and made a *huge* issue about her age and how she hasn't even graduated from high school yet—which I did *not* appreciate by the way."

I snort a humorless laugh. "Are you sure that wasn't more of a dig at me, than her?"

"Yeah, I'm sure," Remy growls. "It made shit awkward as fuck for her the last week of school. She didn't want to do a damn thing for graduation."

"I'm sorry." *Fuck this.* Remy's taking too long to get to the point. I need to hear Molly's voice and know she's okay. "Is she there? Can I talk to her? Is she upset about the car? Tell her it's not a big deal, I'll fix it for her as soon as I get home."

"I don't give a fuck about the car, Griff!" Remy explodes. "Shut the fuck up and listen."

Remy used to blow up like this all the time when we were kids. These days he's usually more in control. The ball of dread in my stomach tightens. "Where's Molly?"

"She's not here. You'll understand why in a minute."

"Go on."

"With the other girls, Kiki's always talking about *you* or that other dumbass, Naptime."

I groan. "He's such a tool. I didn't know she was going after him too."

"So you know she's into you?" Remy shouts.

I shrug, even though he can't see the gesture. "I assumed it's just for the show."

"Yeah, well she can't stop yapping about how *hot* you guys are. How much she wants to fuck you. Maybe both of you at the same time. Says nasty shit about *you* having a little girl back home and how you need a *real* woman."

I roll my eyes to the ceiling. *Fuck me.* "Seriously? She said something like that to me the night I met her. I told her I wasn't interested. They didn't show me turning her down?"

He scoffs. "The whole she's not my prison, she's my peace thing? Yeah, they got a lot of mileage out of that quote."

"I meant it, you dick."

"They've been flashing Molly all over the beginning of every episode. That release they forced her into signing apparently gave them permission to show her face and say whatever the fuck they want about her in every episode."

The dread I was feeling shifts into simmering anger. "What are they saying?"

"It doesn't matter anymore."

"No, tell me what they're saying." *So I can go fucking kill someone right now.*

"It's more like implying that she's dumb and that's why you're with someone so young. Or that she's slutty. Honestly the stuff that's said online about her is worse. But the show definitely provides the ammunition."

"Online?"

"Yeah, bonehead. I tried to fucking warn you this show was a bad idea. I was worried about *you*. I had no idea how much all this exposure would harm Molly."

Goddamn it. I should've forced Diane to delete that fucking release she tricked Molly into signing. This was my choice, not hers.

"I'll see what I can do about that. Get to the part about Kiki."

He snorts. "I doubt you'll be able to do sweet fuck-all about anything. The damage is done, Griff."

"Remy, so far you haven't told me shit. Why do you think I slept with Kiki?"

"I saw it. We all saw it."

I wince at his harsh tone. "Who's all?"

"Uh, all of Molly's friends. They've been coming over to watch the show with her. Eraser and Ella were here too. Vapor's been boycotting the show on principal."

Sounds like Vapor. My mouth quirks to the side. I miss that moody bastard. "Jesus. Eraser's going to give me shit when I get home, isn't he?"

"Eraser might kill you when you get home. If I don't get my hands on you first."

"Remy, what the fuck?"

"Griff," he says slowly, "you're not hearing me. The footage from the bedrooms is black-and-white. Grainy, shitty quality."

"Good to know."

"It's black-and-white in the living quarters but clearer outside the rooms. There was a clear shot of Kiki at your bedroom door and you with your hands all over her."

"The fuck there was!" I blink and run my fingers through my hair. "Wait, yeah, she got shit-faced after one of the nights out. But I walked her to *her* room. I never went inside. And she's never been in my room that I know of."

He's silent again. Thinking over my words? Plotting to kill me? I can't tell.

"*Shiiit,*" he groans, dragging out the word. "I get it, bro. You're in a weird situation. Locked up. Isolated from people you know.

14

You're probably uncomfortable as fuck. And she keeps throwing herself at you..."

Remy knows me well. Except for the whole falling into bed with a stranger just because I'm having trouble coping with my new environment.

"Just tell me the truth," he pleads.

"I am telling you the truth!" Shit, I can't have Jordan or someone else overhear me. I lower my voice. "I'm not *you*—I don't need to fuck every skank who strokes my ego. I can't believe after all these years you think I'd fucking lie to you. Especially about this."

"The way it was edited...It sounded like you. Then the voice-over..."

"What *exactly* did you see?"

"They showed *you* and Kiki stumbling to your door. Then it cut to a commercial break. All week long the show was advertising some 'big bad thing' happening in the romance department."

"Christ," I groan. "As soon as those girls showed up, I knew this was fucked. No one ever told us they were adding the weird dating angle. I thought it was all about the fighting and training."

"I hate to break it to you, but the fights are nothing but fluff. The focus is the drama in the house. A little bit about the rivalry between the two groups the fighters have split into. Otherwise, there's very little about the fighting or training—except for a lot of shirtless beefcake shots."

"Well, *that* I expected."

"It's more like a reality soap opera with some fighting for background noise."

"Really?" On my end, it's hard to tell because we're constantly filming. If the film crew isn't around, the hidden cameras capture every moment. Every time I leave my room, I have to make sure my mic pack is strapped on, and some assistant stops me to check the sound. "Okay, so then what happened?"

A twist in my gut warns that whatever else Remy has to say will alter my life in an extremely bad way.

"When they came back after the commercial break, there were two people in a bedroom."

At least he said "a" bedroom and not "your" bedroom. Small distinction but I'm grasping at straws here. "And?"

"It was a guy and girl, *in bed together*. Clearly fucking."

"Bullshit!" I explode out of the chair and pace as far as the ancient, corded phone allows. "It wasn't me."

"Well, the implication was that it was *you*. Moans, groans, and nails digging into your back. It was dark, grainy, hidden-camera footage but two people fucking."

My heart stops.

Just fucking stops.

Molly saw *that*. She saw "me" in bed with another woman on television. Watched it with her friends. And her brother.

My sweet, shy girl who needed months to be comfortable enough to get that intimate with *me*, thinks I betrayed her in the most humiliating way possible.

I did my research after Diane first approached me. Watched a few shows this company produced. I figured they'd use tricks to manipulate the footage—but I thought they'd rig the *fights,* not fuck with relationships outside of the show.

I guess I should've done better research.

"Where's Molly now?" Defeat colors my question.

Remy sighs. "Gone."

"What do you mean, gone?"

"Let me finish. After the hidden-camera fucking, they cut to a clip of Kiki bragging about how happy she is and how much she wants this to last beyond the show. Griff, it really looked like—"

"I think I'm starting to understand what they made it look like," I groan.

"I don't think you do," he snaps in his shut-the-fuck-up tone. "After Kiki, they interviewed *you*."

"Me? Saying what?"

"How you were mad at yourself for not trying harder and you didn't know how you were going to explain it to Molly."

I'm too stunned to speak. What the fuck did they do? Put words in my mouth? Fake shit?

Then it hits me.

The fight with Hammer Fists that didn't seem to have a clear winner.

"What'd I look like in that interview?"

"Sweaty."

"'Cause I just went a few rounds with Hammer Fists."

"That big fucker? So what? You're faster than him. And you don't lose fights."

"I've never gone up against a fighter like him. Yeah, he's slow but he's fucking strong. He could've cleaned my clock if they'd let us finish the fight."

"What do you mean, you didn't finish the fight?"

"Have they shown me going up against him yet?"

"Not yet."

"Well, that's what I was upset about in the interview. There didn't seem to be a clear winner. I was worried I might get sent home and I didn't know how the fuck I'd explain that to Molly. I came here, spent all this time away from her, and then lost right away. I was fucking embarrassed, not feeling guilty about cheating on Molly."

Remy curses and there's a crash in the background.

"They really didn't show that fight?" I ask.

"Not yet. Just that guy Bear Trap and that annoying sleepy dude."

No wonder I haven't been sent home. They're fixing the show in several different ways. "Christ, this is more rigged than I thought."

"Shit, Griff." Remy sighs. "I'm sorry."

An apology from Remy—don't hear those often. "I'm the one who's sorry. I never should've done this. I thought it was a quick, easy way to get some serious cash, but I should've known better." If my life has taught me anything it's that there's no shortcut to success. Only lots of hard work, pain, blood, and sweat. I close my eyes and grit my teeth.

Just once I wanted to get ahead.

"Griff, you've been hustling and working hard your whole damn life. We know plenty of fighters who've made careers out of similar situations. It wasn't a *bad* idea." Oh, sure, *now* Remy's full of pep talks. "We should've prepared better. I shouldn't have let Molly watch the show. She just wanted to support you."

Of course she did. "Molly knows I love her and I'd never cheat on her." As the words pour out of my mouth, I realize they might not be true. I had a reputation before her. We hadn't been together as a couple long before I took off. She's so damn young. Inexperienced. Unsure of herself and how much she means to me.

If these fucking producers edited the footage a certain way...yeah, the longer we're apart, the more I can see her doubting everything.

"She was rattled," Remy says.

"Where is she now?" I ask again.

"I don't know. I talked to her before she went to bed but when Jerry called me this morning, I realized she was gone."

"Are you fucking kidding me?" I could fucking murder Remy right now. "You're busting my balls when you should be out looking for her?"

"Don't you dare fucking yell at me. What was I supposed to do?"

"Turn off the television and tell her I'd never cheat on her. Be my fucking friend. Act like her big brother. I don't fucking know. Anything but let her go off thinking I betrayed her, you fucking asshole! She's been out all night, and you don't know where she is?"

"She's eighteen! What the fuck am I supposed to do, put a bell around her neck? She snuck out. I thought she was asleep."

"You should've told me that first."

"Why? What the fuck can you do about it? I can't even call you like a normal person. Thank fuck Jerry's guys called the damn cops, or I'd still be trying to figure out a way to reach you."

Cops. Molly's car. "Remy, what else happened? Tell me the truth."

"Well, Griff," he says, dragging out my name like he's talking to an annoying child, "it's obvious where she went after she left the house."

My throat tightens. If I had any tears, I'd probably let them loose right now. "She's the one who destroyed the car," I rasp.

"Took your trusty old bat to it," he confirms.

"Fuck," I breathe out. Unimaginable sadness hits, so heavy it pulls down on me until I fall into the chair behind the desk.

Molly loved the car.

Every moment—from the sweet look of surprise on her face when I gave it to her for her birthday to the night we finished bolting on the mirrors and made plans to take it to the drive-in flash in my mind.

The Molly I know has too much respect for things to destroy them. One time she traded paint with some guy at Zips when she was racing my car and was in tears when she showed me the simple scratches. No big deal. Happens all the time. Yet, she kept apologizing and trying to pay me for the damage for months after I fixed it.

Praying he's wrong, I ask, "You're sure it was her?"

"Who else would do it?" He sighs. "After she went Carrie Underwood on the car, I have no idea where she went."

Molly is missing. But the girl I knew is also gone.

Being on this show has changed *me* in ways I don't like.

And now it's changed her too.

CHAPTER THREE

Molly

"MOLLY!"

I squeeze my eyes shut and curse under my breath. How'd he find me already?

Remy's boots thud-squeak over the highly polished white tile floor as he hurries toward me. I set my coffee on the bench next to my leg. As I stand to greet him, Remy's in my space, wrapping his arms around me.

"What the hell are you doing here?" he shouts, loud enough to draw the attention of several people nearby.

I struggle to breathe under his crushing hold. "How'd you find me?"

"Miss, is everything all right?" Nathan asks.

Remy turns and scowls at the security guard. "This doesn't concern you."

"I'm not asking *you*. I'm asking *her*," Nathan says in a low, warning tone.

I wriggle out of Remy's embrace and tug on his hand, hoping he'll sit on the bench next to me instead of launching the punch he's so clearly dying to land on Nathan's face.

"I'm fine, Nathan. Thank you," I say quickly. "This is my brother."

Nathan's gaze slides between Remy and me. Remy finally seems to chill, his posture relaxing. He squeezes my shoulder and drops down on the bench next to me, blowing out a relieved breath.

"Thanks for looking out for her," Remy says to Nathan in a tone that actually resembles gratitude.

Nathan gives us one more assessing look then walks away, heading toward the escalator.

"Making friends already?" Remy asks but there's no teasing in his question.

"I think he was worried I was carrying a bomb or something."

Remy snorts. "More like he was working up the courage to ask for your number."

I tug on my ratty ponytail. "I doubt that. How'd you find me?"

"The text alert from my credit card for the Uber." He hands over his phone and I stare at the screen with a map of the airport and a little blinking red dot. "And *find my phone*. We're on the same account, remember?"

Damn. I usually just tell Remy where I'm going, I never thought about him using the app to track me down. Or that he'd do it so quickly.

He slides his warm hand over mine and gently asks, "What are you doing here, Molly?"

Tears sting my eyes again. A lump in my throat keeps all my jumbled thoughts inside. I open my mouth once, close it, then try again. "I wanted to start over some place new. Where no one knows me."

Instead of laughing at my poorly thought-out plan, Remy sucks in a breath.

"You were going to leave me without a word?" Sadness roughens his voice and tugs on my heart. He genuinely seems upset at the thought of losing me. "Not even a goodbye?"

Shame burns my cheeks. "I'm sorry." This time I can't stop my tears. Remy pulls me into his arms, shielding me from the curious stares of people walking past us.

"Molly, you're going to be okay." Remy rubs a soothing hand over my back. "I know it hurts but it's not the end of the world. I promise."

He has no idea how much I hurt. My shoulders ache so bad I

can't even wrap my arms around him to return the hug. "I know," I sob.

"You're tough. You're a fighter just like me. When life tries to knock a Holt down, we get right back up and keep swinging."

I wince at his choice of words. I came out swinging all right—a baseball bat right into the car Griff gave me and spent so much time and money restoring.

Ugh. Why do I feel so bad about the car? It's the least of what I should've done after being humiliated like that. But I can't tell Remy what I did. He'll be disappointed in me. Or send me to a psych ward for an extended vacation.

"Where were you going, anyway?" he asks.

"I can't afford to go anywhere." I let out a sad laugh and pull away. "That's why I'm sitting here on a bench instead of on a plane right now."

Remy frowns at the reminder that he could've arrived too late.

"I don't want to go home," I admit. "Everything will remind me of him."

The enormity of everything I've lost rolls over me. No more hanging out at Zips racing cars on the weekend. That's the first place Griff and I said "I love you" to each other. So many places hold memories of him. Even my own damn house.

"I'll take a few days off. We can't go anywhere too exotic," Remy says. "Jersey Shore for a few days?"

"Ugh, I don't want to run into Griff's mom."

"It's a big shore, Molly." He sighs. "We could go up to Maine," he says with more enthusiasm. "You loved the beaches there when you were little."

That brings on a wave of fond, Griff-free memories. Holding my mother's hand as we waded into the water. Jumping waves with Remy. Happier times.

Money's tight and taking multiple days away from the bar isn't easy for my brother. I appreciate his offer to indulge my little tantrum more than I can express. "It's okay." I squeeze his fingers. "I have to face it sometime, right?"

"We can go to Lake George," he suggests. He lifts his eyebrows and uses a coaxing tone I haven't heard since I was eight. "Six Flags for the day. Ride the Steamin' Demon until you barf Twix bars all over me."

"One time!" I squeal, socking him in the stomach. "Who fed me all the Twix bars?"

Relief softens his tense expression, and he chuckles. "I paid for it."

"I felt really bad that I did that to you."

"I know you did." He pats my leg. "Let's go. Nosy Nathan's about to make another stop here."

"Cut it out. He was nice to me." I turn slightly and pick up my iced coffee. "He gave me a gift card for Starbucks."

Remy rolls his eyes. "Of course he did."

"You do realize some guys can be nice without ulterior motives, right?"

"Haven't met one yet."

"So you stopped to help Mrs. Hollister fix her flat tire because you wanted to get in her pants?"

He chuckles. "That's different." His gaze narrows in Nathan's direction. "Actually, I'm glad he was keeping an eye on you. Never know what kind of creeps are trolling the airports looking for lonely runaways to exploit."

"Jesus, you're dark."

"The world is dark, Molly." He stands and holds out his hand to me. "I worry about you all the time. Can't protect you if I don't know where the hell you are. Scared the shit out of me when I saw your bed was empty and Griff's car was gone."

I drop my gaze to my sneakers to hide the guilty expression creeping over my face. Remy knows I took an Uber here but hasn't asked me what I did with Griff's car that I'd been driving since Griff left for the show. Does he already know I parked and left it right next to the garage where I destroyed *my* car? Shoot, leaving it at the scene of the crime was probably a dumb idea. Everyone knows I'd been driving Griff's car for the last few weeks.

"Well, I'm fine," I mumble.

"Still don't need guys trying to pick you up right now—"

His abrupt stop prickles against me. What else was he about to say? "Wait. Do you think I'm so desperate and heartbroken that I'll

24

jump on the first guy who pays attention to me? To get even with Griff or something?"

Guilt crawls over his expression. "Not exactly."

"Sheesh." I press my fingertips to his chest and push, not that he goes anywhere.

"Your first real breakup." He shrugs. "And everything being so..."

"Public?" I finish for him. "Look, just because you like to swoop in and bang girls on the rebound, doesn't mean every girl responds to a breakup that way." *No, some of us take a baseball bat to a perfectly beautiful, innocent car.*

He frowns and plows his fingers through his hair. "I'm not even sure what to say to that."

"Aww, Remington Holt—speechless. Don't see that every day."

"Don't get used to it." He slings his arm around my shoulders. "Let's get out of here. We can talk more on the road."

I cast another longing glance at the ticket counter. Someday. Right now, I need to focus my energy on bettering myself. I'll leave town on my terms—when I go to college in the fall.

CHAPTER FOUR

Griff

"GRIFF, WHADDYA WANT ME TO DO, HERE, SON?" JERRY asks.

"Huh?" Remy must've handed the phone back to Jerry when I wasn't paying attention. "Is Remy still there?"

"No, he got some sort of alert and said he had to go. Took off like a bat outta hell."

I hope that means he knows where Molly is and she's okay.

"I can't put Sheriff Davenport off any longer," Jerry says in a low voice. "He's doin' me a favor lettin' me and Remy talk to ya first. You gotta talk to him."

"Yeah, I'm ready."

"All right. Here's Sheriff Davenport."

I don't recognize the name but that doesn't mean I haven't had a run-in with him at some point. He asks a bunch of questions. Doesn't seem too impressed I'm filming a reality show—can't blame him.

Finally, our conversation comes down to one thing.

"It seems to me everyone knows who damaged your car, Mr. Royal, including you." He pauses, probably waiting to see if I'll fill the silence. "If you want to file an insurance claim, you're going to need to press charges."

"Sir, I'm not planning to bother the insurance company with this. And I'm not pressing charges against anyone." I don't bother correcting him—that the car's actually Molly's. She doesn't need the hassle. "I'm sorry your time was wasted with this today."

"It's my job." There's a slapping noise on his end. "No damage to the garage or anything else. Seems like the vandals exercised a lot of restraint. Someone got a grudge against you, Mr. Royal?"

"Probably. But like I said, I'm on a locked set, four hours from home, so there isn't much I can do about it right now."

"Uh-huh. When will you be home?"

"I don't know, yet."

He releases an annoyed sound and I add, "I'm not trying to be evasive. I really don't know. I could get sent home tomorrow or be here until the end of the summer."

"Fine," he grunts in surrender. "If you change your mind, you have my number."

"Thanks."

There's a rustling and a few seconds later, Jerry returns on the line.

"Look, Griff, don't worry about anything. I got your car stored here. It's safe. Your buddy said he'd take care of the other one. It's all good. Keep your head in the game, all right?" He hesitates. "Don't get suckered by any distractions."

Great, Jerry must think I slept with Kiki too. Fan-fucking-tastic. "Thanks, Jerry. I'm sorry for all the extra trouble."

"Not a problem." He coughs. "Be smart, kid."

"I'm tryin'."

We hang up and I sit staring at the phone.

Rage, slow but hot, builds in my veins. A cloud of anger pushes all rational thoughts out of my mind.

Dread tightens my stomach into a knot.

What the fuck am I going to do?

Irrational rage wins.

I launch myself out of the chair and storm out of the office, not bothering to make sure the door closes behind me. *Fuck it.* I hope everyone in the house discovers the secret room and calls home. Then they can all find out how we're being fucked over.

The show's already airing. How is that even possible? Is that why I haven't seen Diane since the first week? Is she out there somewhere trolling for new suckers to embarrass and destroy their lives?

If Kiki really hooked up with someone, wouldn't we have heard about it? Deadass, Naptime, Pirate, none of them would be able to keep their damn mouths shut.

So who was in the video?

It wasn't me. That's all that matters.

Snorting like a bull, I storm through the maze of hallways and pound down the stairs in search of the editing room Jordan mentioned earlier.

I spot him in the hallway outside the gym.

My feet thunder over the tile floor as I charge him.

"We need to talk." I grab his sleeve, spin him around, and throw him against the nearest wall. He jerks away and I pin him with a hand to his chest.

"Help!" Jordan shouts. "Help!"

Imagine working on a show with a bunch of street fighters and being afraid of your own shadow.

"Quit whining." I jerk him forward by his shirt collar, slam him into the wall again, then release him. I lean close. "How can you look me in the eye after the bullshit lies you've been broadcasting?" I whisper in his ear. "And don't you dare try to deny it."

His eyes widen.

That's right motherfucker—I know.

"You can't tell the others," he warns.

A sneer turns the corners of my mouth, but the wide-eyed look of fear on Jordan's face stops me from saying anything else.

Control. Get control of yourself. Breathe. You're smarter than this.

I don't know what I'm dealing with. There were a lot of contracts and documents I signed for the show. Hope, the lawyer I spoke to, tried to warn me most—if not all—of the contracts wouldn't be in my favor. Who am I kidding—everyone in my *life* tried to warn me that coming here was a bad idea. I went ahead and signed my life away anyway.

No one could've predicted this level of fuckery, though.

All I wanted to do was make Molly's life better. Instead, I made it worse. Forget the car. I hate that I made her last few weeks of school miserable because all her friends and classmates were watching the show.

And she never said a word in our brief phone calls. She couldn't. But I should've been able to tell something was wrong.

That I might have lost her for good, doesn't enter my mind. Molly *knows* me. Once I'm able to see her and talk to her, she'll understand it was all fake.

Everything will be fine.

"I'm serious," Jordan warns in a low voice. "Don't." He flicks his gaze to the ceiling. "Or at least be careful where."

His cryptic warning isn't hard to untangle. There are cameras recording us everywhere in this damn house.

While I had him on the phone, I should've asked Remy if they show footage from the bathrooms.

I'm losing my mind.

"I won't," I promise. Jordan's not the one I'm mad at. He's trying to earn a paycheck like everyone else. "Sorry."

Racing footsteps squeak over the polished hallway floor behind me. I hold my hands in the air and take a few steps back. I glare at Jordan who's shaking and looking anywhere but at my face. "Get me someone in charge to talk to—right fucking now."

"What's going on?" Venom says from behind me.

I turn and find his big frame blocking two of the camera guys and a production assistant from getting too close. It's a small gesture but after the conversation I just had with Remy, gratitude floods my system. At least not everyone's trying to stab me in the back. I nod my thanks to Venom, but Jordan's warning still echoes in my ear.

"Nothing. I just need to talk to someone."

There's still a chance I can salvage this situation. Turn it around to somehow work in my favor. Repair my relationship with Molly. Or maybe I'm fucking delusional, and I've already lost everything.

I still have to try.

Our standoff in the hallway lasts for a few minutes. Enough time for Jordan to pull out his cell phone and frantically tap out a text. A few seconds later, he places a call.

I back away, giving him the illusion of privacy.

"What's going on?" Venom murmurs close to my ear.

"I can't talk about it." I meet his eyes, hoping he'll understand that if I could tell him, I would.

He nods slowly. "You better not be leaving."

No words come to me. It would take too long to explain. I shake my head.

"All right," Jordan snaps. "Paul's going to meet us."

I can't remember which one of the many producers, production assistants, directors or whatever-the-fucks who have been wandering around the set Paul might be, but the tight set of Jordan's mouth says he's not happy about the visit.

Good, must be a suit with some juice.

"Let's go." Jordan tilts his head toward the hallway. To everyone else he says, "Go back to whatever you were doing."

I nod at Venom. He frowns and backs away slowly. I wish I could warn him. Would the producers really stoop so low and fuck with his marriage?

No time to worry about Venom. I can't help anyone if I don't handle my own business first.

I follow Jordan to the other side of the house where there are fewer cameras and lights stationed in every corner. An area the contestants aren't supposed to visit.

Apprehension thrums through my veins. This could be the end. The hard work and sacrifices I've made over the last few weeks could mean nothing if I get sent home.

Maybe that wouldn't be the worst thing.

Jordan stops at a door and knocks, then pushes the door open.

I vaguely recognize the guy behind the desk. A bland and unremarkable face to go with his potato-shaped build. Even his short, curly hair is the color of a russet potato's skin. His tan suit doesn't help, either. Arrogance surrounds him like a cloud of Axe body spray.

To the potato's right, the show's host, Matt, is awkwardly crammed in behind the desk. Potato didn't even move over to make room for the star of the show. He *must* be important.

We usually only see Matt when someone's getting kicked off the show. Even though there are no extra cameras in the office filming this showdown, it doesn't mean I'm safe from getting sent home.

"Where's Diane?" I ask, resting my hands on the back of the chair in front of the desk.

Potato's lips tilt in an evil villain way I don't care for. "We had a difference of opinion on the direction of the show." He flicks his hand toward the closed door. "She's off scouting new talent for another project. That's really her area of expertise. Not this."

Maybe Diane didn't set me up after all. Or she doesn't give a fuck.

Potato stands and stretches his hand across the desk. "Paul Simplot." He rattles off a long title that doesn't mean a damn thing to me other than he's the one in charge. "I'm the one you want to speak to, anyway."

"And me," Matt adds in such a needy, pathetic tone, I cringe with secondhand embarrassment for the dude.

I lift an eyebrow at Paul. He subtly lifts his shoulders in a lets-humor-him gesture that doesn't put me at ease. We're not on the same side here.

"What's on your mind, Griffin?" Paul points at the chair across from him and takes his seat behind the desk again.

"I found out that the show's already airing. *And* it seems to have nothing to do with what's actually happening here." I stab my finger toward the floor. "It's causing havoc for the people I care about at home."

"How did you...Who let you..." Matt stutters.

Even though I threw Jordan up against a wall less than fifteen minutes ago, I'm less eager to throw him under the bus with his boss. "Don't worry about that. The point is, the show's airing lies and it needs to stop."

"This is unacceptable," Matt snips. "He should be sent home, now. He's violated the rules."

"Easy." Paul holds up a hand. "We send him home now, we lose a lot of viewers." He turns his cold, flat brown eyes on me. "And *you'll* lose out on a lot of money."

"No amount of money is worth having my reputation torn to shreds."

"Reputation?" Matt snorts. "How is fucking that young, hot Barbie look-alike going to ruin your reputation, stud?"

So, they know exactly why I'm here and why I'm pissed.

My hands curl into fists but I don't so much as flick my gaze in Matt's direction. I continue as if he hadn't even spoken.

"I don't give a fuck what contracts I signed. You can't keep me here against my will," I warn in calm, confident voice, even though I'm making shit up as I go. "As far as I'm concerned, you're breaking your end of the bargain by telling those lies."

Paul's lips twist with annoyance but my words seem to be hitting their target.

"If I have to walk my ass back to Johnsonville, I will," I add. "Feel free to sue me for my collection of vintage T-shirts."

Paul steeples his hands in front of his face and leans forward. "You think that's the worst we can do to you? I'll keep you tied up in litigation for the next decade. Garnish your wages for the next *twenty* years."

"I got two lawyers in my family ready to go, so do your worst." *Small lie.* The two lawyers I know are wives of officers in the Lost Kings Motorcycle Club. But I've been invited to family dinner night at their clubhouse. That's close enough, right?

Paul hesitates, as if he's actually worried about my toothless threats. "Name your demands. I assume you want to be the last one standing?"

"I don't want to win something that's rigged," I protest.

Paul rolls his eyes. "You must be the first."

I glare at him.

"Fine, what *do* you want?" he asks. "We need you to stay until you're sent home. You're in the unique position of holding some leverage here."

Leverage. Huh. Never had any of that in my life before.

"One—stop showing footage of my girlfriend. That's nonnegotiable."

Paul leans forward. "I'm entertaining your little tantrum because you've grown a pretty solid fan base, but don't push it."

"Trust me, when I'm having a tantrum, you'll know." I lean forward, so we're almost nose-to-nose over his desk. "Stop showing Molly's face. I don't give a fuck about the release Diane tricked her into signing. Molly is *not* part of this."

A slight smile—that should probably warn me something's not right—tilts the corners of Paul's mouth. "Fine." He sits back against his chair. "We don't need her anymore anyway."

Wasn't expecting him to agree so quickly. "Stop insinuating that I fucked Kiki. You know that's not what happened."

Paul shrugs and raises his hands toward the ceiling, proclaiming his false innocence. "Who can really say with all the footage we have to go through. Maybe we got mixed up."

Fuck, I want to punch this guy.

"That's it?" Paul lowers his hands to the desk and clasps them in front of him again. "You really aren't going to ask to win the show and all that money?"

"No." I frown. After all the interviews and psych tests I had to do, these guys didn't learn a damn thing about me. "I'm the best fuckin' fighter in this house. If I win, I want to win fairly."

"Sweet summer child," Mark mutters.

Paul smirks but doesn't say anything.

I tap my fist against the desk. "But all right, since we're talking about money—the show's paying to fix the car my girlfriend destroyed when she saw the last episode."

"Holly shit." Jordan whistles, startling me. How'd I forget him standing against the wall like a creepy statue? "Why didn't we think to get a camera crew up there when that aired? What a missed opportunity."

A sinking feeling settles in my stomach. I should've kept my mouth shut about the car.

Paul slowly turns toward Jordan and Jordan's eyes bug out from having his boss's full attention laser-focused on him. "That's a good question. Why *didn't* someone set that up?"

Jordan shrinks back, as if he's trying to become one with the wallpaper.

"I told you we should've taken our time with everything," Matt says to Paul. "But *nooo.* You wanted to rush the premiere."

"We had a slot to fill," Paul says without looking at Matt. "And we needed to try something new. Keep things fresh."

My head's going to explode if I have to sit here much longer. Why the fuck did I have to tell them about the damn car? Did I really think anyone connected to this show had human emotions and might feel bad for all the problems they caused? What a joke.

"Fine," Paul says. "We'll cover the repairs. Regardless of any winnings from the show." He slides his sneaky gaze Jordan's way. "But you'll have to sign another release not to sue for any damages."

"Whatever," I mutter.

How much more of my life am I going to sign away to these vultures?

CHAPTER FIVE

Molly

SPENDING THE DAY WITH REMY BOTH HEALS AND HURTS. Even before Griff and I became a couple, the three of us spent time together. It's hard to be with Remy and not think about Griff. The two of them have been inseparable since we were kids.

But Remy's patient and sweet to me all day. He doesn't bring up Griff and he doesn't razz me for my stupid plan that took me all the way to the airport.

It's not until the next day that Remy drops a bomb on me.

The scent of vanilla waffles tickles my nose. Part of me's a little insulted Remy's babying me. The other part really wants some waffles. I hurry downstairs and into the kitchen.

After breakfast, Remy pushes his plate away. "I need to talk to you about something."

"Okay." I glance at the clock. "I'm supposed to be at Miller's by noon. Then, after my shift, I was thinking about stopping by the bar to help you out."

I brace myself for him to say no.

"Yeah, I'd like you there." He rubs one hand over his chest. "I should start teaching you the ropes. You can help me decide what we're going to do with the place, eventually." He leans forward and pats my hand. "But I need to talk to you about something else."

The waffles I just inhaled do an unhappy tap dance in my stomach. "What?"

"Jerry called me yesterday."

I fidget at the name of Griff's boss. The owner of the garage where I left Griff's car—and smashed mine to bits.

"That's when I realized you were gone."

I swallow hard. "What'd he have to say?"

Pain ripples over Remy's expression, looking a little too close to pity for my taste. "What do *you* think he had to say?"

I lift one shoulder. "I dunno."

"One of the other mechanics noticed Griff's car parked oddly out by the garage. They saw broken glass. Investigated a little more. Found *your* car vandalized."

My lower lip trembles. "Really?" I squeak.

"Molly." He sighs. "Jerry saw the show."

I squeeze my eyes shut. Damn. Jerry must think I'm horrible. I'll never be able to look him in the eyes again.

"He figured you probably did it, but it was too late," Remy says gently. "The other guys called the cops to report a break-in."

My heart thuds. "What?" I glance up and meet Remy's intense, blue-eyed stare.

"They had to get ahold of Griff. That's why Jerry called *me*."

I shift my gaze away from Remy's face. "What'd Griff say?"

"He declined to press charges." Remy's voice falters. "I talked to him. Explained that we saw the show and what he did."

"What'd you do, congratulate him?"

"Molly." He lets out a louder sigh. "You know I didn't."

"Sorry," I mumble. Remy was ready to kill Griff the other night. I bet he vented some of that rage once he got Griff on the phone. "What'd Griff say?"

Remy hesitates, then shakes his head. "He says he didn't do it."

"What a load!" I jump out of my chair and point toward the living room. "We all saw it."

"Molly," he says in his irritatingly patient voice. "He didn't know the show was airing, yet."

"Yeah, so? That doesn't mean he's innocent."

He squeezes his eyes shut for a few seconds. "It sounds like what's happening on set, and what the show's been airing, are two different things."

I drop back into my chair. "That doesn't prove anything."

"I know."

"Did you tell him..." I lower my voice and glance away. "All the awful stuff the show said about me? And all the crap being posted about me online?"

"I did," Remy says. "He didn't know about any of it. I don't think they would've been able to show that footage if you hadn't signed the release."

Once again, Remy's giving me grief over something I did when I was caught off-guard and just wanted to support my boyfriend. "How was I supposed to know they'd use it that way! I thought I was helping Griff."

"I know that." The slower and more patiently Remy speaks, the angrier I'm getting. "And *he* knows that. I don't think there's a lot we can do about it now."

"Maybe we can tell the show I signed it under duress. Because I *did*."

"We can talk to a lawyer about pursuing that. But it's probably going to take a lot of money."

"That's not fair."

"Not many things in life are fair, Molly."

"Yeah, I should know that by now," I grumble. "Now that Griff knows what the show's doing, will he leave and come home?" I hate the pitiful note of hope coloring my voice. I don't want to see Griff or talk to him ever again.

Liar.

I don't want my brother to know how bad I want to see Griff.

Remy presses his lips tight and flashes his pity eyes at me. "I don't know if he can."

"All he has to do is lose a fight."

Remy shakes his head. "He says he already didn't do well in one of the fights and he was surprised they *didn't* send him home."

"But that's...that's crazy. The show's supposed to be a fighting com-pe-ti-tion." I sound out each syllable as if it will somehow make a difference.

"That's what he thought too." Remy glances toward the living room. "But obviously it's more than that."

"So, is Griff lying? Or is the show rigged?"

"I think it's clear by now, the show is fucked." He shrugs. "Except when you two were sneaking around behind my back, Griff's never lied to me."

I glare at Remy. How dare he throw that in my face now of all times. I should've known he'd end up taking Griff's side. "We didn't *sneak* around. Does it make you feel better now? You were right all along. We never should've been together. Happy?"

"I didn't say that, Molly." He glares at me. "No, I'm not happy about any of this."

"Let me get this straight." I stand and lean over the table. "With your own two eyes." I point two fingers at his eyes and then toward the television. "You saw your best friend in bed with another woman in black-and-white. And after *one* conversation with him, you're ready to take his side. You're trying to tell *me* maybe it's not what it seems. That I didn't see and hear him in bed with someone else. Do I have that right?"

Remy's not a fan of being spoken down to by anyone. He stands and leans over the table so we're almost nose-to-nose. "There are no sides, Molly. There's the truth. And there's whatever agenda the show is trying to push."

"Bullshit! We all saw it. If Griff really didn't do it, why hasn't he tried to call me and explain himself?"

"He can't let them know we talked about the show with anyone on the outside."

"He talked to *you*! For a long time, apparently."

He throws his head back and stares at the ceiling, pure frustration tightening his jaw. "I only got to talk to him because the cops reached him on set. The show couldn't listen in on the call with the cops, so as soon as I got there, Jerry gave me the phone."

"Oh." I blink and sit back down, pulling my chair closer to the table.

Remy takes his seat again, too. "We couldn't talk long. I let him know I had strong feelings about what he did."

I roll my eyes.

"I told him about the show and all the bullshit being said about you. How they kept showing you in the opening credits. The shit people are saying about you online. He had no idea."

Mortification heats me from head to toe. Remy told Griff how dumb and slutty the world thinks I am? I better get used to it. Those clips of me will live on into infinity. "Was he mad?"

"Of course. He's furious. He never wanted you brought into any of this."

"I only signed that dumb release form to help him."

"Your heart was in the right place."

"My heart is stupid," I grumble.

"The interest in you will die off eventually."

I don't believe that for a second. Especially if Griff stays on the show, or worse, *wins.* They'll ask him to come back for reunion shows, spin-offs, and who knows what else.

I would've been there to support him through all of it.

Now, I can't wait to leave for college and never come back to this awful town.

CHAPTER SIX

Molly

Now that I know Remy's spoken to Griff, I unblock his secret number and wait to see if any texts or calls come through. He'd at least send me a text, right?

G: Don't take it too hard. He was bound to find a real woman once he left home. Virgins are only fun for a little while. Luv, Kiki.

I blink and stare at my phone.

This can't be real.

Just as I was starting to believe everything Remy told me, I get this?

Someone at the show found Griff's phone.

Or he gave it to Kiki.

No. Griff wouldn't do that.

But he obviously told her I *was* a virgin. That he...that we... Embarrassment slides over me like hot lava. He'd share something so personal about me with a stranger?

It just doesn't seem like Griff. He's private. Doesn't like to talk about himself all that much. Did I not know him at all? Has being on the show changed him that much? Did he lie to Remy?

Me: Don't worry. He's all yours.

There. If that was the show's goal, they've got their wish. I never bought a ticket for this crazy train and now it's time to get off the ride.

I block the number again and shut off my phone. That's enough outside communication for me. I need to get ready for work anyway.

I CAN'T ESCAPE the stares and whispers when I clock in to work. Does everyone in town watch that stupid show? Stupid question. Of course they do. Our hometown hero is starring in it. *Puke.*

The front-end manager, Stacy, is waiting at the window with the till for my register. The eager-to-chit-chat smile stretched across her face turns my stomach. She chews a wad of gum with her mouth so wide, I can count the silver caps on her back teeth. Every few seconds she snaps it with a loud pop that sets me on edge.

"How's it going, Molly?" *Snap. Chomp. Pop.*

I can count on one hand the number of times she's asked me anything personal. I steel myself for more probing questions.

"Fine." I force a quick smile and grab my till.

"Isn't your boyfriend on that reality show?"

"Yup." I clutch the till tighter, the hard plastic biting into my stomach.

"Did he really sleep with that Kiki girl? Or is it a strategy—like, did they team up to win the show?"

I frown as my brain processes the questions. "What?"

She shrugs. "Those shows are crazy. People do stuff like that to win. Form an alliance. Then when everyone else has been eliminated," her eyes narrow with a strange sort of glee, "the bloodshed begins." She cackles.

"They're not in competition with each other." Was there a cash prize for the ring girls? Since the "romance" angle had been pushed so heavily, I never paid attention to what else the girls might win on the show.

"They're all fake anyway." She pops her gum again. "You can't trust anything you see on reality shows."

I can't tell if she's trying to cheer me up, but I actually take comfort in her words. "Thanks, Stacy."

She nods. "Register one's free. Ann went home early."

Ann's the crankiest cashier and she guards register one like a junkyard dog. It's the best register. The buttons don't stick, the scanner actually works, and best of all there's a big pillar with a bunch of fake plants hanging from it that I can hide behind. Today must be my lucky day.

God, my life is pathetic.

"Great. Thanks." I turn and hurry through the produce department, dodging a cart of big red, yellow, and purple heirloom tomatoes. *Ooo, those look good.* I should bring a few home tonight.

Don't think about Griff. Don't think about Griff.

It's going to be a long night. A long summer.

I need to work hard. Save my money. Toughen up. Then leave for college and never return.

CHAPTER SEVEN
Griff

THE GYM FEELS CHARGED WITH A MIX OF ANTICIPATION and frustration this morning. In the days after my showdown with the head producer, the atmosphere in the house seems to have shifted a lot.

Two new coaches were brought in to work with us. Instead of the loose, self-motivated, training schedule we had, we're now required to be downstairs by six a.m. and the rest of our day is just as structured. The crew wakes us by banging on our doors and setting off an earsplitting alarm throughout the house. It's like the producers want us moody, sleep-deprived, and pissed off before we meet downstairs to spar with each other.

It hasn't been a problem for me—at home I keep a tight gym schedule and work full-time. But for the guys in the house who stay up drinking and fucking around all night, it's been an issue. Their constant bitching and moaning get old fast.

This morning, Venom and I paired up to work on our grappling skills. We're both eager to test and improve our moves, not show off for the cameras.

Somehow, I block out all the noise around me and lose track of the lenses constantly encroaching on our space.

We start on the mat, each of us battling for control. I lunge forward. *Too soon.* The big bastard easily rolls me to my stomach. His arm locks tight around my neck.

"What's going on? You've been...off since the day you got into it with Jordan," Venom says in a low voice against my ear as if he doesn't have my head in a brutal choke hold. He wraps his other arm around my ribcage like a fucking python.

"Can't." I gotta focus on breaking loose before I pass out.

I squirm and wriggle, enough to get my knees under me. Christ, he's a heavy fucker. It's a risk, but I roll him and finally plant my heels, gaining enough leverage to break free.

"Fuck." I struggle to my knees, gulp some air and tackle him, wrapping my legs around his and pinning him to the mat. "Can't... talk...about...it."

I *want* to tell him what happened. Keeping all the betrayal, despair, and anger locked up is clouding my mind. I want to warn him in some way. But this could be a trap by the show to get me kicked off.

"Garden. Past the pool house. Safe zone." He breaks free with disturbing ease. I hit the mat with my shoulder and roll to my back.

"Time!" our new coach shouts. Underhill's a respectable former UFC fighter. A few years into retirement, he remains in top shape. I still haven't figured out if his appearance was always in the script or if something *I* did triggered his arrival. Does the show have enough connections to get someone like him as a coach at the last minute?

It doesn't matter. I need to survive, win, and go home. We *still* haven't been matched up according to size and weight. It doesn't bother me—mostly because I've avoided pairing up with Hammer Fists—but some of the smaller guys seem to be struggling. The more embarrassed they get, the more they run their mouths to prove how tough they are. The relentless trash talk seems to be pushing each of us to the edge. Snorting Bull is the worst. What he lacks in height, he's made up for in bulk. Dude looks like a slab of concrete. He could probably bench press *me*. But all the bulk makes him slow and his more flexible opponent, Rumbling Thunder, keeps getting the upper hand. Amusing to watch. Annoying to listen to.

"We all have things to work on," Venom says to Snorting Bull in his usual calm, zen-like tone. "No need to get belligerent."

The other guys cackle like hyenas. Snorting Bull stomps over the mat, squaring up to Venom, even though his head barely reaches Venom's neck.

Not wanting to inflame the situation with all the wisecracks I'm dying to let loose, I step back and swallow my jokes.

"Say it again, snake boy." Snorting Bull bumps his chest into Venom.

I flick my gaze to the ceiling and sigh. I'm starving and want to get lunch, not sit through another man-baby fit. But I need to show everyone that I have Venom's back. Not that he needs my assistance.

Woolly bumps my arm and plants himself right next to me. "It's embarrassing for a bunch of grown-ass men to behave this way."

"And predictable," I agree.

Even Underhill seems annoyed. He shakes his head and storms out of the gym.

The camera guys swoop closer, pushing most of us out of the way so they can circle Venom and Snorting Bull. How any of this looks "realistic" is beyond me.

"Over here." Jordan squeezes my shoulders and tries shifting me to the side.

"You touch me again, you're not gettin' those hands back," I warn the producer, stepping to where he's pointing.

Woolly snickers and moves next to me, shooting Jordan a challenging glare.

Jordan rolls his eyes and moves on to annoying the other contestants. He arranges Deadass and Naptime into a huddle, then the remaining guys into another clump, so we're all in "teams" watching the drama unfold between Venom and Bull.

Venom shifts his gaze to the cameras and then to me. The corners of his mouth turn down—like this is the last damn thing he wants to deal with. I shake my head slightly and cross my arms over my chest to let him know I'm sticking around and have his back.

That slight moment of distraction is all Bull needs. He charges into Venom, knocking him back a step.

The unprovoked attack seems to flip a switch in Venom. Up until now, I've only seen him calm and methodical—even in the cage.

Now, Venom narrows his dark eyes on Bull. "You need to settle the fuck down," he warns.

Bull postures and puffs up his chest. "The fuck you say, ya big monk?" His left hand flies up as if he's going to shove or slap Venom.

He's too slow, though. In a blur, Venom strikes, plucking Bull's hand out of the air. He grabs Bull's knuckles, then rotates his hand palm down, trapping Bull's wrist and bending.

Bull's knees hit the mat.

"Ow! Ow! Ow!" Bull screams as Venom applies what looks like light pressure but must hurt like a motherfucker.

"Don't fuckin' come at me like that again," Venom warns. He releases Bull, who cradles his arm to his chest and falls flat on his back.

"You still can't knock me out! Your wussy little hand holds are nothin'!" he screams from the floor. "No one knocks out The Bull!"

I step forward. "Dropping you to the floor wasn't enough punishment? You're begging for a KO, too?"

"Fuck off, Stonewall. No one asked you." Bull kicks out at me, missing my shin by a mile.

The other guys hoot and jump around. The camera guys zoom in on Bull's pained expression. I shake my head and back away.

"You couldn't go a little more?" Jordan asks Venom.

Venom snarls. "Would breaking his arm make good television?" He walks off before Jordan comes up with an answer.

Outside the gym, Woolly and I catch up to Venom.

"That was epic." Woolly thumps Venom on the back. "Been dying to shut that motherfucker up all day."

"What got into him?" I ask. "Seemed more agitated than usual all morning."

"Producers probably had a talk with him." Venom glares at one of the hallway cameras as we pass it.

"They'll keep pressuring us to get into these petty fights outside of the ring," Woolly says. "You did good, Venom. Chose the time and place."

Venom scowls. "I didn't really *choose* either one. I wasn't gonna let him hit me, though. I ended it the quickest way I could think of."

"You're going to need to show me that wrist lock." I bump my elbow into Venom's arm. "You moved so damn fast, I couldn't see how you rotated your hand to trap his wrist."

"It's a waterfall lock. I wouldn't try using it in the ring when you're both moving so fast. You can really hurt someone if you're not careful. But it can be good in certain situations."

"Like a bull comin' at you?" Woolly quips.

"Yeah, like that."

"Food's here!" someone shouts, the words echoing through the house.

"I wanna get there before Deadass touches my sushi." Woolly slaps my shoulder and jogs ahead of us. "I'll guard your grub!"

Venom stops a few feet from the turn that will lead to the kitchen and dining area. It's a dead zone where there don't seem to be any cameras. "Grab our food and meet me out back. Behind the pool house, there's a table. None of the camera guys are ever out there. Leave your mic inside."

"That where you go to meditate in the afternoons?" I ask.

"Yeah, so don't tell anyone about it."

"Okay." I glance down the hall. "You want me to bring Woolly?"

He stares in the same direction. "Not yet. You seem like you need to unburden yourself. The fewer people you have observing, the easier it'll be."

"Unburden?" I lift my eyebrows. "What makes you say that?"

He flicks his gaze to me and tilts his head.

"Yeah. All right."

I have to trust someone here eventually.

TWENTY MINUTES LATER, I slip out of the house, carrying a bag of food. Feeling like a criminal, I walk a wide circle around the pool, hoping to avoid the cameras. I clear a row of low hedges and dip into a garden area with trees and flowering bushes that provide privacy.

Seems like the perfect setup. Make us think we're safe from the microphones and cameras, then catch us talking strategy.

This place is turning me into a paranoid lunatic.

Venom's sitting cross-legged in the grass, head tilted toward the sky, eyes closed.

Not sure how the fighter will react to being startled, I clear my throat while I'm still out of striking range.

He slowly opens his eyes and lowers his chin. A faint smile ghosts his face. "Feels good to touch grass after being cooped up all morning."

"It does." I wiggle my toes in the thick, cool, green carpet.

He gracefully stands, then plops onto one of the picnic benches. I drop the bags of food on the table and start pulling items out of my bag.

If nothing else, the show feeds us well. We're able to ask for whatever we want and usually have it by the next mealtime. We still have to prepare it ourselves. No fancy chefs or anything like that. But I've been feeding myself since I was eight. Some of the other guys have never seen the inside of a kitchen and it shows.

I hand Venom a round container of salmon, quinoa, and sweet potatoes that he measured and prepared last night. It's cold but he doesn't seem to care.

"Thanks." He rips off the lid and grabs a fork.

I dig into my own container of spinach, chicken, and hard-boiled eggs.

"Kelly makes this for me all the time." Venom taps his fork against the pink fillet of fish. "She does it much better."

The mention of his wife brings a stab of unease to my chest. It must show on my face.

"We don't have long. Tell me what's going on?" Venom asks.

I take a deep breath. What's the worst that could happen? They kick me off the show for telling Venom? No, they could kick *both* of us off the show.

I lean across the table and lower my voice, forcing him to lean in too. "If I tell you, it could get us both sent home." I stare him dead in the eyes so he understands I'm serious. "Still want to know?"

His eyes narrow slightly. A flicker of concern creases his brow before he masks it with a casual chin lift. "Spill."

So, I tell him everything I learned from Remy, leaving out the part about Molly destroying her car.

He sits back, takes a sip of coconut water and stares at me. "How'd they let you talk to your friend?"

Fuck, now I *have* to explain about the car and the cops being called.

Slowly, I unravel the whole story.

"Fuuuck." Venom's jaw tightens and he stares at the table. "No wonder Kelly's been weird on all our calls. I thought she was just anxious because we're being recorded."

"She probably doesn't like you makin' friends with a lowlife who cheats on his girlfriend."

He grunts but doesn't agree or disagree. "Did Remy say if they showed anyone else in the house hooking up with the bunnies?"

"Honestly, I was too fucking pissed to ask."

"Don't blame you." He frowns and doesn't say anything for a few beats. "I knew this was probably bullshit. Especially after the girls showed up. But I thought that might be a side story, not the main event."

"Same."

"Don't take this the wrong way, but you're kinda fucked."

"Thanks. That hadn't occurred to me." I stab my fork into a piece of chicken and shove it in my mouth, chewing viciously.

"I mean, if you *do* get sent home after the next fight..."

I swallow and take a sip of water. "Everyone back home thinks I'm a cheater *and* a loser, I know."

He huffs a silent laugh. "Well, yeah. Who do you think was actually in the video?"

"I don't know."

"Gotta be Naptime or Deadass. They're roughly your size, although Deadass is covered in all those hideous tattoos."

"It doesn't matter."

His lips pinch tight, as if he wants to disagree. But he picks up his fork and finishes eating. I do the same. We can only be out here for so long before someone in the house notices our absence.

"We'll figure out something," Venom says as he stuffs his empty container in the bag.

"What's there to figure out? I'm just gonna keep grinding like I always do. Work hard. Keep my head down." I throw a few punches in the air. "Fuck shit up in the cage."

"They want the drama, though. You can't hide and expect to make it to the final four."

I glance toward the pool. "I can't get drunk, run around in my underwear, and piss in the pool like those other jackasses. I'd rather leave with no money, than leave without my dignity."

He rumbles with laughter. "Fair point."

"What about you? Gonna strap into a banana hammock and put on a show for us later?"

"Fuck no." He scowls. "Dropping Bull to the ground should be enough for a few days."

"Cameras sure got lots of footage," I agree, collecting my trash and stuffing it into one of the bags.

We walk into the house together. Loud voices and noise from the direction of the kitchen greet us.

"You good?" Venom asks. "I gotta run to my room for a minute."

"Yeah." A flicker of unease creeps over me. Is he going to find someone from the show and rat me out?

Too late now.

Gritting my teeth, I head to the kitchen. Woolly's perched on a stool at the long counter that separates the kitchen area from the rest of the open room. He rocks sideways and almost falls off when he sees me.

"Stonewall!" he shouts. "Where'd ya go?"

A prickle of guilt jabs at me. I should've told him to join us. "Just outside for a minute."

As one of the camera crew members turns in my direction, I quickly skirt by a bunch of guys and toss my bag in the overflowing can. The kitchen's trashed. Food and garbage scattered everywhere. *Fuckin' slobs.*

I grab a water from the fridge and take the stool next to Woolly. "What'd I miss?"

"Not much." He gestures toward Deadass. "That one whipped out his dick and tried to piss in Thunder's Mountain Dew bottle."

"For fuck's sake." I scrub my hands over my face. "That's fucking disgusting."

Woolly shrugs. "It's basically piss anyway. He wouldn't have noticed."

Naptime must've been listening in on our conversation. He grins and points at Deadass. "His dick's the only one skinny enough to fit in the top of a soda bottle."

"Wow." I widen my eyes and stare at him. "That's information no one needed."

Venom joins us, slapping both of our shoulders. "Underhill wants us in the living room. We're going to watch footage of our fights."

Thank you, Jesus. The way this conversation's headed, Deadass and Naptime are two seconds away from whipping out their dicks and slapping each other with them.

"Just in time." I slide off the stool.

"We gotta spend time getting to know our opponents," Venom encourages.

My gaze narrows on Deadass. I catch him anywhere near my food, I'm gonna kill him. "I already know everything I need to know about these clowns."

"Let's go!" the coach shouts, clapping his hands like a deranged drill sergeant.

I hustle the few feet over to the oddly arranged couches so I can get a seat that actually faces the screen.

The first footage shown is mine.

"Of fuckin' course," I grumble, sliding down in my seat.

I stare at the screen. Where'd they even get this from? It's an older fight. Maybe last year? It's not at The Castle—thank fuck. But it's fuckin' creepy that the show went to so much trouble to track it down. My opponent's some college kid on the wrestling team who thought his grappling skills were better than my boxing technique. Boy fucked around and found out I'm superior in *both*.

"Bro, what the fuck is that?" Woolly giggles, drums his feet on the floor like a little kid, and points at the screen.

Venom thumps his hand against my back. "I've been calling it the *Stonewall Slap*. Cracks me up every time you do it."

I wasn't aware I displayed *the slap* all that often. But apparently, I do it enough Venom's given it a name.

Our coach picks up the remote and rewinds the footage, narrowing his eyes on the screen.

Sure, let's watch it again. I squirm and sink lower into the couch.

Naptime laughs and points at the screen, then me. "You look like a tiger swiping his paw at his next meal."

"That's right." I sit up, raise my hand, and sweep it through the air, stopping an inch from Naptime's cheek.

"It wasn't a compliment." Naptime ducks away, falling into the chair next to me.

"It's a legit move," Venom says without taking his eyes off me. "But if you're within slapping distance, you could probably land a punch..." His voice trails off, not asking the obvious question.

I shrug. "I don't know." I slide my gaze toward the other guys, but Naptime and the coach have moved on to studying the rear naked chokehold I used to force the kid to tap out thirty seconds into the second round.

An uncomfortable sensation crawls over my skin. Having people intensely scrutinize my skills isn't my favorite thing. Especially since the other guys are going to use it against me or copy my style.

Shaking off the unease, I return to Venom's questioning face. "The slap—it's more like I do it out of frustration?" Shit, I've never admitted that to anyone before. A wicked smile curves my lips to hide what I just revealed. "Or it just pisses off my opponent and makes him do something stupid."

"See, I knew there was more to it." Venom snorts with laughter. "It *is* a bit humbling to be at that level and then get bitch-slapped. Also, unexpected."

"Exactly." He gets me.

"Yo, Venom, why you swinging from your boy's nuts? You got mad skills yourself," Deadass shouts.

"Now who's nut-swinging?" Pirate quips.

Venom rolls his eyes and shakes his head. "I'm too old for this horseshit," he mutters.

"Don't blame it on age," I protest with a teasing pat on his shoulder. "You don't hear me engaging in the petty trash talk."

"That's why I like *you*."

"Aw, you wanna be alone? Should we leave and give you two the couch?" Pirate pouts at us and tilts his head like a sad toddler who had his Cheerios taken away.

"Low-key homophobic 'jokes.'" Venom curls his fingers into sarcastic air quotes. "How original and clever."

I mash my lips together, but harsh chuckles spill out anyway.

"No judgment here. If you're gay just say so, Pirate," Thunder says in his low, serious rumble. "All those playground insults are starting to sound like projection."

Finally. I'm getting tired of being the only one to put these assholes in their place when they say stupid shit. I swear half these guys already have advanced brain damage, even though no one in the house is over thirty.

"Focus," Coach says. "Let's move on to Venom and Thunder's last match."

Venom's jaw tightens and he turns toward the screen. Guess he doesn't love being judged either.

CHAPTER EIGHT

Griff

I ALMOST LOST OUT ON A PHONE CALL THIS WEEK. THE producers pretended to bend to my demands when I confronted them. But now that I know the show is airing and Remy's been watching it, they won't let me talk to him. Molly won't answer calls from anyone. Knowing my girl, she probably blocked anything with a Long Island area code.

Finally, I get the producers to allow me to talk to Vapor and Juliet after they've been cleared. Thank fuck Vapor's been boycotting the show.

"Thanks for doing this, brother," I say, once I'm handed the phone and Jordan clears the tiny "confessional" booth. "Sorry if they asked a bunch of invasive shit."

"Not a problem. You all right?" Vapor's low voice is full of concern. He's always been almost too sensitive for all the shit the world's put him through.

"Questioning a lot of my life decisions lately, brother," I answer honestly.

"I bet you are." It's not said in a mean way. Just stating a fact.

"Workouts are gettin' harder." I hold my breath, waiting for someone to cut off our call. They killed one of my calls with Molly for saying a lot less. "Kinda reminded me of when Eraser and I took you to the gym at The Castle to teach *you* how to fight."

He chuckles, even though it's probably not a great memory. "Yeah? Who are you torturing in this story?"

"Honestly? I'm *you* in this tale. Been getting my ass kicked."

He laughs harder. Honest laughter that brings on a wave of longing for home—nights at Zips, racing cars, grilling good food, and bullshitting with each other.

"Christ," he laughs. "I never knew so many types of planks existed until you two sadistic bastards got your hands on me."

"You never backed down, though."

"Good thing, too." His voice lowers, turns harder. "Probably the only reason I survived that place."

That's a conversation killer.

"How's little man?" I ask, refusing to use Vapor's son's name when someone's probably listening in.

"Good. Butterfly's got him all signed up for nursery school." Obviously, he's decided to use his nickname for Juliet, so he doesn't expose her to any of the insanity Molly's had to deal with.

"Shit. Already?" Is Atlas even old enough for school? "You're making me feel old."

"It's only three days a week. Let him hang with other kids his age." In the background, there's a rustle and a whisper. "Hang on. Someone wants to talk to you."

I'm expecting Atlas to babble a happy greeting at me, but it's Juliet's soft voice that comes through the line.

"Hey, Champ. How you holding up?" she asks.

"Can't believe you're willing to talk to me."

She scoffs gently. "I know you, Griff."

At least someone does. I'm trying hard not to judge Remy. I wasn't there to see how everything went down, but it's still pissing me off that he was so quick to assume I did whatever the show says I did.

Can't think about that now. Focus on what's in front of me.

"How are things?" I ask.

"She's okay," Juliet says. "Everything's...well, as good as it can be."

"Thank you." For the first time since I spoke to Remy, I can actually take a breath.

We talk for a few more minutes. Nothing substantial. And

nothing juicy enough for the show because they cut me off before my time is up.

A heavy silence settles over me as I stare at the phone. I want to smash it into the wall—or someone's face.

The list of all the things I'm missing out on continues to grow. The time I'm losing keeps expanding.

I sigh and close my eyes for a few seconds. The ache of longing that's been following me for weeks returns. I can't throw a fight. As much as I want to go home, I can't lose a fight on purpose. Fuck the money. It's just not who I am.

So until someone defeats me or the producers lose interest, I'm staying in this mansion that feels more like a prison.

Molly

Something about old men celebrating a birthday by getting drunk in a bar seems rather sad. But at least it's business, something Remy says we desperately need these days, so I lock down my opinions and serve the drinks.

"Why aren't you wearing a skirt?" the man who's old enough to be my grandfather says to me with a leer at my jeans-covered legs.

"I'm here to work. Not be decoration," I retort, forcing myself not to give in to the nervous smile threatening to yank the corners of my mouth up. "That's why."

Remy warned me if I wanted to work at the bar this summer, I had to be ready to fire back a good comeback. Never show weakness.

I set the man's glass of water on the counter with a hard thump. Droplets splish-splash over the sides, wetting my hand.

"Everything all right?" Remy's hand lightly touches my back.

"No." The old man laughs. "You should make the gals wear skirts here. Give 'em a uniform." He vaguely gestures to my legs again.

Weirdo.

Remy's body stiffens. He lays his thick forearms on the bar and leans over. "That's not some 'gal.' That's my sister. Watch your fucking mouth."

His face pales. "I, uh, uh," he stutters.

"Go sit your ass down." Remy points to the man's table.

The guy shuffles away, glancing back once as if he's checking to make sure Remy didn't hop over the bar to chase him into his seat.

"See, that's why I've been hesitant to have you working here," Remy says without taking his eyes off the guy.

"He's a dumbass." I glance down at the floor. "My legs would get all sticky if I came to work in a skirt."

"I doubt he was concerned about your comfort." Remy pats my shoulder. "You okay?"

"Yeah. I had it. I told him I wasn't here as decoration."

"Good, but"—he points to the opening of the hallway leading to the office, kitchen, and basement—"I could see your shoulders crawl up to your ears from there. That's why I came over."

"Thanks."

"I need to get someone else in here on the weekends. Starting to realize how much I—" he stops and clamps his mouth shut.

Pain pokes my chest. "Depended on Griff to help you out around here?" I finish for him.

He shakes his head. Of course he doesn't want to admit that to me.

"I'll be right back," he says. "That guy bothers you again, aim the soda gun at his face."

Chuckling, I nod and pick up the sprayer. "Got it."

Remy turns and pulls out his phone, swiping and tapping over the screen while he walks to the other end of the bar.

I keep busy by cleaning. The counter has a layer of something sticky that's probably been there since my grandparents opened his place decades ago. Lots of scrubbing to do.

Sweat rolls down the side of my face and I flick my fingers against my cheek.

The door swishes open. I tip my head to see who our new customer is and smile at the tall guy walking inside. His bright, almost-orange hair sticks up in all directions. Eraser's cousin, Torch. Our eyes meet and he lifts his hand, waving. He hooks his thumbs in his pockets and approaches the bar.

"Hey, Molly. I didn't know you'd be here." He settles on the stool in front of me.

"Remy's actually letting me help out now." I sweep my hand toward the beer taps. "What can I get you?"

"Whatever's on tap." His eyebrows pinch together. "Are you *allowed* to serve me?"

That question could have a few different meanings and answers, but I supply the most obvious one. "Yup. I'm allowed to serve beer."

I pull the beer and pass him the mug, then stand there awkwardly. Go back to cleaning...or make small talk?

"Your hair looks different." He ruffles his fingers through his own hair and nods at me.

Surprised he even noticed, I tug on my ponytail. "Uh, I trimmed it and lightened it a little. For summer," I hurry to add, desperate to hide the truth—that I thought a change might stop people from recognizing me as that-poor-girl-whose-boyfriend-cheated-on-her.

"You doing okay?" A hint of pity colors the question. Great, if he hasn't watched the show, I'm sure Eraser told his cousin all about it.

"Yeah. Fine." I smile all the way up to my eyeballs.

"Torch." Remy clasps his friend's shoulder in a tight grip. "Thanks for stopping by. How you been?"

Torch swivels the stool toward my brother. "Not too bad. What'd you need?"

Ah, so Remy called Torch to come in? Interesting. Torch is in Remy's friend circle, but I never thought they were particularly close. More like, he tolerates him because he's Eraser's cousin and Pax's nephew.

Remy turns and points at me. "Jigsaw's supposed to stop by. Have him sit at the bar. I'll be back in a few."

"Uh, okay." Jigsaw doesn't seem like the kind of biker who wants to take instructions from a teenager but whatever.

Torch slides off the stool and pulls out his wallet.

"Bro, it's fine," Remy protests.

"For my lovely server." Torch holds out a twenty to me.

"I can't." My nervous gaze darts to Remy who shrugs.

Torch sets the bill on the bar and sticks his glass on top of it.

"Thanks," I mutter, scooping up the twenty.

The two of them disappear down the hallway. Remy better not go too far. The old guys keep glancing at me. I avert my eyes and return to scrubbing the counter.

"Miss?" someone calls.

Crap.

I turn and find someone else from the party on the other side of the bar. "Can we get another pitcher?"

"Sure. I'll bring it right over." I tilt sideways to check if the table needs anything else. Maybe some nuts to soak up all the beer.

I pull a pitcher and shake some mixed nuts into a bowl, then carry them over. Avoiding the guy who'd been so concerned about my wardrobe, I set the pitcher in the middle of the table.

The front door swishes open again but I don't bother looking over to see who it is.

"Took long enough," fashion-police guy grumbles at me.

"Cut it out, Bob," one of his friends scolds. "Thanks." He lifts the nuts. "For this too."

I let out a relieved breath. "Do you want to order anything from the kitchen?"

"Nah, we're good."

Something grazes my leg, behind my knee, then travels higher. Hard enough to feel it through my jeans.

I turn. "What—"

The touch disappears.

But not because of anything I did.

No, there's a tall, muscled, scarred, and pissed-off biker standing behind me with one hand tightly coiled around my customer's wrist as he drags it away from my leg.

"Jigsaw!" I squeak but he doesn't take his eyes off the man.

"Touch her again and you won't be getting these fingers back." Jigsaw slowly pulls a hunting knife out of the sheath clipped to his belt and brandishes it in front of the shocked customer. "Understood?"

"I...I...I..." he stutters.

"He won't, he won't," one of the man's friends says.

"Nah, I need to hear *him* say it." Jigsaw lowers the knife but doesn't put it away.

"Yes," the man finally says.

"Good. Glad we straightened that out." Jigsaw releases the man, tucks the knife into its holder, and focuses his attention on me. His intensity dials down a notch. "You all right?"

I bob my head up and down.

"Your brother got any of those chocolate chip cookies tonight?" he asks.

I blink. Did he just threaten to cut off someone's fingers and then casually ask me for cookies? "Uh, yeah. I think so."

"Great." Expectation glitters in his eyes.

Oh, he wants me to get the cookies right now.

I glance at the customers again, but they're fixated on the table, not daring to look anywhere else.

Certain they won't be leaving a tip or a positive Yelp review, I return to the bar. Jigsaw shadows me like my own personal guard dog.

"Where the fuck's your brother?" Jigsaw slides onto a stool and rests his elbows on the bar.

"In the back with Torch." I duck down and search for the box of cookies Lynette left for me earlier.

Jigsaw leans over the counter. "Are they like your personal cookies or something?"

"Kinda." I grin at him. "But I'm willing to share them since you just rescued me."

"Rescue." He snorts. "You weren't drowning, little girl. You shoulda kicked him in the nuts."

I grab a plate and set four cookies on it, then pass it to Jigsaw. "That would've been difficult." I lift one leg and kick at an awkward angle, as if lashing out at someone sitting in a chair.

He chuckles and snatches one of the cookies off the plate. "Funny." His gaze never wavers from my face. After a few seconds of scrutiny, I squirm.

"Want anything to drink?"

"Coke."

"Okay." I slide down a few feet and grab a can from the fridge under the bar. As I turn to get a glass, Jigsaw raps his knuckles against the bar.

"Can's fine."

I slide the can to him and he pops the tab.

"How come you're riding alone tonight?" I ask. I almost never see one Lost King brother without another close by.

He shrugs. "I was out this way when your brother called." He glances down the hallway. "How come you're working here, now?"

"Remy finally unclenched and agreed to let me help out." I stand straighter. "This was my grandparents' place."

A faint smile ghosts his lips. "I've heard."

Maybe that's a weird thing to brag about but I'm proud of what my grandparents built together. "I have another job I'm working during the day. And I'm still at my part-time job at the grocery store." Why do I feel compelled to share so much?

"You should hang out with my sister more." He circles his finger between us. "Maybe some of your work ethic can rub off on Jezzie."

Remy walks up behind Jigsaw in time to hear that last part. "Did you bring your sister with you?"

Jigsaw swivels on the stool. "Don't worry about where *my* sister is. Why aren't you lookin' after your own sister?" He jerks his thumb toward the rowdy grandpas. "Caught one of them old fucks grabbing her leg when I came in."

"What the fuck." Remy's startled gaze shoots to me. "Are you all right?"

I nod quickly, not sure I like Jigsaw blaming my brother for what some dumb customer did.

The two of them move to the end of the bar for a conversation that seems kind of intense. Every now and then they both glance over at me. Great. One grabby-handed customer might convince Remy to not let me work here anymore.

While they talk, I stare at the small television in the corner. An ad for *Supreme Underground Fighter* flashes on the screen.

Nope.

I grab the remote and turn the channel.

I can't wait to leave for college.

Until then, I'll immerse myself in work. Keep my mind so busy, I don't have a spare minute to think about Griff.

That *has* to be the remedy for healing my broken heart.

But deep down, I know it isn't.

CHAPTER NINE

Griff

EVERY WEEK I'M SHOCKED I'M STILL ON THE SHOW. HALF the time when we have our supposed "face-offs" it's never clear who's the winner.

Hammer Fists is eventually sent packing, so I guess I won *that* fight.

"You've gotta distinguish yourself from Naptime," Venom says to me after a particularly harsh training session.

"Uh, I'm not a douche who runs around yelling out a catchphrase. Isn't that enough?"

He chuckles. "No. That shit gets him noticed. It's entertaining." He roughs his hand over my hair. "Maybe we should shave your head or dye it purple or something."

"The fuck you're touching my hair," I growl, shaking him off.

"All right. Everyone get cleaned up," Jordan shouts. "You guys did good. We're going on a field trip today."

"Aw, shucks." Woolly chucks his arm in the air and pulls a doofy face. "My mom forgot to pack a lunch for me."

"Har, har." Jordan rolls his eyes. "Come on. You guys have been working hard. We put together a fun surprise for you."

I roll my eyes toward Venom. "This is sounding worse by the minute."

He chuckles and shoves me toward the hallway. "Stop dragging your feet. I want to see if the outside world still exists."

"Good point."

"Is it girls?" Deadass shouts. "I'm gettin' tired of seeing the same raggedy bitches every day."

Thankfully, I haven't talked to Kiki since I had it out with Paul the Potato. Either they told her to leave me alone or she finally took the hint. She and the other girls usually spend the day sunbathing by the pool. Since the pool's basically a big tub of piss at this point, it's not hard to avoid that entire area.

I only have one girl on my mind.

Molly.

I want to win this thing and get home to her.

That's what drives me.

Winning means I can take care of us. I can handle any petty bullshit they put me through here, as long as I can take care of my girl in the end.

"Stonewall!" one of the crew members barks. "Let's go."

The camera guys follow us to our rooms as everyone whoops, slaps lighting fixtures, and for some reason, punches the walls.

Shaking my head, I step into my room and quickly change.

I end up being one of the first ones outside. A row of four or five sport bikes line the small circular driveway along with the two vans we took on our last outing.

Afraid to get my hopes up, I ask Jordan, "What's this?"

Venom and Woolly join me, their enthusiasm obvious from their quick steps and wide-eyed appreciation for the machines.

"Oh, fuck yeah." Woolly claps his hands and rubs them together. "Please tell me we get to ride? You didn't just bring them here to tease us, did you?"

"Well, you three have your Class M, so yes. Pick one out. Thunder should be able to ride too. The rest will be behind you in the vans."

"You trust us not to take off?" I circle one of the Kawasaki Ninjas. "The ZX-14R's engine is a beast. It's supposed to do zero to sixty in under three seconds. You won't be able to catch us."

"Don't even joke about that," Jordan warns. "We have road clearance from here to the place we're going. Let's not test local PD's patience."

"Road clearance?" Woolly asks. "So this is a stunt for the show?"

"No, we thought we'd spend all this money to rent the bikes and turn you loose on the town for no reason," Jordan retorts, his annoyance obvious as he rolls his eyes and storms inside the house.

"Heh," Venom chuckles. "About time they do something besides antagonize us."

"Guys." I point to the bikes. "Dibs on blue. Keys are right there." I tilt my head toward the road. "Just sayin'."

"You planning to smash through the gate?" Woolly nods to the closed wrought iron barring our exit.

"Honestly, right about now, I might." I gesture toward the house. "You realize it's going to take another hour to get everyone down here, get the camera crews ready, wait for them to line up their shots. This is torture."

"Quit whining and go run some laps or something," Venom says, nodding at the path circling the house.

"No way." I throw my leg over the bike I've claimed. "You just want to steal my ride."

"Green's more my style." Venom rests his hand on another Ninja.

"I thought you were a Harley guy?" Woolly squints at me.

"Anything with wheels. And I'm not kidding, I'm dying to get out of here for even a few minutes."

Our conversation's interrupted by two of the camera guys coming out of the house to film "candid" shots of us studying the bikes. Hard to "act natural" with a camera up my ass.

As I predicted, it's another hour and a half before we're on the road.

Straddling the sleek Ninja is a whole new world. Instead of the familiar rumble of my Harley, the Ninja has a pleasant throaty growl that only suggests the power waiting under my fingertips. The bike's nimble, different from the weighty foundation of my usual ride.

I kick mine into gear first, eager to dart forward. But we have to wait for a pickup truck to take the lead so one of the camera guys can film us while he hangs over the tailgate. Annoyed, I flip the visor on my helmet down.

Relief, excitement, and a surge of adrenaline spiral through me as we clear the gate. The Ninja effortlessly responds to my touch. I'm eager to open it up, zip around the truck and speed the fuck out of here. Maybe home.

Venom rolls up on my right. I've ridden in formation plenty of times. With guys I know and trust. Being boxed in—the truck with an idiot and a camera hanging out the back—in front of me, Venom on my side, two more bikes behind us, and the vans all keep me from pushing the bike too hard.

Even riding while boxed feels good. I didn't realize how much I've missed being out on the open road. Training and winning have been my sole focus.

Are we headed toward some twisty roads? I'd love to hit some wicked curves. Bet the Ninja would handle them effortlessly.

The truck speeds ahead, putting distance between us. With two fingers, Venom signals for me to take the lead.

Wind rushes past me, whipping my T-shirt against my sides. I open up the throttle, catching up to the truck in seconds.

This is such a tease.

After a few miles, the truck signals to turn left and slows. I hit the brakes harder than I meant to. The tires grip hard and screech against the pavement but I keep it under control, gliding through the turn.

A small, white building with sliding windows in front and a long counter running underneath stands in the center of the parking lot.

I roll the bike to a stop next to the truck and shut off the engine. I wait for the camera guy to focus on someone else before taking off my helmet.

Venom's sneakers crunch over the gravel and he stops next to me. "Did they take us to get ice cream like we're a bunch of five-year-olds?"

"Looks like it." I glance at the building. "Maybe if we ask nicely, Jordan will buy us a cheeseburger too."

He snickers into his hand.

"The fuck is this?" Woolly walks up to us and gestures toward the ice cream shop. "Our first outing in weeks and we're gettin' ice cream cones?"

I turn my head and scan the parking lot. Except for the crew and other fighters, it's empty. Inside the shop, the lights are on, and I can make out two figures. "Maybe they decided we need part-time jobs?" I joke.

"I hope this isn't some bullshit test to see if we can pull ice cream and mix milkshakes." Venom scowls. "I already worked that summer job when I was sixteen."

I glance at the van where Naptime's scratching his armpits like a monkey. "If it *is* a test, not everyone's gonna pass," I say.

"No joke." Woolly holds his hand up high.

I roll my eyes but slap his hand.

"Nice!" one of the camera guys shouts.

"What are we doing here?" I shout.

"Outing." Jordan waves us toward the building. "Order whatever you want. Tables are out back."

"Hope he brought producer daddy's credit card." Venom rubs his hands together. "I'm gonna make him regret that 'order whatever you want.'"

"Amen. Let's eat."

At the window, I hesitate. We're in the middle of training. We all have matches coming up on Sunday. Is *this* the test? Seeing how disciplined we are? How committed we are to winning?

I bump Venom's arm with my elbow. "You think *this* is the test?"

"Seeing how much garbage we'll put in our bodies?" He sighs. "Then when we don't perform well on Sunday, they'll blame it on our inability to control ourselves?"

Not *exactly* how I would've put it. "Yeah."

"Probably." He squeezes his eyes shut for a few seconds. "I'm so tired of the head games."

"I'm still getting a cheeseburger." I step up to the window and place my order. Two cheeseburgers and a strawberry milkshake. I'll work it off later. Venom and Woolly order similar meals.

Thunder must've come to the conclusion that we were being tested too. He places a modest order. The rest of the guys order every single deep-fried item on the menu. While I'm waiting at the pickup window, my gaze lands on Jordan, watching Deadass and Naptime with a slight smirk stretched across his lips as they double-fist ice cream cones.

Definitely a test.

"Order up!" The girl behind the counter shoves a bright orange tray at me.

"Thanks." I grab it and head around the side of the building.

I'm alone for a few minutes and take a second to absorb the humid, summer day. The air's heavy with the scent of fried food and road fumes, reminding me of summer afternoons and evenings spent at Zips. I'd give anything to be there right now. Helping Pax at the grill, racing Molly's car—well, we won't be able to do that until I fix it. No one told me how much damage she did. A baseball bat in Molly's hands...probably a lot of cosmetic stuff. The glass will be a pain to replace but I'll get it done. Small price to pay for everything I've put Molly through this summer.

Fuck, I want to go home.

"Why the long face, Stonewall?" Thunder slaps my back and drops his heavy frame onto the bench next to me. He tears into a burger, making loud, obnoxious chewing noises that increase my annoyance.

Venom and Woolly sit on the bench across from us. Venom scowls at Thunder, then swings his gaze my way. "You're lookin' kinda murdery over there, Stonewall. Burgers no good?"

I huff a laugh. *This fucker.* If he gets kicked off the show any time soon, I'm doomed. "They're not bad."

I bite into one and stare past the building at the road. How far does it go? Since I was busy adjusting to the unfamiliar bike and following the truck, I didn't get a good look at our surroundings.

I'm finishing my milkshake when two angry male voices ripple through the air. I turn, seeking the source of the disagreement. Naptime and Bull trading insults. They're getting louder by the second, putting on a good show.

The camera guys move in closer, circling the two meatheads.

"What're they bitching about now?" Venom says to me.

"Probably arguing over who has the skinnier dick," Thunder mumbles.

"Or who greases up their hair better," Woolly adds. "Have you sparred with Naptime, yet? He's greased up like a Thanksgiving turkey."

"Figures," I mutter. Here I was worried about his obnoxious personality in the ring. "Can you even understand what either of them are saying?"

"Nah, bro." Woolly shakes his head. "Bull's been skull-punched one too many times. He's just speakin' gibberish." He belts out a few curses in a pitch-perfect impression of Bull's distinctive squeak.

"Eh, I don't think he can help that." I shrug.

Woolly reaches over and rubs his hand over the top of my head. "Such a softie."

I smack his hand away. "Won't feel soft when I knock you out."

Venom nods at the two fighters, then at me. "Go on, get in there," he jokes. At least I hope he's joking. I'm not embarrassing myself by getting in the middle of their petty complaints.

Bull jumps and catches Naptime in a sloppy chokehold. The whole scene—two bigmouths tussling in the grass behind an ice cream stand, with video cameras pointing at them—is so ridiculous, I burst out laughing.

Unfortunately, that draws the attention of one of the camera guys. "What's so funny, Stonewall?"

Aw, fuck. I don't want any part of this. "Just enjoying the show."

"You gotta start mixing it up, bro," Venom says under his breath. "Stand out."

I flick a fuck-off glare at him. "I'll choose a better moment."

Bull ends up submitting Naptime with the chokehold, leaving the taller fighter panting hard in the grass.

"That was unexpected." I nod.

"No one knocks out The Bull!" Bull roars, raising his fists above his head.

Naptime glares at him but he's still struggling to breathe. Jordan crouches next to him, concern etched on his face. I can't hear their conversation, and honestly, don't care.

"All right. Let's wrap it up," Jordan orders.

I toss my trash.

Walking to the parking lot, a sense of suffocating frustration grabs me. I tip my head back to stare at the deep blue sky. It's such a perfect day.

An intolerable level of rage bubbles up inside me at the thought of returning to the mansion. To be trapped with these guys for who knows how many more days before they let us out again feels like being buried alive.

I pull the keys out of my pocket. The Ninja shines in the afternoon sunlight. Enticing me to take it on the road for a quick straight-line frenzy. I glance behind me. The camera crew guys are at the corner of the building packing away their equipment. Jordan and the other fighters haven't reached the parking lot yet.

Now or never.

I slip the helmet on and straddle the bike.

"Stonewall?" one of the crew members calls out. "Where ya goin'?"

Venom said I need to mix it up, right?

CHAPTER TEN

Griff

SPEED KILLS. OR SO I'VE HEARD.

The Ninja has a large engine that easily goes zero to sixty in less than three seconds. I push it there in two-point-five.

First, I did a lazy circle in the parking lot, giving the camera guys a chance to get their equipment ready but not enough time for anyone to stop me.

Not that anyone could catch up to me if they wanted to.

The road's straight. No clue where I'm going. I'm not even sure where I *am*. Jordan handed me my license before we left the house. But I don't have a cell phone or any damn money on me.

Would getting lost be the worst thing in the world?

The bike's more comfortable than expected. It's bigger than other sport bikes I've ridden, allowing me to stretch out a bit. For a longer ride, I think I'd still prefer the Harley.

But for a quick escape, this is perfect.

I twist my wrist just a little. The speed increases. Scenery blurs. Thank fuck for the helmet or my eyeballs would be flattened to pancakes.

The big engine smoothly zips to over a hundred miles per hour. A hundred and ten. The bike's so smooth, the speed creeps up fast.

Wind rushes around me. All my senses heighten. I'm in a commercial area that doesn't seem to have a lot of traffic.

Now that I've put some distance between myself and the crew, I ease off the throttle and fiddle with the gauges. The fuel line is barely above the red zone. Can't go far. Figures.

On my right there seems to be an empty parking lot. The tires bite into the asphalt and I ease off, slowing enough to make a wide turn into the lot.

I check the controls again. *Traction control.* I flick that off then head back the way I came.

This time, I'm in danger of getting pulled over for going under the speed limit, not over it. Dread crawls over me the farther I ride.

Quit being a baby. Boo-hoo, you're homesick. Get over it, Royal.

Why the fuck am I doing this to myself?

Money. Molly. Our future. That's why.

I'm the best damn fighter in the house. I'm sure as fuck more disciplined. *I can win this.* I've already come this far.

The sign for the ice cream stand comes into view—a sun-faded, plastic picture of a dancing ice cream cone hugging a cheeseburger. I slow the bike.

Everyone seems to be clustered around the edge of the parking lot.

One of the camera guys spots me and runs into the road.

You want some footage? Here ya go. Enjoy.

I blip the throttle once, then again, and keep the gas steady. I pop the clutch and tap the rear brake. The front wheel lifts. My stomach swoops. Heart hammers. Muscles strain to keep the heavy machine balanced. The front lifts a few more inches.

Dropping six hundred pounds of machinery on my balls isn't going to prove anything. Or help me win.

I let off the throttle. The front tire wooshes towards the pavement. Bounces hard, jarring my teeth.

Oops. Hope I didn't blow out the fork seals.

Jordan's outraged scowl warms my heart as I pull into the lot. Too bad he can't see me grinning behind the dark visor.

"Yeah!" Venom stretches his arms over his head and jumps like he's dunking a basketball. Woolly's standing next to him, clapping like a seal. The rest of the guys shake their heads and load into the van.

"How was it?" Venom shouts.

I nod and flash a thumbs-up.

"What were you thinking?" Jordan yells.

He and our coach, Underhill, run toward me, their sneakers sending gravel skittering. The camera guys follow.

Time to shine.

I take off my helmet, set it on the seat, and grin. "Did you miss me?"

"You're in big trouble!" Underhill shouts in my face, like he's the dad in a bad nineteen nineties teen drama, and I'm the wayward son who snuck in the house after curfew.

I pat the seat of the bike. "Just took her for a little ride."

"You broke the speed limit!" Jordan yells.

Guess I have two dads in this skit.

"Dude, he broke the sound barrier," Woolly hollers.

Jordan whips around and points at Woolly. "You, stay out of this!"

I duck my head and snicker.

The camera guys circle us while coach and producer scold me. I smirk, roll my eyes, and nod along.

"Drop and give me twenty," Underhill orders, stabbing his finger toward the ground.

Wait, am I in an Army sitcom now?

"Seriously?" I glance at the gravel. "Here?"

Underhill just keeps pointing at the ground.

I ease onto hands and toes. The big stones dig into my palms as I crank out twenty pushups.

When I'm done, I pop up and grin at the coach.

"Try to show a little remorse," Jordan mutters.

I slide an insolent look his way. "I'm not that good an actor."

Underhill lets out a disgusted snort and stomps away. One camera guy chases after him.

"We got some good footage." Jordan claps my shoulder and squeezes. "No bullshit on the way back, though."

It's getting hard to tell if he means it.

Or if he wants me to do the opposite.

AFTER AN UNEVENTFUL RIDE back to the house, a new sense of determination settles over me.

"That should be enough to keep you here a little longer." Venom slaps my back as we walk into the house together. "Much more exciting for viewers to watch you race off and pop those wheelies than two meathead fighters...*fighting over who ate the last french fry.*" He punctuates the dig with an eyeroll.

"Is that what they were beefing over?" Woolly asks. "Forget the van, they should've ridden in a clown car."

"I don't know." Venom laughs. "Probably."

"You got somethin' to say?" Bull stomps over and chest-bumps *me*. "You talkin' shit on me? Think you're the golden boy 'cause you zipped around on some lil' crotch rocket?"

I lean down until my forehead's an inch from his. "You better back the fuck up."

"You back up." His palms slam into my chest and he shoves.

For fuck's sake.

I grunt at the blow but don't move an inch. "You sure you want to do this?"

"Didn't you get enough humiliation when Naptime got you in that bulldog choke?" Venom asks.

"Fuck that. I finished him."

Woolly slides his fist in the air in a jerk-off motion. "I'm sure you can go finish him again right now if you want."

I duck my head and laugh.

Bull's hands strike my chest again. "Think that's funny?"

"Don't. Fucking. Touch. Me," I warn.

Like a toddler who skipped his afternoon nap, he pokes me in the chest. "Touching you." Poke. "Touching you." Poke. Poke.

You've got to be kidding. I flick my gaze past Bull's shoulder. One of the camera guys from our outing has his lens on us. Two of the regular house camera operators scurry over to fan out around our circle. Someone else aims a beam of bright, white light our way. I squint and shift to the side. Wouldn't want them to miss my fist cracking Bull's jaw.

"What's wrong, Stonewall?" Bull taunts. "You know I'll kill you in the cage."

"Of what?" I open my mouth wide and yawn. "Boredom?"

"Let's go. Let's go right now." Warm flecks of spittle land on my face. I force my body to stay rigid and ready. "You can't knock out The Bull!" He steps close again.

My hand curls into a low fist and slices through the air in an upward motion.

"You can't—"

Blam!

The uppercut lands square on Bull's chin.

His heavy body crumples to the floor like a sack of wet cement, the impact reverberating through the room. Pain slashes across my knuckles while satisfaction rings in my chest.

Venom whistles. "That has to be the cleanest knockout I've ever seen. You didn't even throw a jab first."

I shake out my hand.

"That's twice," Woolly shakes his head, "no, *three* times, he's stepped to someone and been put in his place." He glances at Bull's prone body. "Think he's learned his lesson?"

"Probably not." I study the unconscious fighter, taking note of the slight rise and fall of his chest.

Jordan rushes over and kneels next to Bull, checking his pulse. When he's satisfied, he peers up at me, widens his eyes and ever so slightly tips his head toward the camera. I blink into the glare of the lights.

Better make the most of this.

Leaning into this cheesy spectacle, I swallow my dignity, flick my gaze to the camera closest to me, flash a cocky grin, and say, "Maybe the third time's the charm."

CHAPTER ELEVEN
Griff

SIX WEEKS LATER...

And then there were two fighters in the house.

One by one, the other guys were eliminated.

Naptime and I are the only ones left.

No matter what, I'll be going home with a hefty chunk of change.

But I want the *big* prize. What the hell was the point of this torture if I don't come home the champion? The weight of that possibility presses in on me from all sides, keeping me awake at night, and fueling me throughout the day.

Nervous energy pulses through my veins. I'm charged and ready. Almost frenzied with the need to pound my fists into Naptime's annoying face and go *home*.

Now that it's just the two of us, the show's officially keeping us separated. The early alarms have stopped too. Underhill collects me every morning and makes me run laps outside, then we train in the gym. There he has two instructors—one black belt in Brazilian Jiu Jitsu and one boxing coach—work me to exhaustion. They push me to my limits, leaving me exhausted but ready to do it all over again the next day.

This morning, someone knocks on my door earlier than expected. I crack open the door. Bright lights sear my eyes. I blink and squint. Through the glare Venom and Bear Trap come into view.

"Holy shit." I stagger backward and pull the door wider. "What are you two doing here?"

"Here to train you for the big fight." Venom steps over the threshold.

After I won *our* match, by using a submission technique *he* helped me perfect, I didn't think Venom would return, let alone return to help *me*.

Is it a trap? Part of a larger plot to sabotage me? To get even for losing?

Nah, Venom hates Naptime as much as I do. Even helped me shave Naptime's head one night after the jackass got wasted and passed out on the patio.

And even though I won our match, Venom had still hugged me goodbye and wished me luck.

This fucking show has made me question everything.

I can't afford to get lost down a rabbit hole of doubt and mistrust.

Bear Trap follows Venom inside and pulls me in for—what else —a big bear hug. His ring name makes so much more sense. I'm almost sorry we never had a chance to face off in the cage.

"You're back too?" I slap his back and motion him farther inside, to make room for the two cameramen.

He leans down and in a low voice says, "Hell yeah, I'm back. As long as they don't stash me in that fuckin' hotel again when we're done, I'll stick around."

I rear back and stare at him, a frown creasing my forehead. "What?"

"Yeah, you didn't know that?" Bear Trap says. "Total media blackout until after my episode aired." He shoots a death glare at Camera Guy Mike. "Fucking bullshit."

"Hey, I just capture the footage," Mike protests.

"I didn't get to go home yet, so I'm guessing my dismissal hasn't aired." A sly smile curves Venom's lips. "But at least they let Kelly come stay with me."

Bear Trap grunts and rolls his eyes. "Yeah, and based on what came through the hotel's thin walls last night, he's desperately trying to impregnate her."

Venom slowly swivels his head Bear Trap's way. "The fuck you listening for, perv?"

My remaining doubts ease into gratitude for their presence. I burst out laughing and step between them. "I'm so glad you guys are back." I lean sideways and stare into the hallway. "Woolly didn't come with you?"

"Nah, man. He had *enough*," Venom says. "Soon as they said he could bounce, he was gone like Tigger the Tiger."

"Thanks for coming back." I pat Bear Trap's shoulder. "You've been gone for a while. I thought you would've forgotten all about me."

"How could I forget you?" His voice and posture vibrate with enthusiasm.

We spend a few minutes catching up but it's awkward with the cameras guys circling us like hungry turkey vultures hoping to pick our carcasses clean.

Underhill's been a good coach but having my fellow fighters back to support me means a lot more.

"Let's get this done, Stonewall!" Venom pulls Bear Trap and me in for a bowed-head huddle. Something I'm sure the cameras are enjoying since they zoom in close.

"Something, something profound, something meaningful something encouragement," Venom mutters.

I snort-laugh at his nonsensical mumbling for the camera. The corner of his mouth quirks but he doesn't open his eyes.

Venom lifts his arm from my back, ending our huddle.

"You've got this, Stonewall!" Bear Trap knocks his fist against my shoulder.

Venom pats the top of my head. "I can't wait to see you twist that pink-mohawked motherfucker like a pretzel."

THREE DAYS. I'm given three days to train with my former housemates. That's it.

Technically, I've been training since I got here.

I'm beyond ready.

The show delivers several pairs of purple-and-gold fitted compression shorts a few days before the final fight.

On fight day, though, Venom shows up in the gym where I'm trying to work on some breathing exercises with a purple satin robe.

I squint at it. "The fuck is that?"

"For you. Paul says you get to make a big entrance, with pyro and everything."

"For fuck's sake." I roll my eyes and take the robe from his hands. "I'm gonna look like a freaky-ass cult leader wearing this."

He presses his palms together and bows. "Ah, mighty Stonewall. We pray for you to kick Naptime into the next universe."

"Shut up." I whap him with the robe. "Where's Bear Trap at?"

"You don't want to know."

Coach comes in and gives me a few last-minute pointers. Then the cameras arrive. Like a good little fighter, I put on a show of sparring with Venom.

"Still quick on your feet," he praises. I swear, Venom's been a better coach than the actual coach. "Your grappling is even better than when you kicked my ass."

A shade of guilt falls over me, but he doesn't say it with any animosity. He almost seems proud. "Thanks."

"You've got this."

"No, I mean it." I motion him closer. "Thank you."

He rests his hands on my shoulders and squeezes. "Clear your mind. Don't be afraid to adapt or change your strategy, okay? Be fluid."

"Like water," I agree.

"That's it."

"Let's roll." Venom holds out the shiny purple robe to me.

Fuck it. I slip it on and pull it around myself.

Bear Trap meets us in the hallway. I stop and take in his purple sweatshirt embroidered with a big, gold crown on the front. Same shade of purple as my shiny robe.

He grins at me. "Wanted to make it clear who I was rooting for."

"Thanks." I reach out and hug him quickly. "Any advice?"

Everyone else seems to have wisdom to share.

"Well, he knows you're a good grappler. He'll probably try to land some punishing body shots as early as possible. So be nimble."

"Nah, Stonewall's a damn good striker too," Venom says.

"Aw, guys, you're making me blush." I duck my head and laugh.

"All right, enough jerking each other off." Underhill claps his hands. "Let's move."

"Yes, sir." Bear Trap raises his hand in a salute that ends with his middle finger in the air.

Underhill shakes his head and mutters to himself.

I walk behind the others, trying to center myself and clear my head. In the van, I take the seat all the way in the back and close my eyes. The others seem to respect my need for distance. Their combined chatter fades into the rest of the noise—the grind of the van's engine, the rumble from the road.

Deep breaths. In and out.

This will be unlike any other fight. Low-quality, bootleg clips of my fights at The Castle or other places back home have been posted online for years—that's how Diane found me for the show. But this time, the whole event will be aired. Every drop of sweat and splatter of blood. Every punch, kick, and move I make will be dissected and analyzed by people I don't even know and will probably never meet. Every moment—including me sitting here with my eyes closed—will be aired for the world to mock, judge, or admire.

I doubt Molly's still watching the show, but if she is, I want to make her proud. I don't want her to think I did all of this for nothing.

If Remy's watching, I don't want him to be embarrassed that he knows me. Fuck it, probably too late for that.

As the van eases to a stop, I open my eyes. The darkness of an underground parking lot surrounds us with only a few pools of light to lead us inside.

The more I try to calm myself, the faster time seems to move. I'm hustled inside to a locker room where cameras keep filming everything. People give me pep talks, but all the noise fades to a low hum—like I'm drowning.

I'd like music and headphones to block out the commotion but even today, I can't have any electronics.

I've never dealt with this kind of build-up and anticipation before a fight. Or had so many people around to bother me. Usually, it's Remy and me in our locker room at The Castle, trading insults or giving each other pointers. Sometimes Eraser joins us to share things he learned about an opponent. Jake and Murphy would hang with us when they used to fight there. We have Lost Kings providing security in case things got out of control. On my home turf, I'm surrounded by people I've known for years. People I trust to watch my back no matter what.

Here, in this alien environment, who can I trust? Underhill? He's not a coach I chose to work with. His loyalty is to the show. Venom? He's here as my friend but up until a week ago, he was my competition.

I've already made so many mistakes and miscalculations about this show. Underestimated how devious these people are.

The boxing coach joins us to tape and wrap my hands, momentarily giving me something else to think about.

Underhill supervises. The worried frown creasing his forehead doesn't do anything to ease my pre-fight nerves. "Naptime's biggest asset in the ring is his attitude," he says.

I raise both eyebrows. "You mean his annoyingness is a *strength*?"

Underhill points his finger in my face. "That. Right there. Let that shit go, Stonewall. Clear your mind of all thoughts and emotions. When you're in the ring, you're above that. You're a better fighter than him every day of the week. Don't let his cockiness distract you."

That's the most words I've ever heard come out of Underhill's mouth at one time. "I won't. Thanks, Coach."

"Done." The boxing coach taps my knuckles. "Go for the KO early. Land a bomb and finish him."

"I'll do my best," I promise. "Thank you."

Underhill checks my hands. "Don't let his antics get to you," he warns me again. He must *really* hate Naptime.

"I got it." I've fought people who were more annoying.

Time keeps ticking down.

Breathe. You're fine.

I inhale, long and deep, hold for a count of five, then let it out slowly.

Think of a word. That's the kind of new age bullshit Eraser would tell me when we were locked up as kids. Fuck, I miss him. I've never been more thankful for all the visualization exercises he's had us do over the years.

Thunderstorm. That word fits what I need to be tonight. Intense, powerful, unpredictable. Move fast. Unleash raw power.

Thunderstorm, huh. Isn't that full circle. Molly and I got caught in one the night before I was whisked away to the house. My heart pounds faster. I wish she was here. But I'm also not sure she could handle seeing me fight. Not like this.

Eyes closed, I stand and throw a quick sequence of jabs, concentrating on each movement.

A surge of determination grips me.

Slowly, I open my eyes.

Everyone's staring at me.

Feeling more confident by the second, my mouth tilts into a cocky line. "I'm ready."

A guy from the show knocks on the door. "Time to go."

Underhill grips my shoulder. "They're gonna want you to do a stare down for the cameras. Just look that soulless punk dead in his squinty little spider eyes. Don't flinch."

Oddly specific description. "Uh, dead-eyed stare. Got it."

"Make me proud." He leans in so we're almost nose-to-nose and pats my cheek. Christ, I hope he's not planning to kiss me next.

We're led down a long, brightly lit corridor. Underhill stops at a corner and holds out his arm. "We wait here," he says.

To our left, there's another long hallway, leading into the opening to the arena. I stand in the shadows, studying what I can see of the seats and cage. It's not completely full but people have been crowded into the seats in the immediate area around the cage. With some clever camera work—which I know these guys are more than capable of—they'll make it look like a packed house.

If the show brought Molly down here to see my final fight, or Remy or Vapor, they would've let them come see me backstage, right? Not blindside me when I'm about to go in the cage.

"Where'd they find all these people to come see this?" I ask Venom.

He stares at me for a few beats. "Probably people who work for the company or friends of the execs? Or paid actors. Who knows. It fucking sucks, though. They wouldn't let me bring Kelly, but they let in all these strangers."

Whatever hope that Molly, Remy, or any of *my* friends from home might be in the crowd as some sort of last minute "surprise" by the show dies a quick, painful death.

My disappointment seems to be misinterpreted by Venom. He grabs my shoulders, forcing me to look at him. "Hey, you've got this. Seriously. You were already good when you came to the house. But you trained like a beast. You were more focused. More driven. And improved the most out of anyone else there."

My throat's too tight to respond but I nod vigorously.

All this waiting is fucking with my head.

The opening tones of DMX's *Ruff Ryders' Anthem* pound through the building. What sounds like a cannon explodes. Sparks shoot straight up to the ceiling. Venom squints toward the hallway.

An announcer says a bunch of stuff that just sounds like gibberish from all the way back here.

"Naaaaaptiiiimee!"

"Christ, is that what he picked?" Venom shakes his head. "How does a guy with the ring name *Naptime* not go with *Enter Sandman* for his walkout song?"

I chuckle and throw my hood over my head. *It has to be close to go time.*

"*Ruff Ryders* always makes me think of the brand of condoms," Bear Trap shouts. "Which is appropriate since Naptime's dad definitely shoulda worn a rubber."

I burst out laughing. "Fuck. Stop making me laugh. I'm trying to focus," I scold.

Bear Trap grins at me.

Shaking my head, I roll my shoulders and bounce on my feet. My stomach twists with the need to purge my last ten meals.

Christ, I've never been this nervous before a fight. Is this what turning pro would be like? Or is it the pressure of all the people watching?

The usual detachment I find in the minutes leading up to stepping into the cage keeps escaping my grasp.

You've done this hundreds of times. This is just a bigger audience. That's it.

The opening riff of the song I chose for tonight pierces the air.

"That's my cue." I point to the ceiling and start moving along the path, following Coach Underhill and the camera guys in front of me.

"Excellent choice." Venom nods in time to Rage Against the Machine's *Fistful of Steel.*

"I would've pegged you as a *Calm Like a Bomb* kinda dude, but this works," Bear Trap adds.

I tap my fists together, then pop them against my cheeks a few times.

Why do I do this again?

I duck my head to avoid the glare of the lights and stare at the black slides on my feet.

One foot after the other.

Music continues to blare from the speakers. It's not doing anything to pump me up for the fight, though.

"Stare the camera down," Venom says against my ear.

I lift my gaze and stare into the black lens a few feet ahead of us.

Sparklers go off at the end of the hall. Heat from the arena prickles my exposed skin. We enter the main floor and the stands explode into a frenzy of movement. People lean forward waving their arms and shouting my name. I reach out and brush my fingers against a few outstretched hands.

What are the chances Naptime forfeits the fight and we can all go home?

Probably slim.

I briefly sweep my gaze over the crowd. A sea of unfamiliar faces. Mostly men. A few women. A few kids. Who the hell brings little kids to a cage match?

I flex my fingers testing the limits of the wrap job.

Block. Defend. Block. Strike, strike, strike.

AUTUMN JONES LAKE

"You know they green-screened a crowd behind us in the matches all season long?" Venom shouts in my ear. "This match won't be weird and silent like the others were."

"That's okay." It's nothing but noise I can easily block out. Better than the eerie silence of the earlier matches.

All the ring girls from the house are prowling around the outside of the cage in tiny gold shorts and barely-there tops.

None of them better come over here and bother me.

I'm stopped by an official-looking guy in a black suit who points to a black rubber mat for me to stand on. I shake off the robe and hand it to Venom, then kick off the slides. Bear Trap picks them up and backs away.

The ref joins us and nods at me. "Mouth guard?"

I hold it out for him to check, then pop it in.

"Arms up." He lifts his hand in case I'm confused about what he means by *up*.

I hold my arms out at my sides and stare straight ahead, not really taking anything in. He runs his hands under my arms and down my sides, pats my legs and checks my feet for hidden paper clips or razor blades, I guess. Then he skims his hands over my shoulders, arms, and elbows to make sure I'm not greased. He checks my gloves, then someone hands him a tube of Vaseline and he smooths a bit over my cheekbones, forehead, and nose. At The Castle we let someone else do this for the fighters.

You're in the big leagues now.

"You may enter the cage." The suit guy sweeps his hand dramatically through the air toward the open cage door.

"Thanks." I nod at him.

Venom slaps my shoulders. "Get him."

"Keep your fingers out of his butt hole," Bear Trap warns.

The unexpected advice jars me to a stop. "What?" I laugh.

"Stuff happens." Bear Trap shrugs.

Venom hooks his arm around Bear Trap's neck and yanks him backward, then nods to me.

Shaking my head, I step toward the cage. One of the ring girls wearing what amounts to three glitter-coated napkins jiggles close to me, blocking my way.

94

"Good luck, Stonewall!" she squeals in my ear. She leans in, her heavy perfume choking off my air for a second as she reaches up and plants a sloppy kiss on my cheek, stopping to rub her barely covered breasts all over my chest and arm.

Fucking great. Sure the cameras caught all that.

I practice my dead-eyed glare on her, and she backs away quickly, almost tripping in her glittering heels. Someone grabs her by the elbow and yanks her farther away from the cage.

Shaking my head, I step up and into the cage. Naptime skips to his corner and paces back and forth, pretending not to notice me. Stupid fucking hot-pink mohawk makes him look like a rooster who'd been raised next to a nuclear waste dump. Can't wait to get him in a headlock.

I study his movements as he paces his section of the cage. Chicken legs. I should target there first. With a good sweep I can probably crack those little toothpicks.

Still studying Naptime, I retreat to my corner.

Underhill's on the ledge, and he reaches through, patting my shoulder. "Tire him out with those snappy punches. Watch his feet."

I nod and accept the bottle of water Venom passes me over the cage. I take a bit, wet my mouth, and hand him the bottle back.

"Go." Underhill presses his hand to my chest and shoves.

A horn blares and the ref calls us to the middle of the ring.

The announcer does his long-winded, annoying spiel. He's so loud and there's so much blood rushing through my ears I barely hear the words. But when he looks my way and what sounds like my name comes out of his mouth, I raise my fists in the air and turn for everyone to take a good look.

People scream, shout, and wave stuff in the air.

The calm I've been seeking all day descends slowly. Only three people matter right now. The three in the ring—me, the ref, and Naptime—the guy who wants to punch me unconscious.

"Mr. Royal, right here." The ref points to a spot on the floor. He places Naptime across from me and asks us to lift our fists. I stare Naptime down. His dark eyes are flat and lifeless, but he doesn't flinch.

"All right," the ref says. "Clean fight. Listen to my instructions. Defend yourself at all times."

I nod to let him know I got it. We'd had the rules drilled into us all week. They weren't that complicated.

"Tap gloves now if you want." The ref presses his fingers to our fists. It's basic respect for fighters to touch gloves before a fight.

Naptime glares at me, curls his lip, and shakes his head. "Nah."

Well, fuck you, too.

"Fight!" The ref quickly backs away.

The room erupts in shouts.

I put my fists up and circle to Naptime's right, my bare feet sliding smoothly over the padded canvas. He lashes out with a fist that whizzes by my cheek. The missed blow rocks him off-balance.

"Over-extend much?" I taunt, pivoting out of range.

He threw everything into that first punch.

Cheered by his mistake I throw a quick double jab. My fist glances off his chin. He grunts and absorbs the blow. I cross and jab again, then shuffle to the side, light on my toes.

His square jaw works from side to side and his eyes light up with anger. What'd he think I was going to do today—pet his pink hair and tell him he's pretty?

He attacks, coming straight at me, throwing a combination of jabs with full force. I slip and weave away, managing to avoid most of the barrage while landing a few shots of my own.

Damn, I've been dogging Naptime the whole time I've been here. His annoying personality and willingness to ham it up for the cameras hides the fact that he's skilled and fearless.

He comes at me fast, throwing more jabs, testing my response. Running on all the rage I've stored up over the last twelve weeks, I lash out with a quick one-two-three combination, ending with a right hook into his cheek.

His head whips around. Sweat or spit sprinkles my forearm.

"Yes! Get him!" Venom shouts.

Naptime throws his left fist. I weave to the side, missing it, but he's quick to catch me with his right, snapping my head to the side.

Fuck, that stung.

Pissed, I charge, throwing several punches to his solar plexus. Relief courses through me as I finally have a way to set free all the fury I've been storing. In the ring, my anger has purpose—to win big —and I don't hold back.

Naptime backs up quickly, his feet squeaking against the canvas. He throws a tentative test punch. I respond with an open-faced slap to his cheek, whipping his head sideways.

"Yeah! *Stonewall Slap!*" Venom cheers.

Naptime growls with frustration.

"Like that?" I taunt, holding out my hand like I'm gonna slap him again.

In a blur, he whips his body in a circle. His foot flies forward and collides with my temple.

The kick rocks me backward.

My vision blurs and for a second, I'm thrown back to the night Molly saw me fight and I absorbed a similar blow.

All this time I've been training, I should've worked harder on blocking kicks.

Coach warned me not to get distracted.

The seconds of hesitation cost me. Naptime advances, pushing me into the cage wall.

Nope. Not getting clinched yet.

I raise my knee, but he blocks with an elbow. *Fucker.* I hammer my elbow into his gut. He doubles over and I throw a punch at his cheek but end up hitting his shoulder.

He grunts and tries to punch but can't get the angle he needs. I risk a quick kick to the side of his leg. It works and I break free, dancing to the center of the ring.

Naptime hops on one foot and dives at my midsection.

Oh, you wanna wrestle? Let's do it.

Forget a KO, I'm dying to choke this motherfucker unconscious, make him feel every ounce of humiliation right until the moment he blacks out.

My back hits the canvas with a hard thud. Naptime lands on top of me, heavy and sweaty, struggling to pin my legs. I throw a few punches to his sides, but from this angle, there isn't enough power behind them to do real damage.

Fuck this. I seize the moment. Hugging his arms to his sides, I roll us and flip him. Straddling his legs and keeping him pinned, I lean in and pummel his face. He balls up like a turtle, then bucks and wiggles, freeing his legs. With a bit of distance between us now, he kicks out, his foot catching me in the ribs. I roll backward, ignoring a slight pop in my knee.

I manage to keep my butt from hitting the floor by sheer force of will, and power to my feet. Fists up, I circle Naptime. *Kick him? Tackle?* I'm not ready to go to the ground again.

Naptime staggers to his feet. Warily, we circle each other.

He throws a jab.

Whoosh—over my head. The missed punch gives me an opening to close in and hammer his sides. I put everything into each blow.

His fist slams into my temple and I stagger back.

Stayed inside too long. Should've moved away faster.

Damn. I shake off the sting. His fists have more bite than I expected.

"Ninety seconds!" Underhill shouts.

Naptime throws a punch that sails by my ear. I pop him on the chin.

"Don't over-extend!" his coach shouts.

Naptime's going all out in this first round. I tuck my chin and lift my fists, slowly circling him, searching for an opening.

"Time!" the ref calls, sending us back to our corners.

I back away and drop onto the stool. Underhill gets in my face, checking my cheek and chin. He applies an icy eye-iron to my cheekbone where I caught one of Naptime's fists. "He's coming at you full power. Missing most of his shots," Underhill says in a low voice. "Let him tire himself out. Keep your guard up. Turn your shoulder and extend those punches."

I nod through the tips, not sure how much of it is sinking into my racing brain.

"You look good. He's already out of breath," Venom says. "Keep picking him apart with those strikes."

I tip my head back so I can see him better and nod.

The ref calls us to the center again. I launch myself off the stool and get back to work.

Round two is a grind. For every two hits I land, I take one. My left side stings. I struggle not to favor it in any way that will give Naptime incentive to keep hitting me there.

"Shoulder!" Underhill keeps shouting.

No shit. I'm tryin'.

The ref calls time and I limp my way to my corner.

"You all right?" Underhill crouches in front of me and dabs at my eyebrow.

I must look as bad as I feel. "Ribs," I mutter.

He of course probes me there.

I suck in sharp, painful breath and glare at him.

A frown creases his forehead. "Can you continue?"

"I'm fine."

I hiss as he rubs the cold eye-iron to my face again. Another guy joins us and presses something into my eyebrow. A sharp sting pinches the spot he's fussing with. He pulls away a small white stick covered in red.

"Just a small cut," he assures me.

"I like to draw first blood," I joke.

"You did." Underhill grins. "Got him right under his eye."

"Take him down," Venom says. "You can easily dominate him, tire him out, and score more points."

I turn to look at him. "Nah, I thought we'd try breakdancing next."

He snorts. "Finish this asshole."

The ref calls us back.

"Watch his feet," Underhill warns me as I stand.

I jump up and down a few times and shake my head from side to side. My second wind billows through me and I tap my fists together. Ready for war.

The crowd screams as I approach Naptime.

I size him up. How am I going to disguise my takedown? He's too good to fall for a double leg shot. Let him come at me with some punches, then duck, catch his leg and drag him to the canvas?

I'd like to punch him a few more times. Wear him down before I take him to the floor.

My fist connects with his chest, then his chin. He staggers backward and I keep the pressure on, landing blow after blow.

The roar of the crowd intensifies.

Naptime bobs, weaves, and tries to block my strikes.

Damn, he's fast with his feet. I lean in for another combination. He dodges and kicks out. Pain slams into the side of my knee. My ass hits the canvas hard, jarring my spine. I pull my legs in and kick, catching Naptime's thigh.

He slams onto the floor next to me.

Party time.

He rolls and scrambles away.

Oh no you don't. "Get back here." I dive for him, sweeping and rolling him to his back. His eyes widen and he kicks and flops away like a fish trying to get back to the river.

The fuck?

Is his ground game that bad?

I trap and isolate his legs and pound him with my fists. Anywhere and everywhere. He defends and blocks, not letting me get close enough to apply arm pressure. I just need an opening to secure a choke and force him to submit.

He squirms and flips.

Perfect. I cover his back and slip my arm right under his chin, tightening and cranking his head to an awkward angle.

The crowd loses it—screaming, stomping feet. I block out the noise and keep applying pressure.

Naptime chokes and burbles but doesn't give up. He grabs at my arm and pulls. I tighten the choke.

His body stills.

Where's the fucking ref?

Naptime taps my arm. *Once. Twice.*

Finally.

Panting hard, I loosen my grip but don't totally release him. The ref saw Naptime tap out, right? Why isn't he coming over here? He should've pulled us apart by now.

Naptime wriggles out from under me. Pain explodes along my jaw. I raise my arm to block. He elbows me again, this time catching my wrist.

Dirty fucking cheater with the fake tap out.

He never made the third tap. I can't believe I fell for that.

Furious, I charge him, throwing punch after punch. Fuck a submission. I'm aiming for his chin and a knockout.

Hot pain sprays over my temple. My vision blurs red. Blood drips down my cheek, splattering on the canvas. *Fuck.*

Now that I'm freely bleeding, he aims for the spot again and again. I get my knee up, hitting him in the gut and throw more punches to his ribs and temple. Fury obliterates my last bit of restraint. I go after him with everything. Strike after strike.

He turns his back and I tackle him in another chokehold, wrenching his arm until something pops.

He struggles and kicks back, striking my knee. I grunt and force the pain away.

A bell screams.

"Time!" the ref shouts, grabbing my arm and pulling me away.

Naptime falls to the ground.

The ref helps him up and we both stagger into the middle. I spit my mouth guard into my hand and run my tongue around my mouth. The tang of blood coats my tongue but none of my teeth seem to be loose or missing.

Underhill runs over and cleans my face, wiping the blood out of my eye. "Good job," he says.

I nod, waiting for the decision.

Breathing hard, I stare at my feet. Bright red *drip, drip, drips* onto the floor. *Huh.* Is that coming from me? Am I still bleeding?

I had to have won, right? Especially the last round. I landed more strikes and I dominated the ground. If Naptime hadn't suckered me with his fake-ass tap out, I definitely would've won. The judges saw that, right?

"We have a winner by split decision!" the announcer shouts.

"What?" I look up and frown, pain slashing through my forehead.

Underhill's scowling at the ref. "That's not possible. Royal won. It's so fucking obvious."

A sick feeling rolls through my stomach that has nothing to do with the blood loss.

The announcer reads the results. The first one awards Naptime the win by a razor thin margin. The second one is for me by a much larger spread. The third goes to Naptime.

Shock rolls through my body in waves. But I smooth my face into a mask of indifference. I turn, arm outstretched, even though I'd rather chew rocks than shake Naptime's filthy, dirty, cheating hand. But it's the honorable thing to do. Win or lose.

Naptime's dazed eyes drop to my hand.

His body sways.

He clutches his shoulder and keels over, hitting the mat with a thud that reverberates up my legs.

Did he have a heart attack?

I look past him to the three judges sitting at a table right outside the ring. Their jaws drop and their eyes widen. None of them will meet my stare.

Kiki rushes into the cage, her entrance so dramatic, it deserves its own theme song. She falls to her knees and starts wailing, her tear-streaked cheeks aimed at the cameras.

Guess now I know who she hooked up with.

Matt actually steps over Naptime's prone body and shoves a microphone in my face. "Lost the fight and the girl. How do you feel, Stonewall?"

I glare at him and bite back the *fuck you* I'm dying to spit out.

How do I feel?

Like this was rigged all along.

No. Don't say that. It'll sound like the whining of a bitter loser.

Chin up.

"I feel good." I force a pained smile. Blood and sweat sting my eyes and blur my vision. "I fought hard. Naptime was a strong opponent." *And also a dirty fucking cheater.* I glance over my shoulder. "I guess when he wakes up from his nap you can ask him what *he* thinks."

Matt's jaw drops and I take that moment to walk away. If he'd put the mic in my hand, I'd throw it at his feet. I'm out and don't give a fuck if he's done with his asinine questions or not.

Venom meets me at the cage door. My body sways to the side as I step down. *Huh.* Those steps didn't seem so wobbly when I went into the cage.

I plant my feet on the concrete floor of the arena, but the wobbliness doesn't go away. Is this place built above a train station or something?

"You all right, bud?" Venom frowns and peers into my eyes.

"Fine."

His frown deepens.

"Split decision. Utter bullshit," Venom mutters. "You clearly had the better moves. You landed double the hits. You dominated him on the ground. He tried to flop away like an eel." He shakes his head. "This is how they wanted it to go."

That's my gut feeling too, but I'm a little too close to the matter to be objective.

"What the fuck?" Bear Trap yells, running up to us but staring at the commotion still going on inside the cage. "There's no way he won. Zero. None. The fuck is wrong with those judges?"

"Let it go," I mumble. There's nothing I hate more than a sore loser. The judges gave the fight to Naptime. I *refuse* to argue or complain. It won't change the outcome. It'll only make me look like a whiner.

Underhill's voice booms through the crowd. We turn in time to catch him shoving the ref against the cage wall.

Apparently other people have no problem arguing about the result. *Heh.* Who knew Underhill cared about me that much?

As the adrenaline slowly leaks from my body, pain races in to replace it. Confusion scatters my thoughts. Blood drips from my chin, rolling down my chest.

"Stonewall?" Venom shouts. "You okay?"

"I'm good."

Underhill's somehow next to me again. He wraps a thick arm around my waist, holding me up. "Let's get him checked out. He needs stitches."

"On my face?" I mutter.

"Yeah, you'll still be pretty. Don't worry." Harsh laughter brushes close to my ear. "You fucked Naptime up good. He's still out cold."

"Then *how* is he the winner?" Venom shouts.

"Don't get me started," Underhill seethes.

I dig deep but can't find any compassion for Naptime's condition. "He fought dirty," I mumble.

"Yeah. I saw the fake tap out," Underhill says.

At least I'm not crazy.

Anger roughens the coach's voice. "Ref blew that one."

Two paramedics with a stretcher rush into the cage. My gaze follows them for a few seconds. Maybe a ride on one of those things wouldn't be so bad.

"He's gonna need some painkillers tomorrow," Bear Trap mutters.

Huh. When'd he get here?

"No painkillers," I murmur.

I close my eyes and rest my head on Venom's shoulder. Just for a second.

"Shit. He needs to go to a hospital." Venom's worried voice sounds so far away.

Hospital sounds good.

CHAPTER TWELVE

Griff

IT'S A LONG NIGHT AT THE CLINIC THE SHOW HAS ON standby.

After the doctor finishes stitching my eyebrow, takes a few X-rays, and decides I don't have a concussion or any broken ribs, he says I'm free to go. I'm handed a book's worth of paperwork on how to treat my various aches and pains, decline a prescription for Vicodin, sign a bunch of papers and hobble outside to a waiting car.

The ride to the house is a blur. I think I passed out. But at some point, I stumble into the big mansion. Silence follows me through the long hallways. Every cell in my body throbs with pain.

This is it. I'm free. I'm finally going home.

I groan as my gaze lands on a concerned Jordan pacing in front of my door.

"What?" I mumble through sore lips and an aching jaw. Every part of my body is a hot needle of pain.

He lifts his head. "Final exit information for you."

"Now?" I shove the door open and walk directly to the closet.

"It's late, what are you doing?" he asks, peering around the corner of the closet door.

"Packing my shit." A wave of dizziness turns my head inside out. I stop and draw a ragged breath. "I want to go home."

He blinks and stares at the bundle of clothes clutched in my right hand.

"What?" I groan. "I'm not allowed to take this shit home?" I don't feel like sorting through and separating the clothes I brought with me from the ones the show gave us through different sponsors.

"No, no. It's all yours. I'll get you a bigger bag or a suitcase." He steps back. "You can't leave until tomorrow morning at the earliest."

"What?" I drop the backpack and clothes on the floor. "Why not?"

He gestures toward my forehead. "We need to monitor you and arrange transportation."

"I'm tired of being 'monitored' every second of my life." I also don't think I can stand on my own two feet much longer. "I just want to go home."

"Please?" he says simply. "I don't want to send you home and have you collapse."

He almost sounds guilty. Why? This is what fighters sign up for. It's not like I didn't know serious bodily harm was a predictable consequence of getting in the ring.

"Fine." I'm too tired and in too much pain to argue with him.

"I need to get you set up with someone to monitor your kidney function over the next few weeks too," he says, following me into the bedroom. "The other guys did it here since they were sequestered—"

Hell, no. I'm not getting stuck in that hotel. Venom made it sound awful. "I'm going home."

"Yes, yes," he hurries to agree. "You still have to return for the reunion show. We won't have a date until Naptime's out of surgery."

I've never taken pleasure in injuring an opponent. It's not like I'm some deranged, blood-thirsty sicko who gets a thrill from hurting people. It's a fight. We get in the ring, trade blows, and shake hands afterward. Nothing more. Nothing less. The only people I've ever held any animosity toward were the ones who forced me into a fight or fought dirty.

But after the sneaky moves Naptime pulled, never mind his general assholery over the last few months, a faint ember of satisfaction smolders in my chest at the thought of him laid up for weeks. Recovering from the beating I gave him. Hope he pictures my fist flying at his face every time he wheezes in a breath.

"Fine." I stare at him.

"You'll get half of your winnings tomorrow, plus your KO bonuses."

"My what?"

"Every time you knocked someone out in the house, you earned an extra five thousand."

"Well, fuck. If I'd known that, I woulda been knocking out people left and right."

He grins. "That's why we don't tell you. But you knocked out Bull the day you took your joyride." He skewers me with a scolding stare. "I should subtract five thousand for taking off on the Ninja the way you did."

"Oh, come on," I scoff. "Bet that was one of the highlights of the show."

He chuckles. "Yeah, it got a lot of attention."

"Anything else? I'd like to take a shower and go to sleep."

"Uh, yeah. I'll have some stuff brought up. Painkillers—"

"No. Tylenol or Advil are fine."

"Okaaaay." He stares at me. "Well, then...ice packs. Food. Whatever you need."

There isn't an icepack big enough to cover all my aches, but I thank him anyway.

"Oh, you can have these back now, too." He picks up a bag by his feet and hands it to me.

I peer inside. My phone, charger, and the burner phone I'd had stashed away until it mysteriously "disappeared" rest at the bottom.

"Same rules. You can't talk about the show at all. Normally, you'd be at the hotel with the others but because of the—"

"I got it. No talking about the outcome. Wait, what about the audience?"

He waves off the question.

"After the reunion show." He hesitates. "They're going to go over all of this with you tomorrow, but I wanted to warn you, so you're not surprised."

I sense he's trying to genuinely be helpful. So instead of shoving him out of my room, I drop the bag with the electronics on the nightstand and sit on the edge of the bed. "Yeah, okay. Give it to me."

I attempt to wiggle my fingers, wince at the pain, and drop my hand into my lap.

He grabs a small chair by the closet door and drags it over until he's sitting in front of me. "You're still under contract with the show. That means no social media posts. No interviews. No photographs, appearances, YouTube. Nothing."

I circle my hand in front of my face. "In case you haven't guessed, I'm not real eager to have my picture taken."

Although...maybe I *should* take some photos to document what I looked like after the last fight. In case the show tries to come after me for something later. I reach over, take my phone out of the bag, uncoil the charger, and plug it in.

"We can't stop you from seeing friends and family, of course. But try to limit what details you give them about your time here."

"Only details I'll be sharing are how I *didn't* fuck Kiki," I remind him. Highly doubt the show ever cleared up that lie.

His lips twist into a guilty frown. "Well, yes. I can understand that but still..."

My eyes keep wanting to close but the rest of my body wants to stand under a warm spray of water for at least an hour. "Anything else?"

"That's the basics. I'll be downstairs and some of the other crew members are still around, so you won't be totally alone in the house."

"Good to know."

"All right." He stands and nods. "I'll let you rest. If you need something, let me know."

"Thanks." I don't have the energy to walk him out, but the door closes behind him with a click.

I strip down, no longer caring if the camera's still recording, and shuffle into the bathroom. While I was at the clinic someone filled the tub with ice. It's melted enough for a cold plunge, but my most sensitive parts are strongly opposed to the idea, even if it might help speed up the healing process.

Instead, I hobble into the shower, flip on the hottest water I can stand, and get in.

Thirty minutes later, I return to the bedroom. Damn, I'm going to miss that shower. The hot water never seems to run out.

Someone stopped by while I was turning myself into a prune. A bunch of stuff that wasn't here earlier is scattered over the desk and chair.

I tuck my towel around my waist and shuffle across the room. An industrial-sized bottle of Tylenol. Tubes, bottles, and tins of pain relief creams, gels, and ointments. Ice packs of various sizes shaped for different parts of the body. It's like the world's most depressing gift basket. At least the ice packs are cold. And a low, unfamiliar hum draws my attention to a slim refrigerator/freezer combo now installed in the corner of the room.

"That would've been helpful three months ago," I grumble as I walk across the room to check it out.

It's stocked with a tray of cold cuts and cut fruit, hard boiled eggs, bottles of muscle milk, juice, and water.

I grab an egg and water, choke them down, then hit the Tylenol bottle.

The freezer has another set of ice packs up top. I grab one designed to wrap around the ankle, one for my knee, and one for my shoulder and carry them to the bed.

Once I have the ice packs arranged on my aching parts, I pick up my phone and turn it on. A barrage of texts flash on the screen. Several from my mother—at least she's alive—who apparently forgot I told her I'd be away at the reality show and needed money. None of her many messages ask if *I'm* okay. I don't bother replying.

None from Molly. Not even a "fuck you for cheating on me" text. Maybe that's a good sign? Probably not. She knew I wouldn't have my phone on me.

I'm too tired to look at anything else. I send a group text to Eraser, Vapor, and Remy to let them know I should be headed home tomorrow.

I tap out a text to Molly and my thumb hovers over the send button. Finally I hit it.

Me: On my way home tomorrow. Miss you bad.

Three dots *blink, blink, blink* as if the message isn't going through.

I check the text I sent to the guys. That was delivered.

Vapor: Let me know when.

Me: K

Remy: I'll stop by your place on my way to work and leave keys.

Me: I'm fucked up. Not going anywhere.

I snap a pathetic selfie, send it, then set my phone down.

The ice packs are more annoying than helpful now. My bleary eyes swing toward the fridge. I should toss the packs back in the freezer but it's too much trouble to get up.

Sleep.

I click the lamp off and roll over.

The Tylenol barely dulls the pain but at last I fall into the frantic tumble of sleep.

CHAPTER THIRTEEN

Griff

THE DRIVER ROLLS THE BLACKED-OUT SUV TO A STOP AT the curb. He turns his head and lifts his eyebrows as if to say, "you live in this dump?"

"This is it."

He shifts into park and steps out.

My gaze searches the parking lot, instantly recognizing two cars that don't belong here. I groan and open my door. I'd sent Eraser and Vapor a text when I finally escaped the mansion, and it looks like they timed their arrival perfectly.

The driver's lining up my bags on the sidewalk. Before I got in the SUV, Jordan instructed the guy to make sure I made it to my front door. Doesn't look like the dude plans to follow through.

Doesn't matter. Two seconds later, Eraser's big voice breaks the eerie, early-afternoon silence.

"Welcome home, superstar," he greets with his sarcasm dial jacked to eleven.

"Think if we ask nicely, he'll give us an autograph?" Vapor says in fake-hushed tone meant for my ears.

I turn and attempt a snarky greeting of my own.

Vapor's playful grin melts clean off his face. "What in the chicken-fried fuck happened to you?"

"Happy to see you too, brother."

Ignoring my sarcasm, he peers into my eyes and frowns. "They get someone decent to stitch you up?"

"Why? Does it look bad?"

"Nooo." He frowns as he stares at my stitches, not really making me feel better about my appearance. "Doesn't look great, though."

"Thanks. The doc went over me." I groan and reach into the car to grab my backpack and drag it out. "I put the other guy in the hospital. So I can't complain about a few stitches."

"You look like shit," Eraser says, taking the backpack out of my hands and hoisting it over his shoulder. "What'd your opponent do —try to make hamburger with your face?"

"Thanks." I gently probe my bottom lip and jaw, then the stitches over my left eye. "Your concern warms my heart."

"Stop picking on Griff." Ella points to my bags on the curb and slaps Eraser's back. "He needs to get inside."

"Inside would be nice," I agree.

"Is that everything?" Eraser asks the driver.

The guy nods and stands outside the driver's door. "Are you good, sir?" he says to me.

"I'm fine."

He stands there for another few seconds. If he's waiting for a tip, he can kiss my bruised ass.

"I can't believe they sent you home like this," Vapor says.

"I've taken worse," I say. Not since we were all locked up at Castle Correctional, but I don't have to say it. They know.

"I assume you won?" Eraser asks.

The disappointment of the judge's decision rings through my head. "I'm not allowed to say."

"Am I right?" He tilts his head.

"Seldom," I answer.

The guys chuckle at that. Normally, they'd throw a light punch or slap my back, but everyone looks like they're afraid to touch me. Like, I'll shatter into a million pieces from any contact.

They might not be wrong.

Juliet slams her car door and hurries over to me. "Griff." Her voice comes out as a high, strangled plea. "Oh my God."

"It's worse than it looks." I wince. "Promise."

She moves closer, opening her arms like she wants to hug

me, then reconsiders. I give her a slow, one-armed hug. "Happy to see you," I murmur against her ear. "Thanks for taking all my calls."

She touches my back gently—she might've found the only non-bruised part of my body. "Of course we took your calls."

When she pulls away, her eyes are glossy and as happy as I am to see her, I wish Vapor and Eraser had come without their wives. "I'm really okay, Juliet." I grin wide even though my jaw fucking aches. "Got all my teeth and everything."

Instead of laughing, she sighs. "Come on. I bet you need ice and a BenGay bath."

"Uh, I don't think you're supposed to bathe in it."

"You're not. But *you* might need to."

Vapor's head swivels between the bags on the curb and me. "I'm not sure if I should carry your stuff or carry *you* upstairs."

"I can walk." I half hobble, half shuffle onto the sidewalk to prove it. "Sort of."

"Good God, Griff, come here." Ella ducks under my arm and wraps her arm around my waist.

I lean on her a little more than I want to in front of everyone. Juliet takes my keys and marches ahead. The guys grab my stuff and coax me into the building.

Inside, I stop and give the staircase a long look. It looms like a mountain. Why the fuck do I have to live upstairs?

"Can you do it, Griff?" Eraser asks, all hint of joking gone. "Otherwise, you can come stay at our place. We only have the two steps on the front porch."

"Nah, I got it. Just give me a minute."

"Take your time," Ella says.

"Guys, I'm fine. Really." I release Ella's shoulders and test putting more weight on my knee. "Go on ahead."

"Like fuck," Vapor says, dropping my bags at the base of the stairs. "Come on."

Juliet returns, standing at the top of the stairs. "How are we doing this, guys?" she calls down.

"Slowly," I answer, gripping the handrail. It's like my knee's on vacation and doesn't want to function.

Eraser murmurs something to Ella I don't bother listening in on and she grabs two of the bags and heads upstairs ahead of us.

Vapor grabs the rest of my stuff and watches me with concern.

I don't have the energy to tell him I'm fine.

Eraser stands behind me while I grip the handrail and drag myself up one step at a time.

"They should've given you crutches or something," he murmurs.

"Nah, I'm fine," I grit through clenched teeth.

"Yeah, real fuckin' fine," Vapor grumbles.

Juliet's waiting in the hallway outside my open door when I finally make it to the top of the steps, wheezing like an eighty-year-old man who spent his whole life smoking three packs a day.

Almost there.

If my friends weren't hovering over me like I'm about to die, I'd crawl the last few feet to my apartment. Nah, that'd probably hurt even more.

I finally step over the threshold and practically cry with relief when I sink into my nubby, old couch.

"It was kind of stuffy in here, so I opened some windows," Juliet says.

"Thanks."

Vapor closes the door behind him and drops my bags on the floor with a thud.

Eraser perches on the couch next to me. Ella squeezes in by his side. Vapor takes the chair to my left and cranes his neck to watch Juliet in my kitchen.

Everyone's just...staring at me. Too stunned to speak? Waiting for me to entertain them? I don't know.

"So, what happened here?" With monumental effort, I rub my hand over the top of Eraser's unusually short hair. "Give yourself a haircut with a butter knife while I was away?"

He ducks away from my touch. "You keep touchin' me, you're gonna need more stitches."

Ella laughs and curls her arm around her husband's waist, then reaches up to smooth his short, chopped hair. "His favorite barber shop closed and he doesn't want to find a new one, so he's been doing it himself."

"Bro, I'll do a better job than that." I scissor my fingers together. "Soon as I can move my arms."

"You really think you're one to give out hairstylin' advice?" He flicks his fingers near my ear. "You came home lookin' like a mangled sheepdog."

I snort and lift my arm to run my hand over my hair. Pain sizzles from my shoulder to my elbow. I stop midway and rest my arm on the couch cushion instead. "Venom told me I needed to stand out more in the house. Naptime and I looked too much alike. So one night when all the dumb fucks got drunk, I shaved *his* head—"

"We saw," Ella says. "It was one of the show's highlights."

"Shit, I keep forgetting…" I shift my gaze to the wall. I've never felt so awkward around these guys.

Juliet returns to the living room and holds out an ice pack to me. "I don't even know where to put this first."

I take it from her and rest it over my knee. "I've got more." I tilt my head toward the bags Vapor dropped by the door. "They're in the black bag but need to go in the freezer."

"I'll do it," Eraser volunteers.

The couch shifts as he stands. He grabs the bag and heads into the kitchen without a word.

I glance at Ella. "Your husband still mad at me?"

She shrugs.

"Are *you* mad at me?"

She stares at me for a few uncomfortable seconds. "No."

"Let's not." Juliet, the peacemaker of our group, holds her hands in the air. "We have Griff back in one piece. That's all that matters right now."

It hurts too much to smile, so I dip my chin. "Thanks."

Eraser returns and plops down on my coffee table, gently shifts my foot a few inches to the right, then rests an icepack over my ankle.

"Besides the thing we're not going to talk about right now," he shoots a pointed look at me, "you did us proud."

A huff of bitter laughter eases out of me. "I don't know about *that*."

"You were the most 'professional' fighter there." Ella exchanges a glance with her husband.

"I tried," I mumble, embarrassed. I don't even know what they saw of my time there. Which carefully chosen snippets of all the weeks, days, and hours of my life were splashed on television for the whole world to see.

"He needs to rest now." Juliet nods at Vapor. "Help him into bed."

"He's twice as big as when he left." Vapor slaps Eraser's shoulder. "Get up. This is a two-man assignment."

"I'm not twice my size," I protest. "And I can get myself off the couch by myself. Unless you're gonna help me take a piss next?"

Juliet glances at Vapor. "You might want to make sure there's no blood in his urine."

Vapor opens his mouth—hopefully to protest—but I cut him off.

"Absolutely not." I shake my head. "I'm fine. I got an appointment with a local doctor later in the week to test kidney function. It's not like I haven't been here before."

"I haven't seen you this fucked up since the nights we were fighting for our lives in the basement, brother," Eraser says in a solemn tone rarely heard from him.

"Thanks." I attempt a withering glare. "Why don't you take your cheerful ass home and let me suffer in peace now."

"I don't think we should leave you alone," Juliet protests. "What if you have a concussion?"

"I got checked out by the doc after the fight. Slept fine last night." I reach over and squeeze her hand. "Thanks, though."

She bites her lip and flicks her gaze to Vapor. "All right." Obvious reluctance slows her words. "We're stopping by tomorrow morning right after we drop Atlas off at school, though."

"Okay," I agree, not that she's giving me a choice. My eyelids drop. "I'm beat."

Eraser stands and nods at Vapor. "Let's get him into the bedroom."

"Are you planning to tuck me in like a toddler?" I grumble.

Eraser leans down, shoving his big, bushy bearded face in mine. "Yeah, little buddy. You wanna go potty first?"

Ella snickers. Juliet smacks Eraser's arm with the back of her hand.

I slowly push myself to the edge of the couch. *Fuck, that hurts.* I shouldn't have sat on my lumpy couch for so long. I might need them to carry me after all.

"Come on." Vapor slips his hand under my arm.

"Uh, uh," I warn. "My shoulder and wrist are fucked, too. Let me do it."

After choking down several yelps of pain, I finally make it into my bedroom. Eraser and Vapor hover behind me like mother cats the whole way.

"I'm fine." I use one arm to try and lift my T-shirt off and immediately get stuck.

"Jesus." Vapor helps me ease out of the fabric and tosses it aside. "Eraser can do your pants."

"I can get the pants." God, I hate this. "But if you'd dig a pair of sweats out of the third drawer over there, that'd help."

"Fucking hell, Griff." Eraser stands in my doorway staring at my bruised torso. "You crack any ribs?"

I twist and stare at my right side. Deep purple bruising stains my skin from hip to armpit. "Felt like it. But they checked. No."

After a lot of unmanly whimpers, I finally change and slide into bed. The mattress squeaks and dips. After sleeping on that fancy cloud bed for so long at the house, my own feels like laying on a mound of dirty laundry. But it's home. Relief washes over me. I made it home.

First thing I'm doing with my winnings is buying a new bed.

The edge of my covers rustle. There's a clink and rattle next to my head.

"I think he's already asleep," Juliet whispers.

"No," I mumble.

"I left a glass of water and a bottle of Tylenol on the nightstand." Something warm and coco-nutty covers my face. Soft lips graze my forehead. "I'm glad you're home," Juliet whispers. "Rest up."

If I could move my arms, I'd hug her. "Thank you."

I'm vaguely aware of their low, concerned murmurs fading and my front door clicking closed.

Then I'm out.

Home sweet home.

Bright light punches me in the forehead.

I groan and try to throw my arm over my eyes, then moan at the pain in my shoulder.

"You alive?" Remy's gruff voice forces my eyes open.

"Satan? That you?" I mumble. "Did I end up in hell?"

He rudely rips the covers off. Cold air races over my skin.

"Motherfucker," he breathes out. "Are you okay?"

"I *was*." I groan and sit up. Boulders of pain bounce around in my skull. "I was enjoying some healing, restorative sleep until I was rudely jarred awake."

"Juliet was worried about you and texted me." He backs up so I can stand. "Now I understand why."

I grunt at him and shuffle into the bathroom, praying he won't follow.

When I emerge, he's on the other side of the door. "Did you want to hold my dick for me?" I ask. "'Cause I'm not into that."

"Shut up." He lifts his fist, then drops it at his side. "Come on. I brought food. I want you to eat something, then take more pain stuff. I assume you went to an actual doctor?"

"Yeah." I shuffle behind him as he walks down my short hallway and turns toward the kitchen. "Some special clinic."

"They give you anything useful for the pain?"

"Bro, you know I won't swallow anything harder than Tylenol." Too many addictive genes in my DNA to take the risk. I'd rather suffer through the pain.

He grunts a sound of grudging agreement.

Despite every part of my body throbbing or aching, my stomach rumbles. That's gotta be a good sign.

"Sit." Remy orders.

I ease into the chair by the window so I can keep an eye on him. "Yes, Dad."

"Don't 'dad' me." He opens my cabinets, searching for plates, rinses one off, then sets it on the counter. "I can't believe they sent you home in this condition."

The scent of roasted chicken teases my nose and my mouth waters in anticipation. "Bro, this is what we do. We literally run an underground fighting ring."

He sets a plate of chicken, macaroni salad, and cornbread in front of me. My stomach roars to life and I pick up a chicken leg, taking a vicious bite.

"We never let a fight go this far." He waves a disapproving finger at my injuries—my entire body. "What the fuck was the ref doing—taking a nap?"

"He wasn't the best," I admit, setting down the chicken leg, picking up my fork, and stabbing into the macaroni. "Other guy needs surgery last I heard."

"Good." He sets a glass of water in front of me. "You get knocked out?"

"Not once." I turn my head, showing off my jaw. "Concrete chin saved the day."

He slides into the chair across from me. "You're done with this now, right?"

I set my fork down with a slight clink against my plate. "Done with what? Fighting? Or the show?"

"Both."

"No. And not quite."

"What the fuck does that mean?"

I take a sip of water, then shake four Tylenol out of the bottle and pop them in my mouth. After swallowing, I look him in the eye. "It means, if I want to collect the rest of my winnings, I have to make an appearance at the reunion show."

"What kind of bullshit is that? How are they getting all the other guys who *didn't* win anything to come back?"

I shrug, then wince at the pain slicing down my back. "They're fame whores? I don't know or care about anyone else's motives. I just want *my* money." Should I tell him there's some extra cash if I convince Molly to go with me? No, it's her decision to make. I'll discuss it with her.

"All right. As long as they're not going to trap you in that house again. Or make you fight."

I stare at him. "You know you're not *actually* my dad, right?" Maybe that was too harsh. "Did you really miss me that much?"

"Yes, bonehead. Besides all the other stuff—that I'm not going to mention until you're feeling better—you were missed."

Not by everyone, I bet. "How's Molly?"

"She's fine." He waves his hand in the air as if he's dismissing the question. "She comes home on the weekend sometimes."

"Don't tell her I'm back yet." I point at my face. "I don't want her to see me like this."

"You assume she wants to see you at all."

Already tired of this conversation, I slam my fork down. "Remy, I didn't sleep with that girl. You really didn't tell Molly—"

"Yeah, I told her," he says, his voice thick with annoyance. "But you not coming home to set things straight," he shrugs and shakes his head, "didn't sit well with her."

"I couldn't!" I explode, then falter as pain flares in every part of my body.

"Stop." Remy holds out his hands. "Finish eating. I think you should come stay at the house with me. At least until you can move without looking like you want to cry."

"More like scream," I mutter, shoving more chicken in my mouth. Do I want to stay at Remy's to recover? Having him in my face constantly lecturing me about my recent bad choices isn't all that appealing. But staying *here* by myself isn't exactly a thrill, either. "You gonna feed me like this every night if I come stay at your place?" I tap my fork against my almost-empty plate.

"No, but if you behave, I'll bring you leftovers from the bar."

"How tempting." Exhaustion tugs at my eyelids. "I'll think about it. Right now, I don't think I could make it back down those stairs."

"Jesus," he breathes out. "What are you going to do about your job?"

"I just need to heal for a few more days and I'll be fine."

Remy stares at me. "You look like you need at least six weeks of recovery."

"Hey, guess what? You're not my dad *or* my doctor." There's no way in hell I'm admitting to Remy that the doctor I saw advised I take it easy for *eight* weeks. Not even light training or cardio for at least a month, he'd said.

"How dumb do you think I am?" He scowls at me. "As you pointed out, this is what we do. Of course I know how much recovery time you need, dipshit."

"We can argue about it another day." I swipe a paper towel over my mouth and push my plate away. "Right now, I just want to go back to bed."

He stares a hole through my face. "All right. I'll be back before I open the bar to check on you."

"Juliet said she'd stop by in the morning, so you're off the hook."

"I'll still check in."

"Great." I roll my eyes. "I'm not a little kid."

"Griff," he says in a dead-serious tone. "You look two steps away from death."

"You should know by now that I'm stronger than I look."

"You are." His gentle, pity-filled voice would irritate me if I had the strength for it. The desire to throttle him—just a little—twitches my fingers. My aching knuckles diffuse the urge. Lucky for Remy.

"I'm all right." Who am I trying to convince? Remy or myself? "I just need more sleep. Maybe an ice bath." *Or ten.*

"I can bring you ice in the morning to fill the tub." He stands and collects my plate and silverware. "I'll take care of this. Go on."

Emotion chokes the words from my throat. What the fuck is wrong with me? One minute I want to kill Remy, the next I'm ready to blubber all over him like a baby. Maybe one of those fists to the skull really did scramble my brain.

Slowly, I pull myself out of the chair and onto my feet. "Thanks, Remy. I..." What else can I say?

He turns and leans against my counter. "Figured you wouldn't have any food." He tilts his head toward my fridge. "There's hard boiled eggs and yogurt in the fridge. And I'll wrap up the rest of the chicken so if you're hungry in the middle of the night, you've got something here."

I swallow a lump of emotion. Food delivery options around here are pretty limited, especially at night. Remy's a lifesaver. "Appreciate that."

"You'd do the same for me."

Of course I would. Tired of the pity and talking about myself, I ask, "How's the bar? Everything okay there?"

"It's been fine. We can talk about it later."

"All right."

That's only one of many things we need to discuss.

CHAPTER FOURTEEN

Griff

EVERY DAY, SOMEONE'S AT MY APARTMENT TO CHECK ON me, bringing food and light doses of verbal abuse.

Wednesday, Remy shows up early to take me to my doctor's appointment.

"Let's go, princess," he shouts.

"I can't wait until we can get in the ring and do some sparring," I mutter, hobbling to my front door. I grab a sweatshirt off the hook on the wall and slowly ease my arms into it. Remy stands and watches with a grave expression I want to punch right off his face. "Thanks, I got it."

He flicks his serious blue eyes up. "You need me to zip it up for you like you're headed to kindergarten?"

"No, jackass." Gripping the tiny zipper with my still-sore fingers takes a few tries but I finally get it done. *Biggest accomplishment of the morning.*

At the top of the stairs I stop and reconsider my plan to leave the building.

"Just take it slow," Remy says, holding out his arm.

Shame prickles over me. I shouldn't still be this fucked up almost a week later. But at least Remy doesn't crack any jokes as I grip the railing and ease myself down the stairs, keeping as much weight as I can off my fucked-up knee.

"I know this visit is for your kidneys, but you might need to see someone about that knee," Remy says when I finally land on the first floor.

"They x-rayed it down there. It's fine." Fifty-fifty chance it doesn't need surgery.

Black Beauty's sitting in the first parking spot, gleaming like Remy ran her through the car wash before picking me up. "I figured you might not want to climb into the Bronco." He holds out the keys to me. "You can drop me off at the house when we're done."

I wave them away. "You better drive." I ease into the passenger side and run my hand over the dash. "How's my baby?"

Remy slams the driver's side shut and snorts. "Fine. I've been taking her out once a week or so. Otherwise, keeping it in the garage out back."

"Thanks. I don't even want to think about what would've happened to it if I left it sitting here." I gesture to the apartment building's small parking lot as Remy fires up the engine.

I cock my head, listening to the throaty rumble, a slight smile tugging at the corners of my mouth.

"Told you I took care of her." Remy shifts into reverse and eases out of the parking spot.

"Thanks." I clear my throat. "Molly's car still at Jerry's?"

"Yup." His tone's clipped, intended to stop any additional questions.

"I'll need to go look at it and—"

"It's been there all summer." He flips the blinker on and makes a left out of the lot. "It'll be fine for a few more days."

"I guess."

"Eraser and I cleaned up the mess."

Well, shit. Now I feel bad for ragging on Eraser's haircut the other day. "How bad was it?"

"Bad." He blows out a long, irritated breath. "I really don't want to talk about it, though."

Tough shit. I had to go weeks without knowing what the fuck happened. "Jesus, Remy. Did she really go at it with a bat?"

He glances at me sideways. "Yes."

"Did she get hurt?"

"Her arms were sore for a few days." He taps the side of his fist against the steering wheel. "And I think she had a few scratches. But most of the damage was to her *pride*. Oh, and her broken heart," he adds with a murderous glance in my direction.

"Remy, you know I never—"

"You know where I found her that day after I talked to you?" He doesn't wait for me to answer. "At the fucking airport trying to leave town."

I open my mouth, then close it as that sinks in. Molly must've been in a bad way if she wanted to leave home and get on a plane all by herself.

"Then she had to deal with every nosy fuck around here asking her about *you* or the show. She worked three fucking jobs all summer so she didn't have to see her friends."

No, I bet she did that to keep herself busy, not just to avoid her friends. "Where?" I'm ashamed I have to ask the question. That's information I should already know. "Besides the clinic and Miller's Farms?"

"The internship at the hearing aid clinic wasn't so bad," he answers. "Apparently their clients aren't the target audience for cage fighter reality shows."

"Well, thank fuck for that," I mutter.

"She kept her shifts at the grocery store. But so many people bugged her there, they ended up moving her to the flower shop where she didn't have to deal with a lot of customers and the other cashiers."

"Shit."

"Eh." He lifts his shoulders. "She said it wasn't too busy, so she got a lot of reading done."

At least *that* sounds like something Molly would say.

"She helped me out at the bar most nights and on the weekends after Miller's," he continues.

"She always wanted you to let her work there." It's not the safest environment, though. Remy's had his share of unexpected events. "Was she okay? Customers didn't bother her, right?"

"We had a few issues. But they were dealt with."

"Like what?"

"Not your concern."

"The fuck it isn't."

"It's really not." He glances over. "You weren't here."

He's going to throw that in my face forever. "Remy."

"I'm not arguing with you." He turns into the parking lot of the large medical complex, glances at a large board of signs and makes a right turn. "I'm glad you're home. But more than your face and body got fucked up by that show."

"Thanks for the reminder," I grumble.

He pulls into a spot next to Building A. "Sign says it's in there."

Glad one of us was paying attention.

"You want me to go in with you?" he asks.

"Not really." I draw a lazy circle in the air with one finger. "This has all been humiliating enough."

He hums a thoughtful noise. "I wish they hadn't made it so... personal. Gone after Molly the way they did."

Guess that's his way of telling me he'd have more compassion for my situation if the producers hadn't fucked with his sister. "You and me both, brother."

The door squeaks as I open it. Gonna have to take a look at that soon.

In the waiting room, the receptionist points me to a chair and hands me a stack of forms to fill out. "People still do this on paper?" I lift an eyebrow.

She scowls at me. "Just fill it out. Payment has already been arranged but we need your signature on those forms."

At least Jordan did what he said he'd do. I'd half expected the producers to fuck me over and get handed a massive bill at the end of this appointment.

After filling out the forms and handing them back to the receptionist, she again tells me to take a seat. I park my ass in the corner and pull out my phone.

None of my texts to Molly have gone through.

I check her social media next. She's never been into it much, but she has an Instagram account.

That I'm no longer able to see.

This account is private.

What the fuck? Her profile picture used to be one of us from prom night. Now, it's her face turned to the side, chin up like she's looking at the sky but most of her features hidden by her hair or obscured by some filter. But I know my girl. It's definitely her.

Did she lock down her account to hide from *me*? Or because people who were watching the show harassed her?

I check my own account. Diane had "curated" it when I first arrived at the house. As far as I can tell, all that meant is she posted a series of obnoxious shirtless thirst traps of me from different events at the house. It worked, though. Each one has thousands of likes and comments. I'm not even going to bother reading all that shit. How fucking embarrassing.

Any photos *I'd* posted before the show Diane must have set to private. That's probably for the best. My bio still says "in a relationship." Gee, surprised Diane didn't change *that* too while she was busy fucking up my life. I navigate my way through the settings and change my password. Not that it probably matters. Those fucks had my phone for so long, they could've put God only knows what spyware on it. Maybe I should have Remy take me to get a new phone while we're out.

"Griffin," a nurse calls out.

It takes a second to realize she means me. Almost no one ever calls me that. I stand and shove my phone in my pocket.

I hope this isn't gonna take all day.

AFTER THE APPOINTMENT, Remy talks me into coming back to the house with him for dinner. He seemed so annoyed with me earlier, I should probably be more cautious.

We're sitting at the dining room table finishing plates of lasagna when I sit back and take my phone out of my pocket. I check it quickly. Still nothing from Molly.

I clear my throat. "You know, I've tried calling Molly and sending texts." I hold up my phone. "She must've blocked me. None of my texts to her have gone through."

Remy's eyes narrow and the corner of his mouth curls up in a pissed-off sneer. "You're damn right she blocked you, motherfucker. She won't even talk *about* you. She definitely doesn't want to talk *to* you."

"Remy, you gotta—"

"I don't gotta do shit." He aims a blistering glare my way. "I warned you what would happen if you hurt her." He runs his disgusted gaze over me. "Kicking your ass when you're in this condition doesn't seem fair. But keep pushing me, and I'll reconsider."

"Why'd you want me to come over so bad, then?"

He takes a long, slow breath and curls his hands into fists on the table. "You've been my best friend...like my brother for a long time. Even though I want to choke the living daylights out of you," the harsh edge in his voice fades, "I'm also worried about you."

Doesn't that make me feel guilty as fuck. "I'm all right."

"We need some ground rules."

I already sense what he's going to say, but I still ask, "Such as?"

"No more updates on my sister. If you two work things out, great. If not—"

"Wait a second." I lean forward. "Not working things out isn't an option, Remy. I *love* her."

"Well, you have a piss-poor way of showing it, Griff."

"I—"

He holds up his hand, cutting me off. "I won't keep going in circles about this with you."

"Will you at least ask her to unblock me?"

"No." He shakes his head. "You're resourceful. If you really want to talk to her, you'll figure it out."

He's right to a certain extent. I can't ask him to play mediator between Molly and me. I'll have to repair the wreckage I caused all by myself.

Still, I have to know. "Just tell me one thing—is she happy at school? Is she adjusting well?"

The corner of his mouth twitches but I can't tell if it's amusement from thinking about Molly or annoyance at my question. "Yeah," he answers with a heavy sigh. "I think so. The roommate thing has been an adjustment, but she fixed her schedule so all of her classes start after ten a.m. She's pretty excited about that."

I chuckle. Sounds like Molly. And that's all I'm going to ask him about school. Those are stories I want to hear from Molly, not Remy.

"She did okay...working all those hours over the summer?" I ask.

"Yeah." He answers slow, like he's not happy about dipping into this conversation with me. "She's a hard worker. Helped me out at the bar quite a bit, honestly. I probably should've let her work with me sooner."

"Holy shit. I hope you told her that."

His lips quirk. "I might have said it once or twice."

"Wish I'd witnessed that conversation." As soon as the words leave my mouth, the full force of them rams into me with painful clarity. I missed so much time with my friends. The people I love and consider my family. I allowed some show biz weasels to cut off all contact with the only people who have ever mattered to me. It's not even like I was away doing something noble like serving my country. I did it for a cheesy, third-rate reality television show. Disgust blows through me like a tornado.

Fame wasn't even my goal. I just needed to win the money. Improving my skills and getting trained by actual professionals was part of it too, but there are easier ways I could've done that. Ways that wouldn't have included alienating everyone I care about.

And I still don't even know what everyone saw. What Molly saw. Why everyone seems so convinced I'm a cheating asshole.

Remy stands and clears the table. "Go on." He tilts his head toward the living room. "I recorded the Eli/Costa fight. You want to watch it?"

"Sure." A fight's the last thing I want to watch but I slowly make my way into the living room anyway. Fatigue pulls me onto the couch. How am I still so tired when I haven't done anything all week? One visit to the doctor and a few conversations with Remy have me ready to pass out.

A few minutes later, Remy joins me in the living room. He sits in his recliner, and swivels around to face me. "You good?"

"Let me see it." I nod to the television.

Remy frowns. "The fight? Yeah, you sure you can stay awake for it?"

"No, the show. Let me see it."

Remy stares at me as if I've lost my mind. "The show? *Your* show?"

I nod quickly.

His slack-jawed expression shifts into anger. "What the fuck for?"

"I need to know..." I ball my hands into fists. "I need to see what she saw."

"You really haven't seen any of it?"

"No. The place was locked down tight. They took my phone almost immediately." I hesitate, not sure if Molly ever told him I brought a burner phone. "I even had a burner phone hidden but after the day I talked to you, it disappeared."

"What the fuck kind of insanity did you sign up for, bro?"

"I guess I thought it was going to be like one of those training camps." I gesture toward the TV. "Remember that show we saw about how Eli went off and trained with all those kickboxing and muay tai experts and shit?"

"Yeah," he answers slowly, "but that was for an *official* fight. Not a bunch of trailer park, wannabe Conor McGregors living in a house as some trashy social experiment."

Thanks for that oddly specific, but highly accurate description that really drives home what an idiot I am. "I thought it was something simple like that. Each week, there'd be a match and one person would go home. At the end, the top four would all go home with some money and the winner a big prize. That's how Diane explained it to me." I gesture toward the television. "I didn't know it would turn into a circus."

"Yeah, it definitely wasn't what you thought," he says with an edge of you're-an-idiot sarcasm. "I don't know if I can sit through all of it again. Which one do you want to see?"

Now I give him the are-you-stupid stare. "*The* episode."

"Christ, Griff." He swipes the remote off the table next to his recliner and turns the TV on. "From the beginning?"

"Yeah."

An opening montage introducing each of the fighters flashes across the screen, complete with cheesy background music and brief, stereotypical, bordering on insulting descriptions of each of us. Venom is the wise, old sage—who's possibly too old to fight. The dude isn't even thirty. What the fuck? Naptime's described as having charisma as bright as the sun—hard disagree on that one. I supposedly have "classic movie star looks" but my reluctance to say much and blank expression points to not much going on behind my pretty face.

"Seriously?" I wave my hand at the television. "I don't run my mouth like an idiot all the time, so I must be dumb?"

A picture of Molly fills the screen. Tears rolling down her cheeks as she says goodbye to me. Hollow pangs of regret thrum through my chest. If I could go back to that day, there are many things I'd do differently.

"Wait a second, did they call Molly jailbait?" I ask.

Remy glares at me. "That's the nicest thing they said about her."

The show starts with all the contestants prepping for a fight. "This was before they brought actual coaches to train us," I explain.

A *lot* of time is spent on the girls. Their portions must've been filmed in a part of the house I never visited. Kiki's front and center talking about goals for her future. The interviewer gets her to admit she likes me and thinks I'm "husband material."

"Christ, that's creepy," I mutter. "I never knew they were asking them stuff like that."

Remy grumbles an annoyed sound.

Then the footage flips to a day they took us out to get fitted for suits to wear to a dinner. "This was a whole different day." I frown at the television. It's been so long, all the days have blended together but I'm pretty sure the suits and dinner thing happened days before the fight we were getting ready for.

"This is so weird." I flick my hand toward the screen. "We did the suits thing before this particular round."

Remy rolls his head and throws me a sideways glance over his shoulder. "Does it matter?"

"I guess not."

The dinner sequence is worse than I remember. The camera spent a lot of time on Deadass, who didn't know which fork to use and ended up eating with his *hands* at one point. I snicker, remembering how annoyed our host, Matt, had been.

Then it skips to us back at the house. Kiki keeps trying to hang on my arm and I brush her off.

I jump up and point at the television. "You can tell I'm trying to get away from her." On the screen, I clearly shake her off. Then she trips and I help steady her.

She follows me to my room.

"Is Kiki going to make her move tonight?" the voice-over asks. "And will Griff give into temptation just this once?"

"I wasn't 'tempted' by anything!" I shout, frustrated at the way this whole night is framed.

I'm at my door trying to get into my room when Kiki walks up behind me. She stumbles again and I react quickly, stopping her from hitting the floor.

The show cuts to commercial.

"She *never* went in my room," I tell Remy. "She tried. That's why I walked her back to the living room and left her there."

"Keep watching," Remy says in a tight, angry voice.

When the show returns, it's Deadass and two of the other girls splashing around in the pool and eventually making out.

"I'm so glad I never went in the pool," I mutter.

Then it catches up with Venom on the phone with his wife.

"What the fuck?" We were only allowed phone calls once a week. At least, that's what I thought.

"Wait for it," Remy says.

Bull and Pirate appear in the downstairs gym, sparring in a cage. "That's not even the same night." I point at the screen. "I was there for this. Look! You can see my red shirt in the corner, right there."

Remy leans forward and squints. "It could be anything."

"They sure did some creative editing."

The screen switches to the grainy black-and-white footage that seems to be reserved for the personal quarters and bedrooms.

"Wait a minute. Did Griff invite Kiki into his room after all?" the voice-over asks in a dramatic stage whisper.

Two people appear in bed, under the white comforter. Loud moaning.

"Looks like Griff has a difficult conversation with his girlfriend coming up," the announcer says.

"Oh, fuck this guy!" I shout.

Acid crawls up my throat as the camera focuses on the guy's back. The girl digs her nails into his shoulders and they're clearly fucking. Or at least putting on a good show.

"Jesus Christ." I stab my fingers through my hair and fall against the couch. It's worse than I thought. So much worse. I'm not surprised Molly took a bat to her car at all. Shit, I'm amazed she didn't light *my* car on *fire* after watching and listening to *that.*

"Yeah," Remy says barely above a whisper. "You get why we all thought—"

"Nah, bro." I shoot a glare at him. "I'm still pissed at *you* for not sticking up for me. You know me." I shift toward the screen again. "But now that I've seen this, I get why *she* lost her shit."

It stings. But there isn't a single piece of me that's angry with Molly. Mad at myself, sure. Rage and shame keep boxing my heart against my ribcage.

Idiot. Stupid, lazy, foolish. Nothing is simple. Nothing is ever easy. Hard work and working hard—the only true path to anything worth having. I *know* this. How did I let that little pink-haired witch fool me into thinking otherwise?

The moans and whispers coming from the television turn my stomach. *Tough shit. Suck it up.* I force myself to watch. So I know what Molly saw—what everyone in the world saw.

Even though I know damn well I *didn't* sleep with Kiki, watching the footage while listening to the voice-over disorients me. Like, I'm questioning my own fucking memories and sanity as I watch every grainy, disgusting minute.

Thank fuck it's over fast. *Gotta keep the show "family friendly" after all.*

What bullshit.

I open my mouth to say something snarky to Remy but my sweaty face flashes on the screen looking guilty and contrite.

"See." I point at the screen. "I'm all sweaty from the match I thought I'd lost."

"Or," Remy answers slowly, "from some other vigorous activity."

"Fuck off," I snarl, annoyed that he's right. That's exactly how the show set it up to look.

The camera switches to Kiki gushing about how much she's into *him*. Unlike the earlier clip, she never actually says *my* name. But the way the events were edited, it absolutely seems like she's talking about me.

Even so, I point out, "You realize she never actually says my name here, right?"

Remy cocks his head and stares at the screen. "I didn't see this part. Molly had already run out of the room, and I went after her."

Anguish twists my chest. My Molly had her heart ripped out and I wasn't here.

"That's good. I guess," I mutter.

"Don't worry, I'm sure Hayden or one of the other girls blabbed the whole thing to her. People couldn't stop giving her helpful 'updates' all summer long. Why do you think she left for college early?"

"That's why you won't let me talk to her?"

"You haven't exactly put in a lot of effort."

"Bro, you saw how I came home. You literally took me to the doctor this morning."

He shrugs. "Well, I caught you checking out her schedule in the kitchen. You know where she is."

"Fuck off." I gesture toward the television. "This isn't some happy horseshit rom-com. You think me showing up on campus unannounced would be good for her?" I lower my voice. "I don't want to do anything to distract her from school." I swallow hard, fighting off my annoyance with Remy so I can make him understand I'm trying to do the right thing. "I don't want to do anything to hurt her more than I already have."

He stares at me for a few long, thoughtful moments. "You're right." His gaze slips to the side and the corner of his mouth twitches. Guilt? About what, though? "You're not really in any condition to drive, either."

"No shit."

"All right." He finally relents. "I'll tell you the next time she comes home."

My heart stops. *Finally.*

"Pax has been talking about having a costume party at Zips," he adds. "She was excited about coming home for that."

Costume party? Molly probably has an outfit ready to go.

"You should probably think about a costume." He scowls. "Although, honestly, if your face still looks like that you won't need a mask."

"Thanks, fucker."

"I should warn you..." He glances away like he has to gather his thoughts.

"What?" I prompt.

"Pax wants to throw a big welcome home party for you at some point."

"Please, no." I can't have any pictures taken until after the reunion show. Besides that, I'm too fucking embarrassed to show my face anywhere yet. Not because of my injuries. Because I lost to the biggest dumbass in the house and whenever that episode airs, everyone will know it.

"Can we do it sometime when it's just our crew?" I don't need a bunch of strangers in my business.

He tilts his head in his obnoxious way. "Having your moody ass there might be a big draw for Zips. Pax could use some more legit business."

"Really?" I cock my head. "Second-place finisher from a third-rate reality show?"

"This is backwater New York." He cough-laughs. "A D-list celebrity is still pretty exciting."

"More like Z list," I grumble and fall against the couch. Fabric rustles over my shoulders. The blanket Molly and I snuggled under not that long ago in this very spot. Instead of Molly's familiar cherry-vanilla scent, the carefully woven yarn now smells like detergent.

"If you're looking for a pity party, I can't help you."

"I'll tell Pax I need some time. Right now, I look like hot garbage."

"Nah." He waves his hand in the air, dismissing my concern. "You look like a warrior. Girls love that shit."

I glare at him. "Only one girl's opinion matters to me."

He does that guilty shift of his eyes again. "You plannin' to stay over, or you want me to drive you home?"

I toss the blanket toward the end of the couch. "You mind if I stay?"

"Nooo," he answers slowly. "I said you could move in and take over the basement."

"But I'd need to bleach all the surfaces." I blink at him with complete innocence. "And pry the mirror off the ceiling."

He rolls his eyes. "I'd say move into the back bedroom down here, but it's still crammed full of Nana's stuff."

"I don't know if I can do the basement stairs right now."

"You want me to install one of those stair lift things for you?"

I burst out laughing. "What's wrong? Are you lonely without Molly around?"

"Me?" He raises his eyebrows. "Lonely? No."

"I'll think about it." I lift my chin. "Who's gonna help me move all my shit?"

"You mean your one bed, one dresser, sad little collection of clothes, nightstands, and TV? I think we'll manage." He gestures toward the basement. "It's furnished. You can sell your stuff if you want."

"How much rent are you gonna charge me?"

"We'll work something out."

I stand and stretch. "Thanks."

Remy stands and faces me. "For?"

"Watching that with me." I tilt my head toward the TV. "I'm so fucking embarrassed."

He studies me for so long, I drop onto the couch cushions and wait for his judgment.

"They did you dirty, for sure." He works his jaw from side to side. "At the time, I didn't know what the fuck to think. You see how they made it look."

It's not a question, but I nod anyway.

"Then Jerry called the next day about the car," he continues.

"Molly took off...It was a mess. I thought after I talked to you, you'd come home—at least for a few days, to clear things up—"

"I couldn't!"

He holds up one hand to stop my protests. "I think I understand that a little better now. For what it's worth, I *did* tell Molly that you denied it and *I* didn't think you'd do that to her. But when you didn't come home or call again..."

I should've tried harder.

"I talked to Vapor and Juliet," I answer miserably.

"I know." He nods. "Juliet kept me up to date on your calls."

"I couldn't tell her much." I shrug and groan at the pain in my shoulder. "I guess I thought, you guys *know* me. You know I'd never do that. I wanted to get through the filming and the fights, then come home and make things right."

"It's not only the cheating thing. You saw the way the show talked about Molly." He sighs. "Although Ella said after that episode they never mentioned her again."

"I told them they had to knock it off or I'd walk home."

Remy lifts an eyebrow. "You did?"

"Fuck yeah, I did. They threatened to sue me into oblivion. Leaving with no money *and* having to defend myself in a lawsuit against people with deep pockets...seemed like a bad choice."

"Jesus Christ." He blows out breath. "Even if they didn't win, they'd drain you dry with legal fees. And if they got a judgment against you, you could say goodbye to ever buying Jerry's Garage—if you still even want to do that."

"Yeah, exactly." Finally, he seems to understand. "I bluffed my way through it, but they had me by the nuts."

He nods slowly. "That's what happens when you swim with sharks."

I should've known Remy's understanding had limits. "No kidding. I thought I was going to be in *Rocky* and instead I ended up in *Saw*."

He doesn't laugh like I expected. "I know it wasn't you." He jerks his thumb over his shoulder toward the television.

It's not an apology, but I'll take it for now.

There's only one more person I care about convincing.

CHAPTER FIFTEEN

Griff

THIS MORNING, I FEEL ALMOST HUMAN. I STILL *LOOK* LIKE I got run over by a garbage truck but I'm desperate to get out of my apartment and into the fresh air.

I have a particular destination in mind.

First, I stop by the garage. Jerry takes one look at my face and tells me to take a few more days off. Should I be grateful or worried he's planning to fire me?

I can't stress about it today.

My engine thrums beneath me on the highway. Aches and pains still rule my body, but for the first time in months, my mind feels more centered and grounded. Thank fuck I'm home in time to enjoy at least a few weeks of perfect riding weather before I'll have to park my Harley for the winter. The sharp scent of motor oil mingles with the earthier aroma of damp, fallen leaves—my favorite scents of fall.

I tighten my grip on the handlebars and twist the throttle. My shoulder protests the movement and I relax my grip. An urgent need to *see* Molly pulls me along. Even if I don't talk to her or reveal myself to her, I have to know she's okay.

It's loud, but my bike will still blend in better than my vintage muscle car with the identifiable red and purple pinstripes. Not many cars with that color scheme around. I love my Harley but damn, that Ninja I was able to take for a joyride would be a lot more fun for this trip.

I'd peeked at the copy of her schedule Remy had stuck to the refrigerator, then looked up the college online and tried to figure out the best place to catch a glimpse of Molly. I have an idea of where she'll be on the small campus and when. If I know my girl, she'll probably stop for coffee and a muffin *after* class. I'll try the coffee shop that's near her English 101 class first, and go from there.

The ride only takes an hour. I can easily see myself making this trip to visit Molly whenever she wants me to.

If she wants me here at all.

I slow for the exit, guiding the bike into the small college town. Large trees line the streets, their branches meeting overhead, creating an almost tunnel-like feeling as I guide my bike into the visitor parking lot and tuck it into a spot in the back, hidden by a big monster truck and a prickly green bush.

I take off my helmet and slip an old green ball cap over my head —careful to avoid my stitches. My hair's a bit longer—I really need to get it cut—so it sticks out from under the cap, tickling my ears. I zip my hooded sweatshirt. Pulling the hood up will probably draw more attention to me. My disguise isn't great, but it should be enough. Molly isn't expecting to see me here. Hell, I might be overestimating my detective skills and not even be able to find her today. What if she decided to skip class? No, I can't see Molly doing that. She didn't work hard and spend a fortune on school just to blow off classes.

I grab my backpack with my laptop, hoping it'll provide me with camouflage among all the other students. Not like I'd know how to blend in with this kind of crowd. I haven't set foot on a college campus in the daylight since my sophomore year of high school when we all took a trip to the Empire State's campus library. That campus had seemed way too big and overwhelming—like its own city. This campus is much nicer. Smaller. I can picture Molly on these sidewalks, darting between ivy-covered brick buildings to get to her next class on time.

I head to the small cafe in the middle of the campus. It's in the basement of a building. Christ, I'm too big to hide if I run into Molly on the stairs. There's no way she won't recognize me this close up. I move down the stairs as quickly as my bad knee allows and push my way through the heavy glass doors. The scent of roasted coffee beans and cinnamon slaps me in the face. Four people stand in line ahead of me.

There's an empty booth, three empty tables and a long counter with a few unoccupied stools. The only spot that gives me a clear view of the door is the booth near the back. Damn, I hope no one takes it.

The line moves fast. I order a black coffee and a blueberry-lemon muffin. If they serve these every day, there's a good chance this is where Molly stops for breakfast.

I flick my gaze to the menu above my head. For a second, I panic, thinking they only accept student meal cards as payment but when I hand over a twenty, the cashier accepts it without comment and gives me my change. I drop the coins in the tip jar and slide down to the next window to wait for my order. It's waiting for me and I grab it, then hustle to the table in the back.

I slouch down on the bench, take out my laptop, open it, but don't bother turning it on. It's just camouflage.

Eyes on the door, I sip my coffee and break off bits of the muffin and try to ignore the agony in my knee. The ride home's gonna be rough. A steady stream of students rotates in and out of the cafe, their chatter echoing in the small space. People meet between classes, sit at tables and gossip about class. A few kids are busy on their phones, ear buds in, blocking out the world.

After the last few months I've had, I feel like I've landed on an alien planet. None of these kids look like they could last two seconds in a cage without crying for their mom.

I don't belong here.

A heavy knot of doubt creeps up and chokes me lifeless. As much as I hated being at the *Supreme Fighter* mansion, I didn't feel as out of place there as I feel now, listening to this nonstop babble.

The door swings open and my heart thuds faster. Molly.

Her long, brown hair's a little shorter, and is it a lighter shade of brown? It's layered or curled or something...different. But it's definitely her. I've spent years memorizing the curve of her cheek, the set of her shoulders, her every movement.

She's with a tall girl I don't recognize. They seem familiar enough to stand arm to arm in line, talking while they eye the menu.

Molly's making new friends at school. That's good. Does she get along with her roommate? After living with Remy for the last few years, she should be able to tolerate the quirks of any roommate.

A solemn mood seems to cling to Molly. She nods and gives half-smiles to her friend. But her usual grin and laughter seem to be missing.

She's between classes, not headed to a party. Of course she's serious.

With my head cocked like an eager golden retriever, her voice is clear above the other noise as she steps up to place her order. "Vanilla pumpkin latte and a pumpkin spice scone, please."

Scone? The fuck? The girl has never turned down a blueberry muffin as long as I've known her, let alone a *lemon*-blueberry one. It's not like I bought the last one. An entire tray of them were in the case.

I slide down in the booth and tug my cap lower as Molly slowly walks to the end of the counter to pick up her order. The guy who hands it to her greets her by name. He touches her hand way longer than necessary as he passes Molly the bag. She gives an uninterested but polite smile and turns away.

Sorry, buddy. She's mine.

But not really.

Not anymore.

Juliet hinted that Molly had a terrible summer. Remy hadn't been as delicate—he said it had been hell on her after that stupid episode aired.

It looks like things are back to normal for her. She's starting over in a new place. Seems like she's adjusting to college well. What am I supposed to do—approach her like nothing happened and shatter the peace she's found here?

I care about her way too much to be that guy.

Molly and her friend head out of the cafe.

I wait a few beats then shove my laptop in my backpack, grab my coffee and go. That short glimpse of Molly wasn't enough.

Outside, I duck my head out of the building first and look both ways. The girls have moved fast, already halfway down the long sidewalk to my right.

I hurry out, slip my arms through my backpack straps, jam my hands in my pockets and hustle to get closer. Not too close. Just enough to catch Molly's scent in the air or hear her voice again.

Every cell in my body wants to continue following her for the rest of the day. To see where her classes are. Where her dorm is. Who she hangs out with.

No. Confronting her here would be a shitty thing to do. I'm so fucking proud of her and I love her too damn much to do anything that might upset her when she's focused on school.

Even casually dressed in loose green sweats and a big black hoodie, Molly's still the most beautiful person anywhere. My gaze hasn't strayed from her once.

Hoodie. Wait.

I almost stumble over my feet.

That's *mine.* One of the many hoodies she's stolen from me over the years. It's old. A faded roses and brass knuckles design Vapor drew years ago spills over the back of the sweatshirt. If it's the shirt I'm thinking of, *Stonewall* is embroidered into one of the sleeves. She went no contact with me after the Kiki incident, but she brought one of my old sweatshirts with her to college? Molly's way too sentimental for that to be an accident.

She hasn't given up on me. On *us.*

My confidence returns with a vengeance.

I'm going to win back my girl.

Not today, but soon.

CHAPTER SIXTEEN

Griff

THE TRIP TO SPY ON MOLLY WORE ME OUT. I SPEND THE next week planning, plotting, and sleeping. And wallowing. Lots of wallowing.

I swear my bones actually *throb*. Maybe I should've risked it and said yes to the Vicodin prescription the doc offered.

Fuck that. I need to rest and not take long motorcycle rides to stalk my girlfriend who doesn't even want to talk to me.

Still worth it. Seeing her in my hoodie gave me hope. The setback in my recovery is a small price to pay.

But lounging around sucks. I feel like a lazy little pansy.

My mind's racing too fast to fall asleep. I'm sort of hovering somewhere in between.

From the living room, there's a click and scrape. Someone opening my front door?

"Griff!" Remy calls out.

I pull the covers over my head.

The floor creaks as he makes his way through my apartment.

"It's Friday afternoon, what are you doing in bed?" My blanket is rudely ripped away from my body.

"This is getting old," I grumble, yanking the blanket back into place.

"Come on, let's go to Zips." He drops onto the edge of the bed and tugs on the blanket again. "Eraser installed these high-flow fuel injectors in Ella's ride. He wants to test it out."

"So, run it. You don't need me." Who knew there'd come a day when I wouldn't give a fuck about car upgrades.

"Griff." His patient dad tone makes an annoying appearance. "You need to get out."

"I'm not supposed to be seen in public, remember?" I crack open one eye. "I went to the doctor the other day. Visited your house." *Stalked your sister all over campus.* "What more do you want from me?"

"I want you to get your ass out of bed and come hang with your friends for a few hours."

"You mean, everyone who thinks I'm a cheating asshole? No thanks."

"Jesus Christ," he mutters. "No one thinks that."

"Anymore," I correct and then offer my next excuse. "My face still looks like a damn Voodoo doll's."

"Well, it's the costume night I told you about. Wear a fucking mask."

Now he has my attention. I throw off the blanket and ease myself into a sitting position.

"Ohhh, does something about that interest you?" His wide, mocking eyes only make his face more punchable.

I glare at him.

"Molly will be there," he confirms.

I tentatively touch my face. At least it hurts less.

"Except for your eye, most of the bruising has faded." Remy sighs. "It'll be dark enough. She might not notice."

"Get out of my way." I tug on the blanket he's sitting on, trapping me in the bed.

"Why?" he asks with mocking slowness. "Where are you going?"

"To take a shower. I smell like despair and self-pity."

"Got that right." He wrinkles his nose and stands, backing away.

As soon as I put weight on my knee, it buckles. I squeeze my eyes shut and take a deep breath. "She might not notice my face, but this limp is obvious as fuck."

"Nah, it gives you a cool gangster walk."

I stop and glare at him. "You ever say that again, I'm gonna stab you."

"Oooo." He holds up his hands and shakes them like he's warding off a ghost. "Scary gangster threats. I'm shaking in my boots."

"You should be shaking. I'm gonna kick your ass one day soon."

"Bro, a stiff breeze could knock you down right now."

"Not for long," I swear.

As eager as I am to get to Zips, I take my time going down the steps from my apartment a few hours later. Remy left to check in at the bar but swore he'd be at Zips before I get there.

Outside, the crisp air bites my skin and I button my flannel jacket. I slide into the front seat of my car and slam the door. The steering wheel's icy cold. I pull a pair of black gloves from my pockets and slip them on.

It seems to take forever to warm the engine. I pat the dash, trying to encourage Black Beauty. "I dunno, girl. If you keep this up, I might have to think about buying something newer with ass-warming seats this winter."

I swore I wouldn't blow my winnings on stupid shit. But it's not like I'm considering a Lamborghini.

Driving the familiar back roads is comforting after being away for so long. Once I finally have a chance to talk to Molly and explain things, I'll have her sitting next to me on the way home.

Remy wasn't kidding about tonight being a big event. The worn, bumpy parking lot is full of cars, trucks, and motorcycles. Behind the bleachers, a large section is marked with short, orange traffic cones. I guide my car to a spot next to Eraser's truck.

The revving of engines and stink of burning rubber fill the air. I close my eyes and inhale. Smells like home.

Damn, it's good to be back.

I'd rather chew glass than admit it to Remy, but I'm glad he lured me here tonight.

Molly. I slide my gaze over the parking lot, but Remy never told me what kind of car he ended up buying her. I doubt it was something she'd be able to race here.

"Holy shit, is that the shy, savage Stonewall making an appearance?" someone shouts.

"For fuck's sake," I mutter, squinting into the darkness behind the bleachers.

Vapor emerges holding a white sweater in his hand and wearing a smirk on his face.

"Why you creeping around back there?" I ask.

He holds up the sweater. "Juliet dropped this from above."

"You're lucky it didn't land in something disgusting."

"Indeed." He squints and leans in closer. "Your face looks like a peach that got thrown down the stairs." His assessing stare slides to my forehead. "So, an improvement from when you got home."

"Thanks. Very helpful." I glance toward the track. "Is Remy here yet?"

His gaze slides sideways, and he rubs his hand over the back of his neck. "Yeah," he answers slowly. "Saw him a few minutes ago."

"Was Molly with him?"

"Uhhh, no." He waves his hand in the general direction of the track. "She's...around, though. Ran a few laps with Ella earlier."

"How'd the new intake do?"

He widens his eyes with surprise. "Okay, I guess. She won. Then again—"

"She always wins," I finish for him.

"Right." He holds up the sweater. "I gotta get this back to Juliet."

"Yeah, I'll catch you later." I love Vapor, but he's not who I'm here to see.

Tonight, Molly's on *my* turf. Zips. A place we've spent a lot of time together. I rub my palms against my jeans. *Find Molly.* That's my only objective. Talk to her. Apologize. Grovel. Kiss her. Whatever I have to do until she understands I'd never betray her. There is no one else for me.

As I clear the corner of the bleachers and the whole track comes into view, I methodically scan the wide-open area.

Eraser's over by the grill talking to Pax. He lifts his hand and waves frantically, then rushes away from the grill, coming toward me. *Whatever.* I'll talk to him later. I turn toward the food shacks. If Molly already raced earlier, she's probably ordering fried dough and a—

My heart stops.

There's my girl.

Her face is hidden behind what looks like a black leather bunny mask, but I'd know my Molly anywhere. Her long legs are covered in red and black striped tights. A black and red dress, tight up top with a short, loose skirt—her favorite style—flatters every inch of her. Tall, black leather boots lace up to her knees. I'm not sure what the costume is supposed to be but she's sexy as hell.

And...*is she here with another guy?*

Who in the fuck is the tall, skinny dude in a wolf mask touching my girl? Pure rage at whoever he is shoots straight through me.

Hell fucking no. I did *not* go through three months of relentless abuse, isolation, and stupidity to lose my girl to someone else.

She thinks I cheated on her.

Correction. The *whole fucking world* thinks I cheated on her.

Remy might have finally come around and says he believes me. But he's obviously done fuck all to convince Molly that I didn't betray her.

"Bro, please put your murder eyes away." Eraser's low warning isn't enough to make me tear my gaze away from Molly and the wolf I'm about to rip limb from limb.

"Fuck off," I growl.

A fist slams into my good shoulder, knocking me to the side. I rip my gaze away from Molly and focus my rage on one of my best friends.

"Don't." Eraser holds up one hand. "I was there that night, motherfucker. I watched that girl get her heart ripped out. You don't get to come home now and—"

"I. Didn't. Do. Anything," I seethe. "I didn't fuck Kiki." Just saying that girl's name fills me with a volatile combination of fury and shame.

He stares at me for a few seconds, then blows out a heavy breath. "I wanna believe you. But." He closes his eyes and shakes his head. "I saw it in black-and-white."

So, we're finally having this conversation? About damn time. I don't give a fuck what he thinks he saw. It never happened. How can my friends trust some slick editing and camera angles over my word?

"How long have you known me?" I demand.

"I love you no matter what, Griff." He taps his fist against his chest. "But I also don't want to see Molly get hurt any more than she already has. The Kiki shit was bad enough. But the way the show talked about Molly before *that* shitshow was downright evil. She didn't deserve *any* of that. *You* brought that into her life."

I hate that he's right. "I didn't know they'd use her that way." I'm getting sick of listening to my own denials. I *didn't* know. But I *should have* known better.

Nothing in life comes easy.

Everything has a price.

But losing Molly is more than I'm willing to pay.

"I know you didn't," Eraser finally concedes.

Remy approaches us from the right and stops next to me.

Eraser turns and nods. "You got him?"

"Got me?" I sneer. "The fuck you think I am? A rabid bear on the loose?"

"Yeah, kinda." Eraser shrugs then shoots another questioning look at Remy. "I don't need him getting into it with my cousin tonight. Not with all these people here. Pax will kill us all."

"We're good." Remy clasps his hand over my good shoulder.

"You gonna shoot a tranquilizer dart in my ass next?" I shake off his hand.

"Do I need to?" Remy asks.

Apparently satisfied that I'm under control, Eraser nods at us and walks toward the grill. Probably to go warn Uncle Pax that I'm ready to stomp this place like Godzilla.

Wait a fucking minute.

Did he say... "She's with *Torch*?" I search the area for Molly and the tall fucker she'd been with. But they're gone.

I turn and get in Remy's face. "You fucking kidding me? He's at least ten goddamn years older than her."

Remy sighs. Worst of all, he doesn't deny it. "It's complicated."

"The fuck it is," I growl.

"They're just friends. He's not...they're not really *dating*." The first note of hesitation seems to creep into Remy's voice, then quickly vanishes. "He's making sure she doesn't date anyone *else*. That's all."

I stare at him, trying to figure out what the fuck that's supposed to mean. "Is *he* aware of that?"

Remy stalls way too long for my sanity. "He's aware."

Fuck Torch's feelings. What about Molly? "Does *she* know?"

Remy scowls. "Fuck no."

Now I'm pissed for two reasons. "So, once again, you think fucking with your sister's head is the right move? Are you for real?"

One corner of his mouth tilts to the side. "I thought you'd be happy."

"That she doesn't know she's fake-dating Torch?" Did he lose his mind while I was away? "No, Remy, that doesn't make me happy at all."

"Look, we know Torch," Remy says as if he still thinks he can talk me into believing this is a good thing. "And you weren't here. Every time I turned around guys were coming onto her. And she doesn't even realize it—"

"How stupid do you think your sister is?"

"Not *stupid*. But about guys and their intentions..." He shrugs. "She's a little naive."

Molly will be furious if she finds out. Worse, she'll be so hurt and embarrassed. *What was Remy thinking?*

"You couldn't have warned me about this brilliant plan sooner?" I ask. "Maybe when you dragged me out of bed this afternoon?"

"I..." He hesitates, his gaze darting across the track toward where Molly's standing talking to Hayden now. "I didn't think he'd be here with her tonight. Otherwise..."

"You wouldn't have told me to come." Seems Remy lost control of the situation he thinks he orchestrated. "That's just fucking great."

Torch would've heard by now that I'm home. He had to at least suspect I'd show up. And he *still* chose to escort my girl to this party.

"I can't deal with you right now." I sweep my arm against his chest and walk past him.

"Don't make a scene." He grabs my arm and yanks me backward.

"I won't." *Just going to claim my girl and kick Torch's ass if he gets in my way.*

"Here." He sweeps a stupid Ghostface mask out of his back pocket and slaps it against my chest. "If you're really not supposed to have people post your picture online, put that on."

I stare at the black fabric hood and white rubber face with black eyes and nose, and the mouth stretched wide into a permanent creepy imitation of a scream. "Did you wear it?"

"Earlier."

"Great, so it smells like dog breath?" I mutter as I slip it over my head.

"Woof, woof, dickhead."

I can barely see out of the dark fabric covering the eyeholes. "This is bullshit."

I'm not even complaining about the stupid mask. It's everything. The show still controlling my every move. Molly still blocking my texts and calls. My friends thinking I'm an asshole. Losing to a jackass like Naptime—when I know I'm a better fighter. Molly "dating" Torch.

Whatever timeline I've been dropped into sucks. *I want my life back.*

Feeling like an asshole with only my red plaid coat, jeans, and boots to go with the mask, I navigate my way across the asphalt, heading for the racetrack and the food shacks behind it.

I recognize a few people but don't bother saying hello. *Molly.* She's all that matters. I need to get her someplace quiet so we can talk. I need her in my arms. I need to bury my face in her hair and inhale her. Taste her skin. Hear her voice.

Torch, that red-headed motherfucker, took off his wolf mask, leaving his stupid orange hair sticking up all over the place. He's still standing *way* too close to my girl. Thank fuck he's not actually touching her. I'd hate to ruin the party by ripping off his arm and beating him with it in front of everyone.

My boots crunch over a few loose stones, drawing Torch's attention as I close in on them. The corners of his mouth turn down. This mask isn't fooling anyone. I yank it off my head and glare at him as I approach.

Molly turns her head. Even with the black bunny mask blocking my view, our eyes lock. Her mouth falls open and she takes a step back.

No. No. No.

Is she afraid of me? Or just desperate to get away from me?

She glances at Torch, then again at me.

I stop in front of them and drill Torch with a fuck-off stare.

"Leave," I snarl.

He flashes a cocky smirk. "Welcome home, Griff."

"Now."

Torch raises his eyebrows at Molly.

"It's fine," Molly whispers. "We're fine." She nods toward the racetrack where her friends are huddled together watching our showdown, silently asking him to leave.

Torch blows out a breath and squeezes her shoulder. "I'll be close if you need me."

"She *won't* need you." I force as much menace as possible into my voice.

He hesitates for another few seconds, then finally walks off toward the grill.

And I'm finally alone with my girl.

Every minute since I left, I've ached for Molly.

And now she's right in front of me. Why does she still feel so far away?

She stares at the ground while I let my eyes roam over every inch of her. Even though I can only see the half of her face not hidden by the mask, she steals my damn breath.

Her body shivers and she crosses her arms over her chest, drawing my attention to her short costume.

"You want my coat?" I slip the thick, red-and-black hunter's plaid wool shirt-coat off my shoulders. "It matches your outfit."

Her teeth chatter and she hugs herself tighter. Still refusing to look at me, she shrugs.

She lets me drape the coat over her shoulders, and even curls her fingers into the wool to pull it tighter.

That's progress.

Don't get excited, she's just cold.

"Can we talk?"

"There's nothing to say," she rasps in a low, hollow voice I barely recognize.

Is this what I did to her?

The first hint of uncertainty grips me. All along, I thought I'd be able to fix this the minute we spoke. She knows me. She'll understand.

"Let's walk." We're alone for the moment but a lot of people are still roaming around. I don't need anyone else interfering.

She sighs and turns, heading behind the food shacks where a long, grassy path stretches all the way to the chainlink fence that encircles the property.

This is not the loving reunion I pictured with my girl.

"I didn't know you were coming tonight," she says over her shoulder.

Is that her way of saying she wishes I hadn't? Or that she's sorry I saw her with Torch?

We keep walking, slipping between pools of bright light from the shacks and dark shadows behind the buildings. The scents of various fried foods mingle together.

"Do you want to get something to eat?" I ask.

"I already ate."

Did Torch take her out to dinner? Did she eat at the bar with Remy? Grab a burger from Pax before I got here?

The last shack stands empty. The door's ajar and I open it wider, motioning Molly inside.

She frowns and stares back at the path we just followed.

"It's cold out," I explain.

"Okay."

Inside, I flip a switch by the door. Dim yellow light flickers above us, barely chasing away the shadows. It isn't much warmer in here than it is outside. The front windows are shuttered, so no one can see us at least. I push the door closed but don't latch it.

Molly frowns at the door.

I step closer and she backs up until her butt hits an old, wooden counter.

Where should I start?

I clear my throat. "Can I ask you something?"

She lifts her head and I feel the heat of her glare shooting out from behind the mask. I used to think her pissy little death-glares were cute, but that's just because I was never on the receiving end of a serious one before. There's no humor hiding behind her expression. Just raw hurt and disappointment pursing her lips.

"Go ahead," she challenges.

I flick one of the tall, leather bunny ears on her head. "What are you supposed to be?"

Her defensive stance softens a fraction. "A devil bunny."

Leave it to Molly to always come up with something clever from her own imagination. "Ahh, cute but deadly?"

She crosses her arms over her chest. "Yup."

"Can you take it off for a minute?"

She mashes her lips together, like she's about to tell me to go fuck myself with the nearest rigid object, but then she reaches behind her head. There's a sharp click. She carefully pulls the mask off and sets it on the counter behind her, then runs her fingers through her hair.

"Stop." I grab one of her hands. "Your hair's fine."

"It's all flat and sweaty." She yanks her hand away but stops trying to tame her wild waves.

Finally, I can see her face.

There's my girl.

Well, my girl with bloodred lipstick and dark, sparkly shadow smudged around her eyes. I kinda like the elaborate makeup, though.

Molly could wear anything and paint her face any way she wanted, and I'd still think she's the most beautiful woman in the world.

"What'd you want to talk about?" She lifts her chin and the glare returns.

"Everything. I missed you."

You're my girl.

Mine, mine, mine.

Nothing you saw on television was real.

"Weird way of showing it." She shrugs as if she doesn't care one way or another.

"I tried calling and texting you as soon as I got my phone back, but you blocked my number." That sounds weak as fuck, but I don't want to talk about how broken my body was when I returned home. And I'm not ready to admit to stalking her on campus, either.

Her chin trembles. She wraps her arms around her middle even tighter. Like she's doing everything she can to stop herself from coming apart.

"Molly, everything you saw was a lie. I didn't...I'd never..." My words falter as she crumbles. "I'd *never* do that to you. To us. I swear."

Twin tears glisten on her lashes, then spill, dragging inky trails down her cheeks.

"Baby, please don't cry." I cup her face and swipe my thumb over her cheek. "Please." My own voice breaks.

"I can't do this," she whispers.

Her words are a punch in the gut.

"Molly, please," I plead. "All I've wanted to do is talk to you." I snort a humorless laugh. "Without someone listening in."

At the mere mention of the show, Molly's body freezes. The hurt in her eyes hardens into ice. She brushes my hand away from her face.

Wrong move, Royal.

Why'd I have to say that?

"So, did you win the whole thing?" she asks in a caustic tone I've never heard from Molly. "Was it worth it?"

Fuck contracts or lawsuits. Any questions she asks about the show I have to answer honestly. "No."

"Sorry to hear that," she says without an ounce of sympathy behind the words.

"Please talk to me. Tell me about school."

"School's fine." She scoffs. "Thankfully no one's recognized me there. Or if they did, they had the decency not to say anything." She casts a stink-eye toward the door. "Unlike around here."

My stomach knots. "Remy told me how bad it was. I'm sorry. I didn't know they—"

"I can't." She throws one hand up in a clear stop gesture and shrugs off my coat. "Here."

"Wait. Molly, we still need to—"

"No we don't." She shoves the coat at me and swipes the mask off the counter.

I grab the woolen bundle and tuck it under my arm. "You sure you don't want it? It's still cold out."

"I'm fine." She slips the mask over her head and adjusts the snaps in the back.

My turf or not, this was the wrong place to try to talk to her. "How long are you going to be home?"

She shrugs. "I have plans tomorrow."

"With who? Torch?" I gesture toward the door. "What the fuck are you even doing with him?"

Her jaw tightens but she won't even look at me. "None of your business."

Her denial's a match to my own temper. This isn't how I saw tonight going. At all. I know she's pissed but she won't even let me explain?

As she reaches for the door, I slap my palm against it, keeping it shut. "Everything about you is my business."

"Not anymore."

"Molly, I know you're mad—"

"I'm not mad." She crosses her arms over her chest.

No. She's not. She's putting up a brave front. I *know* her. How she protects herself from all the people who've hurt and left her. When she's upset, she either freezes or explodes. I'm usually the one who talks her through it.

Except, now I'm the one who hurt her. "We have to talk this out," I try again.

"No, we really don't. Seeing you fuck some random bimbo you'd known for five minutes told me all I needed to know."

"It wasn't me!" I roar, hating myself for yelling at her. "For fuck's sake. Are you kidding me? You know me better than that."

Her mouth twitches with uncertainty for a second. Brief, but I catch it.

"I thought I did," she finally says.

This isn't getting us anywhere. I step away from the door and open it.

"Let me walk you back," I say even though inside I'm screaming, *back to where—Torch's arms?*

"Okay."

At least she'll let me do that much.

She steps out first. And what do you know, Torch is waiting in the shadows. Leaning against the building next to us. He pushes away from the wall and goes to Molly, murmuring something against her ear.

Eraser's gonna have to kiss his cousin's ass goodbye. This motherfucker's dead.

Satisfied she's okay, Torch turns his glare on me. Remy's dead wrong. Torch's feelings for Molly are way more than friendly.

I pull my shoulders back and glare down at him.

"You fucked up, Royal." He stops in front of me and meets my death glare with a smug chin lift. "Nothing you say to her can fix what the whole world watched you do."

"You better watch yourself, speaking on stuff you know nothing about," I warn. My voice and hard stare don't waver. But his words saw open a hopeless void in my chest.

The truth doesn't matter.

He grunts at me and turns away, draping an arm over Molly's shoulders and steering her away from me.

He's right.

No matter what, people will always think I cheated on my girlfriend. They "saw" it with their own eyes. They'll call Molly pathetic for taking my "cheating" ass back. Strangers will judge us and our relationship. Even people we know will gossip about us.

It doesn't matter.

Molly's all I care about.

Us against the world. She said that once.

How can I make her believe in us again?

CHAPTER SEVENTEEN

Molly

HOW IS MY BODY STILL MOVING?

How do I have any blood left to roar through my ears?

I'm pretty sure I left my heart back there.

My feet keep moving forward through the wet, dewy grass, but the ache in my chest keeps begging me to turn around.

Torch takes my hand. Guilt crawls over my skin. *What am I doing?*

"Hungry?" he asks.

"Sure." I could choke down a burger. Anything to try and appear normal.

He steers me toward the patio and his uncle's grill.

Uncle Pax smiles wide when he sees me. "How you doin', sweetheart?"

"Pretty good." I force a weak smile, wishing I'd opted for a full face mask tonight. "I like the costume night." I tap my bunny ears. "It's fun."

Or it *was* fun until Griff showed up.

"Ella's idea." He grins wide. Eraser always jokes that his uncle likes Ella more than him. "School's good?"

"So far."

"Well, eat a burger or two, you're gettin' too skinny." He drops two greasy patties on a plate and passes it to me.

My stomach tightens as I stare at the food. How can I eat when my stomach's twisted into one giant knot?

Torch carries our plates. He tries to move toward one of the picnic benches near the back. *Nope.* That's where Griff and I sat on my eighteenth birthday. If I sit at that table I'll unravel, for sure.

"How about there." I point out a table with two chairs closer to the bleachers. "So we're not interrupted."

"Sure." He sets our plates down. "I'll be right back." He clasps my shoulder. "You all right?"

"I'm fine." I slide into the metal chair, wincing at the chill on the backs of my legs.

I nibble on the plain burger and squishy bun, barely tasting a thing. My gaze scans the racetrack. Not for Griff. Nope.

Did Remy know Griff would be here tonight? Why didn't he warn me?

All sorts of muddled feelings converge in my chest as I spot Griff crossing the asphalt, heading toward the stands. He didn't bother to put his mask on again. Why was he wearing it in the first place? To ambush me? As if some cheap mask would stop me from recognizing the man I loved with all my heart.

Two girls approach him. Slim and blonde—Heather? The other blonde I recognize as Lyla, a ring girl who hangs around the guys. They giggle, fawn, play with their hair, and touch him in a shameless display.

And he's not exactly telling them to get lost.

Why should he?

A larger crowd swarms toward him. Oh, great. That stupid show made him some sort of celebrity.

Griff turns his head, and across the distance our eyes lock. No joy or spark lights up his face. If anything, he looks tired and annoyed. His jaw tightens and he tears his gaze away, focusing his attention on the blondes.

A bottle of ketchup drops on the table. Torch slides into the chair across from me. "You all right?"

I blink and swallow hard. Did he catch me staring at Griff? "Yup." I grab the ketchup and squirt a big dollop on my burger. "Thanks for getting this."

"No problem. Never seen you eat a burger without it."

My lips curve. "True."

I can't risk letting my gaze stray past Torch's shoulders. Thank God he's tall enough to block the view. The girls could be doing a strip tease for Griff or asking for his autograph for all I know.

"Do you want me to come out and visit next weekend?" Torch asks.

"Huh?" I haven't heard a word he's said since he sat down. "No, I think I'm coming home again."

He breaks into a wide smile. "Yeah? There's a carnival coming into town we can go to. If you want."

My heart stutters. Griff and I were supposed to go to that carnival when he came home. Can I really go with someone else?

Torch watches me with raised eyebrows, waiting for an answer to his invitation. Why can't I feel a fraction of what Torch seems to feel for me?

"Maybe." I force a smile. "I like the games and carnival food. But I never trust the rides at those traveling carnivals. A few bolts go missing and you end up sailing through the air." I swish my hand over the table.

He chuckles. "I think you've watched *Final Destination* too many times."

"It's possible." I grin at him and bite into my burger.

No MATTER how hard I tried, I couldn't stay at the track any longer. I lost sight of Griff but that didn't mean he wasn't lurking in the shadows somewhere.

Hiding at home seems like the safer option.

The ride in Torch's car is full of awkward, uncomfortable silence. Usually, we have plenty of stuff to talk about.

Not tonight.

He pulls to a stop in front of my house.

"Sorry I didn't want to stay longer." I press my hand to my stomach and lie through my teeth. "I think I ate too many burgers."

"Pax makes them with extra grease." He's too kind to call me out. Somehow that makes me feel worse.

I lean over the console to pop a quick kiss on his cheek. At the last second, he turns his head, and our lips meet.

The contact's brief but warm.

He pulls away and lifts his hand to cup my cheek. "You all right?"

"Yes, why?"

He runs his thumb over my bottom lip, probably smudging my lipstick. "Seeing Griff seemed to rattle you."

My heart lurches. *He knows.* He saw right through my act tonight.

"I'm fine." I push closer to show him exactly how perfectly fine and not at all rattled from seeing Griff I am.

He pulls out of kissing range and shakes his head. "I like you, Molly."

My eyebrows pinch together. "I like you too." I force a quick laugh. "Obviously."

The corner of his mouth lifts at my sarcastic tone. "I like all the time we've been spending together."

I sense a *but* coming and fall into my seat. "Me too," I whisper.

Embarrassment prickles over my cheeks. Torch is *ten* years older than me. He's probably used to dating women who are eager to do a whole lot more than kiss his cheek at the end of the night.

And oh, how I'd *love* to get even with Griff by sleeping with one of his friends. But Torch—despite his road name—doesn't set me on fire. My feelings for him are warm. Friendly. Maybe they *could* be more—one day.

I'm not in a hurry to have my heart broken again, though.

"But it's pretty clear your heart's still in Griff's hands," he finishes in a gentle, patient tone.

Misery threatens to swallow me whole. Why can't I get over my boyfriend like a normal person? Who the heck ends up with their first boyfriend forever, anyway? Breaking up was inevitable. Why can't I just move on?

"I don't want it to be." At least that's true. I don't want to feel so torn in two. I don't *want* to have the urge to jump into Griff's arms the second I see him.

I don't want to hurt anymore.

Torch inhales a long, slow breath. "I can't believe I'm about to say this," he mutters.

My heartbeat thuds in my ears. "Say what?"

"Look," he continues in a more confident voice, "I didn't watch the show myself. I hate reality TV. But I've known Griff for years." His lips quirk into a wry hint of a smile. "Even in our little morally gray circle, he's known for his fairness and honesty."

Morally gray circle. What a way to describe my brother's friends.

Torch shakes his head. "Any idiot can see how much he loves you. Even me. Even though I don't want to." He inhales another slow breath. "Are you *sure* you saw what you think you saw?"

I stare at him, slack-jawed. Anger simmers in my chest. Does he think I'm stupid? "The whole *world* saw it, Torch."

"What I mean is are you sure it wasn't a trick of the show?" He grips the steering wheel and drums his fingers against it.

"It's not just the..." I swallow hard. "It's not that he cheated on me. On television."

He clucks his tongue. "Shit, that's brutal."

"No kidding," I snap, then soften my tone. "It's not just that. It's other stuff too."

Stuff I can't even figure out how to put into words myself, so please don't ask.

CHAPTER EIGHTEEN

Molly

Well, that was awkward.

I quietly close the door behind me until it clicks shut. The rumble of Torch's engine increases then slowly fades away. I press my hand against my chest. Why did that talk, hell, the whole night, leave a heaviness clinging to me like heavy chains wrapped around my body?

Low, murmuring voices come from the kitchen. Great, does Remy have someone over? Probably a girl he picked up at the track. There were enough of them crawling around tonight looking for a hookup.

I should run straight to my room, but I'm thirsty. Besides, this is still *my* house. I cock my head, listening. Sounds like another guy. Eraser maybe? I hang my bunny mask on a hook by the door, unlace my boots and yank them off. In my stockinged feet, I slide my way into the kitchen.

At the threshold, I skid to a stop. My hand shoots out and hits the wall.

Griff.

In my kitchen.

With my brother.

Casually leaning against the counter like he's done so many times before.

As if he hasn't messed up my night—my *life*—enough.

"Why are you here?" I blurt, harsher than I meant.

They both turn my way. When Griff's gaze lands on me, the desire to melt into the floor consumes my soul.

Griff stares at me like he's trying to memorize every hair on my head, forcing me to look anywhere but at him. "We have business to discuss."

"Oh." I frown in Remy's direction. They couldn't have talked about whatever at Zips?

"He's buying me out of The Castle," Remy explains.

"What?" My eyes bug. "Why?" They've owned the old building and the property around it for a couple of years now. They hold all their underground fights there.

Oh no. Are they parting ways because of me? I always worried I'd ruin their friendship if Griff and I got involved. I never thought about their business relationship. I try not to spend too much time thinking about their illegal cage fighting as it is.

"Don't worry about it," Griff says.

My temper spikes at his casual dismissal. "What are you going to do with the building?"

"I haven't decided, yet."

Whatever. It's not my business. "Excuse me." I don't want to get too close to Griff but he's blocking my path to the refrigerator.

He slides his body less than a foot away from where he's standing. I shoot a glare at his feet, but he doesn't move another inch.

Heat travels over my exposed skin as if I can feel his gaze on me. I yank open the refrigerator, rattling the bottles in the door. I grab a can of seltzer. "I'll leave you two to your *business.*"

"You going to bed?" Remy asks.

Don't look at Griff. Don't look at Griff. "Maybe."

As if I can sleep knowing Griff's in my house.

I pop the top on my can and take a quick sip. Awkwardness slides over me. My presence isn't wanted or needed here.

"Night," I call over my shoulder.

Tears sting my eyes as I leave the kitchen. Why does seeing Griff twist me up in knots so bad? I'm over him.

Liar, liar, red-striped tights on fire.

I pause in the dining room.

"Did you talk to her?" my brother asks.

My heart thuds so loud I'm afraid I'll miss Griff's answer.

"We talked."

"And?"

None of your business! Why is my brother so damn nosy?

"Not your business." Griff's rumbling dismissal makes me want to punch my fist in the air in triumph. *Hah! Tell him.*

"Dead wrong, bro. My sister is my business," Remy, the caveman growls. "I still owe you an ass-kicking for hurting her."

As annoying as Remy's overprotectiveness can be, love for him swells in my chest.

"Oh, yeah." Griff chuckles, low and rough. "What's stopping you, Ruthless?"

"I was waiting for your Frankenface to heal," Remy scoffs.

Huh? Afraid I'd melt into a puddle at his feet if I looked at him too closely, I'd looked everywhere *but* Griff's face tonight.

The urge to return to the kitchen almost moves my feet in that direction.

No.

I'm going to my room.

Hopefully they don't kill each other.

Griff

My chest's so tight I can barely breathe. Having Molly so close again and not touching her is fucking torture. Why'd I do this to myself tonight? Remy and I could've talked about this any time. It didn't have to be now.

But I needed to see Molly again.

And you wanted to know if Torch dropped her off and drove away or if he came inside.

Thank fuck I heard his car leave.

But now I'm obsessing about her being alone with Torch in his car. It sounded like they sat out there for a while. What the fuck were they up to? What do they even have in common to talk about? Why was her lipstick smeared? *Nope.* Can't dwell on that question too long or my head will explode.

"Oh, yeah?" I poke him in the chest, knowing full well how much he hates that. "What's stopping you?"

He lightly slaps the unscarred side of my face. "I was waiting for your Frankenface to heal," Remy scoffs.

"You're just mad that, *Frankenface or not,* I'm still better looking than you."

He chuckles and backs up a step. "You wish."

I want to follow Molly upstairs. Force her to really talk to me this time. Instead, I'm stuck with Remy insulting my face and threatening to kick my ass.

He cocks his head and his gaze strays toward the living room. "On second thought, I don't think I want to sell off my part of The Castle to you."

What the fuck is he talking about?

"Why?" That was going to be the only way I could give Remy some of my earnings from the show. The stubborn fucker sure as shit won't let me *give* him the money.

"Because I don't want to."

I narrow my eyes and study him. Why's he fucking with me like this? "All right. Well, we should talk about what we want to do with it, don't you think?"

He reels back as if I'd slapped him, which I haven't ruled out yet tonight. "You don't want to host fight nights anymore?"

I run my fingers through my hair and stare at my boots for a few seconds. "As you've so charmingly pointed out," I wave my hand in front of my face, "I might draw unwanted attention to our little operation now."

"Oh," he sighs. "Right. So be a silent partner."

I cock my head and give him my best *are you stupid* face. "Because I'm so good at staying silent?"

"Well what else do you want to do with the place?"

"Fix it up and use it as our clubhouse. Have a base of operation for our support club." I had a lot of time to think about it over the last few months and it makes the most sense.

He stares at me for a few beats and now I'm getting the *are you stupid* vibe. "You think making a bigger commitment to the Lost Kings right *now* is a good idea?" He waves his fingers in front of my face. "In light of all your newfound fame and all?"

He's got a point.

"Besides," he continues, "I thought that's the last place you'd ever want to spend another night?"

"That's why I said fix it up."

"Not what I meant, and you know it." He frowns as if he's actually considering the idea. "That's going to cost a fuck ton of money."

"It doesn't have to. If we do some of the work ourselves."

"Because we're such good contractors and have so much free time?" He raises a skeptical eyebrow.

"Don't be a dick. I'm serious." I take a beat and brace myself for the reaction I'm going to get to the next thing I want to tell Remy. "There's some talk about a professional fight I might be offered. In Vegas. They're throwing around some big numbers just for me showing up."

He stares at me.

And stares.

Finally, he opens his big, opinionated mouth. "You're not seriously considering taking it, are you?"

"Uh, six figures, fuck yes, I'm considering it. You wouldn't?"

He's silent for so long, he doesn't have to answer. Of course he would say yes.

"*Actual* fighters don't make that kind of money. What's the angle?"

That had been my first thought too, but I'm not admitting it to Remy. "It's just because I was on the show."

"Where does this end, Griff?" Remy steps back and crosses his arms over his chest. "You gonna keep stepping in the ring until you end up looking like a splattered jack-o-lantern who speaks like he's got scrambled eggs for brains?"

"Well, that's...insulting." I run my hand through my hair. "And no. I'm sure they'll get tired of me eventually. I might as well ride it and rake up the cash while I still can."

"While you can still *walk*," he says with a dickish scowl. If I didn't detect a hint of genuine concern in his voice, I'd walk out the door right now.

I glance toward the hallway where Molly disappeared. What are the chances she's still awake?

"Don't even think about it," Remy warns.

"Last week you were practically begging me to move in." I give him a wide-eyed, confused face.

"Yeah, well, since you haven't and you still have your own place, I think it's best if you stay *there* tonight." He glances toward the dining room. "I don't want you upsetting her."

Fuck, that hurts. "I fucking love her, Remy. And all of this," I circle my finger in the air between us, "is gonna get fixed."

"Bro, if you think money and more fights will fix things, you don't know Molly very well."

"I never said that. Doesn't mean I'm not still trying to plan for our future."

"God bless you, Griff." He shakes his head. "You're either the most stubborn fucker or the dumbest."

"Stubborn sounds better. Let's go with that."

CHAPTER NINETEEN

Molly

THE THROATY RUMBLE OF GRIFF'S CAR PULLING OUT OF our driveway startles me out of my half-asleep state.

I stare at the ceiling, replaying the night over and over. My eyes drift shut a few times, but I can't seem to hold on to sleep.

Why can't I shove Torch's words out of my head? Remy told me he believes Griff. Eraser seems to believe him too. Neither of them tried to force me into believing Griff, though. Vapor and Juliet have never said anything either way, but I know they were Griff's phone call home during the show.

What do I expect? The five of them have been friends forever. Of course they'd take Griff's side.

But Torch saying it...he has *every* reason to want me to believe Griff cheated. We never spoke about it over the summer. Not once. Then the first time he sees Griff, he tells me to reconsider?

I have to know.

Downstairs seems quiet. None of Remy's usual nocturnal noises. No hum of the television or rattles from the kitchen. Or worse, giggles from some girl spending the night.

I crack open my door and peer into the hallway like a burglar checking if the coast is clear. I tiptoe past Remy's closed bedroom door. No light spills from under the crack and I breathe a sigh of relief.

My heart pounds as I ease down the stairs, avoiding the one near the bottom that squeaks.

Without turning on any lights, I perch on the edge of Remy's recliner and swivel toward the television.

Can I really do this again? Should I wait for Remy to watch it with me?

No. I'm not a kid who needs her big brother to hold her hand.

I turn on the television and flip through the on-screen menus until I find the show. Griff's face flashes on the screen as the cover photo for the whole show. My heart squeezes. I scroll through the episodes until I find the right one.

Am I really doing this to myself? It took me forever to get those images out of my head.

I fast forward through the dumb opening montage that includes *my* face as I tearfully hug Griff goodbye. The *big bad moment* happened near the end, so I keep it fast-forwarding through all the dumb fighter antics, the girls strutting around in their bathing suits, and the outing.

The images on screen shift to black-and-white and I hit play. I mute the announcer's annoying voice and just watch.

Griff and Kiki at his door.

A couple in bed together. The picture is so grainy. Without the announcer *telling* me who's on the screen, would I have assumed it was Griff?

I can't really see the girl, either. It could be Kiki. Or it could be one of the other ring bunnies in the house.

Disgusted that I feel like I'm intruding on what was an intimate moment for...*whoever's* on screen, I shift my gaze to the left. The shadowy shape of the plain nightstand, a chair in the corner, a—wait a minute.

The nightstand.

My heart pounds painfully. Am I crazy? How did I miss this before? Why didn't anyone else notice?

The picture I tucked away in Griff's bag, the one the show mocked in the first episode, isn't on the nightstand where Griff put it, right at the edge, so he'd see it first thing when he woke up every morning.

I rewind and watch again. The quality of the footage is terrible but it's clear enough to see the top of the nightstand is completely empty. Nothing. Not even the tube of lip balm I sent with Griff, which he also left by the bed.

It's not Griff's room.

I grab my phone and Google *"Griff Stonewall Supreme Fighter Cheat Nightstand"* and find an entire sub on Reddit dedicated to the show. Every comment I read makes my heart thud harder.

Episode: Something Big Happens

FlockingFab20: "I hope his girlfriend knows he didn't cheat. The photo wasn't there."

SUF36: *My theory is he removed the picture before Kiki came into the room. Probably stashed in his nightstand so he wouldn't get the guilts.*

FlockingFab20: *That makes zero sense. It looked too spontaneous.*

On and on the speculation continues. Hundreds of different users. Two thousand different comments in this thread alone. They seem split fifty/fifty on whether Griff actually cheated.

Why would any normal person care this much about people they've never even met?

Bile burns the back of my throat. Strangers on the Internet stuck up for Griff more than I did. I was his girlfriend. His friend long before that. I didn't even let him explain. I wouldn't hear him out.

Worse, I destroyed the car he gave me for my birthday. The car he bought for me and so lovingly poured many hours into restoring.

How am I supposed to fix this?

Can it be fixed?

He still chose the show over our relationship. He still told that awful woman intimate things about me. The humiliation burns every time I remember her mocking text. I was so embarrassed, I never told Remy—or anyone else—about it.

"Molly, what are you doing?" Remy's sleep-rough voice sends my heart rate spiking to the sky.

I whip my head around. "You scared the crap out of me."

He opens his mouth to say something, then stops. His eyes widen in horror as he takes in the television screen. I left it frozen on *that* scene.

Shame stings my skin. Why'd he have to catch me watching this? Now he'll know for sure I'm not over Griff.

Remy hurries closer and snatches the remote off the arm of the chair. "Why would you watch that again?" He clicks the television off. Darkness descends around us.

I reach over and tap the lamp next to his chair. A weak pool of light pushes the shadows in this corner of the room away.

"I had to know for sure. To see it again." I can't tell him what Torch said. Remy's always been oddly silent on the topic of me dating Torch. I thought he would've blown a gasket the first time Torch asked me out but maybe he finally realized I'm old enough to make my own decisions about who I date.

He stares at me with his unfathomable blue eyes—a mirror of my own. Pity? Concern? I can't tell what he's thinking. "And what do you think now?" he asks carefully.

"I'm not sure." I don't want to tell Remy my photo-on-the-nightstand theory. It sounds so desperate and childish.

"You should at least have a conversation with him," he says.

"I did." I shrug, striving for the indifference I'm having trouble holding onto. "It didn't change anything."

"You're breaking his heart." His voice drops to an anguished whisper.

How dare Remy try to guilt me. "He broke mine first!"

He holds out his hands like he's trying to tame a wild bobcat. "I know how bad it looks." He glances at the black television screen. "But it's not him. We watched it together not long after he came home—"

"You did? Why?"

"He wanted to see it. I don't think he understood how bad it was until he watched the episode." He shrugs. "It sounds like all sorts of things were taken out of context and edited to fit a certain narrative."

As if I give a cracker about the show's "narrative."

"Did he hear the awful stuff they said about me?"

"Yeah, he saw some of it. He was pissed, Molly. I told him when I talked to him, but I think it was different seeing it for himself."

None of this changes anything. "It doesn't matter now."

"Of course it matters." He drops his shoulders, relaxing his posture from protector to comforting big brother. "If you really don't think you can repair things, that's fine—"

"But?"

"No buts." He gestures to the television again. "Maybe tell him you believe him, though."

My face hardens.

"Or not." He holds up his hands again.

"What about you two?" I ask. "You're not really selling your part of The Castle, are you?"

"Nah." He shrugs. "I thought about it for a second."

"I never wanted...I don't want to be the reason you two aren't friends."

He's quiet, thinking that over. "I really hate that he hurt you. Even if it wasn't intentional."

"Grief's the price we pay for love. I'm fine now."

He tilts his head, silently calling me out on my big, fat lie.

"Okay, maybe not *fine*. But I'm getting there."

He nods slowly. "I'm proud of you. Just focus on school, for now. If you two are meant to be together, then it'll happen."

I shake my head. "I think Griff was only meant to be a chapter, not my whole story."

Why does saying that feel like throwing the whole book in the fire?

CHAPTER TWENTY

Molly

I'm up and getting ready to leave for Hayden's early the next morning. If Griff decides to drop by our house like he used to do on the weekends, I'd rather not be around.

Downstairs, Remy's lacing up his sneakers, getting ready to go on his morning run. He tilts his head my way. "What're you doing up so early?"

"Going to hang with the girls at Hayden's before everyone leaves." It's rare we're all home at the same time. I should've stayed at Hayden's last night. Then I could've avoided running into Griff again.

Remy nods at the television. "Did you give that any more thought?"

He doesn't have to specify what *that* he's talking about.

A mix of anxiety, confusion, and guilt bubbles in my chest. "Why?"

"Because I care about you." He stands and rests his hands on his hips. "And I should warn you, I asked Griff to move in. He's probably going to take over the basement."

"Ew, you'd make him live in your sex cave?"

His jaw drops. "What are you talking about?"

"You think I don't know that's where all the ding-dongs you bring home sneak out of in the mornings?"

At least he has the decency to blush. "It's not a 'sex cave.' Grandpa and I fixed it up when I moved in with him and Nana. So I'd have my own space." He frowns for a second. "Or maybe so I wouldn't hear them in *their* room," he says slowly as if this is the first time that possibility has occurred to him. "They were always kinda frisky."

"Ew! Remy!"

He shakes his head quickly. "I only moved upstairs when Grandpa was sick, so I could hear him if he needed me."

Picturing them alone in this house together, with Remy taking care of our grandparents all by himself hurts. My eyes burn. The little bit I did help Remy doesn't seem like nearly enough.

"Anyway, it's not a sex cave, you little smartass."

"Whatever," I say. It stings that Remy would ask Griff to move in after what happened. Almost like he's taking his friend's "side" over his own sister. But that's unfair, so I shove the feeling away. "Just give me a heads-up if he actually *does*."

Remy's forehead wrinkles with concern. "You won't stop coming home, will you?"

I hesitate for a few seconds. Stay on campus instead of coming home just because I might run into Griff? "No."

He still seems uncertain but since I'm miffed about the new possible housing arrangement, I don't offer him any more reassurances.

"I..." Remy holds up his hands. "He came back really fucked up, Molly. Juliet, Vapor, and I took turns checking on him the first few days. I drove him to his doctors' appointments." He hesitates. "He looked *so* bad, I was legit worried he might drop dead."

A hot poker of fear jabs me in the ribs. "He was that bad?"

Remy nods. "He's been banged up at The Castle plenty of times. But this...this was like the ref was looking the other way or something." He shrugs. "*That's* why I asked him to move in."

Great, now I can't even be mad at my brother. "Then why the hell was he at Zips last night?"

"To see *you*."

Instead, he saw me with Torch. "Oh." I frown. "You should've warned me."

"I didn't know Torch was going with you."

"He's always at Zips." I can't keep the exasperation out of my voice. "We planned our costumes together."

"Yeah. I'm sure his wolf mask from the Dollar Tree took lots of planning." Remy's voice drips with sarcasm.

"Because your Ghostface mask was so original?"

One corner of his mouth lifts. "It served its purpose."

"Ugh. I don't even want to know."

He chuckles. "You want to go for a run with me?"

"The only way I'm running is if I'm being chased by a herd of flesh-eating zombies."

"By then it'll be too late," he teases. "You won't have the stamina to outrun the zombies."

Despite myself, I end up laughing.

GUILT and a few other complicated emotions snake their way through my chest as I drive over to Hayden's house. Maybe I'll stay with her tonight and go back to campus early tomorrow. Then I can avoid Griff *and* my brother.

Hayden's driveway is packed. I must not be the only one who couldn't sleep. Or some of the girls are leaving early for their longer drives back to campus.

Hayden answers the door in bright-pink, satin pajamas with her hair still coiled around one long, pink silk-covered foam roller draped over the top of her head like a crown.

"Morning, Goldilocks." I tap one end of the long curler. "This is a cute look."

"Ugh, Jenn said I can't take it out yet. Come in." She stands back and holds the door wide. "It's freezing out."

I hustle inside and close the door behind me.

"We're in the kitchen. Kyla's making blueberry pancakes," Hayden calls over her shoulder.

"Ooo, I got here just in time." A sweet, sharp scent stings my nose as we close in on the kitchen. Is Kyla making pancakes or burning them?

"Hey, Molllllleee," Darcy sings as soon as I step into the kitchen. "Where'd you disappear to last night?"

"We saw you talking to Griff," Kyla says without looking away from the stove. "How'd that go?"

"No comment." I pull one of the stools at the long counter out and pop my butt on it.

Hayden squeezes onto the stool next to me. "Come on," she pleads. "You wouldn't talk about him all summer. Did you unleash your fury on him? Turn him to actual stone with the power of your eyes?"

"I wish." I heave out a deep, annoyed breath.

"Was he mad you were there with Torch?" Kyla asks with wide eyes and a devious smile. "That was seriously the best revenge."

Revenge? Whatever it was, it didn't feel good.

"I don't understand why you won't just fuck Torch to get Griff out of your system?" Hayden suggests as if it's nothing more than sticking my feet into a new pair of shoes. "He's obviously up for it."

"I can't do that." I wrinkle my nose.

Darcy leans her elbows on the counter. "I thought you liked him?"

"I do." I shrug and shift my gaze to the kitchen window where morning light seeps in through the edges of the blinds. Maybe I should've stayed home and risked running into Griff. "He's nice to look at. And he's been really sweet. But I don't feel that..." I circle my hand over my heart, unsure of how to express the lack of something *more*.

"He's not Griff?" Kyla lifts an eyebrow.

"Yes...but it's more than that."

"Aww, we have ourselves a little demisexual in our group." Hayden claps her hands together and nudges me with her elbow.

"Look at you, learning big words in college." Kyla leans over the counter and slow claps in front of Hayden's face. "So proud of you, blondie."

I frown at both of them. "What?"

"You need more of an emotional bond before you want to sleep with someone?" Jenn asks with more tact than her cousin.

"I guess." I shrug. "Doesn't everyone?"

"Nope." Darcy waves a spatula in front of her nether region. "I'm open for business to anyone who lights my fire."

"I wouldn't run around announcing that," Kyla mutters.

"I think that just means you're slutty," Hayden adds.

Jenn flicks her gaze to the ceiling.

I kick my foot out and poke Hayden's shin with my socked toes. "Don't be gross."

"Especially since she's just as *sluuuuttty* as I am." Darcy runs around the counter and taps Hayden's butt with the spatula.

Hayden reaches behind her and yanks the spatula out of Darcy's hand. "Am not."

"Anyway," Darcy says, returning to the stove to push Kyla out of the way, "we were talking about Molly and Torch going down to fuck town."

I blink, not sure how I feel about discussing this. "We're not going anywhere," I mutter.

"You need to do stuff with more guys than just Griff," Hayden says.

"I've done...*stuff*." I sigh and tap my nails on the counter. "It was just so underwhelming I didn't want to do *more*."

"I take it everything about Griff is *over*whelming." Darcy slaps her hand over her mouth, smothering a loud snort-giggle.

I flick my gaze to the ceiling and don't bother answering. But heat creeps over my cheeks. *Overwhelming in all the best ways.*

"Hey." Kyla reaches over and taps my hand. "So, you went off with Griff for a while. What'd he have to say?"

All the complicated emotions I've been carrying around since last night tighten into a knot of pain in my chest. Unable to form any words, I shake my head.

"Aw, Molly." Kyla circles the counter and wraps her arms around me. "It's okay. Maybe talking about it will help."

"Come on," Hayden prods. "What'd he say?"

"He said the same thing Remy tried to tell me," I finally whisper. "That he didn't—"

"But we all saw it!" Darcy shouts, waving a different spatula in the air.

I sniffle and nod. "I know." I take several deep breaths. "Torch even suggested maybe the show set up Griff?" My voice is tentative, almost like I'm testing the theory out on my friends to see if they'll say I'm crazy for believing that.

Hayden's eyes widen and she sits back. "He said *what?*"

My shoulders lift slightly, and Kyla releases me, backing away. I reach out and squeeze her hand to let her know I wasn't shrugging her off.

"I retract my earlier statement," Hayden says. "You should *not* bang Torch."

A sad chuckle eases out of me. "I don't think that's going to be a problem." I suck in a deep breath. "But I couldn't stop thinking about what he said. I mean, of all the people in the world, he has the *most* reason to want me to keep thinking Griff cheated."

"True." Hayden tilts her head to the side. "Damn. Okay. He gets some decent guy points for that."

The attention's thankfully taken off of me for a few minutes while Kyla and Darcy set a plate with a huge stack of pancakes on the counter in front of Hayden and me. Jenn leaves her perch by the kitchen table and passes plates out to everyone.

Hayden pokes at one of the pancakes with a fork and wrinkles her nose.

"Just eat around the burned bits." Kyla flings the top two pancakes onto Hayden's plate.

Chuckling, I jab my fork into the next pancake and drag it onto my plate. "They look fine."

"You can have the syrup first," Kyla says, passing the big, tan jug to me while giving Hayden a stink-eye.

"You and Darcy should've gone first since you made the pancakes." I quickly drizzle maple syrup on my pancake and push the jug into the middle of the counter.

I scrape a piece of pancake from the top layer, careful to avoid the thick, charred bottom and stick it in my mouth. Sweet, warm blueberries and cinnamon bursts over my tongue. "Mmm, they're good," I say around my mouthful.

Kyla sticks her tongue out at Hayden.

Before they can get into it again, I take a sip of water and announce, "So I couldn't stop thinking about what Torch said and I ended up watching *that* episode again last night."

Everyone stops eating and stares at me.

"Molly, no!" Kyla gasps and slaps her hands over her mouth, like I just announced I murdered a baby bunny. "Why?"

I trace my fork in a wavy pattern through the maple syrup on my plate, then stab a stray blueberry. "I don't know. Remy believes him too."

Darcy announces, "Bros before—"

"He's literally *her* bro." Hayden glares at Darcy, then nods at me. "Go on."

"They're all being weird about it or at least weird around *me* about it, but I think Eraser and Ella believe him too." I flick my gaze at Hayden. "And you remember how pissed they were that night."

Hayden shrugs. "But they've all been friends a long time. He didn't cheat on *them*. He cheated on *you*."

"Allegedly!" Kyla announces.

"There's nothing *alleged* about it," Darcy counters, holding her curled hands up to her eyes like a pair of binoculars. "We *saw* it."

"Nope. No way." Kyla shakes her head violently. "We all saw Griff on prom night. He never took his eyes off Molly. And he was so sweet to *us*, even though we barged into their room. I refuse to believe he did that to her."

I stare at her in wide-eyed shock. Kyla spent a good portion of the summer consoling me, but she never voiced any of this. Now that I've given her an opening, apparently, she's airing out all her doubts.

She crosses her arms over her chest and continues, "Besides, I don't trust any of those so-called 'reality' shows. You remember that stupid one we watched with the washed-up rock star who was supposedly looking for love? That dude in a whole-ass relationship with his baby momma the entire time. Both seasons!"

"Oh yeah!" Darcy's eyes widen. "How embarrassing for his family."

"That happened on *Matchmaker Mansion* too." Jenn snaps her fingers. "One of the women trying to date the bachelor was actually married to a woman."

"What season?" Hayden pushes her plate away, picks up her phone, and starts swiping her fingers across the screen.

Jenn shrugs and stabs her fork through three layers of pancakes. "I don't remember."

"Don't they make them sign agreements not to talk about the show and stuff?" Darcy asks. "How do you know if that's even true?"

"Technically, it *wasn't* talking about the show, if other people came forward and said, 'hey I attended that chick's wedding last year, why is she on a dating show now?' Right?" Jenn lifts her eyebrows for emphasis.

"Okay, fair." Darcy nods.

All of this is giving me a headache. I wish I'd never opened my mouth at all. In fact, if I'm wishing for things, I wish I'd never gone to Zips last night. No one—*except Griff*—understood my stupid devil bunny costume. Everyone else thought I was some weird dominatrix with a bunny fetish. Forget the costume. Seeing Griff again after so much time had flipped my heart upside down.

"Well, Griff wasn't supposed to be on a dating show at *all*," I remind them. "It was supposed to be about becoming the best *cage fighter.*"

"Hey, remember *Redneck Roadhouse*?" Kyla says with an eager edge to her voice. "The one your friend Shelby Morgan was on—"

"She's not *my* friend," I correct. *Friend. I wish.* I've gotten to talk to Shelby once and I made a total ass of myself. "Remy knows her fiancé."

"Yeah," Darcy says slowly, her eyes widening as she comes to a realization about something. "Shelby ended up in the middle of a love triangle with Ruby what's-her-tits and that other guy while she was on that show."

"No," Kyla says. "Shelby did an interview not that long ago and said that was all fake."

"Right! The show said they were going to sue her and then—" Darcy snaps her fingers and lowers her voice. "Dawson Roads told 'em go ahead and try it," she finishes in a terrible impression of the famous country singer's Tennessee accent.

"Why would he care?" Hayden asks. "Isn't he like eighty?"

Darcy shakes her head. "He's like thirty something."

Hayden shrugs. "Old dudes don't interest me."

"Shelby's on his record label now," Kyla answers, ignoring them. "Told them he had better lawyers."

"Who knew you cared this much about country music," Hayden mutters while scrolling through her phone.

"I read everything *Sippin' on Secrets* posts about everyone." Kyla lifts her chin, not embarrassed.

"Please, she stalks their IG so much, they blocked her." Darcy giggles and shoves Kyla.

"They did not."

"How is any of this helpful?" I ask, poking my fork into my pancake.

"Ah-ha!" Hayden lifts her hand in the air to get our attention even though we're all less than three feet away from her. "That Sidespeed Salmon Productions or whatever company that produced Griff's show, also produced *Matchmaker Mansion*. I *knew* I'd seen that big tacky house before. It was decorated totally different inside but the pool, two gyms, the sauna, it all looked familiar."

"No way." Darcy grabs Hayden's phone and stares at the screen.

"So what?" I swivel on the stool and cross my arms over my chest. "Who cares?"

"They're devious. They've been sued a bunch of times by former contestants." Hayden holds out her phone to me, but I shake my head.

Who gives a pickle about lawsuits? "Are there more pancakes?" I ask Kyla, lifting my chin at the stove.

"Wait." Jenn holds up both hands. "Molly, you said you watched the show again. What do *you* think?"

"Nothing." I shrug. "I'm probably just...seeing what I want to see."

Hayden's busy on her phone again.

"Molly. You are *killing* me." Kyla wraps one of her hands around her throat. "Killing. Me."

"Knock it off, drama queen." I grab my plate and hold it out to her. "And give me another pancake."

She shakes with laughter as she returns to the stove and slides her spatula under a fresh pancake—with no burned bits.

After she sets it on my plate, I say, "Remember the first episode where they made fun of Griff for putting the picture of us on his nightstand?"

Kyla rolls her eyes. "Yeah."

"I don't know if they were making fun of it," Darcy argues. "I thought it was more like they were highlighting how genuine and wholesome Griff is...er, was."

I let out a sad snort-laugh. "Sure, whatever. Anyway." I circle my hand in front of my chest as if that will help unroll the words from my mouth. "When I watched *that* part again..." I swallow down the sourness crawling up my throat. "I noticed the picture isn't on the nightstand."

Kyla's eyes widen. "Noooo. Really? How'd we miss that?"

"Because we were all staring at the couple in the bed?" Darcy swivels her hips in a circle. "Making it rain in fuck town."

She's so ridiculous, a giggle-snort bursts out of me.

"And listening to the announcer guy," Hayden adds. "She's right, look." Hayden holds out her phone to Darcy, then Kyla.

The girls all crowd around Hayden to squint at her phone. I stay right where I am. I've studied the footage on a much bigger screen and still don't know what to think. Of course I *want* to believe he didn't cheat on me. But I don't want to be the oblivious girl who follows her heart and ignores her brain.

"He could've just put it away out of guilt," Darcy suggests.

A few folks on Reddit would agree.

"Maybe," Hayden mutters, staring at the screen. "Damn, we need like a computer forensics team to clean up this footage for us."

Something about that is so absurd, uncontrollable laughter bursts out of me.

"You know, the fact that the film quality is so bad and that they never really showed Griff and Kiki together again, points to it *not* being true," Jenn says.

"Are you sure you want to go to school for cosmetology?" Hayden pats her cousin's head. "You sound like a defense lawyer."

"Wait." I focus my attention on Jenn. "Back up. *You* kept watching the show too?" I shoot a dirty look at Darcy who gave me weekly updates right until I left for college.

"Hell yeah we did," Darcy says. "That guy Woolly is hot as fuck."

"I'd let him ground and pound me any day." Hayden lets out a shrill whistle and claps her hands.

"Traitors." I cross my arms over my chest again.

"I did *not* partake in any more viewings," Kyla says, slipping an arm around my waist.

"Thanks." I rest my head on her shoulder.

"Well, Griff made it to the end," Darcy says.

"Obviously, since he just got home," I mutter.

"Yeah, but they haven't shown the *last* episode yet," Darcy says. "Rumor is someone got injured."

Griff *had* looked pretty bad last night once I really took him in.

Nope. I don't care if he won the show or not. If I never hear about *Supreme Underground Fighter* ever again, it'll be way too soon.

CHAPTER TWENTY-ONE

Griff

STILL REELING FROM SEEING MOLLY AND TORCH together, I take Remy up on his offer to move into his basement apartment. At least this way, I'll get to see her whenever she comes home.

Of course, if she's still "dating" Torch, seeing them together might make my brains melt and leak out of my ears from the exertion of not murdering him.

It takes less than four hours for Remy, Vapor, Eraser, and me to move what little I have. The next day, I'm sorting through boxes when I find the burner phone I took to the show with me.

Everything was so fucked up, I never bothered to turn it on after Jordan gave it back to me.

I plug it in and wait for it to have a decent charge before turning it on. My short text exchange with Molly has been wiped clean, except for one final text from her.

M: Don't worry. He's all yours.

"What the fuck?" I mutter. Who—no, *what* was she responding to?

That slimy fucking show. It was bad enough that they found and confiscated the only way I had to communicate with Molly. They had to stir up more trouble by sending her fuck only knows what kind of text?

He's all yours. She wasn't responding to me.

"Fuck!" I throw the phone back in the box. I can't even ask her about it. Who knows when the fuck she'll be home again. And I still can't fucking call her.

I need to get out of the house. See if I still have a job. Although I still feel and look like shit, I need to see Molly's car and assess the damage.

But first I need to apologize to my boss for all the trouble I've caused him.

I step out of my car and squint at the sky. Another beautiful fall day. It's so good to be home.

The parking lot's quieter than I'd expect midweek. Maybe that's for the best. I don't need to draw attention to myself.

I swing the front door open, the bell dinging its familiar greeting. Jerry's behind the counter and glances up.

A welcoming smile spreads across his face. "If it isn't the best damn fighter in the country." He steps out from behind the counter and holds out his hand.

"I don't know about that." I shake his hand quickly. "How's it going?" *Do I still have a job?*

"Lil' slow," he says, never one to sugarcoat anything. "But nothin' I'm worried about, yet. Good to see you." He narrows his eyes on my forehead. "You all right?"

"This?" I graze my fingertips against the side of my head. "It was worse."

"Jesus. You look like you went to war."

"I guess I did." I run my hand over the top of my head. "I'm not quite a hundred percent to come back—"

He gives me a slow once-over. "Obviously."

"But I wanted to apologize—"

"Get outta here." Jerry waves a big, oil-stained hand in my face. "Apologize to me for what?"

"Uh, the inconvenience of being gone so long? Having the cops here about Molly's car." I hold out my hands. "Pick one."

"Eh." He shrugs that off too. "Gave the locals something to do."

More like gave the cops something to gossip about. One of the local sheriffs actually fights at The Castle some weekends. Christ, I hope

Brady wasn't one of the ones who came here. He'll be busting my balls all damn night next time I see him.

"You sort things out with her?" he asks in a stern, fatherly tone.

"Not yet."

His face scrunches into a disapproving scowl. Jerry's obvious displeasure needles me unlike anyone else's. I've worked for him for a couple of years and have a lot of respect for him. Otherwise, I wouldn't bother trying to explain myself.

"It was a lie," I say. "The show made up a lot of stuff."

He blows out a thoughtful breath. "It's nonna my business, Griff. What you do on your time is all you." He shrugs. "But she's a sweet girl." He waves a hand out toward the garage. "Came here and apologized for the inconvenience she caused me. Her brother didn't make her do it, either. She came all by herself."

I squeeze my eyes shut for a second. That must've been hard for Molly. Embarrassing as hell. But it definitely sounds like something my girl would do. "I'm not surprised."

He grunts at me. "Honestly, didn't think you'd be coming back. Since you're a big star and all."

Cold fear seizes my stomach. Is he going to let me go? I wouldn't blame him after being gone for so many months. Am I kidding myself that I'll ever be able to go back to a normal job? A normal *life*?

"Of course I'm back," I answer. "That was always my plan."

He nods slowly.

"I'll understand if you don't have room for me now. I never thought I'd be there the whole time." I touch my cheek. "And I came back in rough shape."

"You're still in rough shape." He runs his disapproving gaze up and down me again. "Look like someone went at *you* with a bat."

"Just some fists."

"Of course I've always got room for you, Griff." He clucks his tongue. "Can't find guys who work as hard as you do and are actually good at the job."

"Thanks." Shit, I really don't want to ask him for more time off but the longer I wait, the worse it'll be. "Uh, I may still need a few more days off. I have to go back to film a reunion show."

The Vegas fight isn't anywhere near a sure thing, yet. So, I'll keep that to myself for now.

"I figured." He shrugs. "Just let me know when. Thinking of spending my winter in Florida if you think you can handle things around here?"

"Me?" My eyes widen. "Yeah. Absolutely."

"All right. We'll talk when it's time. I haven't decided yet. Looks like you need to spend some time recovering anyway." He waves a hand at me. "Go have a look at the car."

I nod at him and exit through the front door, circling around the building to avoid the open garage doors. No reason to talk to anyone else now. The back lot's clear and I make a beeline for the building where I stored Molly's car.

I unlock the door and roll it up. Weak sunlight spilling in from the open door illuminates the space. Remy and Eraser cleaned what they could. No glass crunches under my feet. The garage floor's spotless.

A cardboard box sits on the floor. I squat down and carefully pick through the contents. The casing of the side mirrors Molly and I installed right before I left. The glass is long gone. A door handle. A metal piece from a headlight.

I turn and look at the car. *Fuck*. The passenger window's gone. The images from the episode replay in my head. Just as I bet they did for Molly each time she smashed the bat into the car. Door dented. A small crack in the windshield. Both headlights gone. Anger at the show's producers for engineering such a stupid "plotline" for the show boils my blood. For what? Ratings? Molly was the only one who was going to be hurt by that. She was innocent—why do it? So much pain caused for no fucking reason.

I continue circling the car. Back windows are intact. Actually, nothing from beyond the front doors has been touched.

All right. Okay. I can work with this. It's not too bad. Better than I expected, honestly.

Shit. The damage was probably contained to the front of the car because Molly hurt herself smashing it up. Going at the car with the aluminum bat probably seemed like a good idea, right until she hit something solid with it. Didn't Remy say she hurt her arms or got scratched? She's lucky glass didn't get her in the eye or face.

I make a list of the parts I'll need to order. Glass will be a bitch. That'll take the longest to get my hands on. But there's a good chance I can have it ready to give to Molly for Christmas.

Wait. Should I even bother giving her the car again? What if every time she looks at it, she's reminded of "seeing" me "cheat" on her? What if it brings up all those awful feelings? I don't want to give her something that makes her unhappy every time she sees it. Besides, Remy said he ended up buying her a car for school. Something small with all-wheel drive. She doesn't need this anymore.

I glance at the Malibu again. Do I *want* to work on it, if it's not for Molly? Even with the damage she did, it's in better shape than when I bought it. If I want to turn a profit, though, I should fix it. Or maybe I'll sell my car. I can put both of them up like some two-for-one sale.

It's just a car. Molly and I will own dozens of them over our lifetime.

But it still feels like one more thing the show stole from us.

CHAPTER TWENTY-TWO

Molly

THE FOLLOWING WEEKEND, I'VE HAD ALL I CAN TAKE OF the skunky aroma of cheap weed. I'm eager to get away from the dorms and have some peace and quiet at home.

Remy's truck isn't here, so I pull my car as close as I can to the back porch.

Home sweet home.

I haul my backpack over my shoulders and drag my five-foot, blob-shaped bag of laundry out of the cargo area. It lands on the grass with a *splunk*. With some effort, I pick up the bag with both hands and waddle up the porch steps with it.

I fish my keys out of my hoodie pocket and find the one for the back door.

The door swings open before I have a chance to slide the key in.

My gaze lands on Griff.

No, on Griff's shirtless chest.

The loose track pants slung low on his hips.

What the hell?

He's been on my mind non-stop since last weekend and here he is standing in front of me like a dream. My greedy eyes gobble him up, cataloging all the familiar things and all the ways he's changed. He seems broader through the shoulders, taller even. The tight cords of muscle flex in his arms as he stands back to let me inside.

I slick my tongue over my bottom lip.

His hair is longer than when he left, curling slightly at the ends. He's always worn his hair on the shorter side, but I kind of like it longer. More to run my fingers through.

No.

Not mine.

Never again.

I don't even believe he cheated on me anymore.

I never should've believed it.

Now I feel so guilty I can't even look him in the eyes.

"Griff? What are you doing here?" I drag my bag of laundry closer, but he slides by me and grabs it out of my hands.

"Uh, I live here now." He hauls the bag inside, closes the door, and drops the bag at his feet. "Thought you knew that."

He runs his hot gaze over me, and I back up a few steps. The weight of my backpack throws me off balance and I bump into the counter.

"I guess Remy mentioned it. I just didn't..." *Expect to find you shirtless in my kitchen.*

He raises a cocky eyebrow and crosses the kitchen to lean on the opposite counter. "What?"

"Nothing."

"What are *you* doing here?" He pours thick white liquid from the blender into a tall cup but still somehow manages to keep his eyes on me.

"It's my house."

Ignoring my caustic tone, he flashes a tight smirk. "I thought you lived in the dorms now?"

"I do. But I still like to come home on the weekends."

He takes a quick sip of his drink, still staring at me. I slide my backpack off my shoulders, setting it on the floor. My phone buzzes and I pull it out of my jeans pocket.

Torch: *Are you home yet?*

Guilt wraps its fingers around my throat. I can't answer him now. I shove my phone back in my pocket.

"Don't worry, princess." Griff's voice drips with uncharacteristic sarcasm. "I won't get in the way if you want to have Torch over."

If he hadn't almost choked on Torch's name, I'd be furious.

Instead, embarrassment heats my skin. How'd he know that's who texted me?

I lift my chin and glare at him. "Don't worry. We're supposed to go to the carnival this weekend. If I have him over after, we'll stay in my room. Wouldn't want to discourage the ring-bunny fan club I'm sure *you'll* be inviting over now that you're bro-mates with my brother." I'm shaking so hard, I can't even take pleasure in the fury lighting up his eyes.

"That's it." He slams his cup down, splashing protein shake all over the counter, and closes the distance between us.

I back up, almost tripping over my backpack. My butt bumps into the refrigerator door, rattling the big, old appliance in place.

"You know full fucking well I'd never do that to you." He stares down at me, almost pinning me to the refrigerator but not quite touching me.

But I feel him *everywhere*.

No, no, no. Why is he so close? Why does he smell so good? And why isn't he wearing a shirt?

"I do." I stare at my sneakers, the only place that seems safe right now. "I shouldn't have said that."

He sucks in a deep breath and lets it out slowly. "Molly, can we please talk? I didn't—"

"I know," I whisper.

"What?" He steps back, giving me space.

Stop being a coward. I lift my gaze and meet his concerned stare. "I watched that episode again." I haven't talked about it since last weekend with the girls, but I'd thought about it an awful lot this week.

"God, why?" He plows his fingers through his hair in frustration. "Why would you do that to yourself?"

"Because. After last weekend...I wanted to see it objectively." I shrug, trying to figure out what to say. I don't want to tell him Torch is the one who planted the first seed of doubt. "Or try to. I watched it without the sound on." I wave my hand around my head. "Without all the other noise polluting everything. I don't know. I don't think it was you anymore."

"Thank God." He sighs.

"Griff, I should've known. I feel terrible—"

"I don't *want* you to feel bad, Molly."

"But," I mumble.

"I watched it with your brother when I came home. And it was weird as hell for *me* to see. I get it. I'm not mad at you," he adds in a gentler voice.

Why does that make me feel even worse? "You should be." *I didn't believe you and I destroyed our beautiful car.*

"I could never be mad at you." He holds out his arms to embrace me, as if everything is solved now.

"Okay, so truce," I suggest, shying away from his hug. "Since you're living here and I guess we'll see each other a lot."

"Yeah, we're going to see each other a lot." Pure confusion twists his handsome features, then the realization that we're *not* back together slips over his expression. "Wait. You still don't...I'm home. I'm not leaving. I love you. What's the problem?"

How can he not see what happened?

"You hurt me! And I know that's not fair. I know you didn't mean to." Burning with frustration, I wave my hands in the air, unable to find the right words. I wasn't prepared to do this today. "You thought you were helping but you *ruined* us."

His jaw drops. "I ruined us?"

He really doesn't understand? "You made the choice to leave and be on that show. I barely had a chance to understand what it meant before you left. I wasn't prepared for what happened. It made my life hell, Griff. And you weren't here."

"I wasn't prepared either, Molly."

"Yeah, but *you* chose to be a part of it. *I* didn't."

"You, you," he sputters. "You said you were on board!"

"Because I had no choice!" I lower my voice and force some calm into my words. "I wanted to support *you*. I didn't want to be a part of that circus."

"I didn't know it was going to go down like that."

Calm leaves my body in a violent rush. "But you should have!" I explode. "You didn't look into that company even a little bit before you signed their stupid contract. How could you not see that it would expose our lives to the whole world?"

"I thought—"

"I know what you thought." I take a breath and try to speak like a rational human. "But even once you knew what was happening, the lies they were telling, you *still* didn't come home. Remy told you what happened. I know you talked to him." My voice breaks. It still hurts so much that he didn't just *leave*. "And you chose to stay."

"Molly." His voice roughens with emotion. "I tried. I couldn't leave without losing everything. I don't mean the time I wasted on the show or the prize money. They threatened to sue me and keep me going back to court for years if I broke that contract."

Too choked up to say anything, I shake my head.

"So that's it?" He sounds so defeated I want to hug him, but instead I move farther away. "You hate me now?"

No matter how mad or hurt I am, I can't let him think that. I lift my gaze and stare into his sorrowful eyes. "No, of course not."

"But you don't love me?"

"I didn't say that either," I whisper. "But it's not enough."

"What else is there?"

"If you really wanted to come home, you would've found a way." I swallow over a painful lump. "You chose the show over *us*. Over you and me."

"It's not that simple." His jaw tightens. "I couldn't pick up and leave without facing real consequences. If you can't understand that, then maybe you're too immature to be in a relationship."

Ouch, calling me immature pokes at every single one of my insecurities about us as a couple.

"Maybe you're right." I lift my chin and try to hide how much that comment hurt. "But staying had consequences too." I suck in a sharp, painful breath. "You lost me."

CHAPTER TWENTY-THREE

Griff

MOLLY'S STUBBORN STREAK RUNS DEEP. ALWAYS HAS.

But she's not wrong.

Neither am I.

I step closer. "Is that how you really feel?"

She lifts her chin, staring me in the eyes. Bold and beautiful. But her bottom lip wobbles, betraying her bravery. "Yes."

"You know I never meant to hurt you. Embarrass you. Or anything like that."

She glances away. Toward the door. Her eyebrows draw down. Like she wishes she'd never come home. "What do you want from me?"

I want you to love me again.

Or admit she never stopped.

"I want you to talk to me," I say instead. "Tell me about college. Do you like your classes? Do you have a roommate? Are you happy there?"

"Yes, yes, and..." She hesitates, frowns again. "I guess so."

"You don't sound so sure about that last one."

She shakes her head and glances at her sneakers. Her shoulders lift. "I thought I'd be happier getting away from *here*."

"Something new like that. It's a big adjustment."

"I never realized how much I like my...space." She sighs. "I kinda hate the whole communal bathroom thing and the dining hall."

"Yeah? Too crowded?"

"Sometimes." She finally shifts her gaze to me again. Her defensive posture relaxes. "I like Denise—my roommate—but we don't have a lot in common. And all the other girls on my floor...it's like it's the first time they've been away from home, so they kinda act like children? They can stay up and be loud all night because Mom and Dad aren't around to scold them?"

"And you passed that stage of life a long time ago," I say gently. "Living with your brother and his lax rules?"

She chuckles. "Yeah, I guess. Does that make me sound like a cranky old lady or something?"

"Not at all." I almost add, *that's how I felt living in the house with all the other fighters,* but I don't think she's ready to hear any of my reality show complaints, yet. She's talking to me and that's huge. Don't want to do anything to ruin this moment. Or remind her of all the reasons why she should hate me.

"I like coming home on the weekends, because all they want to do in the dorms is get drunk or high," she continues, "or hook up with random guys."

My stomach clenches but I try to keep my face neutral. "You like your parties to be a little more high-octane?" I tease. "Racing cars with a side of fried dough?"

She grins. "Yeah, that's a lot more fun to me."

I don't dare ask if she also comes home to visit Torch. I really don't want to know.

Her phone buzzes again. Annoyed and frustrated by the intrusion, I wait while she checks the screen, then flicks it off without replying.

I just *know* it's that orange-haired fucker.

"Torch come visit you at school?" I blurt out.

Stupid. Fuck. Why'd I ask?

"What?" Her eyes widen and she slides the phone in her back pocket. "Uh, yeah. He came out with Remy when I moved in."

He's been in her dorm room. He's seen her bed. Touched her stuff.

Wait, Remy was there. Nothing happened. Probably.

"Eraser and Ella came too," she adds.

Even better.

"How much stuff did you have to move in?" I was aiming for a teasing tone but sounds more like I'm hacking on every word.

She gestures to the bulging bag of laundry and the corners of her mouth turn up in a shy smile. "All my clothes."

"You're not just rolling into class in sweats every day?" I can't stop picturing her strolling around campus in those loose green sweatpants and *my* hoodie.

She laughs a little more. "Well, yeah." She shrugs. "But sometimes I like to look nice."

For who?

No. Do *not* say that. Molly's always liked putting together cute outfits. Just because I enjoy the hell out of them doesn't mean she was doing it for my—or anyone else's—benefit.

"You always look nice," I say instead. Thank fuck some of my brain cells are starting to function again. "No matter what you're wearing."

Pink spreads over her cheeks. "Thanks."

"I wish I'd been there to help you move in."

Her body freezes and the soft expression on her face goes stone cold. "Well, you weren't."

Damn, why couldn't I keep up the normal small talk?

"Molly, I fucked up." My voice drops as emotion chokes off my words. "I'm so sorry. You have to know that."

Her shoulders drop and a tear rolls down her cheek. "Okay."

None of this is okay.

"Tell me what I can do." Somehow we moved from easy small talk to me practically begging her to forgive me, and I don't even care.

"There's nothing to do, Griff." She shrugs like she's helpless to come up with a single thing. "It's done."

Done?

In no way will we ever be done.

"Are you really going to the carnival with Torch?" I ask. "That haunted carnival I said *I'd* take you to when I got back?"

She nods quickly and swipes the back of her hand over her cheek. "I don't know. Maybe."

I can't do this with her. Talk to her about dating someone else, like it's fucking normal and not ripping out my heart.

My inner asshole's so close to telling her Remy's the one who asked Torch to "date" her. But I can't do it. Sure, it'll make her mad at Torch and she'll probably never want to see him again. Win for me. But more pain for Molly. It'll make her mad at Remy too, which he fucking deserves. But I don't want to cause problems between them either.

Maybe the truth will come out eventually, but it can't be from me, out of jealousy.

CHAPTER TWENTY-FOUR

Griff

Heavy thudding above my head pulls me upstairs a few hours later. Remy's still at the bar. It has to be Molly. What the fuck's she wearing, cement shoes?

I quietly creep into the dining room, leaving all the lights off. If she comes in here, she'll bump right into me but for now, she's facing the front door and too busy furiously tapping on her phone to notice me.

Molly...Fuuuck me. I don't know what she's supposed to be but she's wearing a short, black velvet dress with a high collar of ivory lace. Frills and ribbons decorate the long sleeves. The short, flared skirt has layers of black lacy ruffles peeking out from underneath it. Black fishnets cover her legs and black platform Doc Martens boots give her a few extra inches of height. That's what made all that racket.

Between the outfit, the black ribbon in her hair, and her dark purple lipstick, she looks like some sort of grown-up, goth Alice in Wonderland.

Sexy beyond all reason.

I'm instantly rock hard.

It's been way too long without her.

Blood rushes through my veins and my chest rises and falls in an erratic rhythm. The urge to pull her closer, kiss her until she's dazed, flip up her skirt, and bend her over the dining room table beats through my blood.

Fuck. Fuck. Fuck. What if Torch has the same thoughts when he sees her? How could anyone *not? Jesus Christ,* what if he touches her sexy legs? Every awful possibility flips through my head like a nightmare I can't escape.

I curl my hands into fists at my sides.

There's a strong possibility that I'll kill Torch tonight.

"You look..." *Mouthwatering, too sexy to leave the house...* "pretty," I say, stepping out of the shadows into the hallway.

She jumps. "Why are you skulking around in the dark?" Her pretty face wrinkles into a scowl. "And why don't you ever wear a shirt?"

I glance down at my bare chest and then at her bright pink cheeks. "Why does it bother you, Muffin?" I ask in a low voice.

"It...N...no."

I slide my gaze over her outfit, lingering on her legs. "Why don't you ever wear longer dresses?"

She sucks in an annoyed breath, then slowly lets it out. Her hands drop to the skirt and all the lacy layers underneath, and she lifts the material a few inches.

Fire races over my skin. If she lifts any higher...it's game over.

"Why, Griffin? Does it bother you?" she asks in a mocking but also somehow sultry tone.

I tear my gaze away from her legs and meet her challenging blue-eyed glare. "Yes."

"Too bad." She lets go of the dress and spins around, plucking a small black nylon backpack with skulls printed all over it off the hook by the door.

"Is Torch picking you up?" I ask.

"No." She stuffs her phone in the front pocket of the backpack and marches past me.

Her cherry-vanilla scent compels me to follow her into the kitchen.

"We're meeting there," she says. "I'm heading to Hayden's first."

"Hayden's going too?" Good, so it's not just Molly and Torch.

"And Kyla and Darcy."

Praise Jesus. The more, the merrier.

Molly opens the refrigerator and pulls out a bottle of water. "We're all going as our version of a fairy tale character."

She turns and faces me, raising a questioning eyebrow. Silently asking if I can guess her character.

"And you chose Goth Alice in Wonderland?"

She beams at me. "How'd you know?"

Pleased I put that smile on her face, I shake my head. "I don't know. It was the first thing that came to mind. I love how creative you are."

She glances down at her dress and tugs at the skirt. "I don't know if I'd call it creativity. More like an excuse to wear my weird outfits."

I lift one shoulder. "My only talent is punching people, so yeah, I think you're creative. And definitely *not* weird."

"Thank you." Her gaze darts to the back door, then to me. "I have to go."

I nod slowly. "Have fun."

She opens her mouth, then closes it and shakes her head.

Then she quietly walks into the night without another word.

I don't even wait for her to start the engine and back out of the driveway before I jog downstairs. I tear through bags of clothes I still haven't unpacked yet, find an oversized black, hooded sweatshirt, and throw it on.

Like fuck is Molly walking around some creepy carnival all night dressed like that without someone looking out for her.

And whether she knows it or not, that someone's going to be *me*.

CHAPTER TWENTY-FIVE

Griff

IF I'M GOING TO CONTINUE THIS NEW HABIT OF following my girlfriend around, I really need to invest in a more stalker-friendly vehicle. The distinctive throaty rumble of the Chevelle forces me to keep too much distance between Molly's car and mine. Thankfully, I know where Hayden's house is and which roads they'll take to the Old Miller Farm where the carnival's being held.

Remy's Ghostface mask sits on the seat beside me. Can't have Molly see me following her around like a guard dog. Or worse, have anyone recognize me from the show.

The girls take two cars. Hayden's BMW follows behind Molly's little Bronco, and I try to stay a few cars behind them which isn't easy on the narrow town roads. Once we get on the highway that leads to the farm, I'm able to stay back. Traffic gets heavier closer to the farm. This carnival has to be the most exciting thing that's happened in Johnsonville in years.

I make the turn for the bumpy dirt road. Two cars ahead, Hayden slows to a crawl. The guy in the car in front of me lays on his horn.

Hayden's middle finger appears out of the driver-side window. I huff a laugh at Hayden's brazenness and reach behind my seat, quickly curling my fingers around my baseball bat in case the impatient asshole ahead of me decides to confront the girls.

Several sloppily marked rows have been designated with orange traffic cones and some kind of solar lights. Christ, we do a better job directing traffic and have better equipment out at The Castle. A guy dressed as a bloody gingerbread man waves a light stick and directs Molly to the left. Hayden follows her. The honker gets sent to a middle row. I ignore the gingerbread man and take the farthest lane.

The bumps and uneven ground rattle my teeth. Rocks ping and scrape the undercarriage. I reach forward and pat the dashboard. "Sorry, Black Beauty. I'll make it up to you tomorrow."

I park in the first space I find, grab the mask, and slip it on. A quick glance in the rearview confirms I look just as stupid as I feel.

"Fuck it." I step out and slam the door, then throw my hood over my head, check I've got my wallet and keys, then weave through the parked cars, headed in the direction Molly went.

I find the girls close to the entrance to the carnival. They're clustered around Hayden's car, talking and fixing their makeup, I guess. Hayden's dress is similar to Molly's, except it's a baby pink with white and black trim. Kyla's in a long, red gown with a wide black belt. Darcy's in a black see-through dress with crazy straps wrapping around her torso and feathers on her shoulders. I can't even guess what any of the other girls are supposed to be.

Maybe it's because I'm so fucking obsessed, but Molly stands out like she has a ray of light beaming down on her.

Why am I torturing myself like this?

Like a proper stalker, I keep my distance behind Molly and her friends as they go through the ticket booth and pay their entrance fee. I'm sweating inside the mask but keep it in place.

Without taking my eyes off of the girls, I hand over my twenty and have an orange bracelet clamped around my wrist.

"Have a ghoulishly good time!" the attendant shouts.

I roll my eyes and walk through the makeshift gate. For a traveling carnival, it's rather elaborate. Much larger than I expected. People are hidden by masks of every horror movie character from the last forty years. Sinister-looking clowns mix with Jasons, Freddies, and Michael Myerses. I pass at least seven different Ghostfaces before I hit the midway.

At least I blend in with all the other basic bros who found a mask and called it good.

I pass by a few couples that went all-out planning their matching costumes. A Barbie and Ken. Kermit and Miss Piggy.

Not one costume is as adorable or clever as Molly's.

The girls are to my left, buying funnel cakes, corn dogs, fried Oreos and other fair-style food. Molly wanders over to a different booth and buys something that looks like a waffle cone. When I pass the booth a few minutes later, the sign says *Fried Mac-n-Cheese*. My stomach growls. I haven't eaten since the morning and the mask isn't food friendly.

Suck it up.

I spot Molly ahead of me.

Her short skirt and all the layers under it swish from side to side with every step she takes. She keeps slowing down to take bites of her cheesy waffle cone, forcing her friends to drag her along.

They finally duck into a tent set up with picnic benches to eat their treats. I keep walking and pretend I haven't been following them for the last half hour.

No sign of Torch anywhere. What'd he do? Stand her up? *What a dick.* I should kick his ass for hurting her feelings.

Pick a lane Royal. You can't be pissed she's "dating" him and mad that he stood her up at the same time.

I just hate it when she's unhappy.

Then again, his absence tonight probably saved *my* sanity.

Molly

"See, we're having fun without any boys!" Kyla screeches in my ear, stealing the last of my cheddar waffle cone out of my hand.

"Hey!" I snatch an extra sugary piece of funnel cake off her plate and stuff it in my mouth.

"Did you hear from Torch?" Darcy asks me, as she also picks off a chunk of Kyla's funnel cake. Kyla slaps her hand away.

No need to check my phone again. "Yeah, he's not coming." My voice sounds as disinterested as my heart feels.

Hayden snickers into her giant cup of cherry icy slush. "He's probably terrified Griff will kill him."

Is Griff the reason Torch canceled on me at the last minute? He'd sent me the original "probably won't make" it text when I was home. Griff was there too, not out terrorizing Torch into breaking our plans.

"I don't think so." I didn't tell them about my earlier run-in with Griff. But I haven't stopped replaying it in my head either. I *should* have invited him to come with us.

"Well, Wade blew me off too," Hayden says.

"I'm glad it's just the four of us." Kyla wraps her arm around my waist.

I lean my head on her shoulder. "Me too."

"Don't let me forget to bring a bag of cotton candy home for Jenn," Hayden reminds us for the fifteenth time.

"We won't," Darcy groans. "Why don't you just get it now?"

"Nah," I say. "It'll be all melty and gross by the time we leave."

Hayden sucks the rest of her drink down in one long, noisy rush. "All right. Let's check this place out."

The carnival is larger than I expected. The Millers let whoever runs the thing use a lot of their acreage. Or maybe it seems huge because it's dark and overwhelming.

We find our way into a circular area of booths housing dozens of typical carnival games. Except, these aren't typical. Each one is horror themed. And the prizes range from decks of Tarot cards to cute and creepy-looking stuffed animals.

"Ewww," Kyla squeals. "*Zombie Brain Toss* looks revolting."

"I think that's the point." I stop and watch some of the players use a mallet to launch little jiggly "brains" into the open skulls of giant Zombie mannequins. "It looks hard too. There's no good way to aim that thing."

"These games are always rigged," Kyla says.

"Yeah, but we've seen people walking around with stuffed animals and goldfish all night." I nod to a group of younger teenagers carrying a huge stuffed unicorn skeleton.

"I guess," she sighs.

We pass *Frankenstein Operation* where you have to put organs back into a giant Frankenstein strapped to a bed. Graveyard ring toss, zombie shooting alley, and finally one that looks like something I might be able to actually do.

Skeleton Ball. The prizes are all stuffed and squishy animals with creepy eyes and little colorful stitches.

"Oh!" Kyla points to a row of black plush bats and kittens. "Look at the bat. He's so cute."

The operator of this game is probably a few years older than us. He's tall and almost thin enough to pose with the row of animated skeletons behind him. His jet-black hair sticks up in shiny spikes. As he approaches us, he bites on a small silver ring through his bottom lip.

"Greetings, ladies." He holds out a ball shaped like a skull. "Would you like to sink the bone in the hole?"

Ewww.

Behind him, I spot a lone black, cartoonish-looking, stuffed rabbit with long black ears and a red X for one eye. The perfect mix of macabre and adorable. I point at it. "What do I have to do to win the bunny?"

Skeleton-man walks backward and snatches the bunny from its hook. "You've got thirty seconds to sink one ball in each basket." He points to one of three fifteen-foot-tall animated skeletons holding a wide basket in each hand.

I glance at Kyla. "That sounds easy enough."

"It's like double basketball with a countdown clock." She shrugs. "Right?"

The operator grins. "More or less."

I can't tell if he's naturally creepy or if it's an act for his job. But dammit, I want that bunny.

"Five chances for five dollars." He holds out his hand.

I pull a five from my purse and set it on the counter.

"You've got this, Molly," Kyla says. "You always crushed it in gym when we played basketball."

"That's being generous."

"Positive vibes, Molly." She waves her hands over and in front of me like they're two sage sticks.

The operator lines the skull-shaped balls on the counter in a neat row. I pick one up, testing its weight. It's almost squishy but kind of hard in the middle.

Now that I'm actually trying to launch a ball into the basket, the opening looks so much smaller. I aim for the basket on the left and throw. It hits the skeleton's hand, then bounces away.

"Har, har, har, is your batting average legally drunk?" the animated skeleton barks while its lower jaw hinges up and down with more mechanical laughter.

"What the—!?" Kyla presses her hands over her mouth and laughs. "It heckles you too?"

"Twenty seconds," the operator reminds me.

Oh crap. I forgot about the time limit. I pick up the next ball and quickly throw it at the right basket. It bounces wildly off the rim.

Shoot.

Ignoring the inane insults from the mechanical skeleton, I aim for the left basket again. It hits the rim of the basket, rolls in, then bounces out.

"What the heck was that?" Kyla yells. "That counts, right?"

"Nope. Gotta stay in the basket," the operator says.

I throw my last two balls at the left basket and miss both times.

Well, that humbled me fast.

The operator holds five more balls in his hands. "Wanna go again?"

"Sure." I slap another five on the counter.

The third ball actually lands in the left basket and stays there.

"Ah-ha!" I punch my fist in the air. "Right basket, you're mine now."

I line up my shot so carefully, trying to remember exactly how I got the one to stay in the left basket. I throw the ball with a perfect arc. It hits the rim, rolls around it, then bounces out onto the floor.

"Oh, come on!" Kyla shouts.

"Five seconds..."

Dammit. I throw the last ball without thinking and it ends up hitting the skeleton in the jaw.

"Har, har, har. Were you throwing with your feet?"

"Grrr." I can't believe I fell for this.

"Tell you what." The operator steps closer to the counter,

holding the bunny in front of him, waving it side to side, like he's about to hand it to a toddler. "My name's Bram, I'll let you have the bunny if you give me your phone number. Maybe I can take you out while we're in town."

I stare at the bunny for a second. It's cute but not *that* cute. "No thank you. That's okay."

I grab Kyla's hand and pull her away. She runs to catch up, giggling. "Oh my God, Molly. I think Bram *vants to suck your blood.*"

"Hilarious." I stop and side-eye her. "So glad we watched *Dracula* over the summer."

She hugs me. "Aww, don't be sad. Those games are rigged. Another fifty bucks, you probably would've had it."

My attention's drawn to a tall guy dressed in black wearing a Ghostface mask walking by. Swear he's staring at us through those creepy black eyeholes.

Griff?

No, that's stupid. He wouldn't come here alone. And definitely not in costume.

"What's wrong?" Kyla nudges me with her elbow.

"Oh, that Ghostface guy reminded me of Griff."

She turns left and right. "Which one? I've seen like fifty of them tonight."

"Uhh..." I turn in a circle, but she's right. Five different people have the same mask. "I don't know. Let's go find Hayden and Darcy before they get into trouble."

We follow the widest path through the carnival. Eerie music blares from different booths. Voices over loudspeakers invite us inside to witness horrible things. Characters jump in our way and try to scare us.

A big red-and-white tent stands in the center, but it's crowded. In a quieter section shops and activities line both sides of the wide aisle. Face painting, a crystal shop, clothing, and other vendors I can't read the signs for.

After all the walking and weaving through the crowd, an annoying painful rub starts aggravating the backs of my heels.

"I can't walk another step," I whine to Kyla, stopping in my tracks. "My feet hurt."

We step out of the flow of traffic and lean against one of the buildings.

"I'll let Hayden know where we are," Kyla says.

Standing on one foot, I unlace my boot and carefully slide it off, then peel my sock down. "Oooo." I suck in a sharp breath at the gory state of my foot underneath my fishnet stockings.

"Molly! Shit. That looks bad. Hang on." She digs through her tiny red purse and produces a Band-Aid. "Will that help?"

"Oh my God, you're a life saver." I pluck it out of her hand and peel it open. "I don't suppose you have another one?"

"Just one." She glances down. "Which foot do you like better?"

I snort and rip a hole in my tights, peeling the material away from my oozing skin. I apply the Band-Aid carefully over the painful wound. "I already have this boot off, so this foot wins."

By the time I have my boot in place, Hayden and Darcy have found us.

"What's wrong?" Hayden asks.

"Blisters." I point to my feet. "I thought boots were smart for tonight but apparently not."

"You know what was a *really* dumb choice? Open-toed, high-heeled sandals." Darcy holds out one foot, showing off her ruined black satin strappy sandal and her bare, mud-caked toes.

"I tried to warn you," Hayden sings. "And what did you do? You made fun of my sneakers." Hayden points to her bright-pink Converses that are also now covered in mud.

"Where did you two go that you got so...muddy?" I ask.

Hayden waves her hand toward the big tent. "This haunted house thing. It's really cool but the ground is a mess over there."

My aching feet force us to walk at a slower pace. But it gives Darcy and Kyla time to dart in and out of the small shops and let us know if there's anything good inside we need to check out.

"Ah! That place has clothes." Darcy points to a brightly colored tent up ahead. "Let's see if they have some cheap shoes." She grabs Kyla's arm and starts dragging her away.

"We'll catch up." Hayden stops walking.

I stop my pathetic limping and turn toward her. "What is it?"

"We *have* to do it, Molly." She clasps her hands under her chin. "Please?"

"Do what?"

She thrusts her arm out and points at the narrow red tent in front of us.

Madame Nova Darkwater, Fortune Teller is printed in gothic script on a sign.

I side-eye Hayden. "You've got to be kidding."

"Come on, it'll be fun!" she pleads, tugging on my arm.

"Fine," I groan.

"Welcome, ladies," a woman greets us as we push our way through layers of sheer curtains. Soft, colorful lighting floats in the dim space, giving it an otherworldly feel.

The woman's sitting at a round table with two stools on the opposite side. She's wearing a long-sleeved red dress with silver embroidery. A matching silver scarf's tied around her head, hiding a good portion of her long, wavy red hair. Large gold hoops swing from each ear. Pretty much what I'd expect a carnival fortune teller to be wearing. There's no crystal ball on her table, though. Just a thick, dark-red velvet cloth and a deck of Tarot cards still in the box.

I plop down on one of the low, red velvet stools and Hayden sits on the one next to me.

The woman stretches her arms across the table with her hands up and lifts an eyebrow at me. After a second of hesitation, I rest my hands on top of hers. She gently wraps her soft, warm fingers around mine.

"What do you seek to know, Molly?" she asks.

Her skin's smooth and unlined. She's younger than I'd expect. Maybe my brother's age? But she speaks with the attitude of someone much older.

Wait, how'd she know my name?

I open my mouth to ask, and she shakes her head. "Focus on the question."

"I don't know." I tilt my head toward Hayden. "She made me come in here."

One corner of the medium's mouth lifts. "At your age, I assume it's about a boy." She closes her eyes, her face settling into an impassive mask. "Ah, *two* boys. Interesting. One you love deeply who broke your heart. And the other one you like but..." She stops, *thank God.* "You still love the first one. There was a misunderstanding? You were embarrassed very publicly. Betrayed." Her carefully groomed eyebrows pinch together. "So much *guilt.*"

Whose guilt? Griff's or mine?

Her accuracy is so damn freaky. Did Hayden set me up?

The woman opens her eyes. Even under the odd lighting inside the tent, her blue-green irises shine like sea glass, staring straight through me.

"Holding onto all this unresolved anger and shame is much like sitting in the middle of a fire and hoping those who wronged you are the ones who will get burned," she says. "Tell him the truth. *All* of it."

This isn't fun anymore. I yank my hands away from her voodoo table, praying it breaks whatever psychic connection we've established. "Thank you for the advice." I shoot a glare at Hayden. "It's *your* turn now."

The medium smirks. "Follow your heart, Molly."

"My heart is unreliable," I mutter.

Not deterred by my super-specific reading, Hayden happily lays her hands on the table and the medium takes them.

"You've begun a new path recently," the woman says, closing her eyes again. "But you don't feel like you're where you belong?"

I stare at Hayden. Is she having trouble adjusting to college?

Hayden blushes and averts her eyes.

"You worked hard to get there," the woman continues. "And even though it's a sacrifice for your parents, you *are* worthy, Hayden."

The medium opens her eyes. "That'll be twenty dollars, each."

I pry open my wallet and peer into the almost empty cash slot. "You should've gotten the money upfront," I joke, handing over a twenty.

She winks at me. "I knew you were good for it."

Hayden pays her and we both hurry away from the table. At the tent flaps we stop and share a look.

"We never speak of this," she says.

"Deal."

CHAPTER TWENTY-SIX

Griff

MOLLY SPENT THE NIGHT AT HAYDEN'S AFTER THE carnival. Did she always plan to stay there or was it to avoid me? Whatever the reason, I left a surprise on her bed. I'm hoping she sees it before she leaves.

I keep busy raking leaves, taking care of the pre-winter yard maintenance Remy won't have time to get around to. The dull aches in my shoulder and knee keep reminding me not to get carried away.

Around one o'clock, Molly's car pulls into the driveway.

I glance over as she steps out wearing a hot-pink, velvet tracksuit with a red sequined heart on the front and pink flip-flops so small, her toes hang over the front.

Our eyes meet and I bite my lip, trying to hide my laughter.

"Don't you dare say anything," she warns, her voice carrying through the backyard.

"What in the early 2000s *Legally Blonde* are you wearing?" I manage between chuckles.

"Shut it!" Ignoring my amusement, she pulls a bag out of her back seat, then rips off the flip-flops and tosses them inside.

I rest my rake against a tree and hurry to help her.

"Want me to take that?" I lift the heavy bag out of her hands and catch a glimpse of her balled-up black velvet dress and boots inside.

"My beloved boots betrayed me last night." She lifts one foot, showing me the large Band-Aid across her heel.

I wince in sympathy. "Ouch. You all right?"

"I'll live."

I follow her into the house.

In the kitchen, she takes the bag from me. "I need to sort this stuff and then pack to go back to campus."

"Already?" I can't hide my disappointment. I thought she'd at least stick around for dinner. Is she leaving because of me? Am I making her uncomfortable in her own house?

"I have some stuff to do to prepare for tomorrow," she explains.

"Okay. Remy know you're leaving?"

"I said I'd stop by the bar on my way out."

"That's good."

She hesitates, lifts her bag, then sets it down.

"Did you eat?" I ask.

"Oh yeah." She rests her hand over her stomach. "Lots of pancakes." She turns away. "I have to go pack my stuff."

"Yeah, yeah." I back away slowly. "I'll be outside."

I *want* to follow her upstairs. But I force myself into the yard again. My knee throbs in protest. I stop and study the yard. Still plenty to do but I put a good dent in it. I gather the tools I used and return everything to the shed.

The screen door screeches open. "Griff?"

Molly steps onto the porch, now in jeans and a purple sweatshirt. Her feet are still bare and her long hair's pulled into a messy ponytail. The black stuffed bunny I left on her pillow dangles from one hand. She lifts it and waves it at me.

"Thank you."

I spread my hands wide, feigning confusion.

"It *was* you who left it, I hope?" Her smile falters and she lowers the bunny to her side. She steps down into the grass.

I lift my eyebrows, still playing confused.

"Stop it. I know it was you." Her expression softens as she comes closer. "I have a question, though."

"What's that?" I cross my arms over my chest, my heart quickening.

"How did you know I tried to win something *just* like this last night?"

It's not "like" it. It's the *exact* one she was trying to win from the creepy dude running the skeleton toss game.

"I was out and saw it." *Not a lie.* "It reminded me of your devil bunny costume." I shrug, as if I hadn't watched her try over and over to win the creepy little fluff ball.

She laughs and holds it up and examines it. "I guess you're right."

"So you like it?"

"I do." Her smile fades. "Thank you."

She waves her hand around at the piles of leaves. "I'll tell Remy you've been busy here."

"Tell him he needs a leaf catcher attachment for his lawn tractor, too, while you're at it."

"Suure, I'll get right on that." She glances down at her bare feet. "I need to find some shoes that won't bother my heels." She mumbles a hasty goodbye and hurries into the house again.

A few minutes later, I go inside too.

In the mudroom, she has her bags of clean laundry lined up. The rabbit's sitting on top of her backpack. I grab her stuff and haul it out to her car.

I load everything in the back, then set the bunny on the front seat and pull the seat belt around him.

When I'm done, I stare at the back porch. No sign of her yet.

I can't do this.

I can't watch her leave when we haven't fixed anything between us, yet.

And I can't make her stay here, either.

I go inside and grab my keys off the kitchen counter. I wait a beat. Scuffling and banging echoes from upstairs. She must be tearing her closet apart looking for shoes.

Grabbing my jacket from the hall closet, I slip out the front door. My car's parked at the curb. I slide behind the wheel, fire up the engine, and get the hell out of there.

HOURS LATER, I'm back in Remy's house, going out of my mind with boredom. Definitely overdid it this morning.

Resting and recovering, hell, just sitting still in general, have never been easy for me. My knee's cursing me out for all the yard work, and fire burns from my shoulder to my wrist.

By the time I hear Remy's car in the driveway, I'm jittery as all hell.

I limp to the front door and open it before he has a chance.

"Jesus Christ," he breathes out. "You're supposed to be my roommate, not a butler. What're you doing?"

Feeling like an idiot, I step back and shrug. "Trying to be nice. Sorry that's such a confusing concept for you. Thought you might have your hands full."

He holds out his empty hands. "Is that your way of saying you ate all the eggs?"

I snort. "No. I ran to the store this afternoon and bought groceries."

"Good roomie." He pats my head like I'm a damn golden retriever. "Yeah, Molly said you took off before she left."

I shrug, not really wanting to explain myself to him. "I had stuff to do."

"You mind?" He sweeps his hand through the air, indicating I should move away from the hall closet.

"Are you always this grumpy when you come home?"

"Probably." He opens the closet door and stares. "Fuck."

"What's wrong?" I step behind him, expecting to find a colony of mice living in his coveralls based on his expression.

"We're supposed to get a lot of snow this week." He gestures to the coats neatly hanging in the closet. "Molly didn't take her coat *or* her boots."

"I'll run them out to her." The words pop out of my mouth without a second thought.

He turns and rolls his eyes at me. "Really? You're going to drive *allllll* the way out there to give her a coat and shoes?"

"Well, yeah. If it's really going to be that cold..." I shrug. Who am I kidding? Of course I'd drive out there to bring her anything she needs no matter what. Remy has to know that.

"Maybe they cancel classes for snow," he mutters.

"It doesn't matter. I'll take them out to her." I squint and jerk my head toward the door. "Are you sure, though? It's kind of early for snow, isn't it?"

"Nah. Remember that one Halloween my mom sent us out trick-or-treating in snow boots?"

How could I forget? "Yeah, you kept bitching they ruined your Spiderman costume."

He chuckles at the memory. "You were such a suck-up. 'Yes, Mrs. Holt, I'll wear my boots,'" he says in a high, mocking tone.

The bittersweet memory stings less over time, but I still miss Remy's mom more than I ever talk about. "I wouldn't have *had* any winter boots if it hadn't been for your mom. So, yeah, if she wanted me to wear them, I was wearing them." My own mother barely knew if I was alive from day to day, let alone if I had weather-appropriate clothing. Even when Mrs. Holt was sick, she always made sure her kids had what they needed. Thankfully, she included me too. And later, so did Remy's grandparents.

The teasing smile melts off his face. "She loved you too."

Other kids might have gotten jealous about the attention Remy's mom showered on me. But he never did. If anything, it made him happy she treated me like one of her own. "I know."

He pulls out his phone and taps out a quick message. Then stares at the screen while he waits for a reply. I jam my hands in my pockets. His phone buzzes and he sends another text.

Done with the exchange, he glances up. "She says Tuesday would be better. There's a cafe she likes near her dorm. Meet her there at nine? Is that too early?"

Too early? I'd go set up camp there right *now* if I could. "No." I lift my chin at the phone in his hands and stuff down my annoyance that she answered *his* text so fast when she still hasn't unblocked me. "Are you going to tell her I'm coming instead of you?"

"Nah, bro. I actually *want* her to get her stuff and she'll probably dodge you if she knows you're the one delivering it."

"Thanks," I grumble. "We got along okay this weekend."

"Yeah, and then you took off before she left."

"Was she that mad about it?"

He shrugs. "I don't know. More like, confused? Hey, if she gets mad when you're there instead of me, just toss the stuff at her and run." He taps his fist against my arm and heads into the kitchen.

Using deception isn't how I wanted to repair my relationship with Molly. But now I feel even shittier for not saying goodbye to her. This visit can be a sort of a do-over.

Besides, my desire to see her again outweighs my guilt about Remy tricking her into the meeting.

CHAPTER TWENTY-SEVEN

Molly

EXCITEMENT AT SEEING MY BROTHER PROPELS ME DOWN the stairs of my dorm. I have an hour to spend with him before class. He hasn't visited me since he helped me move into my dorm room. I'd like to take some time showing him around campus, but we won't have enough time.

The sidewalks are crowded enough that I veer onto the grass. I pass a few people I recognize and wave a quick hello. My backless sneakers crunch and crackle through the fallen leaves sprinkled all over the lawn.

Seeing Griff this weekend wasn't as awful as I thought it would be. At least I finally told him how I felt and heard his side a little bit. The night of the carnival is where it turned awkward. And the day after.

As much as I hate admitting it to myself, I miss him so much. I've thought about unblocking him and sending him at least a text a million times. But every time I try, all the hurt and embarrassment comes rushing back and I can't.

Then he went and gave me the bunny. I wanted to thank him again, but he left the house before I had a chance. After packing my car for me. I hated that he left without saying goodbye, but I guess I deserved it.

He's home now. Living at my house. But for how long?

According to all the *Supreme Fighter* gossip sites that I have absolutely not spent any time obsessing over, *Stonewall* was the "fan favorite" of the show. Everyone liked how "real" he was. How he seemed kind of shy and didn't participate in a lot of antics in the house but was savage in the cage.

Mechanic in a small town? Or professional fighter with adoring fans all over the world? The choice seems pretty obvious.

So no matter what he says, I'm not eager to have my heart broken again when he inevitably leaves.

Enough about Griff. I spent my whole summer trying to get over him. College was supposed to be a new beginning. It *has* been a fresh start.

Until Griff came home and forced me to confront all the feelings I've been trying to escape.

I reach the cafe and stop to glance around. Remy's kind of hard to miss. I pull out my phone to check if I have any messages from him. Remy's usually on time. Should I wait outside?

Nothing.

Fine. I'll be able to buy *him* breakfast for once. Introduce him to scones. Cheered by the thought, I pull the door to the student union open and trot down the short flight of steps to the cafe. The rich scent of coffee and pastries tickles my nose as I step inside.

My eager gaze scans the small cafe, searching for Remy.

And lands...

...on *Griff*? Sitting at a table, straight ahead and to my right, watching the door.

I blink. Is this a joke? I was thinking about him on my way here. Did I manifest him into existence? Am I hallucinating?

Our eyes lock and he lifts his hand. A sheepish smile curves his lips.

My phone buzzes in my hand.

Remy: Something came up at the bar. Griff's meeting you.

I want to answer with a row of middle finger emojis. Instead, I don't bother responding *at all*, and stuff my phone in my pocket.

I force my feet to move in Griff's direction but it's like willing them through wet cement. My heart pounds harder and my stomach twists with each step. Why am I so nervous? I just saw him two days ago.

Griff stands to greet me.

I stop at the chair across from his and curl my fingers over the cool metal back. What am I, a lion tamer? Am I going to thrust the chair at his midsection to keep him at bay?

"What are you doing here?"

My harsh tone wipes the tentative smile off his face. He drops back into his chair. "Remy said you needed some stuff. He couldn't make the drive, so I said I'd do it."

Warmth spreads though my chest. He drove all this way to bring me some clothes? I pull the chair out and slide into it. "Really? You didn't have to do that."

Especially since I was kinda mean to him this weekend.

"Not a problem." He lifts a big black overstuffed tote bag in the air. The blue sheen of my winter jacket peeks out from the top. He leans to the side and there's a crinkle from a paper bag. "Your winter boots are in here. Remy just gave 'em to me like that."

"That's okay. You really didn't have to." I glance at the high, small rectangular window in the corner. "It doesn't seem cold enough for snow."

"Remy was worried about you." He shrugs. "It was a nice drive."

Too stunned by his presence, I just keep staring at him and twisting my hands together in my lap.

He lifts his chin. "How are your feet?"

"Oh." I slide one foot out from under the table to show him my ugly sneaker-slides. "I had to find something backless to wear for now." I nod at the winter boots. "Maybe it's a good thing you brought them. I left my Docs at home after they brutalized my feet."

The corners of his mouth lift. "Are you hungry?"

I drop my gaze to the table as he pushes a plate with a giant blueberry muffin toward me. Then he slides a second plate with a pumpkin scone to my side of the table. "Your choice. Or I can get you something else if you want."

Danger. This is way too familiar. Griff bringing me muffins every weekend for the last who knows how many years. "How'd you know I like their pumpkin scones?"

"They looked good." He lifts one shoulder and shifts his gaze toward the door. "You don't like muffins anymore?"

No, they remind me of you. "I do." I pull the muffin closer. "This is a monster, though. Will you split it with me?"

"Sure." His shoulders relax and he leans back against his chair.

I carefully break the muffin into two pieces, then split the scone in half.

"This is yours too." He curls his hand around a short paper cup with a white lid and hands it to me. "Vanilla pumpkin latte."

How'd he know that's what I like to order here? I tilt my head, the question about to trip off my tongue when he says, "Thought it would go well with the scone."

"It does." I pick up the cup and take a tentative sip. The warm sweet liquid warms my mouth—just the right temp. As I set the cup on the table, thin, black, writing catches my attention.

Griff yur #1 no matter what.
Melissa 518-555-0106

"Uh, I think you have a fan." I turn the cup to show him the message.

He frowns and sits forward. "What the fuck?" Wide, concerned eyes meet mine. "I didn't know...I didn't see that. I never would have...Hang on." He grabs the cup and stands so fast his chair scrapes over the tile.

"Griff, it's fine. It's funny." I force a fake laugh.

"No, it's not."

"You're famous now." I almost gag on the words. I want him to be successful, I really do. But geez, we can't even share a muffin and coffee in peace?

He grumbles something I don't quite catch, then hustles away. "Be right back," he calls over his shoulder.

I twist to watch him approach the counter. He holds out the cup to the manager. Polite anger simmers in Griff's low, rumbling voice but I can't quite make out what he's saying.

Shaking my head, I turn and pluck a piece of muffin off the plate and pop it in my mouth. I better enjoy it now. I won't be able to show my face here again this semester.

A few minutes later, Griff's hand comes into view and sets a fresh, larger cup in front of me.

I wrap my fingers around it and pull it closer, letting the warmth soak into my chilly fingers.

He drops into his chair again.

I pop the lid off to let the drink cool. "You realize she probably spit in it, now."

"No she didn't. I watched the manager make it for me."

I flick my gaze to him. I'm about to make my joke about not being able to come in here again but all the easiness in his posture and joy in his expression has disappeared. His body's strung tight and he's absently rubbing his knuckles like he needs to release some energy on a heavyweight bag.

Oddly, his unease about the situation erases my anxiety. "Griff, it's fine." I push one of the plates toward him. "Eat your scone."

He stops rubbing his knuckles and picks up a piece of the scone. His hand hovers over the plate and little crumbs sprinkle down. "No, it's not fine, Molly. I didn't see the number, or I would've given the cup back before you even got here."

"It's not a big deal."

"Yes, it is." He drops the scone. "I don't want you thinking...after everything..."

"Like I said, you're a celebrity now. Be grateful she didn't hand you her underwear."

His eyes widen in horror. How has none of this occurred to him? His handsome face and gorgeous shirtless body have been plastered on television and online for months and months. Women have dedicated pages and pages of commentary about every aspect of Griff's physique, personality, and what kind of oil they'd like to massage into his skin.

"I don't *want* to be a celebrity." He glances at the counter again, an angry frown creasing his brow. "Shit, I'm not supposed to be seen out in public or have pictures of me posted online or anything."

But he still came to a college campus to see *me*? "They make them lock up their phones in the back while they're behind the counter." I've heard the employees complain about the policy several times now.

He nods quickly but his gaze won't stop jumping around the cafe.

"Come on." I pop the last of the scone in my mouth and wrap the remaining half-a-muffin in a napkin. "Let's go."

Hurt or confusion turns his mouth down, like he's worried I'm telling him to get lost. "Where?"

I nod to the bags sitting on the floor next to his chair. "I don't want to carry that stuff to class with me. Come on, I'll show you my room."

"Okay." He jumps up so fast, the table rocks sideways and he steadies it with his hand.

I grab the muffin and my coffee, then sling my backpack over my shoulder. A second later, the weight's lifted off my back. "I'll carry it," he offers.

"Thanks."

"Lead the way."

I press the lid on my coffee tight and turn toward the exit. The girl behind the counter shoots a glare at me but I ignore her. Griff hurries to open the door for me and stays close all the way up the stairs. Like he's worried I'll change my mind. Or sprint away from him.

Outside, he adjusts his ball cap lower and hikes my backpack higher on his shoulder.

"Your face looks better," I say, resisting the urge to touch his cheek. "Is your shoulder okay?"

He pops the opposite shoulder forward then back quickly. "This is the one I fucked up in the last match."

"Griff," I sigh, hating that he's been hurt at all. "Let me take my coat. You don't need to carry all that for me."

"Don't you have to get to class soon?" he asks.

Split a muffin with Griff, and I forget everything else. I yank my phone out and check the time. "I still have a few minutes. Come on."

He walks on my left and slightly behind me. Like my own personal bodyguard. At my dorm door, I swipe my card against the reader and hold it open for him.

"Am I allowed in here?" he asks, following me inside.

"We can have guests. Just not overnight." Not that the policy seems to stop anyone from having their boyfriends stay every weekend.

"Is it safe?" He glances at the door. "Are *you* safe here?"

Is anywhere really safe? "I think so."

I take the stairs quickly. But when I reach the first landing, I realize Griff hasn't even cleared half the steps yet. He seems to be favoring one knee and gripping the handrail hard.

"Are you okay?"

His pained eyes meet mine. Then his jaw tightens, and he nods quickly. "I'm fine. Go ahead."

"Men," I grumble. "You can't just admit something's bothering you?"

"Yes, my knee hurts." He groans. "I think I overdid it with the yardwork this weekend. But it's still better than it was when I first came home, so keep going."

Wow, never expected him to share that much.

Guilt slows my steps knowing that he's possibly in pain. All because I chose to live on the third floor. "I thought at least I'd get some exercise every day if I have to hike to the third floor a bunch of times," I explain.

He nods once, still concentrating on the stairs. "Solid plan."

My room's at the end of the hall and I hurry toward it, pulling out my key. I knock and push the door open slowly in case Denise isn't in class for some reason. The room's dark and empty. I push the door all the way open and flip the switch on the wall.

"Here we are." I set the coffee and muffin on my desk and stand back, so Griff can enter. "It could fit in my closet at home, huh?" I joke.

"It's, uh, small, yeah." He slides my backpack off his shoulder and sets it on the floor next to my desk. "You share this with someone?"

"Yeah, she's nice, though."

"That's good." He hands me the bag with the coat and I take it out, shaking it a few times before opening my closet door and hanging it inside.

Griff jams his hands in his pockets and awkwardly leans against the wall. He glances at my bed. "Where did you find a purple-and-red comforter?"

I chuckle and duck my head. "I don't want to say."

"Okay. Yeah." He crosses his arms over his chest and shifts on his feet.

Oh, no. He probably thinks Torch bought it for me or something. "I found it in the kid's section of Pottery Barn on clearance," I admit.

A wide, relieved grin spreads over his face. "Nothing wrong with that." He steps closer and picks up the black stuffed bunny he gave me. His grin widens. "She even matches."

"She does," I agree, a little embarrassed he now knows the stuffed rabbit he gave me lives on my bed.

I grab the bag with my ugly old snow boots and stick it in my closet. "I don't know why Remy was so worried. It's not like I plan to go sledding or something."

"Yeah, he seemed really stressed about it for some reason." He clears his throat. "Can I walk you to your class?"

"Oh, shoot! I better get going." I'm torn. I don't want Griff to leave but I can't be late to class. "This professor locks us out if we're late."

"Well, let's go." He opens the door and holds it for me. "I'd hate to have to kick your professor's ass on my first visit."

He says it teasingly but knowing Griff he'd probably go bang on the classroom door if I got locked out. The thought propels me forward.

It's a small space and our bodies brush against each other as I pass. Griff's warm, woodsy scent wraps around me. I close my eyes for a second. So many things have changed between us, but his familiar scent still both comforts and excites me.

Class. I have to get to class.

"You okay, Muffin?" Griff asks.

Why does he have to call me that now? I blink up and find him staring at me.

"Uh, I, yeah," I mumble and duck my head, then hurry into the hallway.

Griff follows, closing the door behind him.

I drag my feet the whole way downstairs—I'm worried about Griff's knee, and I want to delay him leaving as long as possible.

My class is in a brick building kind of shaped like an old church on the far side of campus. "Where'd you park?" I ask Griff.

"In that visitor's lot near the cafe." He waves his arm in the opposite direction of where we're headed.

I stop walking and face him. "You don't have to walk me all the way to class. It's kinda far..."

He glances ahead, as if judging the distance, even though I haven't told him where it is yet. "But I want to see where your class is." He taps the side of his head. "Then I'll know what to picture when I'm thinking of you."

Oh, wow. Why'd he have to say something so sweet now when we have to say goodbye in a few minutes. And I haven't even apologized for how mean I've been the last few times we saw each other.

"Okay." I fight the urge to slip my hand into his as we continue walking.

All too soon, the little building comes into view. A steady stream of people are pushing their way through the red front doors. "This is it," I say.

"It looks like a church."

I chuckle and point to the little wooden plaque above the doors. *Church Hall.*

"Well, look at that." He grins and hands over my backpack. "Hope you have a good rest of your day."

"Thanks."

Awkwardness slides over us for a second.

Griff shoves his hands in his pockets and lifts his brow.

"Thanks for, uh, bringing my stuff. And breakfast."

"Anytime."

I'm almost in the front door when something compels me to turn around. Griff's still standing on the sidewalk, hands in his pockets, eyes watching me. He's as tall and immovable as a statue while students move around him. I push through the clump of guys behind me and hurry down the stairs back to Griff.

Concern creases his forehead. "What's wrong?"

"Nothing." I grip his biceps and lean up on my tiptoes. He bends down, tilting his head as if he thinks I'm about to tell him a secret. But I press my lips to his cheek instead. "Drive back safe."

I kiss his cheek again and hurry away. At the top of the stairs I turn again and he's watching me with a smile this time. He lifts his hand and waves.

I make it upstairs and inside the classroom right as the bell rings. Mr. Katz is already standing by the door waiting to throw the lock.

Phew. Just in time.

I grab a seat in the front row, not caring if that makes me look nerdy. My gaze strays to the window again and again even though it doesn't face the parking lot.

The weekend seems so far away. Paying attention in class has never been so difficult.

Griff

I savor Molly's sweet, brief kiss all the way home. Seeing her, walking around campus with her, talking to her, all of it was so much better than following her around like a damn stalker. She seems happy at school. Comfortable. Even if she doesn't love all the big changes, she's doing well. That's what I want for her.

The drive isn't bad, either. When I'm feeling one hundred percent back to normal, it'll be nothing to run out to visit and take her out whenever she wants.

Remy's still at the house when I pull in the driveway. I pull my car up and around his Bronco, so I'm not blocking him.

In the kitchen, he's busy frying eggs and the sharp scent of burned toast stings my nose.

"Back already?" he asks, throwing a glance at me over his shoulder.

"How many eggs are you making? It reeks in here."

"Well, now you're not getting any." He slides two eggs onto a plate, then flicks his spatula under another egg and flips it. "How'd it go?"

"Fine." I shrug off my sweatshirt and drape it over a hook on the basement door.

"Here." He holds out a plate of eggs and buttered toast.

My stomach rumbles. The bits of muffin and few sips of coffee I had on campus weren't enough. "This for me?"

"Yeah, I assume you didn't eat an actual breakfast out there," he says.

Why does he know me so well? Chuckling, I grab the plate and head into the dining room. "Got that right."

I return to the kitchen for orange juice, coffee, and utensils. Remy follows me into the dining room, setting his own plate across from mine.

My phone buzzes and I pull it out of my pocket. *Please be a date for the reunion show.* I want to get that out of my way and move on with my damn life. Worrying that someone at the coffee shop might have taken my picture intruded on my brief time with Molly and I didn't like it.

I flick the screen on to check the text.

Molly: I am glad you're home.

Relief, greater than anything I felt after winning my fights, sweeps over me.

She finally unblocked my number.

Me: Thank you.

No, that's stupid. I hit delete, then type it out again. I *am* thankful she's willing to talk to me. Might as well just be honest. I hit send and stare at the screen.

No reply.

That's okay. It's a start.

But then it buzzes again. A picture pops up. Molly, nose-to-nose with her stuffed bunny.

Molly: I named her Carnival, BTW.

My heart hammers from a simple selfie from my girl.

Me: Perfect name.

"What are you grinning about?" Remy asks.

I click on the picture and set it as my screen background. "Nothing." I set my phone on the table.

He frowns. It's not like he has a *no phones at the table* policy. His own's sitting right next to his plate. "Who are you texting?" he asks.

Does he honestly think I'd be contacting other girls when I'm sitting at his dining table? When all I've been talking about since I got home is repairing my relationship with Molly?

"Molly unblocked me." I grin even wider, not even caring if it pisses him off.

He flicks his gaze to the ceiling and shakes his head. "Good."

"Do you mean that?"

"Yes." He stabs his fork into a piece of egg and shoves it in his mouth.

Something bugged me the whole way home. And now, the need to question Remy won't leave me alone. "You know, it's weird, I checked three different weather apps and *none* of them said anything about snow this week."

"Huh? Really." Remy scratches his head, a sure sign he's lying, being a sarcastic dick, or some combination of the two. "I definitely saw it somewhere. Maybe that's what they mean about 'climate change.'"

"Weather and climate aren't the same thing." I dip the corner of a piece of toast into my egg yolk. "Try again."

"Weathermen are always gettin' shit wrong."

"Uh-huh." I munch on toast and egg for a few seconds, thinking over my words. Remy returns to attacking his eggs like he has a personal vendetta against them.

I take a sip of juice and set my glass down. "You ever get tired of playing puppet master?"

"Puppet master?" He glances up from his plate. "That's new."

I hold out my hand and wiggle my fingers in the air like I'm making a puppet dance. "You brought those girls over to force me into telling you how I feel about Molly. You set Torch and Molly up." I almost choke on that accusation, I'm still so pissed about it. "Now, you made up a fake snowstorm."

"And just think." His dickish smile increases tenfold. "That's only the shit you know about."

I should've known he'd show no remorse. "For fuck's sake, Remy."

"What?" He holds out his hands in an I'm-so-innocent gesture. "Look at it this way, if you were willing to run that stuff out to her,

I'd know you were serious. Then I would've talked to her about maybe unblocking you."

"But?"

"If you didn't give a fuck, then I wouldn't bother." He shrugs as if the answer should've been simple and obvious.

Could he be a bigger asshole? I tap my phone. "So, this is your doing?"

"Nope. I hadn't gotten around to it." He frowns and checks his own phone. "She still hasn't answered *my* text today."

"I don't think she appreciated you tricking her."

A minuscule flash of guilt crosses his face. "She doing okay?"

"She's good, I think."

"She wasn't pissed you showed up instead of me?"

I blow out an irritated breath. "She was surprised. But not mad."

"Anyone recognize you?"

I roll my eyes. "Some girl wrote her number on the coffee I bought for Molly, so that sucked."

He snorts with laughter. "You're famous now."

"That's what Molly said! It's not true." I set my fork against the plate with a harsh *clang*. "Stop saying that. All this 'fame' feels more like punishment."

"All right. Calm down." He sips his coffee. "What'd you do about the phone number?"

"Took the coffee back and asked the manager to make me another one."

He frowns. "Was Molly upset?"

"No." I grin. "She showed me her dorm room."

His frown deepens.

"She wanted to drop off her coat and boots instead of dragging them to class with her."

"Ah, yeah. Flaw in my master plan." He taps the side of his head.

"You're such a dick."

"How'd you do on those three flights of stairs?" He lifts his chin, indicating my bad knee.

Under the table I rub my hand over my thigh and knee, gently testing the inflamed joint. "Fine. Just took it slow. She showed me where one of her classes is, too. Did you know her professor locks them out if they're late?"

"Yeah, she told me."

"That's some bullshit."

He shrugs. "I told her if he ever pulls that crap on her, I'll have a chat with him. She didn't appreciate the offer."

Since I'm guilty of having the same thought, I chuckle and pick up my fork again. "Her room's so tiny. I can't believe she shares it with someone else."

"Yeah, for the amount they're charging, she could probably rent an entire house. But she wanted the 'full college experience.'" He grins, not at all bothered by the expense.

Remy probably didn't mean to, but he's given me all sorts of ideas for the future.

CHAPTER TWENTY-EIGHT

Molly

"Are you sure you don't want to stick around this weekend?" Denise pleads with me Friday afternoon.

"I can't. I promised to help my brother out at the bar." Guilt prickles over my scalp at the lie. I promised to go with her to a frat party at another school not far from our campus.

But a crowded frat house where I don't know anyone and I have to guard my drink with my life is the last thing I feel like doing with my limited free time. Remy hadn't asked me to help him at the bar but maybe I'll work a few hours there tomorrow night so I don't feel so guilty for lying to Denise.

"But you go home every weekend," she implores.

Only every weekend since I found out Griff was back.

Well, even before Griff returned, I went home on the weekends pretty frequently.

At least Remy doesn't seem to mind that I return so often. Part of me had worried as soon as I moved into the dorms, he'd change the locks and be annoyed if I returned on the weekends. But so far, he seems happy whenever I text him to say I'm coming home. Best of all, he's been keeping his usual parade of one-night stands away from the house when I'm there.

Denise helps me carry my stuff out to my car, making me feel worse for ditching her. "I really wanted you to meet this guy I've been talking to," she says after I slam my trunk shut.

"Are you meeting him for the first time?"

"No." A shy hint of a smile flickers at the corners of her mouth.

"Maybe Thursday? Laura said she wanted to go to trivia night at the Fickle Toad."

She raises hopeful eyebrows. "You'll go?"

"Sure."

"Yay!" She wraps her arms around me for a brief hug. "Drive safe."

"Thanks." Guilt tags along as I slide into the front seat. Why do I feel bad? Denise and I get along but we're not super close. Or am I embarrassed because I'm still homesick so often? I spent years wanting to get away from Johnsonville. How can I want to go home all the time?

Okay, this weekend I want to see Griff.

I haven't stopped thinking about his visit the other day. Haven't been back to the cafe yet, either. Just in case phone-number girl wants to serve me a sneezer-latte.

The reminder of the woman who so brazenly wrote her phone number on a coffee cup for Griff dims my enthusiasm. Why am I torturing myself like this? Griff's time home is temporary. He may not see it yet, but it is. And I'm still so ashamed about destroying my car, I can barely look him in the eye. When he visited me here, it was somehow different. I could almost pretend none of it ever happened.

But when I'm home, it's impossible to forget. It's why, even though I unblocked him and sent him the one text and selfie, I haven't contacted him since.

Except for his short replies, he hasn't reached out again, either.

Worried Griff will be at the house, I stop by the bar to see Remy first.

And promptly run into Griff.

I can't catch a break.

He's sitting on a stool near the front door. A wide smile brightens his face as I step inside.

"Since when do we need a bouncer?" I ask, a bit more snippy than I intended.

His expression smooths into indifference. "Your brother asked me to watch the door. So, I'm watching the door. Why are *you* here?"

I guess I deserve that. Answering that I didn't want to run into him at the house seems obnoxious. "I knew no one would be home, so I stopped by to see if Remy needs help."

He nods quickly and jerks his thumb over his shoulder. "He's in the back."

"I thought you weren't supposed to be seen in public?" Why did that sound so snotty too? We had a nice morning the other day. Why am I so unsettled seeing him here?

He slides off the stool, wincing slightly as he puts weight on his knee. "Unfortunately, it's not that busy yet." He turns away and walks into the main part of the bar.

Not sure what else to do, I follow. He's right. We only have two patrons. But it's still early. People who commute to Empire and normally stop in for a drink on their way home probably haven't even left their offices yet.

I wave to Anderson behind the bar before turning left and heading down the long hallway to Remy's office. The door's open a crack, so I push it wider.

"Hey, big brother. I'm home." I hold my arms open wide and grin at him.

He lifts his head from the piles of papers spread out in front of him on the desk. "Hey, kiddo. How was your drive?"

"Snow-free."

He bites his lip and chuckles. "Come here." He stands and moves around the side of the desk, meeting me in the middle of the cramped office for a quick hug.

"Do you want something for dinner?"

"I could eat a slice of pizza."

He lifts his chin toward the hallway. "Is it still dead out there?"

"Pretty much," Griff says.

I hadn't realized Griff was still behind me. I turn and he's leaning on the doorframe, arms crossed over his chest, eyes on me. Why does such a casual pose make him look so...climb-able?

"Grab a table. I'll bring something out for you," Remy says to me.

"Thanks." I slide past Griff—who doesn't bother moving an

inch out of my way. Electricity skitters over my shoulder as it brushes against his arm.

Anderson's busy with one of the guys at the bar. I wave but keep walking to my favorite booth in the back corner.

I pull my phone out of my purse and aimlessly scroll through Instagram, searching for a new nail or makeup look to try this weekend.

A text pops up.

Torch: You home this weekend?

My thumb hovers over the message, unsure of how I want to reply.

"Order up." A thin crust cheesy pizza on a round metal pan slides onto the table in front of me. I glance up into Griff's stoic eyes. He sets a plate and a roll of silverware on the table.

"Thanks." I drop my gaze to the eight wide slices. "I can't eat that whole thing by myself."

He pulls out the chair on the other side of the table and settles his big frame into it. "I thought you'd never ask."

"I didn't...where's Remy?"

"In the back."

I slide out of the booth. "I'm going to grab a soda." Why am I being so weird? We've split lots of pizzas together over the years. Taking a breath, I rest my hand on his shoulder. "What do you want?"

He places his hand over mine and stares at me like he's reciting every beverage the bar carries, but finally says, "Whatever you're having."

I hurry behind the bar, pull a pitcher of root beer, grab two cups, and return to the table.

He nods at me to pick the first piece. Too nervous to eat now, I pull the one closest to me onto my plate.

Griff doesn't seem to share my nerves. He grabs a slice, folds it in half and takes a big bite.

I pour the soda into our cups and hand him one.

"Thanks." He takes a quick sip. "How was the rest of your week?"

"Good. Busy. You?" I take my fork and knife and cut the big slice in half, then take a small bite.

"Took a few shifts at Jerry's. Felt good to get back to normal."

Another place I'll never be able to show my face again. It'd been hard enough when I went to see Jerry and apologized for the mess I made at his shop. "That's good," I mumble.

"I'm glad you unblocked me," he says.

My gaze flits around the bar. Anywhere but at Griff.

"I...I'm sorry." I should've done it sooner.

"I didn't want to bug you if you were busy, so..." He takes a bite of pizza without finishing the thought.

"Do you want to go to a movie or something when we're done?" He nods to the pizza.

Wait, what? "This, this isn't a...date, Griff."

He scowls and swipes a napkin off the table, quickly dabbing his lips. "I thought we...Molly, what's stopping you now?"

My bottom lip quivers. Dammit, I don't want to cry about this anymore. I'm still drowning in embarrassment that I did something so awful and foolish. "Look what I did. We haven't even talked about it. You've never—"

He frowns in confusion. "Talked about what?"

"My car." My voice breaks. "The car you gave me. Fixed up for me. I destroyed it because I was so mad at you for..."

Griff stares at me in wide-eyed disbelief, then pushes his chair back so fast, it scrapes against the old hardwood floor. He rounds the table and slides into the bench seat, forcing me to scoot over. Pulls me into his arms, sheltering me from the rest of the bar.

"Molly, I don't give a fuck about a few car parts." He blows out a relieved breath, or an amused one, it's hard to tell. "Hell, you had access to my car too. I'm impressed you didn't drop a match in her gas tank while you were at it."

He's definitely making fun of me. I tilt my head and glare. "Don't give me any ideas."

His smile slips. "You don't know how sorry I am, Muffin."

The familiar nickname brings a wave of longing and fondness swelling over me. I can't afford to get caught in the undertow. "I'm so sorry. I should've—"

He pulls me against his chest, cutting off my apology. He nuzzles his cheek against my hair and kisses my temple. Tears well up and burn my eyes.

I bury my face in his detergent-scented T-shirt. Underneath I sense his familiar spruce and soapy scent and breathe in deep.

He holds me tight while tears silently roll down my cheeks, finally handing my pain over to him.

"Please, please don't cry, baby," he murmurs. "I'm not mad about the car. Never." In between words, he kisses the top of my head and strokes my hair. "The only thing I was upset about is that you could've hurt yourself busting it up."

He lifts one of my hands, inspecting it closely before brushing his lips over my knuckles. "All that glass. I was worried you got cut up. That's it. Everything else is just *stuff*. It can be repaired or replaced. You're all that matters."

His easy acceptance and forgiveness only make me feel worse. It's not just stuff. It was a beautiful, thoughtful gift that he put so much time and effort into.

My throat's too tight to form any more words, though. Instead my body shakes with more sobs.

He hums a soothing noise that rumbles deep in his chest. "I'm sorry I wasn't here. If I'd known. *Really* understood, I would've burned down that whole fucking house to come back to you."

Sincerity rings in his voice. I lift my head and sniffle. "You worked so hard. Finding the car. Fixing it. I'm *so* sorry I did that."

No matter what Griff says, I don't think I'll ever live down the shame that I was so destructive. Would I have done it if he'd been home? Probably not. I would've confronted him or hidden in my bedroom until the end of time.

Besides my shame about the car, there's the shame of knowing he talked about me with someone else.

Another woman who wanted to fuck him.

Maybe that's why he's so willing to forgive me about the car? I pull away from him and grab a napkin to dab my eyes and cheeks. I quickly glance around the bar. No one's paying attention to us.

"It's not just that." This is so mortifying. But I can't go on letting him think I don't know.

"Tell me. What else?" He rests his hand on my leg. "Tell me so I can fix whatever it is."

This is humiliating. Heat burns my cheeks, but I push ahead. "Did you...tell anyone about me? About us?"

I might be willing to accept that Griff didn't *sleep* with Kiki but what if they formed some sort of emotional connection in the house? How else would she know such personal stuff about me?

"I tried not to talk about you too much to anyone." He frowns and hurries to add, "Not because I don't love you or I'm not proud you're my girlfriend." He stops as if he's daring me to correct him.

When I say nothing, he continues. "I wanted to protect you." He shakes his head. "I know that sounds weak after what happened, but I didn't realize—"

"No, I mean, more *intimate* details about me. Or about us?"

Confusion wrinkles his forehead. "What do you mean? Like what?"

"The day after...everything...I received a text from your burner phone."

His forehead slashes into a scowl. "They *took* my burner after I talked to Remy and confronted the head producer."

"You confronted the producer?"

"Fuck yes, I did. When Remy told me what happened. What they were saying about you...I know it sounds weak as fuck, Molly, and I didn't understand how bad it was, but I tried to fix what I could."

I nod slowly. Everyone had told me the show never mentioned me again. I'd always wondered if they were only saying it to make me feel better. "At least that was something," I mutter. "Thanks."

"After I came home," he closes his eyes briefly, "I found a text from *you* on the burner phone but everything else, all of our prior messages, had been wiped clean. So I didn't know what you were responding to." His mouth turns down. "I figured it wasn't anything good."

That sounds awfully convenient. "Really?"

He nods. "What'd the text say?"

I close my eyes, concentrating on the memory I've tried hard to bury. "Something about how virgins are only fun for a little while and you couldn't be interested in me for long. Signed Kiki." I finish her name in a snotty singsong tone. "I was hurt you'd...tell someone that about me."

Griff slow-blinks like he's staring at a crash at the racetrack. "What. The. Fuck," he breathes out. "Molly, I never said...I would *never* talk about you like that to anyone. *Ever*. And definitely not with some woman I barely know."

"Well, how else would she know something like that?"

He presses his lips tight like he's afraid I might not like his answer. "I'm sure she guessed. Or the show did. And then they just ran with it."

They *had* made a big deal about my age and that I still hadn't graduated from high school at the time. "Okay, but how'd Kiki know about your burner phone? Did you let her use it or something?"

"Of course not. If I was going to let anyone borrow it, it would've been Venom. But I wouldn't even loan it to him to call his wife, because I was worried he'd turn me in." He takes a breath. "I doubt it was even Kiki who sent the text."

Apparently, he didn't watch many of Kiki's private chats on the show. "Are you defending her?"

"What? No." Frustration roughens his voice. "Molly, I barely spoke to her or any of the girls."

Does he think I'm an idiot? "You were all stuck in a house together."

"It's a big house," he insists. "I trained and did whatever else the show wanted us to do. The ring girls were off doing their own thing in another part of the house. Or they were lounging around the pool and hot tub. I didn't go out there much." He scowls. "Saw too many of the guys get drunk and piss in the pool to ever want to swim in it."

"Eww, that's gross."

He hums a sound of agreement. "I was there with one goal—to win fights. I learned and trained. That's it. The rest was noise to me."

I stare at him, trying to sense any hint that he's lying. But Griff's never been a liar.

"You have more in common with her," I say quietly.

He frowns. "Who?"

"That woman." I wave my hands in the air, refusing to utter her stupid name again. "She's your age. She wanted to run her own business the way you do..."

"Congratulations, you know more about her than I do." He scowls and rests his hand on my leg again. "Molly, I know I'm not perfect. I wish I'd done a few things differently. But I don't *want* anyone else. Never have. Not for one second. You were always the only woman on my mind."

CHAPTER TWENTY-NINE

Griff

HOURS LATER, AFTER LEAVING THINGS UNFINISHED WITH Molly, I'm downstairs on the couch in the basement, watching an old boxing match with the volume down low.

Our conversation keeps replaying over and over. The car, I understand why she's upset, probably still embarrassed. I hope what I said soothed those concerns for her.

But the text? Based on the response she sent, I figured whatever had been sent to Molly had been a childish "he's mine" text. Not a jab at something more personal. For months, Molly's been thinking that not only did I sleep with another woman, but I trashed-talked her while I was doing it. No wonder she's been so uneasy around me.

Thank fuck she finally told me about it. I hope to hell she believed me. That has to be the final thing holding her back, right?

Something creaks above me. I cock my head and mute the television. Is that the back door opening?

Ten to one says it's *not* an intruder, but I ease off the couch anyway. Can't take any chances with Molly in the house.

I take the stairs two at a time and push the basement door open. The kitchen's empty and dark. My eyes take a second to adjust.

As I expected, the back door's ajar.

A small shadow sits on the back steps. Faint moonlight illuminates her shoulders and hair tied back in a low ponytail. *Molly.* What the hell's she doing out there in the dark?

Don't spook her.

I twist the screen doorknob slowly, but still make some noise, so I don't startle her, and step outside. The cool night air hits me in the face. Way too cold for her to be out here. She's on the second step, knees drawn up to her chest with her arms wrapped around her legs. The wooden planks of the porch are rough against the bottoms of my feet as I shuffle closer to her.

I'm done restraining myself. Finished with keeping my hands off of her.

I step down, bracketing her hips with my feet and lower myself to the top step, then wrap as much of my body as possible around her.

"Aren't you cold, baby?" I ask.

She hugs herself tighter, not really accepting my embrace, but not pushing me away either. A soft sigh eases out of her, and she rests her cheek on her knees. "No."

"What're you doing out here all alone?"

"Thinking."

About us? Does she finally believe me? Or is she out here thinking of a permanent way to tell me to fuck off?

"Mind if I sit with you?" I ask.

"You already are."

I chuckle softly. "Fair."

In the distance, an owl hoots his persistent mournful question, but Molly seems to have her own questions.

"You really didn't tell that woman anything about me?" she asks.

That's what has her up in the middle of the night? "No, Muffin. When she hinted that she was interested in me, I stone-cold turned her down. I never knew she was talking shit in her confessionals. I don't even think it was about me."

"What do you mean?"

I let out a heavy sigh. "At the last fight, Naptime passed out after the judges' decisions were read. She rushed into the cage and dropped to her knees next to him like her favorite cat had just been run over."

Molly doesn't laugh. "Huh."

After that we're quiet. What else can I do or say to help her understand how much I love her?

She continues staring into the shadowy backyard. I stare at her. At her tank top with the thin straps that tie at the top of each shoulder, reminding me of her prom dress. Just like that night, I'm dying to tug on the end of one of the bows and pull it loose.

Instead, I trace my finger over her shoulder. How is her skin always so soft and smooth?

She lifts her head and tilts sideways to look at me. "That tickles."

"Yeah?" I wrap her ponytail around my hand and gently tug her head to the side. "How about this?" I lean in and brush my lips against her neck, finally tasting the salt of her skin after all this time. "That tickle too?"

She shivers against me. "What are you doing?"

"Inhaling you. You smell so good. Taste good too." I kiss behind her ear. "I've missed you so much."

She draws in a long shuddery breath. "I've missed you too."

Every cell in my body demands I move the strap out of my way and kiss her shoulder.

But she *finally* admitted she's missed me too.

I let go of her hair and wrap her in my arms like a little package. "Can I hold you for a while?"

Her hair tickles against my arm as she rests her check on my biceps. "I'd like that."

My restraint only lasts for so long. Her familiar cherry-vanilla scent curls around me, stirring a blizzard of memories. "You feel good in my arms." *Right where you belong.*

"Hmmm." She sighs a contented little sound and rubs her hand from my wrist to my elbow. "I like being here," she whispers, so softly I almost miss the words.

I dip down and kiss the crook of her neck again, stopping to lightly suck.

Her body shivers and trembles in my arms.

"Griff." It's not quite a protest or an invitation to do more.

"Tell me what you want."

She presses against me harder, tilting her head and exposing more of her neck.

Now *that* feels like an invitation.

I slide my tongue along the side of her neck, and gently graze my teeth against her earlobe.

The soft swell of her breast barely hidden by her tank top teases and tempts me until I can't resist. I slide my hand over her shoulder and cup her breast through her top.

She gasps and turns slightly, giving me better access. Her nipple is sharp against my thumb, and I stop to stroke it with my fingers. She gasps and arches into my touch. *So sensitive.* I'll never get over how she responds to the lightest of touches.

"Are you cold?" I kiss her temple.

"A little." Her body shudders. "It's okay."

The flimsy tank top gaps, giving me room to slip my fingers underneath. Molly lets out a moan as my rough hand palms her breast again. I want my mouth on her so fucking bad it hurts.

"Come here." This angle and location are too awkward. I need her like I need oxygen. After all this time away from her, furtive gropes in the dark won't cut it.

She turns quickly and lifts herself off the step, then resettles herself in my lap, facing me.

Much better.

I brace myself with one hand behind me. "What're you doing, Muffin?"

She places her palm in the center of my chest. "Warming up. You're like a furnace." She drops her gaze, staring at my pecs, then lower. "A beautifully sculpted furnace."

I'm warm all right. Feverishly fucking warm from having her so close. "I don't know about that. I haven't done jack shit in weeks. I'm gettin' all soft."

Her hand drifts lower, tickling over my abs. "Definitely not soft."

"Keep moving a few inches south and see how hard I am."

She laughs softly and the smile finally lighting up her face and lifting away her sadness is better than anything else.

I cup the back of her head and pull her closer. Her eyes close as I press my lips to hers. *Heaven.* Exactly what I dreamed about for months. She tastes like cherry lip balm and minty toothpaste. I slip my hands under her butt and lift us off the steps.

A quick squeal pops past her lips and she wraps her arms around my neck.

"That's it. Hold on." I don't go far. A few steps back until my heel bumps against one of the old rocking chairs. I lower myself into it, keeping Molly anchored to my lap. The chair tips back wildly, thumping against the house.

I curse and peer up, as if I can see through the walls and into Remy's bedroom and figure out if the noise woke him. The last thing we need is him racing outside with a shotgun.

"Careful." Molly giggles and throws her hand forward, bracing the chair so we don't hit the wall again. "Although," she tilts her hips forward and back, rocking the chair, "this could be fun."

I groan each time she rocks herself against me.

"Slow down." I scatter kisses over her collarbones and stop to nuzzle her neck. "I want to get reacquainted with all the things you like."

"I like you...touching me...so much," she says between choppy breaths.

"Happy to do that." I sneak my hand under her tank top, skimming over her ribs. It feels so fucking good to touch her again.

As much fun as this is—and I'd love to keep messing around in the rocking chair—one of the neighbors could peek outside and get a free show. Not to mention Remy might decide to step outside and wind up seeing more than the starry night sky. I'll be happy to tell him Molly and I are back together, but I'd rather not have him find out *this* way.

Molly dips her head, kissing my neck. Her long hair slides over my chest, tickling in the best way possible.

"Will you come downstairs with me?" I whisper against her ear.

She pulls away and stares at my face. "I guess we shouldn't go upstairs to my room."

At least our minds are both traveling down the same path. "Probably not."

"Okay." She scoots out of my lap and stands in front of me—all sleepy-eyed and kiss-ruffled. The strap of her top hangs off her shoulder and her thin top's bunched under her breasts, leaving a sliver of her stomach exposed. I slide to the edge of the rocker, grab her by the hips and duck my head to kiss above her belly button.

"That tickles." She rakes her nails through my hair and I close my eyes, savoring the shivery sensation that shoots straight down my spine.

"You're awfully ticklish tonight." I kiss her stomach again, then tug her shirt into place.

"Because you're extra tickle-giving tonight." She skitters her fingers over my shoulders and into the crook of my neck, giving me a dose of my own ticklish medicine.

How did I survive so long without having her hands on me?

Never again.

CHAPTER THIRTY

Molly

My heart gallops so fast, I'm sure Griff can hear it. We quietly open the back door and tiptoe into the kitchen. At least, I sneak in like a bandit. Griff doesn't seem concerned that my brother might overhear us.

He opens the basement door for me and I stop, lean up, and kiss his cheek.

"What's that for?" he whispers.

"I love you."

He stares down at me with love-drunk eyes. "I love you too."

Heart racing, I grip the handrail and carefully step down the smooth, wooden steps. The air's warmer than I expected. This part of the house has been my brother's domain since I moved in with him. I haven't ventured into the basement since I was little. All the dark, dusty corners full of spiders deterred my curiosity. I usually picture it as a dark, dank expanse. But as I reach the last step, more of a homey man-cave expands before me. A dark overstuffed couch and large flat screen television are straight ahead. To my left there's one door and to the right two more doors.

"Where?" I ask Griff.

"You haven't been down here?"

"Not in a long time." I glance up at the white drop ceiling that must conceal all the pipes and beams of the house that I remember. "It was more open and spidery back then."

"No spiders," he promises. He touches the door on the left. "That goes to the rest of the basement—furnace, water heater, all that fun stuff."

He taps the first door on the right. "Bathroom."

"So it's basically an apartment without a kitchen?" I say, following him to the next door.

"Exactly." He pushes the door open and holds out his arm, inviting me inside. "Bedroom."

"Right to the point, huh?" I tease.

He flicks on a light switch. "I don't think you understand what you unleashed up there in that rocking chair, Muffin."

That *had* been fun. Teasing him. Feeling his hard body against mine. Letting his warmth seep into my skin. Possibly getting caught by one of our nosy neighbors.

I glance up and find a more thoughtful, almost hesitant expression on his face. "We can slow things down." He takes a step back and gestures toward the couch. "We can watch a movie or something."

That would be pointless. I'm so wound up, and want him so much, I'd probably climb in his lap before the movie starts.

"I'm just happy you're here with me." Longing and appreciation echo through his words.

"Me too." I step into the bedroom and hold out my hand to him. "Touch me."

"You don't have to ask twice." He rests his palms on either side of my face and tips my head back. I stare at him, trying to memorize every line and angle of his face. The fear that he'll leave again continues to hover at the back of my mind.

Not now.

He leans down and brushes his lips against mine. All the bitterness and hurt I've held onto the last few months seems to evaporate.

I sigh and lean into the kiss. I've never wanted anything more than his mouth on mine.

Griff's quick fingers untie the straps of my tank top and the loose, flowy material pools around my waist. Staring him in the eyes, I gather the material and lift it over my head, dropping it on the floor.

Hunger beats a steady pulse at his throat. His chest rises and falls faster while he stares at me like I'm the only drop of water in an ocean of sand.

"I've missed you so bad," he rasps. "Thought about you every day. Feels like a thousand years since I've touched you."

Every word brings on a wave of desire. Then guilt snakes around my heart. If only I'd trusted him. "We could've been here sooner if—"

"No." He presses a finger to my lips.

"Remy said I broke your heart." A soft tremor vibrates through my whisper, so ashamed that I hurt someone I love so much.

"Muffin, you can break my heart," he leans in and kisses my forehead, my cheeks, the tip of my nose, and finally my lips, "over and over again as long as we're together in the end."

"I never want to hurt you."

"I can take it." He cups my breasts. Each brush of his thumbs against my nipples is a jolt to my entire body. He slides his hands over my ribcage and down to my waist like he's trying to map and memorize every inch of my body.

His gaze drops lower and one corner of his mouth tilts. "Are those little cherries on your pants?"

I pinch the loose material away from my legs. "Yes."

"They're really fuckin' cute on you." His fingers play with the waistband. With one swift tug, he pulls the drawstring loose and pushes the pants down my legs. "But I need them off."

"Done." I work my feet loose and kick them aside.

The numbness I've felt ever since Griff left me finally burns away, leaving me wound tight and dying to release the unbearable tension at my core.

His gaze drifts to the little red triangle of material between my thighs. He squeezes my hip, then slides his hand between my legs. I shift my feet apart, giving him room.

He groans a short, appreciative sound and strokes one thick finger over the damp fabric barely concealing me. My breath stutters. How does such a simple touch—over my panties—feel so good?

"You're so hot and wet," he whispers, his palm pressing and covering me.

"For you."

That seems to unlock his slow exploration. He slides one finger up to tease and rub over my most sensitive spot. I gasp and squeeze my eyes shut. My hand shoots out, bracing myself against his shoulder.

"That's it. Hold onto me."

I slide my hand lower and curl my fingers around his bicep.

"Open your legs a little more for me," he demands.

I can't comply fast enough.

"That's it."

"Griff?"

"Shhh. Give me this." His touch turns harder, more focused. He presses a second finger over my clit, slowly increasing the pressure of the circles he keeps swirling. Time spins and stretches. My need grows.

Ripples of pleasure pulse through my body. Building and building. "Griff," I gasp, not sure I can stand on my own two feet much longer.

A rush of liquid heat gathers at my core.

His gaze stays transfixed to where he's touching me. The direction of his strokes changes, sharpening the pleasure. He presses harder, moving faster. I whimper and grind myself against his hand.

"Yes," he encourages.

Pressure continues to build. So intense, I can't breathe. I want him to rip my panties off so I can feel his skin on mine, but I'll die if he stops—even for a few precious seconds.

"Please...don't...stop," I beg.

"I won't." Need that matches my own roughens his voice.

My thoughts swirl into the tornado of desire spiraling inside me. I dig my fingers into his arm, holding on for dear life.

"Griff...I..."

"Yes. Be my good girl and come on my fingers."

Heat explodes over my skin. *Oh my God*. If he called me that under any other circumstance, I'd be furious. Instead my body trembles from his husky whisper urging me to be his good girl. My body bows forward, shaking violently, and I grasp his other arm.

Intense pleasure curls my toes. My legs wobble. I open my mouth, but only garbled sounds scrape against my throat.

"That's it," Griff praises.

I'm coming...and *coming*. Then suddenly, it's too much.

"Ack!" I jerk my body away from his hand and dance on my tiptoes. "That was intense."

"Come here." He wraps his hand in my ponytail and tugs me closer. "Kiss me."

I drop my gaze to his cock straining against his flannel pants. "I don't think I can get close enough."

One corner of his mouth tilts. His erection digs into my hip as I wrap my arms around his neck and kiss along his jaw. I stop to whisper in his ear, "Thank you for the orgasm. My legs are still trembling."

He unleashes a wild grin and slides his hands under my butt, lifting me to kissing level. "I love that I can make you come even with clothes in my way," he says against my lips.

I wrap my legs around him and shamelessly rub myself against his hardness. "Is that weird?"

"It's fucking incredible." He squeezes his eyes shut. "Careful there."

"What?" I ask innocently. I rock my hips against him and a tingling sensation spreads down to my toes. "This?"

"Yes," he groans, carrying me to the bed.

He drops me in the center and falls over my body, kissing and sucking at my neck. One of his hands cups my breast and he bends down to tease his tongue over the tip.

"Ah!" My hips shoot up, colliding with his body. "Griff, please."

"What?" He gathers my wrists in one hand and pins them over my head.

My body twists on the comforter, desperate for more. "I'm feeling very empty."

"We've got all night." He sucks my other nipple into his mouth and lashes his tongue against it. "I want to take my time saying hello to every part of you."

"Okay." I stop moving and stare at him. "Can you take off your pants, first?"

He sits back on his heels. A crooked smile spreads over his lips. "Why? Are you trying to get your way, thinking I won't be able to resist sinking inside your hot pussy if we're skin on skin?"

Fire races over my skin. I want that right now. *Oh no. Skin on skin.* How could I forget? "Uh, I'm not on the pill anymore."

Well, *that* wipes the smile off his face.

"I, uh, didn't..." *need the reminder of* him *every day*. And since I didn't plan to sleep with anyone else in the immediate future, didn't see the point. Heat sears my cheeks. I'm naked and writhing on the bed, aching for him but I'm embarrassed to explain? "It's fine. I'm close to getting my—"

"Hang on." He leaps off the bed, silently landing on the floor and hurries out of the bedroom.

I sit up and squint into the dark hallway. "Griff?"

There's a shuffle and bang, then five seconds later, he returns to the side of the bed. I kneel on the mattress and curl my fingers into the waistband of his pants.

"These need to go." I tug on the drawstring, but he has it knotted tight. I glance up into his amused face. "A little help here?"

He holds out a handful of condoms, then leans to the side, dumping them on the nightstand.

I side-eye the pile. "I'm not even going to ask."

"It's probably better if you don't." He frowns. "Wait, they're not *mine*."

That only leaves one other person they could belong to and the thought of it is too horrifying to contemplate. I stop fussing with his pants and clap my hands over my ears. "No, nope, no way."

His chest jumps with laughter. Shaking his head, he unties the drawstring and stares at me with raised eyebrows, encouraging me to make the next move.

"Yes, yes, yes." Eagerly, I grab the waistband and slide the pants down over his hips, releasing him. A flutter of excitement swirls with a bit of fear. "Wow, you're bigger than I...just...wow." I curl my hand around his thick, steely length.

"That's something I'll never get tired of hearing." He hisses in a sharp breath as I lean forward and swirl my tongue around the tip.

"Fuuuck," he groans and shoves his pants off the rest of the way, kicking them aside.

"I want you in my mouth." I stare up at him and part my lips.

"Take me," he rasps.

I open wide and circle my tongue around the head again, stopping to lick where he seems the most sensitive. A slight tremor runs through his body, so I tease my tongue there again.

His breathing turns ragged. He gathers my ponytail and a few bits of hair that escaped and wraps it all around his fist. Feeling brave, I open wider and suck him all the way, as far as I can go.

His hips jerk and he lets out a wild noise between a growl and a groan. "Ah, fuck. That's so good."

Still on my knees on the bed, I rest one hand on the mattress and curl my other one around the base of him. I experiment, taking as much of him as I can without choking, then slide my hand along the same path, using my saliva to make it easier.

He leans forward, tugging my sheer panties between my cheeks and lightly smacking each one. My body jumps and I suck him harder.

"I don't want to come in your mouth, Muffin." He backs away and I release him.

I sit back on my heels, rest my hands against my thighs and pout. "I wasn't done."

"No, but I almost was." His hot gaze slides over my exposed skin. "I really love those see-through red panties on you but take them off. Now."

I scoot backward and recline against the pillows, pressing my knees together. "Come and get them."

He stares at me with wide, surprised, lust-filled eyes for a few seconds, then climbs onto the bed and rests one hand by my hip. I stretch my legs out but keep them tight together. He hovers over me for a second, then dips down and kisses my stomach.

"Need to taste you," he murmurs.

"Mmm."

He drags his tongue against my skin, right above the elastic of my panties. Tugs at the thin strap over my hip with his teeth.

I can't tease him any longer. I dig my heels into the mattress and lift my hips.

"That's my girl." He grabs the thin band and peels the damp material from my skin.

Fire crackles over my skin as he drags my panties down my legs. He drops them on the floor and hooks one arm under my knee, opening me wide.

"Yeah," he whispers with appreciation, his breath caressing my exposed skin. "You're even prettier than I remembered." He slides two fingers through my slit. "Fuck, you're so wet."

"I want you inside me really bad." I drop my hand to his shoulder.

He kisses along my inner thigh. "Let me taste you first. I've been dreaming about making you come with my tongue for months."

"Really?"

His eyes close for a second. "God, yes."

I shift closer and run my fingers through his hair. "I like your hair longer like this."

He rubs his cheek against my leg, his light beard stubble scratching lightly. "You'll need something to hold onto while I'm eating your pretty pussy."

I flush from cheeks to chest.

He brings his mouth closer, his breath hot on my sensitive skin.

"Tell me you love me." He lifts his chin and meets my eyes. His gaze penetrates down to my soul. Almost like a challenge. Except, I sense he really needs to hear it.

"I love you," I whisper, running my fingers through his hair.

He lowers his head between my legs and swipes his tongue over my clit. My hips jerk and he clamps his arm over my hips, pinning me down. Somehow that excites me even more. I squirm and wriggle, testing his strength. His mouth is hot and insistent, his tongue pulsing against my clit, giving me exactly what I need before I even know I need it.

My body quivers under his touch. He shifts and hooks an arm under each of my legs, dragging me closer. He uses his fingers to gently spread me open and swirls his tongue around my clit over and over. Every few passes he stops to suck and kiss. With every touch, my orgasm builds. Pleasure ripples over my chest and up my legs. Restless with need, I cup my breasts and tug at my nipples.

Griff lets out a groan that vibrates against my core. I flick my eyes to his and find him watching me intently.

"You like this?" I tease my fingers over my nipples.

He flattens his tongue against me and groans with approval. As if he can't take his mouth off me for even a second.

I arch my hips, pressing myself against his face. He nods and makes more encouraging noises, each one vibrating against me, pushing me closer.

He switches to flicking the tip of his tongue against that same, sensitive spot. I moan and try to spread my legs wider, arch my hips higher.

"I'm...oh..." I squeeze my eyes shut, concentrating on the sensations.

Griff slides two fingers inside me, curling and stroking in time with his tongue. It's the last push I need to go over the edge. I let out a wild scream and keep chanting nonsense sounds over and over. He keeps working his mouth against me, drawing out the throbbing pleasure for an eternity.

When I can finally breathe again, I lower my hips to the mattress. "Oh my God," I whisper, covering my face with my hands. "That was so...oh my God."

He grins, pleased with himself, and keeps his palm between my legs, gently petting, like he's keeping me warmed up and ready.

"Griff, I still need you inside me." My want for him is staggering.

"Give me one of the condoms." He jerks his chin toward the nightstand and wraps his free hand around his long, thick cock, and strokes.

I twist and reach, finally capturing one of the gold foil squares between two fingers. I hold it out to him and he reluctantly takes his hand off me to grab the condom.

He carefully tears it open and I watch, fascinated as he rolls it down his length. "Surprised it fits," I whisper.

He ducks his head and laughs.

"I'm serious."

"I know you are." He stretches his big body over mine, resting his arm next to my head, bracing himself to keep most of his weight off of me.

Suddenly, I'm struck with the need to make a confession. "Griff, I need you to know something," I say in a rush. "I didn't—"

"Don't." He closes his eyes briefly. "Say his name."

"But I want you to know, I didn't—"

"I *know*." His low, insistent tone resonates with certainty.

"What?" Why does he sound so confident when he hasn't heard what I'm trying to say? "Griff, please. I need to tell you this."

"Molly, you don't have to tell me anything."

"Yes, I do." I take a breath. "I didn't sleep with Torch...or anyone else."

He dips lower, brushing his lips against my ear. "I know you didn't."

Why does he sound so sure? "How?"

He kisses the tip of my nose. "I know you." His lips curve into a wicked smirk. "And you should know *me* a whole lot better by now."

"Oh, no," I groan, fearing what's coming.

"That's right, Muffin. If I thought he'd touched anything more than your hand, I would've beaten him into a pile of mush."

My nose wrinkles. "That's not very nice."

"Never said I was a nice person."

I press my palm to his cheek. "You're nice to me."

"Because I *love* you." His lips quirk. "Trust me, I'm an unapologetic jackass to everyone else."

"That's not true." I quirk an eyebrow. "You put up with an awful lot from my brother."

He lets out a short rumble of laughter then shakes his head. "Please don't bring him up now."

"Sorry." I wrap my hand around the back of his neck and pull him closer. "I need you so bad."

He presses his forehead to mine and stares in my eyes. I lift my legs, wrapping them around his hips.

"That's my girl," he praises. "Open for me."

Slowly, he presses inside. Inch by pleasurable inch. He watches my face the whole time, backing off with each flinch or frown that crosses my face, giving me all the time I need to adjust and accept all of him.

"I missed you inside me," I whisper, clenching around him.

He groans and pulls back slightly. "I missed being inside you."

I tighten my legs around his waist and roll my hips, meeting him each time he thrusts.

"That's it," he encourages. "You feel so fucking good, baby."

"It's still okay," I lower my gaze to where we're connected, "with the...you know?"

He thrusts harder. "Better than okay. I think, without it, I would've blown before you had a chance to come all over my dick for me."

I shake with laughter and he groans, resting more of his weight on me. Something about the pressure or angle lights a new fuse. "That's good," I whisper urgently. "Don't stop."

"Already?" He lifts an eyebrow.

"I don't know, but it feels good."

He thrusts harder, hitting me just right. How does he seem to *know* exactly what my body likes? "Oh God."

My limbs tremble as sweet release spirals through me.

"Yes," he groans. "I feel you. Come for me."

He slows his frantic thrusting as the pleasure ebbs. His lips trail over my throat, keeping the fire inside me at a slow simmer.

He gently kisses his way to my chest and slides out of me.

Still a bit dazed I blink at the loss of him.

"Up." He grabs my hip and turns me to my stomach, then pulls me to my knees. "Nice." He flattens his hand between my shoulder blades, pushing my chest to the mattress, arranging me the way he wants. "Very nice," he groans and pushes inside me again.

"Oh," I squeak. "This angle's different."

He slows his movements. "Too much?"

"No." I wiggle my hips and move myself back and forth, testing out the slightly different sensation.

"Fuck, yeah." He rests his hand at the small of my back, gently guiding my movements. "That's good. You're so fucking beautiful."

I concentrate on rocking back and forth. It feels good but isn't setting off any fireworks for me, yet.

"Come here." He bands his arm around my middle and, keeping us connected, shifts and turns our bodies.

Behind me, he kneels and urges me, "Up. Up."

Keeping my hips angled so he doesn't slip out, I brace one hand against the mattress. He slides his forearm between my breasts and loosely wraps his hand around my throat, bringing me almost flush with his chest. I rest my hands on his thighs and rock myself up and down.

"Oh. Wow. I like this." I slide my hand over his arm. He feels so solid. "That's good."

He kisses my shoulder and neck. "This way I can touch you all over." He demonstrates by sliding one hand between my legs and gently rubbing my clit. His other hand stays at my throat.

"Open your eyes, Muffin," he whispers against my ear.

I blink, unsure of what he wants me to see.

"Look." He grips my chin, guiding my head straight.

We're facing a mirror over an old dresser. It's only enough to see from my chest up but our flushed, sweaty skin, and the visual of Griff's bigger body looming behind me while his arms completely cage me against him, brings on a new rush of excitement.

"I love you," I whisper.

He kisses my cheek. In the mirror I watch him close his eyes and breathe me in. His lips travel to my neck and he stops to suck my sensitive skin.

I hook my arm behind me, grabbing the back of his head.

"That's it." He squeezes one of my breasts. "Look how pretty you are." His fingers graze my cheek, then glide over my chest. "You're blushing all over. I'm buying a full-length mirror, so we can do this again. You're gonna watch me play with your clit while you work yourself up and down on my dick."

The combination of his slow, cherishing touches and his dirty words quickens my pulse. I rock my hips a little faster. "Yes," I moan.

"Would you like that?"

"Yes." My hand flails from his shoulder to his head, grabbing his hair. He rubs harder between my legs.

"Can you come for me again?" he says in an almost teasing tone.

"I'm...yes."

"Good." He kisses my neck. "Molly?"

"Wh...what?" I'm so close, I can barely concentrate on anything except the energy gathering between my legs.

"Hurry for me. I want to come all over your back."

Holy hell. The raw urgency in his voice undoes me. Nothing has ever sounded so hot. My orgasm descends over me like a summer thunderstorm. A powerful burst of pleasure. When the lightning bolts recede, I let out a soft cry and fall forward. He keeps his arm tightly around my middle, holding me in place. His other hand strokes and soothes between my legs, turning down the flame.

I stretch and crawl toward the foot of the bed and he groans as he slips free of my body. His hand clamps down on my hip. "Where are you going?"

I flip over, resting on my back and spreading my legs wide. "Come on my stomach. I want to watch."

Surprise sparks in his eyes. "Fuck yes." He grabs my ankles, drags me closer and thrusts inside hard and fast. A few seconds later, he pulls out and rips the condom off with a harsh snap. I watch, fascinated, as he grips his cock harder than I'd ever dare and works his hand over it.

"Don't move," he warns in a strangled voice. He hovers over me, pumping hard on his length over and over. His body convulses and shakes. He moans even louder and shouts my name. His eyes squeeze shut as his warm cum lands on my stomach and between my breasts.

When he's finished, I smile up at him. "That's...a lot."

He slowly opens his eyes. The corner of his mouth tips up, then his gaze shifts to my face and a genuine smile curves his lips. "You okay?"

I arch my back, showing off for him. "I feel good."

He pats my leg. "Stay right there. Let me get a towel."

"I'm not going anywhere."

He carefully extracts himself from the bed, but winces as he stands. I frown but, messy as I am, feel helpless to do anything for him. "Are you okay?"

"My leg locked up from kneeling for so long," he explains.

"Why didn't you say something?" I hate that while I was taking pleasure from his body, he was in pain.

"It didn't hurt until I tried to stand on it." He leans over the bed and brushes his lips against mine. "Your pussy feels so good, someone could've sawed my leg *off* and I wouldn't have noticed."

My nose wrinkles. "Ew."

He chuckles and backs away slowly. "Don't move."

"I'll be here." I close my eyes and concentrate on my racing heart slowing back to normal and the warm sticky pool cooling on my skin.

"Here we go." Griff wipes a towel over my stomach and chest, cleaning most of the mess. "Let's take a shower." He holds out his hand and pulls me up and off the bed.

"My legs are wobbly." I squeeze his hand and follow him to the bathroom.

I can't stop yawning and rubbing my blurry eyes while I wait for the hot water to warm.

"You all right?" Griff asks, grazing his knuckles against my cheek.

"You wore me out."

Our shower's quick and to the point. Griff glides his soapy hands over every inch of my body, pulls the showerhead down and rinses me clean. The little stall doesn't leave much room for anything else.

Outside the shower, Griff wraps me in a towel, then dries himself. He rests his hands on my shoulders and guides me back to the bedroom.

"Are you worried I'm going to leave or something?" I ask.

"No. I just like touching you." He pulls the rumpled covers back.

I stare down at the towel knotted over my breasts. "What am I going to sleep in?"

He hooks his fingers in the towel and yanks it free. "Nothing."

"What if my brother comes down here in the morning?" My gaze shifts to the open door.

He walks over and closes the door. "He hasn't yet."

I'm too tired to worry about it more than that. I climb into bed and Griff slides in behind me, pulling me into his arms. His warm, naked body curves around mine and I stroke my fingers over his arm.

Monday, I'll be back on campus. I want to soak up as much time as I can with him.

"I love you, Molly," he murmurs into my hair.

I reach down and touch his granite-hard thigh. "I love you too."

"You my girl again?"

The weight of the question steals my breath for a second. "Yes."

But for how long?

What happens when I go back to school? Is Griff even done with fighting? We haven't talked about his plans. Will he leave to film another reality show? I still can't picture him wanting to stay *here*.

I turn so I can see him and ask the question I shouldn't. "But you're famous now. You can have anyone."

He frowns. His hand cups my cheek. "If I don't have *you*, then I've got nothing."

Sincerity resonates in his voice.

What if he's offered professional fights? He'd have to travel a lot. Train somewhere with bigger and better facilities. Would he want me to come with him, or will I be stuck here, missing him again?

While I'm brimming with worries, Griff's sleepy, sated eyes hold no fear. Just love as he traces his finger over my cheek. "I don't want to sleep. I want to watch you," he says.

"I'm not going anywhere."

Satisfied with my answer, his lips curve and eventually his eyes close.

All the warmth and happiness from getting back together outweigh my fears.

At least for now.

CHAPTER THIRTY-ONE

Molly

THE NEXT MORNING, CREAKING FROM UPSTAIRS PULLS ME from sleep.

Remy must be awake and moving around in the kitchen. No wonder Griff knew to find me outside last night.

Griff's warm body's still next to me. Sometime in the middle of the night I let him have his arm back and it's now tucked under his head.

I trace my finger over his cheek and brush his hair off his forehead. My stomach clenches as I study the angry red scar over his eye. The result of taking one too many blows in that spot.

"What are you doing?" Griff mumbles sleepily.

"Looking at you. I've missed your face." I'm going to miss him so much when I have to leave tomorrow. The fears I fell asleep with early this morning return with a vengeance. "I don't want to go back to school."

His eyelids snap open. "You have to."

"I don't want to leave you."

A soothing sound rumbles in his throat and he cups my cheek. "I'll be right here, Muffin."

"But I want to be *with* you."

He shifts my hand from his cheek to his chest. "You're always with me."

"You're not listening."

"I'm listening," he says a little sterner. "But you're not missing classes to stay *here*."

He's right. I can't do that. And he can't come stay in my dorm room every night.

I still don't like it.

"You're not that far away," he continues in a firm no-nonsense tone. "I'll visit whenever you want."

"You'd do that?"

"Of course I would."

"I'd really like that. I could show you around the campus some more. And the little town nearby is so cute. They have a bunch of bookstores with shelves overflowing with old books. I love it."

A slow smile spreads over his face. "Dinner and old books. Sounds perfect."

Is he making fun of me? That *was* a pretty nerdy suggestion. "There aren't any racetracks or cage fights nearby. That I know about, anyway."

The smile slips off his face. "I mean it. Anything that makes you light up like that sounds like a good night to me."

"Oh, okay."

He brushes his fingers over my shoulder. "What about Thursday. There's a hotel near campus. I could stay there, and you ride home with me after your classes Friday?" he suggests.

"That'll get expensive."

"I don't care."

"Okay." Then I remember my promise to my roommate. "Oh, shoot. I promised Denise I'd go out for trivia night with her. She wants me to meet this new guy she's seeing."

I study Griff's disappointed expression for any hint he'd be willing to go with me. "I don't suppose you'd be interested in something like that?" I hate the pitiful, hopeful rise to my voice.

Relief turns up the corners of his mouth and his eyes widen. "You'd want me there?"

"Yes. I'd like you to meet my roommate." I shrug and drop my gaze. "But I know it's a long drive for something silly that—"

"Molly, look at me." He grazes my chin with one rough finger. "I'll go anywhere. Do anything with you."

Excitement quickens my pulse and I lift my gaze. "Really?"

"Yes, really." He touches a finger to his forehead, right above his fresh scar. "You sure you want your bruised up brawler of a boyfriend hanging around all your college friends, though? I don't know if I'll fit in with the trivia crowd."

Underneath the teasing question, I sense something more serious or vulnerable lurking. "You're not a 'bruised up brawler.' You're my boyfriend and I want you to meet the people I spend time with when I'm not spending time with you." My words come out sharper than I intended but he needs to know I'm not embarrassed that he's a fighter, mechanic, or anything else he might be thinking.

"So passionate," he teases.

"About you? Yes." I close my eyes, remembering an important detail. "But you're not supposed to be out in public, are you?" I can see it now. Some jackass uploading a video to YouTube titled "Stonewall from Supreme Underground Fighter Attends College Trivia Night."

"So I'll wear my hat."

I raise my eyebrows. "It's a hat, not an invisibility cloak."

He frowns. "Maybe you're right. Not this week, but I'll definitely go with you when I can."

That's all I need for now. The promise of normal couple stuff in the future. I tease my fingers over his chest. "That's probably wise. What if we ran into Melissa again and she wanted to give you her number?" I tease in a high-pitched singsong.

He flicks his gaze up. "This show's like a curse that never goes away."

"Understatement of the decade." We haven't talked about any of this yet and I have no idea what his plans are for the future. "But let's face it, you're this big reality star now—"

His harsh laughter cuts through my words.

I smack his chest. "I'm serious."

"It just sounds so ridiculous. And trust me when I say, that's the *last* thing I want engraved on my tombstone. Black belt. Mechanic." He leans in and kisses my forehead. "Molly's boyfriend. Those are the only titles I want."

One corner of my mouth tilts up. "Molly's boyfriend should be first on that list. Just sayin'."

He rumbles with deep, affectionate laughter. "It is. 'Molly's husband' will be even better one day."

"Oh." My heart pitter-patters. "Really?"

"Hell yes." His happy expression fades and his forehead wrinkles into a frown. "I need to talk to you about something."

His grave tone raises the hairs on the back of my neck. I shift away to see his face better, but he tightens his arms around me.

"What?" I ask.

Here's where he says it's nothing bad. Or no big deal. Or tells you he's moving to California to become a professional fighter and we'll see each other during the holidays.

"Uh, so you saying the reality star thing reminded me, uh..." He squeezes his eyes shut and curses under his breath.

My lungs freeze, waiting for him to continue.

"Part of my contract, well, getting the rest of my prize money hinges on me returning for a 'reunion' show."

I groan and roll my eyes. "I'm not surprised."

Relief floods his expression. "It got delayed and put off because of Naptime's surgery."

"What surgery?"

Griff lifts a shoulder and shifts his gaze away from me. "I came home pretty fucked up, but he fared a lot worse. He had to have an operation on his shoulder or something." He blows out a frustrated breath. "I really don't care what happens to that asshole, I'm just trying to explain why I'm still tied up with this thing."

Knowing Griff, he cares a *little* about injuring someone that severely. The guy he and my brother train with always taught them to fight clean and always end a fight with the least damage possible.

A reality show wouldn't care about sportsman-like behavior. Just like they didn't care about destroying our relationship. They'd want the fights to be as brutal as possible. Anything to bring in the highest ratings.

"I'm surprised they didn't make a big deal out of his injuries. They could've given you some spiffy new ring name like *The Bone Cracker*." My voice turns cold and distant.

Instead of laughing, his frown deepens. "Maybe it had more to do with them wanting Naptime to look like the clear winner."

Anger that Griff was robbed from winning the title boils my blood. I don't need to watch the show to know he should have won. *Split decision my ass.*

"Anyway." He reaches for my hand, curls his fingers around mine and squeezes gently. I lift my gaze. His serious expression sends fear pumping through my veins again. "Before I left, I had a sit-down with the head guy. The one I demanded a meeting with after...Remy told me about the episode that—"

"Ruined my life?" I finish for him. Why is he bringing this up now? We had such a beautiful night together. Talking about the show is bad enough. I don't want to be reminded of all that other ugliness.

He closes his eyes for a second, then powers ahead. "They mentioned the reunion episode. Like I said, *I* won't get the other half of my winnings unless I go."

Figures there'd be more strings attached. "I guess that makes sense. They want the whole cast there, I bet. Especially the final guys."

"Right." He takes a breath. "But they dangled another incentive in front of me."

"What?"

His lips part and the cold, awful truth of what he's about to say spills over me.

"No," I whisper.

He nods slowly. "They'll pay you for your appearance on the reunion show."

He names an amount that would be enough to cover my remaining tuition, books, and housing next year—if I'm lucky enough to be awarded the same scholarship money I received this year. That could really help take some of the burden off of Remy. There might even be enough left to make a few of my car payments since I hate that Remy took on that extra expense too.

But sitting on some stage with all those fake people would be like selling my soul to the ghouls who "showed" the world my boyfriend sleeping with another woman.

Or maybe it would give me the chance to repair my image.

Instead of the "dumb virgin slut" the show painted me as, I can present myself on the show as a composed, intelligent college girl.

"Did you tell Remy?" I ask.

"No." He frowns. "It's your decision. Not his."

Well, at least that's something. A couple of months ago he probably would've asked Remy's permission before even telling me about it.

"I wanted to talk it over with you first," he adds.

"But you also know there's no way he'd be okay with it."

"The decision is *yours*. Not Remy's. Not mine." He shakes his head. "*I'm* not comfortable with it."

"Then why *are* you telling me?"

"Why *wouldn't* I tell you? It's a lot of money. It would be shitty to lie to you about something like that."

"What if we hadn't gotten back together?"

"We were always getting back together." He tilts his head and stares at me. "We were never 'apart' as far as I'm concerned." His steady gaze never wavers, as if he's daring me to deny it.

"I'm serious."

He runs his fingers through his hair, messing it up in the most irresistible way.

Focus. Don't get distracted.

"One of the producers probably would've contacted you directly and asked you to come on the show." He lifts one shoulder. "Hell, maybe they'd offer even more money."

"This feels so unfair. They know we're broke. All those fighters in the house needed a way to support their families in one way or another and these sick freaks are basically dangling bananas in front of us and cooing 'dance monkey dance.' It's insulting."

He blinks. "That's nothing new. Rich men have exploited lower classes for blood sports since Roman times."

I narrow my eyes. "You're not low class."

"You know what I mean." He sighs. "You don't have to do it."

I sense there's something he's holding back. "Do *you* want me to?"

"I don't want you around those people. I don't want to expose you to any more of this. Not after what you've already been through."

There's a catch or hesitation in his denials. "I sense a *but*."

He lets out another sigh and rubs his hand over my arm. "I want you with me," he admits in a voice almost too low to hear.

"You do?"

"Yeah, I do." His eyes meet mine. "I really do. And I know that's selfish as fuck."

"Why?" My voice wobbles but I force the question out.

"Because. They tried to break us, and I want to show them we're unbreakable."

I love him so much for saying that.

But we both know it's a lie.

CHAPTER THIRTY-TWO

Griff

I FINALLY HAVE MY GIRL BACK IN MY ARMS.

And I told her about the reunion show.

While she said she wants to come with me, sadness lingers in her expression. It hadn't been there when I woke up and found her staring at me. No, I put it there, by bringing up the damn show again. Worse, I practically guilted her into going.

"Molly, you really don't have to go if you don't want to." Fuck, that sounds hollow after I all but whined that I want her with me.

"I thought you wanted me by your side?" Hurt bleeds into her voice.

"I do. But I'm worried." I roll my eyes. "Except for Venom, Woolly, and Bear Trap, and maybe Hammer Fists and Thunder, the rest of the guys are real assholes. Immature, sloppy drunks and dirty fighters."

Her lips purse into a thoughtful pout. "Maybe that's the role the show 'assigned' them?"

I consider that for a second. She's sweet for suggesting it as a possibility. "Nah, it's probably *why* the show recruited them. Trust me, none of them were good enough actors."

She chuckles. "Well, I only watched until...you know, *the* episode—"

"Baby, I am so—"

"Do *not* apologize again." Her fierce, scolding tone is way hotter than it should be.

"Yes, ma'am," I tease.

"I'm serious." Her expression turns thoughtful. "But they really did want to stick everyone in a certain box." She holds her hands up and forms a square with her fingers. "Even the ring girls." She wrinkles her nose as if it bothers her to defend any of them. "Since they were filming, what, twenty-four hours a day, I guess they had lots of time to cherry-pick their footage."

"They definitely orchestrated certain events. There was no script or anything, but they'd set things up and sort of push us into situations, then run in with the cameras to catch the reactions. They'd even arrange us a certain way to make it look real." Finally, I'm able share all of my experiences from the show with someone.

The last someone I thought would ever want to hear these stories.

But Molly listens intently to every word. I haven't felt comfortable talking about this stuff with anyone else. The show is such a sore subject with Remy and the guys, I've rarely mentioned it. I didn't realize how much I'd stored away until everything starts pouring out of me like a faucet I can't turn off. Molly's right here with me. She laughs, sympathizes, or offers her thoughtful commentary but mostly she lets me purge it all from my system.

When I finally wind down, she rests her hand on my chest. "And they said you were the taciturn, shy fighter."

I lift a questioning eyebrow. "Taciturn?"

"Someone who's reserved and doesn't say a lot."

"I guess that's better than the belligerent blockhead they used to describe that guy Bull." I tilt my head. "Although, honestly, that one was true."

She laughs softly. "Yeah, Darcy mentioned you knocked him out once."

"I'm sorry you still had people telling you about it." I swallow hard. "I'm sorry I just dumped all of that on you."

A little furrow forms between her brows. "I want to hear everything from *you*. Every story you want to share." She flicks her gaze down. "I'm sorry I stopped being your weekly phone call."

I brush my finger under her chin, tipping her head back. "Uh, under the circumstances, I don't blame you one bit." I narrow my eyes, thinking it over. "I still really don't understand why they did it. We weren't supposed to talk about the show on our calls. Would they really expect you to keep calling if you thought I cheated?"

"Sounds like maybe they *should* have had a script."

I huff a sound of agreement. "I think they lost the plot when they added the girls into the mix."

"I like how you, Venom, and Woolly seemed to stick together. At least that was real." She lifts her eyebrows as if she's asking for confirmation.

"I think it was. I feel shitty saying this, but I could never fully trust them. A lot of times Venom was probably trying to give me helpful advice. But in the back of my mind I was always wondering if he was sharpening a knife to jab between my shoulder blades."

"Because they wanted you to turn on each other." She rolls her eyes. "Better ratings."

"Probably."

"I hope I'll get to meet them at the reunion. And Bear Trap. He seemed funny."

I squeeze my eyes shut and rumble with laughter. "Jesus Christ, you know what helpful advice he gave me before getting in the cage for the last fight? To keep my fingers out of Naptime's butt hole." I pull a disgusted face.

She bursts into giggles. "That's priceless."

"It certainly gave me something else to think about besides how nervous I was." Maybe that had been his intention. "I kinda miss those guys."

"Well, have you tried reaching out?"

"Yeah, Woolly started this group text for four or five of us from the show. We've been going back and forth about the reunion and what to expect. I talked to Venom once. Talked to Woolly too. Bear Trap texts me outside of the group chat."

"Well, hopefully you guys can hang out at the reunion."

I love her for saying that, but my first priority will be watching over *her*, not socializing.

"Thank you for listening. I haven't really been able to talk about it with anyone here. And not only because of the show's restrictions."

She tilts her head. "Not even Remy? I thought you two talk about everything?"

I slant a look at her. "Not *everything*. But he was so pissed at me, I don't like bringing it up so he can remind me of how stupid I am for doing it in the first place."

She sighs. "He was worried about you too."

"I know."

She strokes her fingers through my hair. "What do you want to do today?"

I make a big show of looking around the bedroom. "Uh, *this*. Spend time with you. Talk to you. Just *be* with you." *Before you leave me again tomorrow.* "I meant what I said. I missed you."

Her eyes shine with emotion. *No. No. No.* I didn't want to make her cry.

"Actually, you know what we should do today?" I lean over and kiss her shoulder. "Go find that full-length mirror."

She giggles and rolls away, taking the covers with her.

I sit up. "Where are you going?"

"Upstairs to get dressed so we can go shopping."

I lunge off the bed, hug her around the waist and toss her back onto the mattress. "You like that idea, huh?"

"Oh, yeah." She reaches up and runs her fingers through my hair, then over my shoulder and down my arm. "Loved seeing your strong arms around me." She rubs the tip of her finger right between my eyes. "Love the serious face you make when you're concentrating on making me come."

"I take my work seriously. I want to make *giving Molly orgasms* my new full-time job."

She shakes with laughter. "You *do* excel at it."

The covers are bunched around us, obstructing my view. I untangle myself, then peel the sheet down to reveal her body. Her smooth skin seems to glow in the early morning light, begging my fingers to explore every inch. "Love you sleeping naked next to me." I cup her breast, kneading softly, admiring her pretty pink nipples, hard and pointing at my mouth. "Look how perfectly you fit in my hands." I dip down to suck one tight bud between my lips, swirling my tongue around the hard peak.

"Oh, shit." Her back arches. "You *do* have big hands."

All my blood rushes to my groin. I smile against her breast, then move to the other one. "All the better to hold you with."

I slide lower in the bed, kissing and tasting. Her stomach quivers beneath my tongue as I feather kisses around her belly button and keep moving lower and lower until I arrive at my destination.

I flick my gaze up and meet her eyes. She licks her bottom lip as if the anticipation's killing her as much as it's killing me. I rake my fingers over her dark curls, inhaling her scent, and slowly edge my thumb toward her clit. She lets out a shuddery gasp and spreads her legs a little wider.

It's a gift that she's so uninhibited with me. No longer shy. Her confidence keeps growing every time I touch and kiss her. She trusts me with her body. Knows I want to give more pleasure than I take.

I trail kisses from her knees to the crease of her hips. She's panting with desire by the time I bury my tongue in her. She opens wider and tilts her hips, offering herself. I slide my tongue to her clit, teasing with light flicks until she trembles and gasps my name. Her little moans and shudders increase as I keep licking then finally suck her clit into my mouth.

"Oh!" She lifts off the mattress, curling her body forward. I hold her gaze and slide two fingers through her wetness and slip them inside her. Her thighs tremble and she rocks herself against my face. I move my tongue up and down, bury my fingers and curl them, seeking the spot that makes her go crazy. *There it is.* Tension seizes her muscles. She clenches tight, squeezing my fingers. Arching her back, she unleashes a long husky moan I feel in my balls. I flatten my tongue and give her long, slow licks, easing her down.

I slide my fingers free, wet and glistening. Placing one more kiss over her clit, I tear myself away from her long enough to grab one of the condoms. Her eyes sparkle with anticipation as she watches me smooth it on. I kiss my way up her body and settle over her. Mouths inches apart, we stare into each other's eyes. She presses her palm to my cheek. "That was...so amazing."

"Good." I touch my lips to hers and she opens, kissing me hot and deep, like she can't get enough. Crazed with the need to bury myself in her I pull back. "Do that thing where you wrap your legs around me."

She lifts her hips and presses her knees to my sides. "Like this?"

I groan and tease my cock through her wetness. "You're so fucking wet. I love you coming on my face."

She blushes but maintains eye contact. "I was afraid I'd break your nose." She bumps her hips up to demonstrate why.

"You're not going to hurt me." I tap my nose to hers. "It's hot when you're so out of control you're grinding all over me."

She blushes even pinker.

I stop torturing us both and thrust hard until I'm buried deep. Last night I managed to go slow. Give her time to adjust. This morning I'm so desperate for her, I can't think straight. She lets out a squeak of surprise then smiles up at me. I hold still, savoring how good she feels wrapped around my cock. My lips find her mouth again; she opens her mouth and sweeps her tongue against mine, wild and insistent.

I groan and withdraw. Thrust hard. Over and over, establishing a rhythm that pulls the sexiest noises from her throat.

After a few minutes, I squeeze her hips and roll us to the side, urging her on top of me.

"Oh!" She braces her hand against my chest and lifts herself.

"Ride me." Too impatient to wait for her to orient herself, I grip her hips, moving her back and forth. "Just like that."

She leans back, resting her hands on my thighs and slowly rolls her hips, finding her own rhythm.

"Ah, fuck that's sexy." I lick the pad of my thumb and bring it to her clit, slowly rubbing in time with her movements.

"Ohhh." Eyes closed, her head falls back and she moves a little faster, chasing release.

I raise myself on one elbow for a better view of my cock disappearing then reappearing, in and out of her.

"Griff?" Her nails dig into my thighs. Her movements turn frantic and harder. "I'm...you feel so good."

"Keep going." I clench my jaw, trying to hold back.

She lets out a low, satisfied moan and slows her frantic pace. Her body spasms and contracts around me. I seize the moment before she's finished, wrap my hands around her waist and hold her down while I pound up into her.

Her moaning continues and she curls her hands around my wrists. My orgasm slams into me, squeezing my balls. Stars fill my vision and heat shoots down my spine. I groan through my release, holding her tight.

She keeps slowly rocking up and down, milking every last drop from me.

"Come here." I lift her off of me and she falls down by my side, curls her body around my arm and twines her fingers with mine. My racing heart slows to normal and I turn to see her face.

"We should do that every morning," she says.

"No arguments here." I flop my free hand onto my chest.

She nuzzles closer, kissing my neck and along my jaw. "I want to wake up with you inside of me tomorrow," she whispers in my ear.

My cock twitches.

"Or, if I'm up first, I want to wake you up with my mouth on your cock." She teases her tongue at the sensitive spot below my ear.

My cock jerks again.

"What have I done to you, Muffin?" I turn and grin at her. "My shy little virgin is now full of *fantastic* ideas."

Her face falls.

I quickly cup her cheek before she gets the wrong idea. "I fucking love everything you just said." I kiss her hard. "Everything."

I glance at the soggy condom. "Let me go take care of that. Then, when I come back, you're going to tell me every other naughty idea running around your brilliant mind."

Her lips curl into a sly smile. "That might take a while."

CHAPTER THIRTY-THREE

Molly

IT'S EARLY AFTERNOON BY THE TIME WE EMERGE FROM downstairs.

Remy's in the kitchen, leaning on the counter directly across from the basement door. Like he's been posed and waiting for us all morning.

I run my fingers through my hair and adjust the T-shirt I borrowed from Griff. It almost goes to my knees, but my wild sex hair and pajama pants practically announce I spent the night downstairs.

"Good morning." I flash a bright, chipper smile.

"Good *afternoon*." Remy tilts his head and levels us with an exasperated stare. "I assume this means you're back together."

"Aww, you should be a detective, brother dear." I reach up and pat the top of his head.

He ducks and weaves away from me.

Two strong arms band around my middle, and Griff pulls me tight to the front his body, resting his chin on top of my head. "Don't worry. She's going back to campus tomorrow," Griff says.

"*She* is standing right here and *she* will decide when and where *she* goes," I say, slipping out of his hold.

Remy bites the inside of his cheek but a chuckle slips out anyway. "Damn, Griff. That lasted five seconds."

"Yes, I'm going back to campus tomorrow," I say. "Griff said he'll visit me."

"Is that right?" Remy lifts a skeptical eyebrow.

Griff raises his hands. "Whenever she tells me she has time. I won't interfere with her classes."

"You better not."

"Remy!" I snap, tired of him hassling Griff. "This may shock you, but I had a crush on Griff all through high school and still managed to graduate near the top of my class. I'm capable of doing more than one thing."

"Yeah, but now you're actually *with* the bonehead." He slides an annoyed look at Griff. "Again."

"Don't call my boyfriend a bonehead."

"Aww." Griff nuzzles his face in my hair and kisses my cheek. "Thank you, baby." Whether he's sincere or trying to further annoy my brother, I'm not sure. "You really had a crush on me that long?" he whispers against my ear.

"Probably longer." I pat his arm. "Don't let it go to your head."

Both of them rumble with laughter. Griff releases me. Hopefully that means they're not going to continue the verbal sparring.

"Great." Remy claps his hands together. "Now that you've left your cocoon, let's make breakfast."

My stomach growls. "You haven't eaten yet?"

His gaze slides to the door. "Nah, I ran some errands early this morning. Just got back a little while ago."

"All right, what are we making?"

"Omelets," Remy says as if it should be obvious.

"Of course." I smack my hand against my forehead. "What was I thinking?"

"I bought those blue eggs you like from the farmer's market."

I stop and stare at my brother. "You went to the farmer's market?"

"Yes, smart-ass. I ordered something for the bar from one of the vendors." He flicks an irritated look over my shoulder. "Since I had some *time*, I looked for the egg lady."

"Oh boy." I rub my hands together, looking forward to breakfast now. "The scrambled eggs they serve in the dining hall come out of a one-gallon container. They're so gross."

The three of us work as a team and form an efficient assembly line. I beat all the eggs, Griff preps fillings for the omelets and Remy mans the stove. Griff and I work closer together than probably necessary, stopping to touch each other frequently. Remy heaves several exasperated breaths but otherwise keeps his opinions to himself.

Remy gives me the first omelet and I hurry into the dining room to devour it. A few minutes later, Griff sets his plate next to mine and a glass of orange juice in front of me.

"Thanks." I pick it up and take a sip.

"No problem." He leans over and kisses the top of my head. "Need anything else?"

I shake my head.

He makes a few trips back and forth from the kitchen, and I feel a little guilty for sitting down to eat so quickly.

Finally, they both join me.

Griff places a plate of toast in the middle of the table and I wait until they've both taken a piece, then grab one.

Griff's phone vibrates. He picks it up off the table and checks the screen, then shows it to me. It's an email with information about the reunion. I scan it and nod at Griff.

"I'm going to forward it to you," he says.

"What is this?" Remy waves his fork at us. "You going to be one of those couples who have to monitor each other's messages now?"

"What?" I frown at him. "No."

Griff releases a heavy sigh and sets his fork down. "You know how I told you I have to go to the reunion show?"

Remy narrows his eyes and sets his own fork aside. "Yeah," he says slowly. "Otherwise, they won't pay you the rest of your prize money. Which, for the record, is fucking bullshit."

"Agreed." Griff glances over at me and what he's about to tell my brother is written in the way his lips turn down. "Well, they invited Molly too. We're going together."

Invited. He makes it sound so cheery when he puts it that way.

Remy hasn't responded, yet.

But if *nuclear* had a color, it'd be the shade of red on my brother's face.

Griff

"You're taking my sister, where?" Disbelief drips from every word out of Remy's mouth. "Are you insane?"

"I'm going." Molly defiantly lifts her chin. "I want to show those demon clowns that we survived what they tried to do to us."

I snort at *demon clowns.* That's what I'm calling the producers of *Supreme Underground Fighter* from now until eternity.

Remy's nostrils flare in a silent snarl of rage. "This isn't a game. You have no idea what you're going to face." He waves his hand wildly in the air. "I read that the ratings are fucked from them taking so long to air the last episode. They'll want something extra juicy to reel viewers in again."

"Okay." She uses her *let's be reasonable* tone. "But I'll know that going in. We'll be okay."

Remy focuses his glowering stare on me. "Is this how you protect my sister? Drop her into that snake pit? After what they already did to her?"

"Hey!" Molly snaps. "Don't talk about me like I'm not sitting right across from you. It's *my* decision."

Shit, I better intervene before they get into it. "They're going to pay her for her appearance."

If anything, his face turns a deeper shade of angry. Definitely the wrong argument.

"Fuck their money." Remy fumes and turns his relentless stare on Molly. "No amount of money is worth that, Molly."

She glances at the table, like she's carefully considering her words. "It's not about the money as much as, I hate what they did to Griff. And I despise the way they portrayed me as some sniveling little girl. I never had a chance to defend myself. This way, I can."

"You're kidding yourself, Molly." Remy shakes his head. "They will cut and edit whatever you say to fit their story. This isn't a battle you can win. Please don't do this."

"The whole cast will be there," I interrupt, bringing Remy's blistering stare my way again. "Venom's bringing his wife. Thunder will have his wife *and* kid there. Woolly's mom is coming."

"None of those people had the shit said about them that Molly did," Remy points out. "They didn't 'show' Venom fucking some skank. They pinned that on *you.*"

"We're all aware," Molly says. "Remy, I love you for worrying about me so much. And for trying to bring up things I hadn't considered. But I'm not asking for your permission. I'm going."

"When is it?" Remy asks.

I give him the dates.

"Why two days?"

"I assume it'll be a long day of taping." I shrug. "It's like a three-hour drive."

"You have some time," Remy says to Molly. "Please think it over some more." He scowls at me.

I hold up my hands. "If she changes her mind, that's fine. I won't force her to go."

"You're right, Remy," Molly says.

His three favorite words.

"I'll consider it more carefully," she continues. "Try to read some of the fan pages to see what their viewers are expecting from the reunion."

I glance over at her. "That's a really good idea."

She grins at me. "I know." Her smile slips a little. "Have *you* looked at any of them? You've got legions of women ready and willing to do all sorts of gross things to you."

"No. Fuck no. Seriously?"

"You really are a bonehead," Remy mutters.

Molly presses her palms against the table and stands. "I'm going to go get dressed." She rests her hand on my shoulder. "Griff's taking me shopping for a few things I need in my dorm."

Good cover story. I will myself to not react even as I'm already trying to measure in my head how big of a mirror I can fit downstairs.

"Be right back." She leans over and kisses my cheek.

Now that Molly's gone, Remy sits back and glares at me.

"What now? You heard her, she wants to go."

His angry stare burns even hotter.

"I thought you were happy for us."

Finally, he opens his mouth. "While you're out shopping today, consider picking up some soundproof tiles."

"Uhhh…" I don't like where this conversation is headed.

He leans forward and rests his elbows on the table. "Do you have any idea how disturbing it is to hear my best friend knocking boots with my little sister?"

My eyes bug and heat rushes over my forehead and down my face. "Then why were you listening, creep?" I choke out. "You could've, I don't know, *not* been in the kitchen."

"I left the house. Got groceries. Stopped by the bar. Returned to the house. And it was still…" He closes his eyes briefly and wretches. "You know what? I'm not talking about this."

"Good. That would be my preference too." I lean forward and pin him with a *don't fuck with me* stare. "Do *not* tell Molly you heard a thing. She'll *die* of embarrassment."

He stares at me with wide eyes. "Why the fuck you think I waited until she went upstairs, you filthy, sister-corrupting gremlin?"

I cover my mouth with one hand.

"Don't you *dare* laugh," Remy warns.

"Hey, you asked *me* to move in. I had a whole-ass apartment of my own where you wouldn't have heard a thing."

"You're right." He sighs and picks up his plate. "Just, please, for my sanity…I'll be at the bar all afternoon, so go nuts. But…Jesus."

"Wait." I hate that I'm about to ask this. "How bad is it? What's the sound radius we're talking about? Like, could you hear…things… all the way upstairs?"

He grits his teeth. "No. Thank God."

I blow out a relieved breath. "Okay."

He returns to glaring.

A couple dozen smart-ass comments come to mind but I wash them down with another sip of coffee, then stand and clear the table.

CHAPTER THIRTY-FOUR

Griff

WE CAME HOME TOO LATE TO INSTALL THE MIRROR. Especially after Remy's noise complaints. But it's my first project of the day. We'd gone to sleep after some extremely quiet snuggle-fucking.

My room's eerily quiet.

And chilly.

I pry my eyes open. Barely any light filters through the small, high window.

Molly's side is empty.

I sit up, listening for any sounds. She must be in the bathroom.

I lie back down, waiting for her to return. My eyes close briefly, then snap back open.

Throwing off the covers, I roll out of bed and yawn, scrubbing my hand over my face. My girl said she had a very specific way she wanted to wake up this morning.

And she has to go back to school later tonight.

Nope, don't think about that now.

The hallway's dark. "Molly?" She's not on the couch.

The bathroom door's open and it's dark inside.

Where the fuck did she go?

I return to my room and grab a pair of gym shorts from my dresser. If Remy didn't want to hear us, I'm pretty sure that means he doesn't want to run into me with my balls swinging in the breeze either.

Is she having second thoughts? Oh, fuck, I hope she's not upset about going back to campus tonight. She's going if I have to drop her off myself. I will *not* be the reason she starts skipping classes.

I open the back door and peer outside. The porch is clear. Her car's in the driveway.

Moving through the dark house, I check the couch, and the laundry room. It's a big house but there are only a handful of spots where Molly spends a lot of time.

Only place left to check is her room upstairs.

Molly

My door squeaks but I'm in too much pain to bother opening my eyes to see who it is. If it's a murderer, then this is how my story ends.

"Molly?" Griff whispers.

I groan and tighten into a ball.

"Why're you up here? I thought we said we were waking each other up in a certain way?" His voice is light at first, then concern bleeds into his words. "Molly? You okay?"

Bright light floods my room. I shriek and pull the comforter over my face. "No lights," I moan.

"What's wrong?" Darkness returns. I sigh in relief and push the comforter off my face.

The door clicks shut. I open my eyes and Griff's hurrying to my side of the bed. He kneels next to me, resting his hand over my forehead. "Shit, you're kinda clammy. What's wrong? Are you sick?"

Embarrassment scalds my skin. I pull my covers up higher, tucking my arms under them.

"No." My mouth screws into an annoyed pout. How mortifying to have to explain this to my boyfriend. "My body decided that early this morning was the appropriate time to make its monthly sacrifice to the moon goddess."

Griff blinks, then frowns and finally lifts his chin with understanding. "Why didn't you wake me up?"

Huh? "To do what?"

"To tell me you didn't feel well?" Exasperation colors his words.

I vaguely point my chin in the direction of the bathroom. "All my stuff's up here. I wanted to spare you the horror of waking up to a crime scene in your bed."

He bites his lip and shakes his head.

"Don't laugh at me."

"I'm not," he says calmly. "I don't like you feeling that you have to sneak away because of something totally normal. There's nothing to be embarrassed about."

"You don't understand."

"No, not exactly. But I know what it feels like to be in pain. What do you need?"

I flop my arm to the side and point at the nightstand. "My heating pad. And some Advil. There's none up here and I didn't think I'd make it downstairs again."

"Okay." He crouches next to the nightstand and pulls out my old, plaid heating pad. Thankfully it's here and not in my dorm room. "Did you eat something?"

My stomach lurches, rejecting the idea of food. "Ugh, no."

He unwinds the cord and plugs in the heating pad. "Come here." He gently tugs the covers down. My teeth chatter from the rush of cool air. His concerned frown returns. "Are you sure this is normal?"

"Yes." I slide the heating pad out of his hands and arrange it over my stomach. "It got a little better when I was on the pill, but..." I shrug, too tired to talk.

He tucks the blanket around me again. "I'll be right back." He ducks down and kisses my forehead.

"Thank you."

I close my eyes and drift through the red, misty clouds of agony. *Stupid, stupid, stupid.* I should've taken something earlier. I know the longer I wait, the worse it gets.

"Can you sit up for me?" Griff's urgent voice pulls my eyes open.

I groan and throw my legs over the side of the bed. Griff holds out a peeled banana. "Eat that first."

I wrinkle my nose but take it from him and bite off a piece. When I'm done chewing, he hands me a glass of milk.

"Eat a little more," he encourages.

I finish about half then push it into his hands. "I can't."

He pops the rest of the banana in his mouth, chews it quickly, and shakes a few round pills out of the bottle into my hand. I toss them back and he passes me the glass of milk again.

"I'll be right back," he says.

I sit up for a few minutes, letting my stomach settle. Ugh, I want to claw my way out of my skin. Everything hurts so bad. I flop against my pillows and groan. This is the *worst* timing. I wanted to spend my last day home doing stuff with Griff, not have my uterus throw an unauthorized fiesta.

"Any better?" Griff asks as he opens my door. He sets a water bottle on my nightstand.

"No." I reach over and take a sip of water, then groan and press the heating pad to my stomach.

He peels the covers back and climbs into my bed.

"What're you doing?" I ask.

"I'm still sleepy." He shifts his body closer. "And I want to be near you."

"Are you sure about that because it's like volcano week in here." I rub my hand over my stomach.

He frowns at the description for a second, then it seems to sink in. "I'll be fine."

"Well, I tried to warn you." I turn away from him, moving to the edge of the bed.

"Come here." He pulls me against his chest and curls his body around mine, resting his hand over my stomach.

"Seriously, I don't think you understand." I shift my lower body away from him. "Sometimes all the protection in the house doesn't cut it."

"Would you stop."

"Thank God it didn't come earlier. Last night when we were... um, you know."

He shakes with a quick huff of laughter. "Uh, you've seen me fight. I end up covered in someone's blood all the time." He kisses my shoulder. "Yours would be preferable, really."

"Grossss," I whine, but wiggle closer to him.

"That's my girl." He rubs his hand from my hip to belly button, lower, then back. "Where's it hurt?"

"Everywhere," I mumble.

He rubs slow, gentle circles over my stomach. Maybe it's the Advil kicking in, but the pain seems to slip away with every caress of his big, warm hand. "That actually feels better," I murmur.

"Good." He kisses my shoulder again. "Go back to sleep. I'm right here. You need anything, just tell me."

"Okay," I murmur, already retreating into sleep.

Griff

The door creaks.

"Bro, what the fuck?" Remy's harsh whisper pulls me out of sleep.

I untangle myself from Molly, brushing strands of her hair out of my face. "Shh," I hush him.

As lightly as possible, I roll out of her bed, careful not to disturb her. I wave him into the hallway, follow him out, and close the door behind me.

Remy stands outside the door and glares at my bare chest and the gym shorts I threw on earlier.

"I know I said I was fine with you two together. But seriously?" He gestures wildly toward Molly's door. "Can't you two go spoon in your room so I can at least pretend you're not violating my little sister every chance you get?"

I roll my eyes and blow out a long, slow, annoyed breath. "She didn't feel well and wanted to be in her own bed."

He drops the aggrieved brother routine. "Is she sick? She need to go to the doctor?"

"No." Will Molly be upset if I tell him? She didn't want *me* to know. But they've lived together for years. He can't be that clueless. I rub my hand over my stomach. "Girl stuff."

"Ohhh." He nods in understanding. "Yeah, she has it rough sometimes. I'm glad she's home then, instead of at the dorm."

I stare at him. *Why don't I know this?*

He seems to understand my unspoken question. "Why would I talk to you about *that*?"

Good point. I still feel shitty I had no idea.

"Does she need anything?" he asks.

"I think I got everything for her. It was like pulling teeth, though."

"She's very...private about that stuff."

"Why?"

Remy shrugs. "I love Nana but she was kinda past that point when Molly was going through it. I don't know how much she talked to her, other than the basics."

Fuck. Molly's mom had already passed away, so Molly only had her shitbag father, Remy, or her grandparents to help her. Knowing Molly, she just figured things out on her own and suffered in silence. Like she wanted to do today.

Remy glances at her closed bedroom door. "I usually make sure there's cookie dough ice cream in the freezer, ask her if she needs anything else, and she tells me to let her die in peace."

Sounds about right. "Cookie dough, huh?"

"Ben and Jerry's or Stewart's are the only acceptable brands," he warns me.

"Noted." I chuckle. "Thanks."

He lifts his eyebrows. "You're okay?"

"I'm not easily spooked."

"Good." He pats my shoulder. "I'm going for my run, but I'll make waffles when I get back. Tell her I brought strawberries and whipped cream home last night."

"I'll let her know."

Molly's still asleep when I return to her room. At least she seems peaceful now. Do I get back into bed and risk waking her?

Before I make a decision, she moans, stretches, and flips onto her side. Her eyes flutter open. A soft smile curves her lips. "Hey," she mumbles.

I cross the room and sit on the edge of the bed. "Feeling any better?"

"Lots."

"Good." I pull the now-cold heating pad out from under her comforter, unplug it, and tuck it back in the drawer. "Are you hungry? I ran into Remy in the hallway. He left for his run but he said he'd make waffles when he gets back."

She purses her lips and frowns. "You didn't tell him, did you?"

"I...he wanted to know why I was up here. Something about it's easier to pretend we're not knocking boots if we're downstairs." I lift my shoulders in an exaggerated shrug and pull a silly face.

She sighs. "I guess I could eat some period day pity waffles."

I snort and shake my head.

"I need to take a shower first," she says, tugging at her shirt. "I feel gross."

One corner of my mouth slides up. "I can help you with that."

She drops her gaze to my crotch. The thin, shiny material does fuck-all to conceal what's happening in my shorts. I lift my hands, pleading for mercy. "I can't help it. You said shower, I pictured you wet and naked." I point to my dick. "And here we are."

She bursts into giggles. "Well, tell him to settle down. It's shark week."

I close my eyes briefly. "Yeah, that's not a deterrent."

"Really?" She slips out of bed and comes closer. "But I can't..."

I grab her hand and tug her toward me. "I think it's because there's very little chance of you getting pregnant if we go without a condom now," I whisper in her ear.

She bites her lip. Her eyes light with curiosity but she shakes her head. "That's going to be messy." She wrinkles her nose.

"Probably." I tilt my head toward the door. "Shower's a perfect place for messy situations."

"Aren't you kind of...disgusted—"

"No." I cut her off. "Nothing about you is disgusting. Ever."

She bites her lip again.

"We don't have to do anything. Soaping up my girlfriend's beautiful, naked body isn't a hardship."

"Maybe." Her eyes dart to the door again. "Just give me a couple of minutes? When I start the water you can come in."

My heart pounds with satisfaction. "Got it."

She reaches between us and curls her hand around my erection through my shorts.

"Ah, fuck." I squeeze my eyes shut.

"You're really not bothered?" She strokes me harder.

"Not even a little," I rasp.

She releases me and I groan.

"When did Remy leave for his run?"

Who? What? My body's humming and throbbing with need. My mind's already in the shower with Molly and she wants to know where her brother is? "Uh, a couple of minutes ago."

"I'll be quick."

So will I.

I'm like a hound dog with my ear cocked toward the door, waiting for the sound of the shower blasting on.

Maybe I should check to be sure Remy's gone.

I head into the hallway and walk to the top of the stairs. Silence.

The shower screeches on and water patters against the tub, calling me into the bathroom.

Molly's already behind the shower curtain. I drop my shorts, take two steps, and push it back a few inches.

Beautiful. Molly's facing the water, but she turns and her wide eyes meet mine.

"Can I join you?" I lift my eyebrows a few times, hoping to pull some laughter from her.

But tension lines her face as she nods and angles her arms in front of her body, like she's trying to hide herself from me.

Can't have that.

I step in and reach up to adjust the showerhead so it reaches me. Then I wrap my arms around her semi-wet body and draw her closer.

"Griff." She presses her palm against my chest.

"Just kiss me."

She tilts her head back. I lean down and lazily drag my lips over hers.

"Mmm," she sighs with pleasure, her body relaxing against mine.

"That's it." I move my hands to her hips while we keep slowly sliding our mouths together. She opens and I gently stroke my tongue against hers.

Another sigh eases out of her. I move her closer to the spray and rub my hands over her back, down to her ass.

She tilts her hips away from me.

"Get over here." I firmly plant both hands on her ass and pull her flush against me, trapping my hard cock between us. She reaches for me with both hands, curling them around me and squeezing.

Fuuuck. I hiss in a breath.

"Can I?" She braces one hand on the shower wall, like she's trying to lower herself to the floor.

I grab her arm to stop her. "Absolutely not."

"Why?"

"You know my rule."

She tilts her head and stares at me while her maddening little fingers keep rubbing up and down my length.

"Molly comes first."

She frowns. "But I can't."

"Why not?"

"Because..."

"So, you don't actually know?"

She opens her mouth and I press my finger to her lips. "Do *not* utter the words gross or disgusting."

Her mouth closes.

"That's what I thought. Turn around for me."

She gives me one last, long twisty stroke, then turns to face the water. I grab the shower gel, pour some into my hands and lather it up, then rub her shoulders.

"Relax." I slide my soapy hands down her arms, up her sides, over her breasts and down her stomach, then reverse the same path. The water beats down hard, chasing the suds away.

She reaches behind her, curls her fingers around me, and tugs at a slow, maddening pace. I groan against her ear and suck at her neck, while thrusting my hands under the spray, washing off the remaining soap.

"Give me your hands." I nip her earlobe.

"You don't like this?" She squeezes gently.

"I love it. But I need your hands for a minute."

She releases me. I take a breath. Clear my head. She holds her hands in front of her. I gather her wrists in one hand and press them between her breasts. With my free hand I pinch and roll one of her nipples between my fingers. I nuzzle and kiss her neck while teasing her nipples.

She gasps and wiggles against me.

"Do you like that?" I ask.

"Yes," she whispers.

"Does it feel good?"

She nods quickly.

"Do you trust me?"

"Yes." She tilts her head back to see my face. "You know I do."

"Good." I crush my lips to hers and slide my hand between her thighs.

She squeezes her legs tight and breaks our kiss. "What are you doing?"

"Open." I kiss behind her ear again. "I want to play with your clit. I won't go any further unless you ask me to."

Her breathing picks up. She inches her feet apart.

"Good." I slide two fingers down, gently rubbing and circling until I find the way she responds the most. She circles her hips and arches her back, stretching her arms over her head and looping them around my neck. "That's better," I praise. "Nothing to be shy about with me."

Now I'm free to run one hand over every little curvy inch of her while I keep stimulating her clit.

Her body jerks. "Griff."

"Shhh." I kiss her temple. "I've got you."

She starts moaning low in her throat and rocking her hips in time with my fingers. "Oh! There."

"That's it."

Her body shakes. She gasps and pants. Louder moans pour out of her, and she arches her back more. I tap my finger directly on her clit and she goes off.

Fuck, I hope Remy's not back from that run yet.

There's no containing her wild little noises.

Breathing hard, she opens her eyes. Drops of water cling to her lashes. Amazement and uncertainty play over her face. "I want you," she whispers, almost like she's afraid to admit it.

My cock's already rock hard and just waiting for the invitation. "Tell me more."

She reaches down, wrapping her fingers around me and slides her palm up and down the length of my dick. "I want you inside me."

"As you wish." I kiss the tip of her nose. "Brace your hands against the wall for me."

She moves so fast, it's like she never had any reservation at all.

"This isn't going to take long," I warn her.

She arches her back, as if encouraging me.

Careful not to slip in the tub, I grab her hips and pull her closer. "Molly, you're absolutely gorgeous like this."

She hums a needy little sound.

Spikes of heat prickle down my spine as I slowly drive myself inside her. So hot, tight, and wet. Fucking bliss. I grip her hips tighter, piston myself in and out of her, quickly increasing the pace. Our wet bodies slap together under the warm spray. An overload of sensations.

She moans and pushes back against me, asking for more.

"That's my good girl," I praise. "You like this?"

"Yes," she whimpers, clenching tight around me. She dips lower, resting her hands on the edge of the tub, angling her ass up even higher.

"Fuck yes." I drive in even deeper.

"Oh my God!" she whimpers. "Right there."

Pressure tightens at the base of my spine, but I keep grinding into her until she lets out a sharp cry. Her body unleashes a violent orgasm, convulsing and squeezing my dick so hard, I follow two seconds later.

My vision blurs but I hold on tight, working us both through the storm. Sweat pops up on my forehead but quickly washes away.

When we're finished, I pull her up and closer, bending at the knees so I can nuzzle against her neck.

"Oh my God," she whispers. "That was so...intense?" Her nose wrinkles. "Was it okay?"

"Baby." I stroke her cheek, her neck and down to her chest. "Okay doesn't even begin to describe how good you feel wrapped around me. No matter what."

She glances up into my eyes and slides her hands up over my wet chest. "I can't believe I was worried."

I can't tease her with an *I told you so*. I kiss the tip of her nose. "Thank you for trusting me." I spin her to face the shower again. "Now let me clean you up. And let's pray your brother isn't back from his run yet."

"Oh my God!" She laughs and covers her face with her hands as I push her back under the spray. "I guess we're done, then."

I slide my hands over every inch of her body. "Impossible. I'm never, ever done with you."

CHAPTER THIRTY-FIVE

Griff

LATER THAT AFTERNOON, I'M IN THE LAUNDRY ROOM helping Molly pack her stuff to go back to campus. She keeps touching, bumping, or rubbing herself against me every chance she gets and I love every second.

The next time she does it, I capture her in my arms and kiss her forehead. "I loved fucking you in the shower this morning," I whisper in her ear. "You were so sexy making all those sweet little noises. You gonna let me do that again?"

"Anytime."

"Next month." I raise my eyebrows so she knows exactly what I'm asking.

Pink spreads over her cheeks. "Yes."

"Did it feel good?"

Her eyes roll back and she shakes her shoulders like she's possessed. "So, so good. That was insane." She bops her finger on the tip of my nose. "It was so good, I don't even care that you're being smug about it right now."

Rumbling with laughter, I release her and return to laundry duty.

My hand grazes her little sleep top with the straps that tie together. "Can I keep this?"

She blinks at me, a devilish smile curving her lips. "I think it'll be tight on you, but sure."

307

"Funny." I smirk at her for a second. "I want something that smells like you to keep under my pillow."

"Aww." She snatches the top out of my hands and sets it on top of a pile of clothes. "I just washed it, though. How about," she teases her fingers under the hem of her pink T-shirt, "I leave you this one?"

I skim my gaze over the light pink tee with the skeleton ribs and red heart on the front. "You love that shirt."

"I love you more."

"Deal." I hold out my hand.

"Now?" She laughs. "I promise I'll leave it under your pillow before I go." Her laughter cuts off.

"It's okay," I assure her even though it feels less than okay that she'll be leaving soon. "We'll spend all next weekend together. And then the weekend after we'll be at the reunion."

"God only knows what fresh hell that'll be," she grumbles.

She's got a point.

An unfamiliar engine rumbles outside. Too close to the house to just be a neighbor. "Keep packing. I'm going to see who that is." I pat her hip.

"It's probably a delivery from Amazon," she calls after me. "They're always dropping stuff off at weird times."

"Be right back."

Barefoot in my gym shorts and T-shirt I open the back door and step onto the porch.

And find Torch at the bottom of the steps.

We stare at each other for a few seconds. Surprise spreads over his face. Annoyance flows through my body.

"So, I take it you two are back together?" A disappointed smirk tugs at the corners of his mouth. "I should've known when she suddenly got too 'busy' to text me. I thought she was pissed at me for skipping the carnival."

"Nope." My heavy footsteps thunder down the old, wooden steps and the screen door snaps shut behind me. "Your 'hanging out' with my girl days are done, bro."

He holds up his hands in a "no harm intended" gesture. "Hey, Remy asked me for a favor. Who am I to say no to taking his little sister out?"

That only pisses me off more. I lean in close, and I'll give him credit, he doesn't flinch away. "We both know Remy isn't the reason you said yes."

"You've got me." He holds up his hands in surrender, but his lips curve into an even more obnoxious smirk. "What're you gonna do about it? Go full caveman on me?"

The door behind me squeaks open. My eyes close briefly. *Please tell me she didn't overhear any of this.*

"What did you say?" Molly asks in a small, timid voice full of hurt.

I glare at Torch. "You need to leave."

"No," Molly says. "Stay, please." Anger simmers beneath her words. Better than the hurt I first sensed. "Did I hear that right? You were spending time with me as a *favor* to my brother?"

I glance at her on the top step glaring down at us with her arms crossed over her chest.

"I..." Guilt and dread wash over Torch's expression. His sorrowful gaze slides between Molly and me. At least he feels bad about being an asshole.

What the fuck's wrong with me? I don't *want* him to have feelings for Molly. How is *that* better?

I can't stand Molly having her feelings hurt, though.

"It's not like that," he says. "Remy was worried about you." Torch flicks his gaze to me again, as if he's weighing his words carefully. Or maybe he wants to throw the blame on me somehow. Like Molly doesn't know *I'm* the reason why Remy was so worried. "I would've asked you out eventually. Wanted to for a while."

A low growl rips out of my throat. *I knew it.* Knew it at her fucking birthday party when he showed up with his stupid gift card.

Torch backs up a step.

"Suuure you did," Molly scoffs. "What'd my brother do, pay you to babysit me?"

"No." Torch scowls. "Fuck no."

Molly turns her hurt eyes on me. "You knew about this?"

This isn't the time to fuck around with the truth. "Not until the night I saw you at the track."

"But you never told me?"

"*Why* would I tell you something like that?" I fling my hand in Torch's direction. "Besides, I took one look at him and knew Remy was wrong."

Torch chokes on a laugh. "I'm that obvious?"

"Save those chuckles," I warn him. "I haven't decided how many times to punch you, yet."

"Griff!" Molly scolds.

I flash a quick, innocent smile her way. "What?"

"Well, I'm gonna go," Torch says, backing up toward the driveway, one step at a time, keeping his eyes on me. "Glad you're okay, Molly." He points at me. "You punch me, I'm punching you back."

"Give it your best shot, carrot top." I sneer.

He rolls his eyes. "So original."

The door slams behind me. I whip around but Molly's gone. *Shit.*

"Griff," Torch calls. When I turn, he's already in the driveway next to his car.

"You're *that* scared of me?" I taunt. It's not like Torch doesn't know how to handle himself in the cage. "Seriously?"

"Uh, you're a pro fighter now." He wiggles one hand in the air. "Scared isn't the right word. Healthy respect for how deadly your fists are would be more accurate."

First time anyone's called me a pro fighter. Am I? Not really. Doesn't matter. He *should* fear me. When it comes to Molly, I'll do anything to protect her.

He lifts his chin. "Seriously. Tell her I'm sorry."

"Yeah, I'll make apologizing on your behalf my first priority." I turn around, jog up the steps, and pull the screen door open. At least Molly didn't try to lock me out.

She's at the kitchen sink. A large, round, black plastic lid's in one hand, and in her other, a small red tube.

Her tongue pokes out as she concentrates on touching the tip of the tube to the inside rim of the lid.

"What are you doing?" I close the door behind me. Outside, Torch's engine rumbles to life and slowly slips along the side of the house.

"Gluing Remy's coffee can shut," she answers matter-of-factly. "Already did his protein powder and vitamins. Next, I'm stuffing paper in the toes of all his shoes."

"Uh, the protein powder was probably mine."

She flicks a cool look my way. "Oops."

I bite my lip to stop my laughter. She's so cute. And absolutely diabolical. I love her.

She bangs the coffee lid into place and caps the glue. Her wild gaze swings around the kitchen like she's plotting what way to hamper her brother's morning routine next.

"Do you want to talk about it?" I ask.

"Oh, *now* you want to talk? Couldn't be bothered to tell me before."

"What was I supposed to say?" I hold my arms out wide. "I was fucking furious when Remy told me because I knew how you'd feel when you found out. I told him he was an asshole."

She sets the glue on the counter and ducks her head.

I approach her slowly and pull her against my chest. As soon as she snakes her arms around my middle, I blow out a slow, relieved breath.

"I feel so dumb," she mumbles against my shirt.

"Don't. Remy's just being his overbearing self. He thinks he's doing the right thing—"

"Don't stick up for him."

"He's not as clever as he thinks he is." I jerk my thumb over my shoulder. "Torch wasn't lying. I knew he was into you at your birthday party. I'm not surprised he jumped at Remy's suggestion at all."

She squeezes me tighter and shakes her head, her cheek sliding against my T-shirt. "At least now I don't feel bad."

"For what?" Dread fills my chest as I ask the question.

"Not...I don't know." She quickly pulls away.

"Hey." I rest my hands on her shoulders, holding her in place. "You don't have anything to feel bad about, okay?"

"Ugh." She squeezes her eyes shut. "What was he doing anyway? Running back to give Remy updates?"

Probably. "I really don't know."

"I'm so embarrassed." She pokes her fist into my stomach. "Why couldn't you just have said something?"

"Molly." I pull back so I can look at her face. "I would've sounded like a jealous asshole, accusing Torch of doing Remy's bidding. I had enough trouble trying to convince you I didn't cheat on you." I think it through a bit more. "I wanted you back because you wanted to be with me, not because you were hurt by someone else."

She squeezes her eyes shut and hugs me tighter. "I'm sorry."

"Don't apologize. I'm just trying to explain why I didn't tell you. I don't like keeping secrets from you. I thought about saying something the night of the carnival." I squeeze her closer. "But I couldn't stand the thought of being the one to cause that hurt. I'd already done enough."

She sniffles. "You didn't *do* anything."

"Yeah, I did. It wasn't intentional but you still got hurt because of me."

"I was unhappy at the carnival without you," she admits.

"Yeah." Should I admit that I followed her around like a creep? Sure, why not? "You looked like you were having fun with your friends."

"I did..." Her voice trails off and her eyes widen as realization slams into her. "I *knew* it! You didn't 'guess' I liked that bunny. You saw me trying to win it!"

"Sure did. You were cute as hell, trying so hard to sink those little skulls in the baskets."

"Let me guess." She huffs and rolls her eyes. "You won the first time you tried."

"No, it took me two turns." I shrug and arc my hand through the air like I'm playing basketball. "The trick was to gently lob the ball into the side of the basket, so it rolled in instead of hitting hard and bouncing out."

"Good to know for next year." She raises one questioning eyebrow. "If you'll still take me?"

"Hell yeah, I will." I rest my hands at her waist. "Only if you wear that sexy little dress again for me."

"Sexy?" She holds her hand up to her throat. "The one with the high collar?"

"Yup."

"What if I come up with a better costume?" She drops her gaze and flutters her lashes, teasing me.

"You can go with a black bedsheet over your head, and you'll still be sexy as fuck."

She laughs and hugs me tighter. I kiss the top of her head, grateful we moved past the Torch situation and she's not holding a grudge. Against me, anyway.

God help Remy. He's on his own.

CHAPTER THIRTY-SIX

Griff

MONDAY MORNING, I FIND REMY IN THE UPSTAIRS entryway dressed for a run, sneakers in hand and balls of brown wrapping paper at his feet. "Bro, do you know why all my sneakers have wads of paper stuffed in the toes?" he asks.

I squeeze my eyes shut and try to force my laughter back. "Guess you haven't tried to make coffee yet?"

His confused frown deepens. "No, why?"

"Torch stopped by yesterday."

He drops the sneaker on the floor with a thud. "And?"

"He couldn't help mentioning your arrangement and Molly accidentally overheard him."

"I'm gonna kill him," he grumbles.

Not that I feel like sticking up for Torch, but. "I don't think he did it on purpose. He seemed upset that he hurt her feelings."

"No wonder she didn't stop by and see me before she left." He waves his hand at me in an irritated gesture. "Here I thought it was because she was spending every last second with your dumb ass."

"I told her she should still go say goodbye to you. Said I'd go with her. But she didn't want to cause a scene there." I nod to the paper all over the floor. "This is her way to let you know what she thought of your plan."

"Did you help her do this?" he asks.

"Nope. She was done in the kitchen by the time I found her." It's

315

impossible to hold back my smirk. "I didn't exactly stop her when she went after your shoes, though."

"That's just great." He bends over and collects the paper. "What other surprises am I going to find?"

"Now what fun would it be if I ruined it for you?" I cross my arms over my chest. "I think you've learned a very important lesson here."

"Yeah?" He rolls his eyes. "What's that?"

"Your sister has a brilliant, evil side. Don't piss her off."

Even though he's trying to keep a straight face, he shakes with laughter. "Fine." He walks into the kitchen and tosses the paper in the trash and swipes his phone off the counter. "I'll send her an apology."

His phone buzzes in his hand. He checks the message and cracks up.

"What?" I ask.

Laughing too hard to answer, he passes me his phone.

Molly: Happy Monday! I hope you're having the morning you deserve, brother dear!

A row of grinning emojis follows.

"See?" I hand him his phone. "What'd I tell you?"

The rest of the week goes by fast. I spend a few days at Jerry's helping him get caught up on paperwork that he's neglected. I take Molly's advice and call Venom to catch up and to talk about what might happen at the reunion. His take: nothing good.

Every night I talk to Molly for at least a few minutes before she goes to bed, and she sends me texts and selfies throughout the day.

It's not quite the way things were before I left. Actually, except for her being an hour away, things are even better than before.

At the back of my mind, I can't help wondering if the reunion will be the thing that tears everything apart.

CHAPTER THIRTY-SEVEN

Griff

Supreme Fighter mansion—the last place I wanted to return. The actual "reunion" show is being taped at a studio tomorrow. But we were all asked to meet at the mansion the night before to "get into the same head space." If that isn't a red flag that we're being led into a trap, I don't know what is.

They offered to send a car for us. I declined.

Molly was too nervous about navigating the busier roads of downstate New York, so I'm behind the wheel of her car.

"It says it's seven hundred feet ahead on our right." Molly points at the windshield.

The car's GPS system announces the same information a second later.

"None of this looks familiar," I grumble, staring at the perfect green lawns and glimpses of estates hiding behind high privacy walls and iron gates.

"You were in a high pressure, disoriented state when you arrived—"

"And barely conscious when I left." I slow the car and make the turn through the wide-open gates. "The day they let us ride the motorcycles, I was too worried about the camera crew in front of me and the other vehicles behind me."

I guide the SUV into a parking spot close to the gate. Several other cars are already here. The detestable prison-style vans they carted us around in are nowhere to be seen.

"Wow." Molly stares out the window at the sprawling mansion. "It's...even bigger in person. And kinda tacky, honestly. All it's missing is a big, gaudy fountain of cherubs out front."

She nailed in five minutes what it took me weeks to figure out that I didn't like about the place. "Inside's not quite as bad."

"You know Hayden looked it up." Molly presses a finger to the glass. "They actually used this place in another crappy reality show."

"Makes sense. It's probably a tax write-off for some douchebag."

I step out of the car and walk around to open her door. The crisp, late autumn air feels good on my face after the long drive.

"I'll grab our stuff later." Once I'm sure we're staying.

I glance at the open gates and pat the car keys in my pocket to reassure myself I'm free to leave at any time. This time they'll have to pry my license and cell phone from my cold, dead hands. I never want to feel trapped like that again.

Molly curls her fingers around mine. Love for her and overwhelming desire to keep her safe thrums through me.

"Ready?" she asks.

"No." I stare at the huge mansion, its opulence hiding the ugly truth—it's nothing more than a giant shark tank. Inside those walls, blood and lies triggered a feeding frenzy of cameras to capture every moment for someone else's entertainment. "You should take the car and go home. Leave me here. I should've listened to Remy."

What the fuck was I thinking, dragging Molly into this sick world where everyone has a hidden agenda we can't even guess? I'm supposed to protect Molly, not bring more chaos into her life.

I suffered through drama, isolation, and exploitation in this house for months. But *I* agreed to it. Molly didn't. She's doing this *for* me. All because I admitted I basically want to come here waving my middle finger at everyone. Sure, the money's an incentive but it's not worth whatever falsehoods the producers have cooked up in their relentless pursuit of sensational content.

"No." She stares up at me with determination shining in her blue eyes. "They used me too. Projected a persona onto me without ever letting me speak for myself. I want to do this. Show people I'm an actual person. Not a naive little girl who can't think for herself."

"Whatever we say, they'll just twist it to fit their story. There's no 'reality' here."

She shifts her gaze to the house. "I know. But I've been silent for months. Even if it doesn't go the way we want, at least I'll know I tried to speak up for myself."

I can't deny her that chance. I want to protect my girlfriend, but I can't do it by treating her like a little kid who can't make her own decisions.

Dread slows my steps as we approach the front door.

Last time, I was here alone. I made friends in the house but never shook the feeling of impending betrayal.

This time Molly's at my side. I trust her completely.

We're going to get through the reunion. Together. As a team. Then we'll collect our money and go the fuck home. Put this chapter of our lives behind us once and for all.

The door opens before we have a chance to ring the bell. Jordan's mustached face greets us.

"Did you get demoted to butler?" I ask. "Why're you answering the door?"

"Good to see you too, Stonewall." He opens the door wider then drops his gaze to our empty hands. "You don't have an overnight bag?"

"It's in the car." I jerk my thumb over my shoulder. "I'll grab our stuff later."

"Very well." Jordan won't even look Molly in the eye. Guilty conscience? Is he the one responsible for the Kiki storyline? Or did that come from higher up?

I need to chill.

"Well, you'll be staying in your old room if you want to show your girlfriend—"

"Molly. My name is Molly," she says in a firm tone, forcing Jordan to acknowledge her.

"Yes. Right. Molly. Nice to finally meet you."

"Is it?" she asks.

I bite my lip. Damn, she's comin' in hot and I fucking love it.

Jordan takes a deep breath. "I'm sure you have mixed feelings about being here. But the SUF family appreciates your attendance. I think you'll be pleased. We'll be able to set the record straight tomorrow about a couple of matters."

I don't know whether to be happy or terrified.

"A few things." Jordan claps his hands together. "Naptime, Kiki, and the other ring girls won't be staying here tonight."

"Aw, shucks." I pull a fake sad face to go with the sarcastic comment.

A hint of a smile twitches under his mustache. "People are still arriving. You can give Molly a tour of the house if you'd like. We won't be doing any filming until a little later." He leans in and lowers his voice. "All the cameras have been removed from the private quarters."

"All of them?" I ask.

"Yes. Tonight is just a low-key get together." He gestures to Molly. "And to give the families a little behind the scenes look."

Molly nods and lets her gaze wander around the foyer.

"I'll leave you two. If you need something, just let me know."

"Thanks." I rest my hand on Molly's lower back and guide her toward the kitchen and the hallways behind it leading to the bedrooms.

"I like the kitchen." Molly waves her hand toward the long island with a prep sink in the middle and a row of tall stools on the outside. "I'd like a counter setup with stools like that in our house one day."

Such a simple request fills me with happiness. No matter her mixed feelings about this weekend, she's still planning our future. "Yeah? I thought you wanted to live in your grandparents' place?"

"We could always remodel the kitchen one day." She shrugs. "Or not. If you don't want to stay in Johnsonville."

I frown at the suggestion. "Where would we go?"

She shrugs.

We reach my old room and I take a deep breath, then push the door open. "Here it is."

"Oh wow." She walks to the center of the room and spins in a slow circle. "It's even bigger than it looked on television."

"Bigger than I remember," I mutter. Since I left, I've been picturing it about the size of a prison cell.

"I love that chair!" She points to the purple velvet chair still standing in the corner.

"I thought you would." I toss my coat on the bed and she does the same.

She turns and stares up at the corner of the room.

"At least Jordan wasn't lying. See that black mount up there. That's where the camera was."

She stares at it for a few seconds, then glances at the bed. "That's so creepy." She steps closer, rests her hand on my shoulder and leans up to whisper in my ear, "I love you but I am *not* having sex with you here. I don't trust them not to have placed a camera somewhere else." She flits an anxious glance around the room.

Laughing, I lean down and kiss her forehead. "Don't blame you one bit."

Now that the excitement over seeing the room where I spent so much time has died down, I hold out my hand. "Come on, I want to show you something else."

Outside the room, she glances up and down the sterile white hallway. "It's like a maze. How did you remember which way to go?"

"Well, some of the guys drew all over the walls like toddlers, so that helped."

She snorts. "That's probably why they did it."

I touch the wall near my door. "They must have brought painters in after we left."

"They probably should've waited." She snickers into her hand. "Be a shame if the guys draw all over the walls again tonight."

"Come on, I want to show you something before too many people show up."

She links her arm with mine and stays tight to my side as we return to the wide-open room at the center of the house. I continue past the oddly placed flatscreen. "That's where we got to gather around and watch each other's footage."

"Oh, I bet you hated that."

"Sure did." I keep my eye out for any rogue camera guys. But so far, there's no one else here. Even Jordan seems to have gone to another part of the house. Regardless, I lower my voice. "It was extra strange that they went to the trouble of finding old footage from illegal matches for some of us."

She stares up at me. "From The Castle?"

"No, thank God." We turn a corner and enter the area I called the book nook.

Molly gasps. "This is so cute." She runs to the built-in bookcases and starts pulling out different titles.

"I thought of you the first time I saw it. And when I was in a *taciturn* mood, I'd hide out here and think about finding a house for us with a little reading area just like this one day."

Her lips quirk and she slides a book into its place on the shelf. "I'd love that."

Loud voices echo through the house. "I knew we wouldn't be alone for long." I sigh.

A few guys have congregated in the kitchen. I only recognize Pirate. The rest must be camera guys.

"Stonewall!" Venom's voice booms through the space.

My gaze searches the room, finding him sitting on the sectional with a petite blonde woman at his side.

"That's quite a size difference," Molly mutters.

I tip my head down and stare at her.

"What?" She shrugs. "It is."

My face splits into a grin as Venom stands. The blonde scowls up at him. He hurries to meet us halfway. "I'm so happy to see you, brother."

I'm yanked forward for a hug and back slap. "How've you been?" he asks.

"Not bad." I fall back and slide my arm over Molly's shoulders. "Molly, this is Venom—the guy who got me through this shit show and taught me some sick new moves."

A smile curves her lips. "Thank you for helping Griff survive."

Venom glances over his shoulder at his wife, still sitting where he left her, and frowns. He tilts his head toward me. "Kelly, this is Griff. He kept me sane in this bungalow of bullshit."

I burst out laughing. "What an accurate description."

"I know it's not a 'bungalow,' but 'mansion of bullshit' just didn't have the same ring to it." Venom grins. His whole demeanor is so much lighter than when we were living here.

Molly chuckles and squeezes my hand.

Kelly approaches us and forces a tight smile that doesn't reach her eyes. *Great,* she probably thinks I'm an asshole who cheated on my girlfriend, then dragged her here to make myself look good.

"Venom said such glowing things." I offer my politest smile. "I feel like I already know you, Kelly."

"That's nice to hear," she says in a high, squeaky, childlike voice I'm not expecting from an adult.

I blink and try not to react. "Uh, this is my girlfriend, Molly."

They exchange hellos but I don't picture them being besties anytime soon. Then again, this whole situation is so strained. Maybe Kelly's coolness has nothing to do with *me* and everything to do with anxiety about what's going to happen tomorrow.

I can't blame anyone for being nervous about it when I'm ready to bolt home any second, myself.

CHAPTER THIRTY-EIGHT

Griff

THE NEXT MORNING WE'RE UP EARLY TO GET READY FOR the show. The two bags she brought with us should've clued me in that Molly has more than one outfit. I enjoy her fixing her hair and putting on makeup in a sexy red bra and panties, not realizing she hasn't decided what she's actually wearing to the taping.

"Dress or pants and blouse?" She holds up a short red dress—the bottom has little folds that make it look like a tennis skirt. Next she holds up a pair of what look like purple velvet jeans and a silky black blouse with some sort of faint purple pattern on it. Then she gives me five seconds to consider each option.

"The dress is cute." My gaze strays to the other outfit. "But you look really pretty in purple."

She glances at each one. "I love this dress but honestly, I don't know what the seating arrangement will be. I'd hate to accidentally flash everyone and have the cameras catch it for 'bonus footage' or something." She lets out a disgusted snort.

This show has been crass on every level. It wouldn't surprise me one bit if they did something like that. "Pants it is, then."

AT THE STUDIO, we're separated into different rooms. Venom, Kelly, Woolly, Bear Trap, Molly, and I get to hang together in a large room with a long green plaid couch and a few chairs. Woolly's mom was escorted into the audience. Apparently only significant others get the privilege of being up on stage.

The wait is surprisingly awkward. The guys and I had all gotten along so well at the house. But now, everyone's silent.

The door opens. Jordan stands there and flashes a cheesy thumbs-up at us. "How's everyone feeling!" he shouts.

"Great!" Woolly lifts his arms up and down like a bird about to take flight.

Venom groans.

"Let's line up." Jordan's enthusiasm is not infectious. We all march out the door like we're being led to an execution.

Side stage, Jordan stops us. A different producer lines the other guys up. "Each seating placement has a number on the back that's not visible to the audience," the new guy shouts. "I'll hand you your number and you'll sit in the corresponding seat. Everyone clear?"

We give him some version of yes.

"Ladies, you'll met your men and sit next to them."

Molly and Kelly share a look but don't say anything.

I search backstage but don't see any sign of Naptime, Kiki, or any of the other ring girls.

Jordan walks down the line, saying a few words to each fighter.

He stops in front of us last. "Now, Molly's going to stay here and then we'll call her out after your intro," he says.

Molly's scared eyes meet mine.

I glare at Jordan. "I think the fuck not."

"It'll be five minutes, tops." He glances behind him. "Kelly will be with her."

Molly blows out a breath and flashes a brave smile. "I'll be fine."

"Atta girl." Jordan pats her shoulder.

I hold Molly's hand while we wait.

Bright lights spill from the stage to the hallway. Matt's annoying voice echoes through a microphone. Music pumps through the speakers.

One by one, in the order we'd been sent home, each fighter walks onto the stage and takes a seat in their designated spot. The audience cheers and claps a respectable amount for each guy. But when Venom trots out, they explode into cheers and whistles. He grins and waves back.

"Let's welcome Griffin 'Stonewall' Royal back!" Matt shouts.

I lean down and kiss Molly. "Five minutes."

She nods quickly. "Go, go."

I walk out and the roar is *deafening*. The stadium-like seats in front of the stage are full of people. To my right a group starts chanting something that I can't quite make out with all the other noise. It seems positive, so I lift my hand and wave in that direction. The blinding lights don't let me actually see individual people. More like a blur of blobs and colorful shapes.

A long white couch has the number two taped to the back of it right at the end. I almost keep walking, then remember that's where I'm supposed to park my ass.

I hope that entrance looked smoother than it felt.

The couch looks plush but feels like the back is made of concrete. I settle in and flash a smile into the bright lights. As the adoration from the crowd continues, heat crawls over my cheeks. This didn't happen to anyone else.

Venom reaches over and slaps my leg a few times. "They like you."

I smile and nod like a bobblehead but can't think of anything to say besides, "I guess so."

Matt stares at me. With his permanently frozen face, it's hard to tell what he expects me to do.

I turn my head to the right and spot Molly backstage. She flashes me two thumbs-up and claps her hands. To the left there seems to be another backstage area. I catch Naptime standing at the edge with an angry scowl etched into his face.

I don't want to look like that sullen dickhead. Reluctantly, I stand and wave to the audience who's still impossible to see beyond the glare.

Finally, Matt decides to move the show along and asks everyone to settle down.

Relieved the pressure's off, I drop into my seat. We've got ten other guys out here, no reason to keep so much attention on me.

"And finally, the winner of season one of *Supreme Underground Fighter*..."

Does that mean there's going to be a season two?

Naptime walks out from his side of the stage.

The response isn't what you'd expect the winner of the whole damn show to receive. Boos rain down from every section of the audience. A few people chant what definitely sounds like, "Cheater! Cheater!"

Well, fuck. Maybe they actually aired his fake tap-out.

Venom grins and bumps my elbow. "They know what's up."

"Hell yeah." I nod.

Naptime's walking with a limp he didn't have on the show. *Good.* And he's holding one arm like it's been stapled to his side. He drops onto the end of the other couch on my right. Almost close enough to reach out and gift him with a *Stonewall Slap* if he gives me a good reason.

Matt calls Kelly and Molly out. Molly hurries to my side and drops into the seat next to me. I curl my arm around her shoulders and pull her close. "You okay?" I ask against her ear.

She nods quickly.

Behind the couches where we're all seated, a large screen slides down from above.

Matt goes through questions with each fighter. He starts with the ones who'd been dismissed first and works his way up. Scenes that Matt references play on the screen behind us.

The audience laughs or gasps at different antics. I can't see the screen without craning my neck, but the audience seems into it. Women scream at one of Woolly's clips. The whole audience gasps when the clip of Venom dropping Bull to his knees pops up.

I sit there with a barely controlled sneer, hating every second of reliving this.

"Stonewall!" Matt turns his attention to me.

A montage of clips plays on the screen behind me.

Molly and I both turn and stare up.

What.

The.

Fuck.

Clip after clip of me shirtless and sweaty. I'm either working out or training. Several close-up shots of the outline of my dick in gym shorts. To make it worse, each clip is shown in a strange slow-motion that looks more like a trailer for porno about fighters than clips from a reality show about fighters.

"We love you, Stonewall!" someone screams.

"I told you," Molly whispers in my ear.

And here I thought it couldn't get more embarrassing than people thinking I cheated on my girlfriend.

Then the clips of each of my fights start. At least *those* are professional. Who the fuck shot those other ones? Molly winces and squeezes my arm when the footage shows me taking a brutal shot to the face. She gasps at the one where I knocked out Bull. And a little *squee* pops out of her mouth when they show me winning against Venom.

The closing shot is the day I took the Ninja for a joy ride.

"Oh my God," Molly whispers. "I can't believe you did that. Was that staged?"

I lean down and say against her ear, "No. I felt like a dog who'd been taken for a walk on a leash that day and I just snapped."

"Stonewall," Matt says pulling my attention from Molly. "That was a very daring stunt you pulled. What were you thinking?"

I glance back at the screen. It's frozen on a shot of me popping a wheelie. My muscles popping while I balance the heavy machine. "I was thinking if I'd been given a ride with a full gas tank, I would've ridden all the way home to see my girl." I hug Molly to my side.

The crowd lets out a collective murmur of admiration.

Molly shifts and leans up, pressing a quick kiss against my cheek.

The audience responds with an even louder chorus of, "Awww..."

"How sweet," Matt says in a dismissive tone. "Moving on to our winner!"

Naptime's scenes flash on screen next. He's got lots of shirtless close-ups and gym short junk shots too, so at least I'm not special in the embarrassing footage department.

The one where he passes out and I shave his head into a mohawk is my favorite. After that, I face forward again. From the sounds of it the rest of his clips involve him being drunk, training, hitting on the ring girls, or peeing in the pool.

An angry rumble works through the audience while the footage from our last fight plays.

"Well," Matt says. "It looks like you had quite a time in the house."

"Yeah," Naptime grunts into his microphone.

"Did you know it was Stonewall who shaved your head?"

I glance over and meet Naptime's blank stare. "Yeah, I knew."

Matt pauses but Naptime doesn't add anything.

"All right then." Matt holds his arm out to the side. "It's time for our lovely ring girls to make an appearance."

They don't get montages. Matt shows footage of the girls in the hot tub making out with different fighters. Every question is focused on who they did or didn't hook up with.

My stomach clenches.

If that motherfucker says I slept with Kiki, I'm going to kill him. *Wait.* I lean forward, glancing at the other couch and one of the chairs where the ring girls arranged themselves. Kiki's not there. How'd she get to skip out on this?

"And finally, let's welcome America's favorite ring girl!" Matt shouts.

That seems like a bit of a stretch.

Kiki struts onto the stage and aims a cruel smirk at me, then Molly. Molly's body tightens but she casually drapes her arm over my leg, resting her hand on my knee. Maybe not that casual. It's blatant possessiveness. Under any other circumstances, I'd fucking love Molly staking her claim on me. Here, it just saws me wide open. She has no reason to feel insecure. I rest my hand over hers, twining our fingers together.

Naptime stands and holds out his one functioning arm.

These two assholes deserve each other.

Kiki saunters to the center of the stage, her hand gracefully waving at the audience and a broad smile on her face like she's a damn beauty queen.

For the first time today, the audience remains silent, nothing but awkward tension filling the air. They're not as impressed with Kiki as Matt—or anyone else—expected.

"Cut!" echoes for the first time today, breaking the stillness.

Jordan rushes in front of the audience, his arms flailing in the air as he shouts, "Come on! Give us more energy!"

Kiki's smile falters. She hurries backstage and Matt calls her out again. The walk's quicker and she waves a lot less this time.

"Whore!" someone in the audience screams.

Not the kind of energy I think Jordan meant.

I duck my head and pray this is over soon.

Molly

What in the demon clown upside down world have I agreed to be part of?

Given all the shitty things the show did to manipulate everyone, Kiki might not be the one who sent me that final text. She could've had nothing to do with the "cheating episode." What if she's a victim of the show's lies as much as Griff and I were?

I still can't help the little daggers of hate sharpening inside me as she struts onto the stage as if she was the star of the entire show instead of a side piece. And I can't help cringing when people from the audience scream, "Whore!" the second time she walks out.

No one deserves that. Especially if she had no idea what the show did.

Conflicting emotions war inside me but I keep my face smooth and calm. At least, I hope so.

Kiki embraces Naptime. They make an uncomfortable show of licking each other's tongues, and then finally take their seats.

"Well, well, well." Matt paces closer to Naptime and Kiki. "You two seem to be extremely cozy now." He glances at the audience and, I think, attempts to wiggle his eyebrows. "But at a certain point, Kiki, everyone was sure you'd end up with Stonewall. What happened there?"

"Nothing," Kiki says. "Nothing at all."

Thank you!

In my heart, I *know* Griff didn't sleep with her, but I hate that so many people who watched the show think he did. He's not a cheater. In relationships or fights. I cast a stink-eye at Naptime. *Unlike some people.*

"But we caught it on tape." Matt's whispery gotcha voice crawls over my skin like centipedes.

Overblown muffled voices and guttural groans echo from the speakers.

"Shhh."

"Hurry up."

The images have already been burned into my brain. No need to see them again. I stare straight ahead, ignoring the video playing on the screen behind me.

"That ain't Stonewall!" Naptime shouts.

I squeeze my eyes shut. *Thank you.* The more people who say it the better. When we leave here today, I don't want there to be a single doubt that Griff's innocent.

Matt gasps. "It's not?"

"No!" Griff finally snaps. "It's not."

"Oh my." Matt's overstretched lips curve up. "What a grave error."

"Issh bullsheee," Naptime slurs.

"Finally, we agree on something," Griff mutters.

"So, Molly," Mat says in a low voice, as if we're two buddies sharing secrets. "Word is, after that episode aired, you were so angry, you destroyed a car. Tell us about that."

My eyes widen in horror. Do they somehow have a clip of that too? I slowly turn but the screen's still frozen on the image of Naptime and Kiki in bed. I slide my startled eyes toward Griff.

What should I say?

He nods once, silently giving me his strength and encouragement.

Do I lie? Tell the truth?

Griff wanted to present a united front. Wanted everyone to know the lie didn't break us.

Except it did. It broke me.

And I destroyed my car because of it.

That's between Griff and me.

Don't give them the satisfaction of knowing that they got to me.

The perfect answer falls into place.

I push my lips into a warm smile and beam it toward the audience. "I just love spending time in the garage with my man." I reach down and take his hand, holding it up like I'm showing him off. "His hands are as talented at restoring cars as they are at rearranging faces in the ring." I aim a sweet, innocent smile at Naptime, then the host.

Hah! They can interpret that any way they want.

Griff body jolts slightly, his stomach quivering as he suppresses a laugh. He leans in, kissing my cheek. "Love you, Muffin," he whispers, his breath warm against my ear.

A collective murmur of admiration rolls through the crowd.

The host sputters and frowns, then glances at the note cards in his hands.

I pull my shoulders back and lift my chin, striving to project more confidence than I possess.

Turmoil and doubts churn inside me. I'm the lowest fraud. If only I really *had* believed in Griff. After being surrounded by these people for a few hours, it really sinks in how awful Griff's isolation in the mansion must've been. I hate that I wasn't there for him in the last few months of the show. Embarrassment and hurt ruled my actions.

The blade of anger I've been carrying twists inward, pointing at myself. How could I let some sneaky camera angles and slick editing fool me?

I don't belong up here, sitting next to Griff. Acting like I was a faithful, loving girlfriend.

All the awful feelings from that night rush over me. The ache in my arms. My desperation to run away...The buzzing in my head crackles to a stop. Slowly the conversation around me filters back in. I force away my doubts and try to pay attention.

How much longer do we have to be here?

Matt's speaking to Kiki. "But you have to admit, you were really into Stonewall." He points to the screen. I turn and it's the clip of their first interaction playing.

While Kiki's playful and flirty, Griff seems disinterested but trying to be polite.

The video freezes when she touches his chest.

"I mean, just look at that chemistry." Matt's voice oozes with insincerity, his fake smile plastered to his face.

I flick my gaze to the screen again. I don't know how anyone could interpret Griff's stone-cold fuck off stare as anything other than hostile.

Griff sits forward, catching Matt's attention. "Why don't you show the rest of that clip? The unedited version if it still exists."

A wave of interested "oohs" and "ahhs" ripple through the audience.

The video continues. Kiki's voice harsh over the speakers. "Why are you letting some little girl back in your hick town lock you down so young, Griff? You have so much potential. Why shackle yourself to one girl when you can have your pick of any *woman*?"

The emphasis she puts on *woman* makes me want to shrink into the cushions. I have never felt more like a dumb kid in my life.

"You wouldn't understand." Griff's firm tone resonates through the theater. "She's not my prison. She's my peace."

The audience erupts in cheers and whistles.

Warmth flows through me. With all the other ugliness, I'd forgotten that moment earlier in the show.

Griff squeezes my hand. I lift my gaze and meet his loving eyes. He rests his forehead against mine. "That's the truth, you know. I meant it."

My throat's too tight to say a word. Moisture burns the backs of my eyeballs. Griff presses his hand to my cheek, providing me with a shield until I wrangle my tears back. Finally, I nod. "I know."

Mortification chills me to my toes when I look away from Griff and realize everyone is staring at us and several cameras are pointed our way. They probably caught every word.

Every second I'm on this stage, I'm slowly falling apart, like an old book with pages slipping from their binding. My brave front crumbles piece by piece. And the cameras are preserving every moment of my vulnerability.

"Did it bother you to see your man have a connection with another woman, Molly?" Matt asks.

"Knock it the fuck off," Griff says. "There was no *connection.*"

"Do you agree, Kiki?" Matt asks.

I blow out a relieved breath that his attention's off of me.

"No, we definitely had a connection," she says.

Naptime scowls at her and it's the only thing that probably stops me from screaming.

"I thought so," Matt continues, as if he's ever had a serious thought in that empty plastic head of his. "Then things seemed to... fizzle. What happened there?"

Giff sits forward, drawing Matt's attention. "*Nothing* happened."

A low, interested hum moves through the audience.

"Molly?" Matt's gaze locks onto me. "Do you believe that? Deep in your heart of hearts, did you always have faith in your man?"

"I..." My mind races. Everyone back home will know I'm a liar when they watch this. I steal a glance at Venom. Griff confided in him about what happened. He'll know I'm lying too. Griff squeezes my hand, giving me courage.

"Of course," I manage, my voice strained. "We have a *true* connection. We've known each other for years. I knew he wouldn't do that."

Liar, liar, liar. That's what *should* have happened.

"Well, that is a relief!" Matt tips his head back, like he's praising God.

"Of course I didn't screw Stonewall." Kiki tosses her hair over her shoulder and thrusts her chest forward.

Naptime rests his hand on her leg. "Thass right," he slurs.

"Why would anyone think that?" she asks.

"Well, we had it right there in black-and-white." Matt points to the screen, still frozen on that creepy overhead shot of the couple in bed.

"Thass me!" Naptime jumps off the couch and pounds one fist against his chest.

He seems oddly proud of those fifteen seconds of awkward, dull rutting under the covers.

Kiki reaches up and grabs Naptime's hand, pulling him back to the seat next to her.

"Whatever connection *we* shared fizzled out because," Kiki slants an evil glance our way, "once I knew he was one of *those* guys, I lost interest."

Griff snorts.

"One of *those* guys?" Matt asks, a creepy lilt in his question.

She leans forward, staring into the audience like she's trying to become besties with every one of them. "Everyone knows guys who only date virgins are always bad in bed, right?"

Cold shock seizes my insides.

A wild, collective gasp comes from the audience.

Griff's hand tightens on mine.

Fuck. This. Bitch.

What should I do? Defend Griff? Defend myself? Run screaming from the stage?

I don't want to discuss my sex life in front of all these people.

Remy was right. Everything about this is lose-lose.

"This kind of trashy bullshit is why none of us wanted anything to do with your skanky ass," Woolly shouts.

"Amen!" Bear Trap adds.

Griff lifts his fist and nods in their direction.

More of the fighters add noises of agreement. Maybe they're as sick and tired of this being the Griff and Kiki show as I am.

"Who's trashy?" Naptime yells. "Who y'all callin' trashy?"

"You." Venom doesn't need to raise his voice, his deep rumble easily carries over the other chatter. "And Ring Bunny Barbie over there."

Venom's been fairly quiet since I came out on stage. I can't even see his wife on the other side of his large frame. It's probably for the best. She didn't seem to like me much last night. After today, she probably hates me for sure.

"What's wrong?" Kiki jumps off the couch and steps over Naptime's outstretched feet. "Little girl can't speak for herself?"

Is she talking to me?

Yup. Her hot glare burns right into me. I don't even know this girl. Why does she seem to hate me so much?

After years of living in fear of my father's unpredictable temper, Kiki's aggression triggers an immediate response in my body. She's *not* my father—she's a hundred and ten pound-bully in six-inch heels. I spring off the couch, ready to defend myself.

As Kiki invades my personal space, a tug on my pants pulls my attention away.

She's right in my face, taunting me. "Nothing to say? You just let everyone else speak for you?"

I open my mouth, a *fuck off, bitch* burning on my tongue.

But her hand lunges forward.

I twist just in time. The blow misses my face but her palm hits my shoulder. Her long, sharp nails tangle in my shirt.

An explosive surge of rage and instinct sends my fist through the air.

Pop! My knuckles hit her jaw. Kiki's head whips sideways and she collapses on the floor like a bag of rotten apples.

It all happens so fast.

Oh my God. What did I just do?

CHAPTER THIRTY-NINE

Griff

"Oh my God. Oh my God. I can't believe I did that," Molly whispers over and over against my neck as I carry her off the stage.

"Here, follow me," a woman says.

She opens the door to the same room we'd been in earlier. "Take a few minutes to cool off."

Few minutes. Fuck that. I need to get Molly *out* of here. I never, ever should have asked her to come with me. How could I let that woman get so close to Molly?

The door closes behind us and I twist the small lock on the knob.

"It's okay. I got you." I set her down on the long, green plaid couch. She throws her hands over her face and hangs her head, resting her elbows on her knees. "Take it easy."

I reach for a side table and grab a handful of tissues. "Come here." I brush my knuckles against her chin and tip her head up. "You're going to ruin all your pretty makeup." I fold one of the tissues into a square and dab it gently over her cheeks.

She sniffles and closes her eyes for a second. "Thank you."

"Talk to me."

"I'm sorry I lost it."

"Baby, it's okay."

"No, it's not," she cries miserably. "I'm so stupid. I actually felt bad for her at first. Then, I was trying to take the high road." She gestures wildly toward the door. "Now you look like you have a trashy girlfriend. I did exactly what they were hoping for. Behaved as bad as her."

"First, I don't care what anyone says or thinks," I say calmly, looking in her eyes. "She came at you first. You defended yourself. Just like you've been taught. What's my number one rule about fighting?"

"Don't start a fight but if someone else does, finish it quickly?"

"Yup. And that's all you did. Knocked her away from you." *Did she ever.* "You didn't do more than necessary. It's not like you put the boots to her after she was on the ground."

She sniffles again. "No."

"That was the rule when I was locked up too. Remember that annoying cellmate Eraser told you about? Wiggles?"

Her nose wrinkles. "The one who jerked off in his bed every night?"

"That's the one." Even though I hate thinking about that time in my life, I've got Molly focused on something else and she's starting to calm down. "When my mom came on visiting days, he used to talk shit about her."

"Like what?"

I shake my head, not wanting to get that far off course. "Dumb stuff horny teenage boys say."

"Oh." Her eyes widen. "Your mom was pretty before...I mean..."

"I know what you mean." I swipe the tissue over her damp cheeks again. "Anyway, he was younger, weaker, a weird kid. As much as it pissed me off, I'd never hit him just for trash talking."

"He was dumb enough to take a swing at you?"

"Once."

Her face breaks into a smile.

"They put hands on you, it's game over." I rub my palm over her leg. "I'm sorry. I should've protected you better."

"I was already so upset." Her leg bounces and she bites her lip.

"Why?" I lift one corner of my mouth. "Worried the whole world thinks your boyfriend's a lousy fuck, now?"

"What? No. Pfft. That wasn't even worth acknowledging." She

lifts her eyebrows. "Are *you* worried about it? I didn't want to stoop to her level and recite my orgasm stats."

I snort with laughter. "You handled it fine." I rub my hand over her knee. "What else is bothering you?"

Her gaze darts to the door.

"It's locked," I assure her. "Talk to me, baby."

She takes a deep breath and sits straighter. "I feel so fake. I hate the pretending and lying."

"About what?"

"He brought up the car." She inhales and rubs her hands over her pants. "They know they got to me. That I did lose faith. In you. In us. It feels unfair or wrong, disrespectful to you, to sit there and *lie*."

I can't have her think that. "Hey, hey, hey, look at me. That's not true."

"Griff! I took a bat to our car."

She's never going to forgive herself for that, is she? When I've forgiven her a thousand times over.

"You were hurting and you lashed out." I crouch in front of her and take her hands in mine. "But I *know* you never lost faith in us. That part isn't a lie at all."

She blinks. "I wouldn't even talk to you when you first came home. I thought I was dating Torch," she whispers.

"Doesn't matter."

Her eyes widen like she's worried I've completely lost it. "How can you say that?"

My mouth slides sideways. "I have a confession, Muffin."

"What?"

"I rode out to see you when I first got home. I peeped the schedule Remy had taped to the fridge." I tap the tip of her nose. "Since you had me blocked and your social media locked down tight, I was reduced to snooping."

She rolls her eyes and waves her hand toward the door. "Thanks to that circus, I had to private all my socials." Her forehead wrinkles. "But what do you mean you came to see me?"

"I waited in the cafe. Same place Remy tricked us into meeting. I never told him I'd already been there."

"What?" she practically shouts. "How did I not know?"

"I didn't *want* you to know. I tried to blend into the crowd."

She cocks her head. "How?"

"Brought my laptop and set up camp at one of the tables with my muffin and coffee."

One corner of her mouth quirks up. "You didn't get any phone numbers?"

That dims the fun of my story a bit. "No. But I went in disguise."

"Disguise?"

I brush my hand over the top of my head. "Ball cap."

"Great disguise. Why didn't I see you?" She rests her hand on my chest. "You're hard to miss."

"I kept my distance. I didn't want to do anything to upset or distract you from your classes." I stop and can't help smiling as a clear picture of that day comes to mind. "But the second I saw you, my heart fucking stopped."

A hint of a shy smile curves her lips. "Really?"

"Oh, yeah." I curl my hand around hers and bring her wrist closer to brush my lips against her soft skin. "Then to complete my stalker destiny, I followed you a little bit."

"I wish I'd known."

"Nah, once I knew you still loved me," I shrug as if leaving that day hadn't felt like dropping my heart on the sidewalk, "I decided to wait for the right time."

"What do you mean? How'd you know?"

"You looked so cute that day. You were wearing these sexy green sweatpants."

"Sexy sweatpants, huh?"

"On you—definitely. But that's not how I knew."

"How?"

And here it is. The sliver of information that kept me from losing my mind when I saw her with Torch. "You were wearing one of the *many* hoodies you've stolen from me over the years."

"I was?" She covers her mouth and lets out a soft giggle.

"Yup. And right there, I knew if you had lost faith in us, and didn't love me anymore, you would've lit those hoodies on fire. Not taken one to college with you."

"I took more than one," she admits with a coy smile.

"Even better."

She presses her palms to my cheeks and pulls me closer for a kiss. "I love you," she whispers against my lips.

"I love you too. Always will."

"In a way you're right. I brought your stuff with me because I still liked having that connection to you." She drops her gaze. "In my heart, I kept hoping you'd come home and tell me it was all a lie. Even though my head kept telling me how stupid that was."

I lift her hand and brush my lips against her knuckles. "Your heart was right."

She shakes with laughter and smacks her palm against her forehead. "That fortune teller Hayden dragged me to at the carnival even told me to listen to my heart."

"Is that what happened in there?" I lift myself off the floor and settle onto the couch next to her. "You and Hayden looked shaken when you came out."

"Oh my God!" She playfully slaps my shoulder. "I forgot you followed me around there too."

"Can't keep my eyes off you, Muffin."

She launches herself forward, hugging me tight, then quickly pulls back. An excited gleam brightens her eyes. "Did you hear how the audience reacted to you? You were the clear winner in their eyes. They don't seem to like Naptime or Kiki at *all*."

"Can you blame them?" I study her face for any lingering signs of distress. "I'm really sorry it turned into a shit show. I don't know why she went after you like that, Molly. I swear I barely talked to the woman while I was at the house."

"You underestimate your market value." She rubs her hand along my jaw. "And I bet Naptime is a snoozefest in and out of bed."

I chuckle and tilt my head to kiss her palm.

"Wait." She gasps and leans in closer. "The show's paying *me* for being here," she whispers. "What if they paid *her* to pick a fight with me?"

"I wouldn't put anything past these demon clowns," I say,

considering the idea. "I didn't interact with her enough for her to hold that kind of grudge."

"Maybe *any* rejection makes her freak out."

"Seems so."

"Let's get out there." She squares her shoulders and tosses her hair back. "I'm ready."

"I'm sorry I made you do this."

"You didn't *make* me do anything." She slides to the edge of the couch and stands. "I'm glad they finally set the record straight about *you*."

"Me too." I couldn't stand the idea of thinking for the rest of our lives that people see Molly as some kind of doormat who took my cheatin' ass back. And I kinda love that the whole world now knows not to fuck with her.

I curl my hand around hers and open the door first. The makeup artist who helped Molly earlier is leaning against the wall across from us.

"You need a touch-up, hon?" she asks Molly.

"Oh. Do I?" Molly glances up at me.

She looks fine to me, but I want her to be comfortable. "Whatever you need."

"Let me see." The woman steps closer, pulls a puff-looking thing out and dabs at Molly's face, then sweeps something under her eyes. She brushes a few strands of Molly's hair into place and nods. "Good to go." She leans in closer. "Good job out there. That little witch had it coming and you gave it to her."

Molly blushes and glances away. "Thank you."

"Thanks." I nod at her and lead Molly down the long hallway.

Another woman meets us side stage out of view of the audience. "We moved Kiki to the opposite end of the stage," she says.

"You better keep her the fuck away from us," I warn.

"I don't think you have to worry about it." The woman cracks a smile. "She'll think twice about coming at Molly now." She pats Molly's shoulder and gives her a quick nod of approval.

Molly shrugs and ducks her head as if it was nothing. Only I know how much the burst of violence bothers her. I wrap my arm around her shoulders, drawing her closer.

"I've got you," I whisper against her ear. "Obviously, they're not going to stop fights from breaking out. I'll be watching better this time," I promise.

I'm still furious with myself for letting anyone get that close to her.

"Okay, go ahead," the woman tells us.

I keep Molly on my left, shielding her from both the audience and everyone on stage.

The audience claps once they see me. But when Molly peeks around my body and they get a glimpse of her, they absolutely lose their shit. The lights fan out over the crowd, so we can actually see them. Women stand up, whistling and clapping. A few people chant her name. Molly lifts her hand in a quick, shy wave.

We return to our seats on the couch. This time, I keep a bit of space between us in case I need to launch myself into the air and pummel someone. Molly seems to understand my intention and flashes a quick smile at me. I reach over and slide my hand over hers, keeping that connection.

"Everyone have cooler heads now?" Matt asks.

I glare at him. "You tell me."

He clears his throat and focuses on Molly. "That's some right hook you've got, Molly. Is Stonewall responsible for teaching you that?"

"I have a big brother who's always taught me not to take shit from anyone."

"Fuck yeah!" Woolly shouts.

"That's a fighter's girl!" Pirate yells.

Laughter echoes through the studio.

Finally, Matt turns his attention to some of the other guys.

"Venom, you seemed to take on a mentor or big brother role to Griff and Woolly. How did it feel to have the student surpass the master?"

"For fuck's sake," I mutter.

"I'm proud of my teammates." Venom keeps his answers short. "They did good."

Frustrated, Matt prowls around the stage, pestering the other guys with questions. I tune them out and focus on Molly. She seems calm now—her breathing's normal, posture relaxed. But her eyes keep nervously darting around like she's expecting another attack. Every now and then she flicks her gaze toward Matt and whoever he's badgering. A faint smile or a short laugh ghosts her lips but otherwise I don't even think she's listening.

After Matt's spoken to all of the contestants at least once, he stops in front of Naptime.

"All those weeks and you came out the victor. How did that feel?"

Naptime opens his mouth to answer—something obnoxious, probably—but the audience boos him into silence.

Shit, that's embarrassing.

"Wow." Matt wipes his hand across his forehead in a corny, fake-ass move. "Our audience has strong feelings about this subject."

"Fuck all of ya!" Naptime jumps up and throws his hands in the air. "I'll fuck all ya up right now. Come here." He points to someone in the audience. Could be a dad in the second row hurling insults at Naptime or the grandmother waving her middle finger at him in the front row. It's hard to tell which person he's challenging.

A huge guy that looks like he was carved out of boulders lunges out of his seat and runs toward the stage, cursing at Naptime. Two equally large security guards jump into action, capturing him before he gets too close. Another security guard bear-hugs Naptime and drags him back to his chair next to Kiki.

"Everyone, calm down," Matt says. "Phew, well, I guess that explains my next question."

Matt focuses on me.

Shit. I don't want to accuse Naptime of cheating. I know what he did was underhanded. The audience seems to know it. But saying it just makes *me* look bad.

"Well, Griff, as you know Mike 'Magic' Everson has issued a challenge for you to fight him in Vegas," Matt says with that fake, game show announcer voice I've grown to despise.

Molly's body goes rigid.

Fuck me. I've been so focused on this reunion, I didn't mention the Vegas fight to her yet. It's not even a sure thing.

"I'm aware of the challenge," I say carefully.

"He said it's because out of all these *Supreme Fighters*, *you* were the best. 'An absolute savage in the cage,' he said. You're the only fighter he feels right now is worthy of fighting him."

Weird way to insult everyone else. "Uh, I hadn't heard all of that. And while I'm looking forward to punching a hole through Magic's skull, he doesn't know what he's talking about."

The audience roars with laughter. Even Molly chuckles.

I point at Venom two seats away from me. "Amazing fighter. Venom would easily put Magic in a coma. Woolly could probably knock Magic out in round one. Bear Trap would submit him in ninety seconds or less. Hammer Fists would knock that guy into next year." My gaze skips around. Can I say anything decent about the other guys? I don't respect any of them much. "Magic would probably break his knuckles punching Bull."

"Fuck yeah, he would!" Bull jumps up and thrusts his fists into a Y. "Fuck that dude. Stonewall can take him easily."

At least he took what I said as a compliment.

Molly lets out a quick giggle and covers her mouth with her hand. Relief spirals through me. Maybe she won't be mad I didn't tell her about the fight sooner.

Everyone else starts talking at once, bragging on their skills and how they're just as worthy of fighting Magic.

Nope. That fight's taken.

Now that the news about the challenge is public, I want this fight more than I thought. Another chance to prove myself.

I hope Molly's as easy to convince.

When all the chatter dies down, Matt walks closer to us. "You're going to need a coach, a team, a trainer to get yourself to Magic's level," Matt says in a low, dramatic tone.

"I have a good team of people I trust at home." To train with and fuck around in the cage, sure. To prepare me for a Vegas fight, maybe not but I'll figure that out later.

"Stonewall, would it surprise you to know there's a world class trainer who would *love* the opportunity to work with you?"

"Uh, I guess not." My words come out as more of a question.

"Welcome back to our coach!" Matt shouts. "Daniel Underhill!"

"No shit," I mutter.

Underhill walks out on stage and waves to the audience, then to me. "What's up, bro?"

"How you been?" I stand and shake his hand.

Matt doesn't let us talk long. He brings Underhill to a chair in the center of the stage.

"So, you're willing to train Stonewall to go up against Mike 'Magic' Everson. You didn't get enough of him at the house?"

Underhill laughs, a deep hearty sound. Wasn't sure the guy even knew how to laugh. "Hell, yeah. He's an exceptional student and fighter."

"You certainly seemed to have strong opinions about the outcome of Naptime vs. Stonewall," Matt says.

Footage is shown of Underhill attacking the ref after my fight with Naptime. Damn, their brawl was worse than I thought.

"Well, I did, Matthew," Underhill says in his best *I'll fuck you up* tone. "Frankly, Stonewall was robbed. He should've won that fight."

"Fuck you!" Naptime shouts. "You're a loser and your boy's a loser." He points at me and I wave back with my middle finger.

Molly sits up, like she's ready to pounce on Naptime if he comes any closer. I rest my arm against her leg, subtly pushing her back into her seat.

Even though she must have a thousand questions and she's probably not too happy with me right now, my girl's first instinct is to jump to my defense.

I hope she finally realizes that none of this noise matters. Not the show. Not the car or what she did to it. Nothing.

We have always been unbreakable.

CHAPTER FORTY

Griff

AM I FINALLY FREE OF *SUPREME UNDERGROUND FIGHTER?*
It's consumed my life—almost ruined my life—for months.

Hours later, we're finally free to leave the studio.

It's like a huge weight lifting off my shoulders.

Diane—now sporting blue hair instead of the pink she had when she conned me into this ring of ridiculousness—stands next to our car in the chilly evening air.

She holds out her hands in an appeasement gesture as we approach. "I know things weren't perfect, but you have to admit I was right."

I wrap my arm around Molly's shoulders. "About what? Blowing up my life?"

Diane still seems confused by our lack of enthusiasm. She must have lived too long in her reality TV bubble. Her gaze slides to Molly. "You look like you're doing okay."

"Yes, I thoroughly enjoyed having strangers on the Internet call me dumb, slutty, or a combination of the two. It was the highlight of my summer. Then coming here and being physically attacked by an unhinged lunatic was fantastic," Molly says. "Thanks for making me sign that release form. I *really* appreciate it," she adds with generous dose of sarcasm.

Diane's shoulders slump. Is that a sign she actually feels some remorse? "I didn't have anything to do with that." She lifts her gaze

353

and looks me in the eyes. "You know I left shortly after the show started." She glances toward the door we just came out of. "The ladies and romantic aspect weren't a part of the show when I asked you to sign on."

That actually helps me hate her less.

"It really *was* supposed to be about fighting and training together in a closed environment. All the knockouts, antics, and brawls between the fighters was supposed to be the entertainment, not romance or dating."

Hating her a bit more now. "You realize paying us a bonus each time we knocked each other unconscious is fucking psychotic, right?"

"Only if we'd told you that ahead of time." She chuckles. "It's a show about fighting," she says as if I'm dense.

Maybe I am. "Fighting in the ring. Not knocking each other out over who stole someone's French fries."

"Well, from what I saw, you conducted yourself with integrity throughout the whole season." She vaguely gestures toward the studio again. "I think that's why you were the fan favorite, even though Naptime supposedly 'won.'"

At least she seems bitter about that too. "So you know it was rigged?"

"*Rigged* isn't the right word." She shakes her head. "And based on the audience reaction, you came out on top, no matter what the judges decided."

When I don't agree with her assessment, she shrugs. "I'm sorry it wasn't the experience you expected. But you *did* end up winning money." She nods at Molly. "For your future. That's what you wanted, right?"

"Yes," I answer but can't quite bring myself to add a *thank you.*

"I think you'll navigate the newfound celebrity well. You're not going to be out there making an ass out of yourself like so many others I've worked with."

"No, the show already did that for me."

"And all those misconceptions were clarified today." She lifts her eyebrows.

Is she trying to say *she's* responsible for the truth about Kiki and me coming out?

"The fight with Magic could be huge for you," she continues. "I hope you're considering it seriously."

"I am."

"He's a massive douche canoe." She laughs. "Don't get me wrong, he's a good fighter and has a huge following. But his personality...you'll hate him." She waves her hand toward the stage. "He's like an articulate, better-looking Naptime."

"Super. Can't wait." I flash a fake grin.

"But, now that you've recovered, if you resume your training and focus the way you did here, I think you'll beat him easily. Knock him out in round two at least."

"You're not just a reality television fairy," Molly says. "You're a fight promoter too?"

I can't tell if Molly's serious or subtly mocking Diane.

Diane seems to take the question seriously. "Just a fan of combat sports. Who knows people."

"Are you saying you're responsible for the Magic fight?" I ask.

"I didn't say that." The corners of her mouth twitch with secret amusement, then her expression turns serious. "I really *didn't* know they were gunning to set you up to make it look like you were with Kiki. That's not the kind of narrative that interests me." Her gaze shifts between Molly and me. "I actually liked the young love story, thought it would bring a little wholesomeness to what can be a trashy game sometimes. But obviously I was overruled." She grins and reaches out to tap my arm. "I heard you had Paul practically pissing his pants when you confronted him. Good for you."

So Paul must be the one who changed the direction of the show. What an asshole. I should've punched that potato-looking motherfucker when I had the chance. "I don't know about that."

"It's all behind you now. If we get renewed for another season," her voice rises in pitch, like I'm a kid she's teaching to use the potty for the first time, "we might ask if you want to come back as a coach or mentor."

Molly lets out a snort-laugh that sounds a lot like *"hell no"* and I couldn't agree more.

"I wish you two luck," Diane says. "The balance of your money should be deposited in a day or two, Griff. And Molly, you should've gotten a check for your fee before you left?"

Molly pats her purse. "I did."

"Good." She tilts her head, looking at someone behind me. "I need to have a minute with Woolly. Congratulations, Griff."

"Thanks." This time I say it with more sincerity.

Molly just nods at her. Once Diane's distracted with Woolly, Molly shrugs my arm off her shoulders and sends me an icy side-eye.

I need to get her alone so we can talk about the fight before she starts thinking I'm planning to abandon her again and have a repeat of last summer.

"You ready to head home?" I ask.

"Yup."

I hit the unlock button. She jerks the door open, not waiting for me to open it for her.

"You okay?" I grab the door, pulling it wider.

She slides in without looking at me. "Yup."

"Molly—"

She turns her head and stares at me with glossy blue eyes. "Can we please go?"

"I'm on it." I make sure she's tucked in her seat and shut the door.

She's quiet while I navigate out of the parking lot and onto the road that will take us to the Thruway. The last thing I want to do after the day we've had is get lost somewhere on Long Island.

"You okay?" Why am I asking when I know the answer.

"Why didn't you tell me you're going to Vegas? For a big fight?"

No time to have an argument like when we have a three-hour drive ahead of us. "It's just been talk so far. Nothing was confirmed until today."

From the corner of my eye, I catch Molly's bottom lip wobble. All I want to do is pull over, drag her into my lap and kiss her concerns away. The reunion show was stressful enough, without this extra bullshit.

I better start with what I'm sure is her biggest concern. "I won't be leaving again. You heard Underhill, he'll work with me so I can train at home." Shit, that's not entirely true. "Well, I have to go to fight camp three or four weeks before the event—but it won't be like the show. We'll be able to talk whenever we want. It's probably gonna be when you're in the middle of finals, anyway."

"For something that isn't confirmed, you sure have a lot of details," she says, staring straight ahead.

"I'm trying to be smarter this time, Molly. Learn as much as I can before I commit," I explain. "Once you're done with finals, I want you to fly out to meet me for fight week."

She blinks rapidly. "Wait, you want me there? I can come to the fight? To Las Vegas? To be with you?"

"Of course I want you there." I can't stand not having my arms around her another second. I spot a small gas station ahead and pull into the parking lot.

"What are you doing?" she asks.

I stop in a space on the side of the building, out of view from most of the parking lot and turn toward her. "I need you there." I reach over and take her hand. "I won't have a lot of free time during fight week. There's going to be press conferences and stuff. Probably boring as hell. And I'll still be training. But I'd really like you there. After the fight, we can stay for a few days and explore Vegas if you want. Hell, if I win, we can go anywhere you want."

"I don't care about seeing Vegas or anything else." She turns my hand over and traces a soft, ticklish line from my middle finger to the inside of my wrist. "I want to be there to cheer for *you*."

"Thank you. I want you there, believe me." I raise her hand and brush my lips against her knuckles. "While I'm training at home, I *might* not be able to drive out and visit you as often as I have been lately."

Her brow furrows. "Griff, I understand how serious training for something like this is. If you're doing it, then you need to do it a hundred percent."

"I can't do this...I *won't*, unless you're really okay with it."

One corner of her mouth slides up. "Well, from what Diane said, it sounds like this guy is in desperate need of a *Stonewall Slap*."

That's not the answer I expected, but it's definitely the one I needed.

If I didn't know how much Molly wants a small, rose garden wedding one day, I think I'd ask her to marry me while we're in Vegas.

CHAPTER FORTY-ONE

Molly

GRIFF AND I GET HOME SO LATE THAT WE DON'T WAKE UP until the next afternoon.

Wait. I open my eyes. I'm alone.

Where is he?

I grab a T-shirt from one of his drawers, slip on my velvet pants even though they feel gross from wearing them all day yesterday, and head upstairs.

Low, angry voices greet me as I push open the door. Griff and Remy. I roll my eyes and walk toward their budding argument.

"What do you mean she punched someone?" Remy seethes.

They're in the dining room. That's good, at least there's a whole table between them. Remy's back is to me, his neck and shoulders tight with anger.

Griff's facing me and notices my arrival first.

"Good morning, Remington," I say from behind him.

He turns and relief washes over his face, smoothing the angry furrow between his eyebrows. "Are you okay?"

"I'm fine." I show him my right hand. "My fingers hurt a little. I don't know how you guys do that repeatedly."

He gently takes my hand, inspecting for damage, then looks up into my eyes.

Remorse, not smug satisfaction that he was right, shimmers in his eyes.

"You were right," I say. "It was a total shit show."

"I didn't want to be right."

Griff snorts.

"But," I continue before my brother responds, "I'm glad I was there. I spoke up for myself." I shift my gaze to Griff. "And for Griff."

"Yeah, you did, baby."

"And unless they decide not to air it, everyone will finally know that Griff never slept with her," I finish. "Naptime and Kiki confirmed it was them. More than once."

"Griff's reputation wasn't my concern," Remy says.

"Thanks," Griff mutters.

Ignoring him, Remy continues. "Yours is. That video of you punching out that woman on some reality shit show will live forever. You want to work in a medical-related field. What if it hurts your job prospects?"

I blink and stare at him. Why hadn't I ever thought of that?

"Cut it out," Griff says. "Kiki came flying at Molly. She touched her first. It was a clean knockout, not a hair-pulling scratch fest. No one can look at it as anything other than self-defense."

Remy lifts one shoulder. "Okay."

"Well, it's done now." I sigh and round the table, taking a seat next to Griff. "Did Griff tell you he's going to fight Magic Everson in Vegas?"

Remy chuckles softly. "Yeah, he mentioned it. I'm going to have to stop going so easy on him at the gym. And make him come on my morning runs with me now. Build up that endurance."

"I run," Griff protests.

"Bro, you haven't done shit in weeks."

"I've been *recovering*," Griff says, sounding out each syllable. "Doctor's orders."

Laughing, I stand and push in my chair.

"Where are you going, Muffin?" Griff reaches for me, hooking his arm around my leg.

"I need to pack and get ready to go back to school." I lean down and kiss his cheek. "You two try not to kill each other while I'm away this week."

"We'll do our best." Remy focuses his intense stare on Griff and the lingering anger in his eyes doesn't reassure me at all.

CHAPTER FORTY-TWO

Griff

THE NIGHT THE REUNION SHOW AIRS IS ALSO THE official announcement that I'll be fighting Magic in Vegas. My phone starts blowing up almost immediately. Texts from everyone I've squared up with in a cage in the last five years flash over my screen. Notifications from every social media app blink or chirp.

I return the texts to the people I give a shit about and silence the notifications.

Days later, I'm still getting bombarded with questions and tags about the fight.

"It's gonna be like this for the next couple of months," Remy says to me after breakfast. "Surprised you don't have to do a press tour to promote the fight."

If I thought he'd been furious when I told him about what happened at the reunion show, it was nothing compared to when we watched it. They sensationalized the big "fight" between Molly and Kiki, including several slow-motion replays of Molly's fist flying through the air.

He's been a bit sharp with me since then.

I set my phone on the table. "I have to go down to the city for something mid-week," I admit. "But nothing else out of town is on the schedule until I leave for Vegas. The company hosting it is going to send out a camera crew at some point to film me training."

"That'll be fun." He rolls his eyes. "I hope you told Jerry before the announcement was made."

I nod once. "I did. He was cool with it."

"Good." He lifts his chin. "Why don't you come up to The Castle with me later?"

"You're not hosting anything this weekend, are you?"

"No. But you keep saying you want to fix things up there. Let's go. Start making a list of what needs to be done."

"Molly's going to be here in a few hours." I pick up my phone and check for a text from her.

He groans. "Then let's go *now* before you two disappear into your lair of love all weekend."

"Lair of love?" I snort. "I guess it could be worse. There's no disappearing. We've got that thing at the bar tomorrow night."

Finally free of the show's restraints, Remy, Vapor, and Eraser insisted on throwing a party to officially "welcome" me home.

"That'll be a couple of hours max." He walks out of the dining room. "Let's go. And maybe bring your sparring gloves too," he says over his shoulder.

Immediately suspicious, I clear my plates from the table and jog downstairs to find my gloves.

The Castle needs more work than I realized. I have a notebook with half the pages dedicated to lists of supplies we'll need by the time we finish our walk-through.

"Told you it would be expensive," Remy says. "We might be better off leveling the place and starting over." He walks over to the duffel bag he brought with him and dropped off near the octagon-shaped cage in the center of the main room. "Now, what we really need to do is evaluate the cage."

"Evaluate how?" Wary of the shift in Remy's mood, I circle to the other side of the cage and grab my backpack off the steps.

"I think you know how." Remy strips off his shirt, dropping it on top of the bag.

Ahhh, I should've known this was coming. Still, I can't help fucking with him. "How? You planning to give me a lap dance or something?"

He slips on his gloves and stares at me.

All right. I've been getting back to the gym. Slowly starting training again. I might not be quite where I was before my fight with Naptime, but I've got this.

I find my gloves and wriggle my fingers into them.

Remy's feral smile raises the hairs on the back of my neck. He really thinks he's gonna win here, huh?

I lift my shirt over my head and hop up the stairs into the cage.

"Let's do it, bro." I tap my gloves together. They're made for sparring, with more padding than what we'd wear in an actual match. Still won't feel good to get smashed with one. I bounce on my toes in the center of the cage, trying to pump myself up.

I didn't expect this today. But that's always been part of training. You never know when you might encounter a fight. Always be ready.

Remy enters the cage with his hands up, already guarding his face.

"No ground rules?" I ask.

"Nope."

I take a deep breath and knock my gloves together again. "All right then. Come and get it, fucker."

He slowly slides to my right, circling me. The same first move he always makes. His sharp blue eyes bore into me. I stare him down just as hard.

He steps forward.

Whoosh. His fist breezes by my face. Not an actual punch. More like he's testing me.

"You seem to have some big feelings you need to get out, Remy. Let's hear it," I taunt.

My mocking tone drops a match to the gasoline that seems to be flowing in his veins.

"Fuck you for dragging my sister into that snake pit." He lands a solid fist to my gut.

I wheeze a pained breath and back up. That punch unlocks all the fury I've been holding in and trying to forget for months.

"Fuck *you* for not believing me." I smash my fist into Remy's jaw —harder than I'd normally hit him, but fuck it, he started this.

His eyes widen in shock, then narrow. "You're going to regret that."

He sends his fist through the air. Even though it's been a while since we've faced off, I know Remy too well. His moves are predictable. He practically announces his intentions.

I easily duck the blow, then pop back up and punch his side.

"Regret what?" I reach out and tap his face with the underside of my glove—a padded version of the *Stonewall Slap*—just to fuck with him.

"This?" I taunt and tap him again. "Or this?" Another tap on the opposite cheek.

"You watched it," he grunts and sweeps my hand away. "Saw how bad it was." *Punch.*

Weave.

"It doesn't matter." I hit his shoulder. "You should've believed *in me.*"

"I warned you not to do the show." *Blam!* His fist hits my cheek.

It smarts but I shake it off and back away.

"So what? You wanted to teach me a lesson?" I throw a few jabs and he counters. "You let Molly go all that time thinking I'd do that to her?"

"You should've found a way to talk to her *yourself.*" He drives his fist into my gut.

Air whooshes from my lungs in another painful wheeze.

I blink, then laugh in his face. "That's all you've got for me?" I hit his side again.

He growls a curse and hooks a kick, popping me behind my bad knee. The shot almost takes me down.

I glare at him and return the kick. There isn't enough power behind my foot. He grabs my ankle and yanks hard. I hop and wobble. We both tumble to the mat.

The fall's hard enough to jar my bones but I recover faster than Remy. "Been waiting for this, huh?" I easily wrap my legs around his midsection and squeeze.

Remy's always been a slightly better grappler than me, but my time at the house taught me a few new moves.

And I'm about to give Remy an education he won't forget.

He twists and struggles to free his legs, but I'm motherfucking concrete ready to drag him to the bottom of an ocean. Slowly, I twist and unwind, rolling us until I get my arm under his chin in a guillotine choke.

"You like that?" I say against his ear, flexing my arm enough for him to feel it but not completely cut off his oxygen. "Ready to tap out?"

"No," he grunts through clenched teeth.

He presses his palms into the mat, trying to throw me off but I stay on his back like a monkey. He's always been a strong son of a bitch. But I'm stronger.

"Remy, I'll choke you out." I tighten my arm a fraction more.

He launches himself backward, throwing my shoulder into the cage wall. The fence is sturdy but not exactly up to safety standards. It buckles and rattles. I release him from the hold, brace my palms against his shoulders and shove him away from me.

He coughs and sucks in a huge breath, but whips around faster than I expected and fires off a kick to my midsection. I dodge the worst of it but his heel glances off my side and I stumble against the cage again.

I hurry to put distance between us. Regroup. New attack plan.

We circle each other slowly.

Remy runs a lot. He's got endurance. I won't tire him out easily. As furious as I am, I don't want to hurt him more than I have to. But he's obviously not giving up.

Fuck it. I move in, letting him think he has an easy shot at my face. As soon as he cocks his arm I duck and take him down.

"Fucker," he breathes out.

I'm an octopus, wrapping my limbs around him. Locking my legs around his hips and my arm around his neck. A python, squeezing my prey.

He freezes for a second, then lets his body go limp.

"I'm not falling for that." I squeeze him harder. We're ending this now.

"I. Warned. You. Not. To. Hurt. Her." He reaches up and

behind, knocking his glove against my temple. Not enough to hurt. More like the annoying tap of a cat's paw.

"I didn't know..." The protest dies on my tongue. I'm tired of saying it. Tired of defending my actions. I've apologized to Molly and she forgave me. But I hurt Remy too and my pride wouldn't allow me to admit it. "I'm sorry. I'm so fucking sorry. I never wanted any of that."

He taps my arm three times.

Finally.

I release him so fast, his chin hits the floor. He rolls to his back, panting and staring up at the ceiling. I fall down on the mat an arm's length away.

"I'm sorry," I say again.

He rolls his head my way. "You're right. I should have known it was bullshit. I'm sorry too."

My eyes widen and I flick my gaze to the ceiling. "Holy shit. Did you manage to knock me out after all? Am I hallucinating? The great Remington Holt didn't just *apologize*, did he?"

"Christ, you came home a better grappler and a *supreme* asshole. Fantastic."

"Hah. You admit I'm better than you. Finally."

"That's *not* what I said." He groans and rolls to a sitting position, then glances over at me. "But yeah, you're damn good."

I sit up and stretch. "Thank you."

"I hate that you're doing the Vegas fight."

"Why?"

He runs his hand over the top of his head and winces, then shakes out his arm. "I'm worried it's another setup. I don't trust anything that comes as a result of that damn show."

He's not saying anything I haven't already considered. "It's not the same company. But yeah, the way they got Underhill to agree to coach me, means they're probably involved." I stop and consider the bigger picture. "We both know I have a small window of opportunity, though. Once the second season airs, everyone will lose interest in me. Life will return to normal."

He scoffs. "I think you're kidding yourself. But okay."

"I'd like your support."

"You've already got it. You know that." He hesitates. "I'm not thrilled Molly's going with you to Vegas, though."

"I can't do this again without her. It's not fair. It won't interfere with her classes—"

"I'm not worried about that. She'll be done with finals, by then."

"You worried she'll get upset during the fight?" If things get as bad as they did in my fight with Naptime, I don't know if Molly can handle seeing me bleed that much.

"Yeah." He stretches out his arm and waves his hand near my face. "For some reason she likes your ugly mug arranged as it is." He pauses, then adds, "I also don't want any of the fight bros that'll be hanging around the event bothering her. They'll do it just to fuck with your head."

A slow grin slides over my face. "Then come with us, and be my fight bro, *bro*."

He flicks his gaze to the ceiling. "Yeah, I probably should be there to chaperon. I don't want you two getting any ideas while you're in Vegas."

It takes a second for his meaning to sink in. "Molly wants to get married in a rose garden, not Vegas."

He groans and shakes his head.

"We're not ready for that anyway." I cock my head. "You don't need to make up reasons. It's okay to want to be there to watch me win. Just say you'll be my emotional support fight bro."

He cracks up and kicks his foot at me. "Fine, fucker. Yeah, I wanna be there to see you hand that guy his ass. And to make sure no one in his crew tries to mess with you outside the ring."

"There." I roll my head to the side and grin at him. "Was that so hard, big buddy?"

"I don't know if I like this new, cocky Griffin Royal."

"Same guy I've always been."

"Nah, you used to fear me more."

"You want a friendship based on fear?"

He can't seem to come up with an answer to that one. While he's working out a comeback, I peel myself off the floor and hold out my hand to him.

Reluctantly, he allows me to help him up.

"You got me good, fucker." He curls his arm around his side.

This is the real reason we stopped sparring with each other. I hate hurting my best friend. And there isn't really a "nice" way to trade blows with someone. "You asked for it."

"I did." He nods once.

"You went low with that kick to my bad knee."

He grimaces. "That *was* shitty. Sorry."

As much as I try to hide it, I end up limping out of the cage. It's not even the pain as much as my knee just doesn't want to function. I don't want to make Remy feel worse, though, so I do what I always do and power through the pain.

CHAPTER FORTY-THREE

Griff

"AREN'T YOU TWO GETTING A LITTLE OLD FOR THIS?" Molly places her hands on her hips and glares at us.

Molly was here, waiting on the back porch when we dragged our sorry asses home. She had *not* been amused to watch us stagger out of Remy's vehicle.

She herds us into the kitchen, fuming the whole way.

"Old? We're in the prime of our lives. This is what we do." Remy holds his arms wide, then winces.

"Suuure." She skewers him with a scathing look. "Real prime, old man."

"Heh." I limp toward her. "Tell him."

"What are you laughing at, gangster walk?" She scowls and holds out her hand, blocking my hug.

"Hey, now." I cock my head. "Those are fightin' words."

"Look at you." Molly sighs and reaches up on tiptoes to touch my cheek. "Damn you, Remy." She throws a scowl at her brother, then roughly grabs my chin and turns my face. "At least he didn't cut you open."

"I think he cracked one of my ribs," Remy complains.

I roll my eyes. "You were being stubborn."

"Ugh." Molly throws her hands up. "You two can nurse each other back to health. I'm staying in my room tonight."

375

She spins away, grabs her bag off the table and speed walks toward the stairs.

Remy snickers. "I think she's mad, bro."

"We could've done this Monday...or literally any other time, you know."

He grins wider.

"Fuckin' cock-blocking motherfucker," I grumble.

He laughs, then hisses a pained breath. "Ow."

"Feel that?" I point at him. "That's Karma."

"Yeah? What're you naming your aches?"

"Remington." I chuckle at my joke but he just shakes his head, then pulls another pained face.

"Maybe I *should* take you to urgent care," I suggest.

He closes his eyes for a second as if he's assessing his injuries. "No. If it gets worse, I'll go. Right now, I want to shower and sit with some ice."

"All my fancy ice packs I brought back with me are in the chest freezer downstairs." I nod to the basement door.

We both stare at it.

"Think we can get Molly to run down and grab them for us?" he asks.

"Unlikely." I wince. "She's pretty mad."

A few minutes later, Remy and I haven't moved far when Molly stomps down the stairs and into the kitchen again.

"Ugh. I'm so mad at you two." She throws her hands in the air. "But I can't stand knowing you're in pain." She turns and glances at both of us. "What do you need?" she asks me.

"Ice packs." I gesture vaguely to the basement door. "They're in the chest freezer."

"How many?"

"All of them," Remy groans.

Molly growls, a sound that's more adorable than angry, and stomps toward the door.

"This is why I didn't wait until Monday," Remy says. "So someone was around to nurse us back to health."

"You're an idiot." I limp over to the cabinet and take a bottle of Tylenol off the shelf. It takes two tries to twist off the stupid childproof lid.

"All right. Geez, these are cold." Molly dumps an armful of icepacks on the counter. "Who started the fight?"

"Why does it matter?" Remy asks.

"Because whoever started it," she says slow enough to convey how irritated she is with us, "gets last dibs on the icepacks."

I laugh and then wince at the pain spearing my cheek.

"Since no one's answering, I'm assuming it was Remy," Molly says.

"Hey!" Remy protests. "Why me?"

Molly glances at me and lifts an eyebrow.

"I can't rat out my bro." I shake my head.

Ignoring me, Molly turns toward her brother. "Take off your shirt."

"What? Why? Just give me an icepack."

"I want to see how badly you're bruised."

Remy lifts one side of his shirt up. His skin's a pinkish red. Tomorrow it'll probably be black-and-blue. Molly hisses out a pained breath and glares at me.

"What?" I point at Remy. "He started it."

"I knew it!" She picks up the longest icepack and hands it to her brother. *That's my girl.* Not a mean bone in her body. Her worry for Remy outweighs any anger at him. "You need help getting to your chair?"

"No. I'm going upstairs." He presses the pack to his side.

"I'll come check on you and change out the ice pack in a half an hour or so," Molly promises.

"Thanks." He pats her shoulder and walks slowly toward me. "You good?"

"I'll live."

He makes a fist and lightly taps my shoulder. Remy's way of apologizing.

Once he's gone, Molly sorts through the icepacks and finds one designed to wrap around my knee. "Come on. Let's get this on you." She looks at the pile and grabs two more packs. "Couch. Go." She jabs her finger toward the living room.

"Nurse Molly's stern bedside manner is really hot," I say over my shoulder as I hop out of the kitchen.

She grumbles something I can't make out.

Once she has me arranged on the cushions with an icepack on each aching spot, she sits cross-legged at the end of the couch, facing me. Tension twists between us and I shift my body closer to her.

"Griff, can you answer something seriously for me?"

"Always."

She bites her lip. "Don't be mad."

I reach over and rest my hand on her knee. "I could never be mad at you."

"How much longer are you planning to fight?" She waves one hand in the air between us. "Besides Vegas. After that...how much longer do you think you can keep doing this?"

This? I feel like I've been fighting my entire life. I never *wanted* to. I didn't have a choice. "Today wasn't a fight. Just a sparring match that got a little out of control."

She tilts her head and levels me with *who are you kidding* glare. "A little?"

"We had some issues and aggression to work out," I concede.

"About what?"

"Fighter confidentiality." I run my fingers over my lips.

She rolls her eyes. "That doesn't exist." She stares at me for a few beats, more questions brewing in her beautiful blue eyes. "Was it about me?"

I blow out a long breath. "Not exactly."

She seems to accept my non-answer. "Did you sort it out?"

"I think so." I nod once and return to her original question. "Vegas is a lot of money."

"So when you win and you're offered another fight for even more money, what then?"

Shit, she's dead serious.

So, I crack a joke. "I appreciate your assumption that I'll win."

No laughter. Just her unwavering, concerned stare. "All the money in the world can't cure you if you end up with Chronic Traumatic Encephalopathy," she continues.

The full medical term rolls off her tongue easily. Someone's been doing her research. "I've never been knocked out," I say, knowing full well plenty of concussions don't result in loss of consciousness.

She tilts her head, silently calling bullshit on me. "Yeah, and athletes who've never been diagnosed with concussions still get CTE. Strange, huh?"

All right. I need to cut the bullshit. "You're not saying anything I haven't thought of. At the house, a couple of the guys were so hard to understand, I wondered if they already had brain damage."

"Yeah, I remember in the beginning of the show, they kind of mocked Bull." She frowns. "Seemed shitty under the circumstances."

"I'm not surprised." I rest my hand over hers. "Do you want me to pull out of the Vegas fight?"

She's shaking her head before I fully get out the question. "No. Don't put that decision on me. I support you no matter what. But you keep talking about *money* for our future, and I want there to *be* a future for us, period."

"I hear you." I run my hand over the top of my head. What *will* I do if I get offered another fight after Vegas? How much is enough to keep us comfortable for the rest of our lives? "I don't need stacks of cash. I don't have any desire to go dropping a fortune on diamond-encrusted watches or Lamborghinis and yachts." I tilt my head and give her a crooked smile. "Although, you'd look fantastic in a bikini on one of those things."

She flicks her gaze to the ceiling. "You don't need a boat for that. I'll wear one for you wherever you want."

"That so?" We're getting off track. I reluctantly file mental images of Molly in a skimpy two piece to the back of mind to examine later. "I want to work with my hands." I hold them out and flex my fingers, pain flaring through each knuckle. "Building things instead of tearing them apart. My plan's still to buy Jerry's garage and work on cars."

She blows out a relieved breath.

"Fighter wife life, not for you?" I ask.

"Like I said, I want to support you no matter what. But I also want you to take care of yourself." She cuddles closer, allowing me to wrap my arm around her shoulders. "So we can grow old together."

That's exactly what I want too. I kiss the top of her head. "Sounds like a plan."

CHAPTER FORTY-FOUR

Molly

GRIFF'S "WELCOME BACK" PARTY HAS SO FAR BEEN A success. The bar's full of people. No customers, just friends from all the different social circles Remy and Griff navigate.

At the back door, I give Juliet a quick embrace. "Are you sure you guys have to leave so early?" I ask, feeling guilty that I haven't seen her a lot since Griff and I got back together.

She glances out into the parking lot where Vapor's talking to Eraser next to his Harley.

"I promised the sitter we wouldn't be out too late. Let's do something if you come home next weekend?"

"I'd like that."

"Good." She hugs me again.

I hold the door open and watch her cross the parking lot to Vapor's bike. He starts the engine, the distinctive rumble deafening even from half a parking lot away.

I close the door and pivot on my toes, intent on returning to the party.

And smack right into someone.

"Shoot." I glance up into Torch's apologetic face.

"Hey, I've been looking for you."

Oh, this is bad. Embarrassment, guilt, and anger all take a spin in my chest.

I clench my jaw and stare at him. "Why?"

"Look, I'm sorry. I realize what you overheard the other day sounded bad." He blows a puff of air past his lips. "Really, I was just trying to save face in front of Griff." He chuckles. "I mean save *my* face."

My expression stays the same.

"Yes, your brother asked me to take you out. But like I said, I was going to ask you out, anyway. Just maybe not *right* after everything that happened." He waves his hand over his shoulder.

"You could've told me."

He tilts his head.

Right, everyone's scared to challenge Remy.

Everyone except Griff.

Guilt needles me in the ribs. "Well, I'm sorry too."

"Why?" He lifts his eyebrows. "Because you were using me to get over Griff?"

My jaw drops. That's not quite how I was going to put it.

"I don't care, Molly," he continues when I still haven't said anything. "I was fine with it. Figured you'd get over him, eventually. Or not."

This is the worst conversation of my life.

"We're still going to run into each other." He circles one finger in the air. "So, friends?"

What else am I supposed to say? He's right. "Sure."

He opens his arms and leans in like he's going to hug me. *Oh, that's not happening.* I sidestep the embrace.

"Got it," he says.

"I need to get back…" I keep walking sideways. Other people in the hallway glance over at us, but no one says anything.

Ugh, that was awful.

I speed walk into the main room, my steps slowing as I hit the crowd. Bikers, fighters, and racers from Zips fill the space. I recognize a few of the women and wave.

Remy lifts his hand, signaling to me from his place behind the bar. Instead of throwing up the middle finger I want, I glare at him.

Confusion wrinkles his forehead.

Good, let him wonder.

I'm so focused on shooting lasers out of my eyeballs, I slam into someone else. By the height, feel, and arms that close around me, it's Griff.

"I was getting worried about you."

"I'm fine," I mumble against his shirt, taking comfort in his warm, solid presence.

He keeps his arm around me while he signals Remy to hand him drinks. Then we make our way over to my favorite table in the back.

"Hey, Griff." Someone stops us briefly.

Griff keeps moving. "I'll catch you in a minute."

We stop at the table and Griff nudges me to slide into the booth first. Good. It's dark enough in this corner to hide my face. My gaze scans the back hallway I just came from. Did Torch leave? Is that where he was headed when I ran into him?

"Did I tell you how pretty you look tonight?" Griff says, sliding all the way into the booth. I scooch over until I can't go any farther.

My lips twitch. "Yes, but I don't mind hearing it again."

"I'd rather show you." He leans down and presses his lips to mine. Soft and gentle at first, then slowly becoming more insistent. He trails kisses along my jaw, to my neck.

A pleasurable shiver races over my skin, momentarily making me forget where we are.

Griff isn't usually *this* affectionate in public. Hold my hand, yes. Grab a quick kiss, sure. His teeth grazing my neck in front of everyone—not so much.

I press my hand to his chest. Not really pushing him away, more like a reminder to myself to stay in control, since he's apparently lost his *in public* switch. "What are you doing?" My eyelids flutter shut from the shivery sensation of his tongue on that sensitive spot right below my ear.

He dips his head lower, brushing his lips in the crook of my neck. "Kissing my girl."

"In front of everyone?" I pry my eyelids open and stare around the bar. It's kind of dark at our corner table, but we're not exactly invisible. A few Lost Kings at a nearby table glance over and smirk at us, but no one says anything. Some are involved with their own significant others and not paying us any attention.

"Everyone here should know you're *mine*," he whispers.

Is this some weird biker ritual? Or...*oh, no.* Did he see me talking to Torch? Is he worried some guys might think I was *with* Torch? Thanks to Remy's embarrassing plan, everyone probably knows Torch was only "dating" me because my brother asked him to act like my babysitter. Does that somehow make Griff look "bad" to these guys?

"If you're worried about Torch, I'm sure everyone knows he was only pretending to date me," I say, casting another stink-eye toward Remy, even though he's too busy behind the bar to notice this time.

That stops Griff from exploring all my sensitive spots with his tongue. He pulls back, his large frame hiding me from a good portion of the room. "I don't give a fuck about him." His eyes glitter with challenge. "Do you?"

"Not like *that.*" I slide my hand over his heart, feeling the steady thudding against my palm. "I just don't want to feel like a fire hydrant you're marking."

Surprise or maybe hurt flashes in his eyes. "Is that what you think?" He leans close. "I hate to break it to you, but I always have a hard time keeping my hands off of you. And I already told you, it's not true. The only person that orange-haired motherfucker was doing a 'favor' for was himself."

Why bother protesting? Torch just said almost the same thing, but I can't stop wondering if Remy put him up to that too. "Griff—"

"Stop." He slams his lips over mine and slides his hand through my hair, cradling the back of my head.

I'm absolutely breathless when he finally pulls away.

"I love you so fucking much, Muffin." He teases his fingers through my hair, rubbing my scalp with the pads of his fingers in a gentle, hypnotic way. "I'm so happy the show is behind me. I don't have to hide in public or worry about someone taking pictures and posting them online. It's an enormous weight off my shoulders."

I hadn't—but should've—realized the constraints bothered him that much. "You seemed to still go where you wanted."

"Not really, and when I did, I was constantly worried some asshole would grab a picture."

And yet, he still came to visit me at school.

"So, making out with me at your welcome back party is how you want to celebrate?"

His lips tilt into the slow, cocky grin I usually can't resist. "Yeah. I guess so."

"One fight with Remy this month wasn't enough for you?"

He touches his cheek, gently probing the bruised skin. "Yeah, I can't do that again. Glad we finally got it out of the way." He taps his forehead. "I need to be laser focused from now on."

"Me too. Finals are coming up and I'm freaking out a little."

His eyebrows draw down. "Is coming home on the weekends messing with your study time?"

Probably. But I don't want to say that.

"Be honest," Griff warns.

He knows me too well.

"It's loud in the dorms on the weekends. But Sundays, I should probably spend more time in the library."

"If it's that bad on the weekends, why don't you let me rent you a hotel room? You could go there and study."

Is he out of his mind? "I don't want to waste money on that."

"If it helps, you get some work done, then it's not a waste."

"I can study at home too." I poke him in the chest. "I just like spending time with you more."

"And I enjoy spending time with you too." He pulls an exaggerated sad face. "But you know how mad I'll be if you don't get an A in all of your classes because of me?"

"A's in everything is a bit optimistic, but I know what you mean."

Out of the corner of my eye, I catch a man approaching our booth. He stands quietly with his hands folded in front of him like a soldier—if soldiers wore all black and had throat tattoos.

Griff jerks his head to the side, noticing the guy. "Hang on a sec, Muffin." Griff stands to talk to the dark-haired, dark-eyed man who seems vaguely familiar. Their conversation's too low to hear over the other noise, but when Griff moves sideways, I recognize him from Zips. *Black Mercedes Guy.* He races often and frequently loses. Eraser told my brother to keep his eye on this guy at some point. But now he and Griff seem to be pals?

"Is this the girlfriend?" BMG says to Griff.

Griff hesitates, then curls his fingers, motioning me closer. I slide out of the booth, happy I wore jeans instead of a dress since I've gotten in and out of this booth at least fifty times tonight, and stand next to Griff.

"Quill, this is my girlfriend, Molly. Molly, this is Quill. He loaned me the Mercedes for your prom."

"Ah." Quill wags a finger in the air. "I didn't loan it. You *won* it," he says in one of the smoothest voices I've ever heard.

Griff nods and ducks his head. "True."

"Borrowed or won, it was still really nice. Thank you so much," I say.

"Not a problem." He dips his chin. "Nice to meet you, Molly."

Quill slaps Griff's shoulder, then turns and melts into the party.

"He seems nice," I say, then lower my voice. "But isn't he the guy Eraser wanted you guys to watch at the track?"

Griff nods for me to sit in the booth again. "You don't miss anything, huh?"

"I know you guys think I don't listen or pay attention, but I do."

He slips his arm around me. "I'll have to remember that."

"You never really answered my question."

His lips quirk. "Yes, there were some concerns, but I think they have it under control. You forget, I wasn't here for a few months." He lifts his chin at the bar. "If Remy invited him, I assume things are cool."

"Okay."

After a few minutes, Griff's easy attitude slides into something more serious. He pulls his arm away and shifts his body so he's facing me. "Hey, don't get mad, but I need to talk to you about something."

With anyone else, *don't get mad* would be a sure sign someone's about to say something to piss you off. But I trust Griff. Even so, my stomach clenches with anxiety. "What?"

He rubs his hand over my thigh, the heat from his skin warming me through my jeans. It's more of a nervous gesture than an affectionate one, which jacks up my anxiety even more.

"Everything's been so good, I haven't wanted to bring this up.

But now that the reunion's behind us and I'm back to work, I need to know what you want to do about your car."

Guilt punches me in the chest.

How could I forget what I did to my beautiful car?

Griff's right. Things *have* been good. Busy but wonderful. After the reunion and what Griff confessed after I hit Kiki, I haven't thought about the destruction I caused again. How could I forget the mess I left for him to clean up?

"Hey, hey, hey, baby, look at me." Griff takes my hands in his. "I'm not trying to upset you, but I need to know. I ordered everything I need to repair it—"

My eyes flare in surprise. "You did?"

"Well, yeah. If *you* don't want it, I still need to get it in saleable condition."

He should probably sell it to someone who will appreciate it. I don't deserve it after what I did. "I'll pay you back."

"What?" His face screws into a mix of confusion and outrage. "Molly, I don't give a fuck about money. If you keep it, is it going to remind you of that night every time you look at it? Because if it is, I don't want that for you."

I hadn't even considered that possibility.

"I know you've got your little Bronco Sport, which is much more practical for you," he continues, "but you can keep the Malibu to race at Zips or to drive in the summer. Whatever you want."

Hope expands in my chest. "Will you let me help you fix it?" I ask.

His face breaks into a wide grin. "Yeah, of course. It can be our spring break project when you're home from school."

"I'd like that."

"You sure it won't bring up bad feelings for you?" he asks, his eyes boring into me, seeking a truthful answer.

Nothing but love and concern flows through the question. Will I look at the car and remember that awful night? Maybe. But I'll also always remember that it's a symbol of Griff's love and forgiveness.

"No, I think if anything, it'll be a reminder that we really are unbreakable."

CHAPTER FORTY-FIVE

Griff

I DIDN'T WANT TO INFLUENCE HER DECISION, BUT I'M SO fuckin' happy Molly chose to keep her car, and that she's able to see it in a different light now.

I hug her close again. "It's still just a car. Definitely not unbreakable."

She drills one of her poke-y little fingers into my side. "Hey. You know what I mean."

"I do." My smile fades. "And I feel the same way."

"Thank you." She rests her head on my shoulder and we watch the party for a bit. The bar's over capacity. Pretty much anyone and everyone we know is here.

Most of the Lost Kings, from both the upstate and downstate clubs, along with their wives and girlfriends, have shown up. Guys from Zips, including Torch—which irritated me to no end—but so far he hasn't shown his face in this corner of the bar.

Lots of fighters from The Castle have stopped to talk to me. They all want to gas me up about the Vegas fight. One asked how he could audition for Season Two of *Supreme Underground Fighter*. I told him to come talk to me at the gym this week. From their perspective, I'm sure it looks like I have the world by the balls. Went on TV, got famous, brought home stack of cash, and now I'm in a pro fight and earning a *lot* of money. That's the dream, right? I'll never be able to convince them otherwise. But maybe I can help any future fighters prepare for the *SUF* the experience better than I was able to.

Tonight's going so well, I almost feel bad for giving Remy shit about throwing the party. Since it's his place and he's hosting, I didn't want him closing down for the whole night. But our biker friends have been stuffing the tip jars with every order they make. So much so that maybe he'll end up making more than if he'd been open to the public.

"Do you think I should go relieve Remy of bar duty?" Molly asks.

"Uh, absolutely not." I know most of the people here, but I'm not sure all of them are aware of who Molly is or that she's with *me*. A woman behind the bar by herself in a place full of bikers, mobsters, and gearheads could be trouble.

"Griff, I recognize almost everyone here," Molly says. "And if they don't know I'm your girlfriend, they definitely know I'm Remy's sister."

I lean down and say against her ear, "Knowing you're Remy's sister didn't stop *me* from wanting to put *my* filthy paws all over you."

She pulls away and flicks her challenging blue eyes up at me. "And you only get to put your hands on me because you have *my* permission, not Remy's."

She's got me there. "Excellent point, Miss Holt." I slide out of the bench and hold out my hand to her. "Let's go give your brother a break."

"You can't serve drinks at your own party," she protests, slipping her hand into mine.

"I'm not planning to."

"You're just going to sit at the bar like a scary bulldog chasing people away."

I love the way my girl just *gets* me. "Woof, woof, baby."

Her eyes narrow and her lips flatten with the effort of not laughing.

I walk behind Molly, keeping my hands at her waist to help her navigate the crowd—and because I enjoy touching her every second I can.

A large hand with several thick, metal rings on each finger waves in front of my face to catch my attention. Rooster's bearded face grins at me. I stop and tug on Molly's belt loops, so we can say hi to the Lost Kings downstate VP.

"Congratulations." He slaps my shoulder hard enough to knock over a rhino.

"Thanks."

His biker brother, Dex, joins us, also offering a congratulatory backslap. "I tried to warn you that was going to be a shit show," he says, cutting right to it.

I shrug and nod, not really looking for brotherly advice or opinions at the moment. He means well, but I'm not in the mood. "I survived, but I definitely wouldn't do it again."

"Thank God," Molly grumbles.

Dex chuckles. His gaze slides between Molly and me, noting how I've got my arm around her out in the open.

"How're you doing, Molly?" he asks.

"Good. I was on my way to help my brother out." She flicks an amused look up at me. "But someone thinks I need my own personal bouncer."

Dex and Rooster both shake with laughter.

"No comment," Dex says.

"Emily here with you?" I ask him.

"She is." He nods to the far corner, across from the bar. "Playing darts with the ladies."

"Come say hi to me." Molly waves over her shoulder as she continues moving through the crowd.

Rooster eyes me. "We will. Don't go far, Stonewall."

I tilt my head toward Molly, now a few steps ahead of me. "You know where I'll be."

Molly slips behind the counter, picks up an apron and wraps it around her waist. Instead of walking through the crowd again, I also slide in behind the counter, intent on popping out at the other end and perching my ass on the last stool, where I'll have the best view of everyone approaching the bar.

Remy stops me with a hand on my chest. "You done mauling my sister?"

I brush his hand off me, but he's still in my way. "Not even close."

"Griff," Molly rests one hand on each of our shoulders and leans up on her tiptoes, "will you please tell my brother that I can handle things for a few minutes so he can take a break?"

I lift my eyebrows at Remy.

He turns his head, quickly scanning the room.

"Fine." He sets the rag in his hands on the counter. "I won't go far," he says to Molly. "If you get a request for something you don't know how to make, just offer them a beer."

She nods quickly. "I can do that."

I push him down the line and out from behind the bar.

He lifts his head, searching the room or checking to see that everything's still intact. "I'm gonna run in back." His gaze shifts to Molly, then back to me. "You'll—"

"Be right here." I settle myself on the last stool.

He nods once and takes off.

I swivel from side to side on the stool and cross my arms over my chest, trying to look more like a mascot than a guard dog.

A short blonde woman rests her silver cowgirl boots on the lower rung of one of the stools next to me and boosts herself up to lean over the counter. "Can you make me a Paloma?" she asks Molly in a thick Texan accent.

I recognize the accent and the woman it belongs to. "Hey, Shelby. How've you been?"

She whips her head my way, then beams. "Howdy, Griff! I've been lookin' for ya." Her lips quirk with amusement. "Rooster said you came this way. I shoulda been lookin' for Molly, knowin' you wouldn't be strayin' far."

Molly's waiting on the other side of the bar with a frozen deer-in-the-headlights expression. I can't tell if it's because she doesn't know how to make a Paloma or she's starstruck from being face-to-face with her favorite country singer. Probably a little of both.

"Did she ask for a Paloma?" Another girl with long black and rainbow-colored hair slips behind the bar. "I can show you how to make it," she says to Molly.

"Griff," Shelby says to me. "This is Jiggy's sister, Jezzie. Have you met—"

"We've met." I nod once. "How are you?"

"Fine," she answers in a perpetually bored tone.

Like her brother, she's not much of a talker. But unlike Jigsaw, Jezzie's kind and patient, as she shows Molly how to blend the tequila and grapefruit juice cocktail.

Molly's scrunched expression seems torn between thankful for the help and wanting this strange woman off her turf, but she listens to Jezzie's instructions and finally passes the drink to Shelby with a shaking hand.

"Thank you much." Shelby takes a quick sip and sets the glass down. "Perfect."

"So, why were you looking for me?" I ask Shelby.

"Oh! Ha! Vegas. I'm supposed to ask you about Vegas." She takes another sip of her drink.

Before she elaborates, Jigsaw and Rooster approach us. Rooster rests his hands on Shelby's shoulders and she tips her head back to smile at him.

Jigsaw scowls at his sister. "Why are you back there?"

"I was helping." She rolls her eyes. "I've tended bar. I know what I'm doing."

Jiggy huffs an annoyed breath but doesn't argue. The two of them never seem to get along.

"She taught me how to make a Paloma," Molly says.

"Anyone bother you tonight, Molly?" he asks.

"No."

He pats the knife at his side. "Just let me know."

Her eyes widen and then she bursts into laughter. "Will do."

"I'm afraid to ask," I mutter.

"While you were off frolicking with ring bunnies, your girl was gettin' groped by customers," Jigsaw says.

"For fuck's sake," Rooster mutters.

"What?" Jigsaw's eyes widen until he looks like a cartoon of an overgrown, innocent child. "He asked."

"Actually, I said I was *afraid* to ask," I point out.

"Which is code for *tell me more*." He flashes a serial killer smile at me.

"Lord." Jezzie tips her head back and raises her hands toward the ceiling. "I can *not* with him. So rude."

"I'm blunt," Jigsaw insists. "There's a difference."

"Not really," Jezzie says.

Molly shakes with laughter. "Have you met my brother? That's why they don't like each other. They're too similar."

"I take offense to that," Jigsaw says.

Jezzie leans close to Molly. "If you need help, holler. I'll go work the other end."

"Thank you."

Molly moves to the center of the bar to help someone else. Jigsaw and Rooster move in closer, boxing me in, which I can't say I'm thrilled about.

"How's this Vegas thing going down?" Jigsaw asks.

I stare at him, surprised he gives a fuck since he basically just called me an asshole. "Why do you care?"

"Don't get twisted because I busted your nuts." He casts a look Shelby's way. "We all know you've been exonerated from cheating on your sweet little girlfriend."

Shelby's grave face peeks around Rooster's side. "I wish you woulda come an' talked to me before you did that show. I coulda warned you those maggots are devious as all get-out."

One corner of my mouth hikes up. I appreciate the sentiment, but even with the warning, I still probably would've done the show. "Molly likes to refer to them as demon clowns."

She hoots with laughter. "Damn straight they are. Bloodsucking demon clowns. All of 'em. Seriously, though, it musta been rough." She holds out her fist and I tap my knuckles against hers. "Reality survivor club."

"Thanks. Don't tell me you watched it?"

"Hell naw. But I caught some of your fights."

I shrug. "Only parts worth watching."

She nods and swivels toward the bar to talk to Molly again.

"So," Jigsaw says. "I take it you're going to need an entourage with you in Vegas."

I stare at him. "What?"

He lifts his shoulders in an isn't-it-obvious shrug. "All those fight guys travel in packs."

"Because you're so knowledgeable on this topic?" Rooster says, side-eyeing his friend.

"I know things. What're you gonna do, Griff? Show up to fight week with just Remy scowling by your side? You need more people around you." Jigsaw slaps his friend's chest but focuses his attention on me. "We've handled security for Shelby's last two tours. We know what we're doing."

"Security." I slide my gaze between the two of them. "I can't afford that."

"That's where the whole brotherhood thing comes in," Rooster says, as if I'm dense.

"Yeah, but I'm not a patched member of *your* club," I remind him in an equally *are you dumb* tone.

"Bro, you and Remy were there," he lowers his voice and leans away from Shelby's stool, "when Shelby was in trouble. I owe you."

"You don't owe me anything." I snort and shake my head. We didn't do a damn thing helpful on that trip. "We got there after everything went down."

"Yeah, but you came." Rooster's solemn expression doesn't change. "That shit matters."

I *would* feel better going with more people, especially since Molly will be there. I'll be tied up with pre-fight interviews and training. I don't want her to feel abandoned. And let's face it, it's not exactly hardship for a bunch of bikers to hang out in Vegas for a weekend.

While I'm mulling it over, Remy returns from wherever he went. He slaps my shoulder and stands next to me.

"What're you doing with the bar?" Jigsaw asks him.

Remy crosses his arms over his chest. "What am I doing with it for what?"

"When your boy's in Vegas," Jigsaw says. "I assume you're going?"

Not sure how I feel about being called Remy's "boy."

Dex joins our circle, almost like they planned their ambush in advance.

"Where are we at?" Dex asks Rooster.

What the fuck is happening?

"Asking if he needs help covering the bar for Vegas," Jigsaw says.

Remy shrugs. "I'll have coverage. Lynette and Anderson will be fine for a weekend."

"Emily and I can help you out," Dex offers.

Remy frowns. "Does *Emily* know you're offering her services?"

He chuckles. "She likes your place. She's between jobs right now. She won't mind helping a small local business. I'm out this way all the time. It's not a problem. And it's not like I don't have experience."

"Your strip club isn't quite the same as my Nana and Grandpop's tavern," Remy laughs. "But I get your point."

"Yeah, it'll probably be a lot less drama than what I deal with," Dex says.

I glance at Remy. "They did say I can bring whoever I want with me." I don't want to ask for his opinion in front of the Lost Kings and accidentally insult them when they're making a generous offer.

"Eraser's already committed but Vapor's probably not going to be able to go, so the more people the better." He pops his fists together and shoots a quick glare at me. "It'll make me feel better about Molly being there."

"Shelby wants to go too." Rooster rests his arm over her shoulders, drawing her back into the conversation. "If you don't mind."

Have an actual celebrity in my entourage? "No, of course not." Molly will be so excited to hang out with Shelby, maybe she won't worry about me as much.

"Oh, oh, oh!" Shelby leans forward. "I'm supposed to ask you if you need a *sponsor*."

I stare at her, unsure of how to answer.

"Not me." She waves her hand in front of her face. "I told Dawson I know you." She glances up at Rooster as if asking if she should continue. He shrugs. "He sponsors fighters sometimes. *Hates* the guy you're fighting." She snaps her fingers a few times. "Magic?"

I nod quickly.

"He *really* wants to see you punch his porch lights out," Shelby says.

Remy snorts at her colorful description.

This is so fucking weird.

"Well, give it a think," she says. "I'll have him reach out to you."

"All right."

Rooster lifts his chin at me before leaving with Shelby.

"Don't sweat it, Griff." Jigsaw says in a low, confidential tone. "Dawson Roads has more money than he knows what to do with."

"Yeah, but still..." I shake my head like it'll help me sort all the information that's been thrown at me.

But the surprises aren't finished coming.

The shadow of the enforcer for the Lost Kings falls over us. Wrath's big enough to block out half the room. Jigsaw moves to the stool Shelby had been sitting on.

"Welcome back." Wrath stretches out his hand and I give it a quick shake.

"Thanks for coming."

He stares at me for a few seconds. "The fuck happened to your face?"

I shoot a glare at Remy. "Some cocky asshole wanted to go a few rounds."

Remy raises his hand, then winces from his still-sore ribs. "Hi, it's me. I'm the cocky asshole."

Wrath rumbles with laughter. "Good to see nothing changes with you two." His gaze narrows on Remy. "Who won?"

"I tapped out," Remy admits without posturing. "He was three seconds from choking me unconscious."

Wrath has always appreciated directness. He nods slowly, then focuses on me again. "Looked like you learned some new techniques on the show?" He waves his big hand in front of my face. "Besides all that other embarrassing bullshit."

I pinch the bridge of my nose. "Don't tell me you watched it."

"Fuck no. Just some of the highlights Trinity showed me."

"You let your wife watch that?" Remy asks. "A show full of shirtless beefcakes clowning around and showing off?"

Wrath's scary eyes turn toward Remy. He runs his hand over his chest. "She has access to the beefiest of beefcakes. Why would I care what she watches?"

I side-eye Remy. "Does anyone other than cartoon characters still say beefcake?"

One corner of Remy's mouth slides up. "I was trying to pick a word from back in the olden days that he'd recognize."

Instead of punching Remy through the wall, Wrath laughs. "I've forgotten more than you'll ever know, kid."

Wrath shifts his attention back to me. "Where are you going to train for this fight? Sully's place?"

"Seems like the obvious choice since that's where I got recruited for the show. Jake and Sully said they'd both work with me."

"If you don't mind the longer drive, you're welcome to train at Furious too," Wrath offers. "I'm a little rusty on the more technical shit, but I can help you focus on the endurance."

Rusty. I doubt that. Wrath was lethal in the underground circuit years ago. "You mean you'll whip me while I run on a treadmill?" I joke.

"Yeah, something like that."

"He's gonna start running with me in the mornings again," Remy says. "Once he gets clearance from a doctor about his knee."

Oh, that's rich coming from Remy since he *kicked* that knee. I slowly turn and glare at him.

"Get that shit checked out first," Wrath says. "Then stop by whenever. If I'm not there, Murphy can help you."

"Thanks. I would like to split my time."

Sully's gym is closer to me, but it's small and fills up quickly. Wrath's place—Furious Fitness—expanded a few years ago and has a lot more equipment.

"Good deal." Wrath reaches out and pats my shoulder. "We'll help you get ready for fight camp and make sure you win this thing."

After he and Jigsaw leave, Remy and I are alone—at least for now. He quickly pushes me behind the bar and into the corner next to a mirrored shelf.

"What the fuck?" he says in my ear.

"Yeah, no shit. I'm feelin' all kinds of love bombed right now."

"You need an entourage. Let's find you a sponsor. Come train at my gym." He lists off all the things that were just thrown our way.

"It's about them showing us they'll hold up their end of the support if we form the support club," I say.

"Or there's something else in it for them," Remy finishes.

Realization runs over me like a herd of elephants. I've been so overwhelmed with figuring out how to structure my training cycle, I haven't thought much further than the fight itself. Which is really fucking stupid since Remy and I have run an illegal gambling ring for years.

"It's Vegas." How did I not see this coming?

Remy nods slowly. "You're the underdog."

"Fucking seriously?" A rush of annoyance washes over me. I proved myself week after week on *SUF*. It's not like all those fights aren't available for everyone to watch and see what I can do in the ring.

"It's your first *pro* fight. As far as everyone's concerned, you're unproven."

That means I'm right. "So, Lost Kings have a vested interest in my training before the fight and my safety *at* the fight. They're planning to place heavy bets on me to win."

"Then I guess you better win." Remy's expression remains dead serious. "Because I *really* don't want to be chopped into pieces and tossed in the Hudson River."

CHAPTER FORTY-SIX

Molly

ALL WINTER LONG GRIFF AND I WORKED ON RESTORING my car. Every weekend I came home we spent at least a few hours at the garage putting it back together.

I aced my first semester exams, and I'm halfway through my second semester of college.

Griff hums *Happy Birthday* to me as we walk around the Malibu.

Happiness explodes in my chest as my gaze slides over every inch of my beautiful car. "It's done."

"Well, there will always be something to tweak or swap." Griff swipes his hands on a rag and grins at me. "But for now, yes."

"Just in time for spring break." I jump and throw my arms around his shoulders. He catches me around the waist, lifting me.

Eagerly, I kiss his cheek, his beard stubble a slight sting against my lips. He turns and his plush lips land on mine, easing the brief sting.

He lifts me higher, breaking our kiss for a moment. Our mouths collide again. I press harder and he groans against my lips, giving me room to slide the tip of my tongue against his.

Still holding me, Griff walks the few feet to the car, pinning me against the driver's side door. I wrap my legs around him, anchoring myself. His mouth melts against mine. I flick my tongue against his, savoring his familiar taste.

Between our clothes and coveralls there are too many barriers in our way. Certain he has me, I slide my hand to his chest and tug at the zipper.

He pulls back, his lips shiny and tilting up at the corners. "What are you doing?"

"It's hot." I pull at the thick zipper harder.

"You're hot." He sets me on my feet and drags my zipper down the front of my coveralls. They're practically pristine next to his, loudly announcing which one of us actually works on cars and which one tinkers with them.

While I wriggle out of the stiff pants, Griff takes a few steps back and sheds his coveralls. He scoops mine up and sets both on the bench. I lean against the car and crook my finger. "Please come back here."

He scoops me into his arms and spins us in a slow circle. "Don't you want to take it for a ride?"

"I want to take *you* for a ride." I laugh and kiss him again. "In the back seat. Watching *you* work hard all day has *me* worked up."

"You worked hard too." He carries me to the back of the car and sets me on the trunk. "Let me close the garage door. We don't want spectators."

"Hurry." I tease the bottom of my tank top up over my stomach.

Outside, a loud grumbly engine pulls into the parking lot. A small rusty pickup truck that looks like it's being held together with duct tape and coat hangers screeches to a stop.

Griff frowns and moves to the edge of the garage. "We're not open, sir." He edges sideways, blocking my view of the unexpected visitor.

"Are ya sure?" a man says.

"Yup. I'm closing now."

"That's too bad." There's a scraping of feet against gravel.

This guy can't take a hint.

"I really need something," he says.

Griff lets out a weary sigh. "What is it? If it's something small, I can probably—"

I lean sideways to see what made Griff stop.

A skinny, dirty-looking man in tattered jeans and a hole-filled sleeveless shirt thrusts both hands forward. A black pistol's held in his tight grip. Aimed right at Griff's face. "I need you and your little girlfriend to back the fuck up."

CHAPTER FORTY-SEVEN

Griff

"ARE YOU SURE YOU WANT TO DO THIS, MAN?" I SAY IN A low, calm tone.

Behind me, Molly scrambles off the car, landing with a squeak against the concrete. Instead of putting distance between herself and the gun-waving lunatic, she rushes to my side.

I curl one arm back, keeping her behind me.

"You realize this is Lost Kings MC territory, right?" There's a fifty-fifty chance that's enough to scare him away.

He twitches and glances over his shoulder. My stomach drops with every jerky movement he makes while he's holding that gun. "So what? No it's not. They don't run this far west."

"Yeah, they do," I say with exaggerated patience. "And my club's under their protection." We haven't quite *formed* the club, *yet*, but Greasy doesn't need to know that. Anything to get him and his gun away from Molly and me.

"That ain't got nothing to do with me. Or our business."

Fighting the urge to take Molly's hand and run outside, I keep slowly backing us farther into the garage. Lots of tools that could be used as weapons are only a few feet away. If only I hadn't put everything back as soon as we finished.

"Do you have me confused with someone else?" I ask.

"Don't think so." He takes a few steps closer.

Are we being pranked? This lowlife has his hair slicked back with so much gel—or grease—and twitches so often, he's a living, breathing caricature of every strung-out junkie who ever robbed a liquor store on a cop drama.

Those jerky movements are a problem. One wrong twitch and he could accidentally blow a hole through Molly or me. Slow as possible, I hold my arms out in front of me, to show him I have no weapons and ease my body fully in front of Molly's. She curls her hands into the back of my shirt, her warmth and fear soaking into my skin.

"Where's she goin'?" he shouts. "Hey, stay put, bitch."

I grind my teeth. "She's got nothing to do with this." *Neither do I,* but that's beside the point. "And the way you're waving that gun around's making me nervous."

"Aw, that's sweet. You want to play human bullet vest for your little sweetie?" He licks his slimy lips and leans sideways, trying to look at Molly. "I get it. She's a pretty one."

Black dread expands in my stomach. But I keep my face blank. He'll have to put every single one of those bullets in me to get to Molly.

"Just take it easy and tell me what you want," I say, keeping my voice calm and even.

"Fine," he spits. "She can stay back there. But I want to see her hands."

Molly rests both of her hands at my waist, then flashes her palms at him.

"Good." Greasy paces backward and rubs the barrel of the gun across his forehead. If he does that again, I might have time to take him to the ground before he gets off a shot.

No. My gaze pings around the garage. It's too tight in here. A bullet could ricochet and hit Molly. I can't risk that.

He's so careless, maybe we'll get lucky and he'll accidentally shoot *himself.*

"Look," I say, a hell of a lot calmer than I feel. "Tell me what you want, and I'll see if I can help you."

Get him talking. Divert his attention. Grab that fucking gun. If I was the only one here, that's what I would've done by now.

"You're Griffin, right?" He runs his beady eyes up and down me.

"Christ, she wasn't kiddin'. You're a big dude." He lets out an unhinged cackle and waves the gun at me.

"She? Who?" As soon as I ask, my blood runs cold.

Tanya Royal. Who the fuck else but my junkie mother would bring this craziness into my life?

I'm shocked it's taken this long for one of her dealers to show up looking for money. Maybe her lowlife friends don't watch reality TV. I haven't spent a lot of time worrying about it but in the back of my mind, I've been waiting for the day when she—or someone she owes —shows up looking for money.

I guess that day is today.

"Your mother skipped town." He *tsks* at me like a cartoon gangster. "She owes some people money."

Of course she does.

"She says she's clean now," he adds.

Well, at least that's something.

He lowers the gun to mid-thigh. It's still aimed in our general direction but at least it's not pointed at my chest anymore. "That don't mean she ain't gotta pay her debts, you know? Everyone's gotta pay."

"Where is she?" I desperately want to somehow signal to Molly she needs to drop to the ground and take cover behind the car if I make a move. But how? All the training I've done. All the times I've taught her how to defend herself, why didn't we ever come up with some sort of plan or signal for a situation like this?

"How the fuck should I know?" He shrugs, holding his hands—and the gun—out wide.

Christ, if he wasn't armed, I could've taken him to the floor ten times by now. But this isn't a cage match.

I lower one hand and slowly reach behind me, tapping Molly's leg and pointing to the floor. Who the fuck knows if she can even see what I'm doing.

But a second later, she gently squeezes my side.

That's my girl.

I take a deep breath and blow it out slowly. The next time he points that gun elsewhere, I'm going for him.

"So, who does my mother owe?" I ask.

"A guy I work for." He paces closer. "It doesn't matter."

"It matters to *me*. If you expect me to give you money, I want to make sure her tab's paid in full and I don't see you again."

"What? You think I'm gonna give you a receipt or something?" He flashes a dirty-toothed grin.

Behind me, it feels like Molly's sliding down to the floor, using my body and our gunman's inattention as cover.

"How much?" I ask. *Just keep him talking.*

"Twenty k."

I choke on a laugh. "You think I have twenty thousand dollars in my pocket?"

He glances around the garage. "You got tools and shit here."

"This isn't my place."

"Ain't my problem."

My blood's boiling but I pretend to slump my shoulders and look defeated. "If I put together that kind of cash, I'm gonna need some assurances that this won't happen again," I say. "I'm not an ATM for my mother."

"I'll get him on the phone for ya." He reaches in his pocket, lowering the gun in the process.

I'll never have a better chance than this. I launch myself forward, wrap one hand around the barrel of the gun, forcing it down. With my other hand, I grip his wrist and give it a vicious twist, slowly rotating the gun until it's pointing at his stomach. He screams and drops to the floor, his bony knees making a sick thud against the concrete.

"Stop! Stop!" he screams.

In an organized fight, hell, even in an underground match, I would've released him by now. But this is life or death. I yank the gun out of his hand, but keep rotating his wrist until there's a sickening, but satisfying, *snap*.

He screams and his eyes bug as he stares at his hand. I set the gun on the roof of Molly's car and curl my fingers in his shirt, dragging him up. I slam my fist into his face twice, then drop him.

Behind me there's a scraping and a clang. Molly rushes forward, a crowbar clutched in her hands. She raises it sideways like a field hockey stick and plows it into the back of his knee.

He shrieks again, clutches his dangling hand to his chest and half-rolls, half-crawls toward the open garage door.

Molly brings the crowbar down again, smashing his ankle. The tip hits the concrete floor with a hard clang, probably rattling her teeth. The man howls and rolls onto his back.

She opens her hands and the crowbar clatters onto the floor.

I stare at Molly for a few stunned seconds. "I had him, Muffin."

Her wide, unblinking eyes don't seem to focus on anything at first, then slowly slide my way. "He could still walk with a broken wrist."

Who is this woman? "Good point."

Heart still hammering, I rush to the wall and slap my hand over the button to close the garage door.

The guy flops and drags himself faster over the dirty concrete.

He won't make it in time, so I leave him be.

Everyone, even this greasy piece of shit, deserves the delusion of hope.

CHAPTER FORTY-EIGHT

Molly

"IF YOU GIVE GRIFF ONE MORE DIRTY LOOK," I WARN MY brother. My threat's empty since I can't think of anything that would actually scare Remy.

The tension in his face fades into a smile. "What? You gonna stuff my shoes full of paper again?"

"Maybe." I cross my aching arms over my chest, then release them. "It's not Griff's fault." My eyes water and my throat tightens as all the fear of what just happened ripples over me. "He...he put himself between a *gun* and me."

Griff pulls me into his arms, wrapping himself around my body like a cocoon of protection. "Shhh." He kisses the top of my head. "We're okay now. It's okay."

"Why'd you do that?" I rasp. "You could've—"

"That's just how I'm built, baby. I didn't think about it."

He knows he could've been shot, right? His heart thumps wildly against my ear as I press myself tighter to his chest. At least he's not as calm as he seems on the outside.

"I was scared as shit he was going to accidentally fire the gun," he says to my brother.

"Well, he's not shooting anything now."

The robber's zip-tied ten different ways into what looks like an uncomfortable position on the garage floor in front of my car.

Griff's arms tighten around me. "What the fuck made you grab a crowbar?"

I pull back so I can see his face. "We're in a garage. It was the first thing I saw."

Remy snorts. "You're turning my sister into a serial killer."

I turn and glare at him. "I'd argue you've *both* contributed to my serial killer education." I hold up one fist. "Who's been teaching me how to defend myself since I was five?"

"She hasn't killed anyone," Griff says. "Don't put ideas in her head."

"So, what are *we* doing with him?" Remy asks.

"After I called you, I called Jigsaw and Dex. I assume they'll spread the word."

"Thank fuck Jerry's off in Nova Scotia and the rest of his employees are slackers." Griff runs his hands through his hair and turns his head toward the office. "This could've been really fucked if more people were here."

"Guys, aren't we going to call the *police*?" It seems like one of them should've done *that* by now.

Remy tilts his head and studies me for a minute. "Yeah, I'm sure they'll assume Griff's completely innocent."

"He is!"

Tension pinches Remy's expression. "He doesn't need the publicity. Not before the fight."

Griff turns haunted eyes on me. "What am I going to say? My estranged mother almost got us killed because she owes some drug dealers? That's *all* people will be talking about leading up to the fight."

I don't want to do a damn thing that protects his mother, but his concerns are valid. The promoters would love a juicy story to bring more attention to the fight. Anything to sell more tickets. Even if they spin it to make Griff look like a hero, all that exposure will shine an ugly spotlight on his family demons.

"Lost Kings always want to know if anyone's moving product through their territory," Remy says to Griff.

"They might've lost the battle with the hillbilly heroin," Griff mutters. "That shit's everywhere."

Remy shrugs. "They'll still want to question him. Find out who he works for. Anything they can get out of him." Remy slaps his hands together like he's dusting off the responsibility of the robber's dwindling life expectancy.

"Are they going to...*kill him*?" I whisper.

Remy stares at me like that's his last concern in the world.

Griff pulls the magazine from the robber's gun out of his pocket. "It was loaded, Molly. He could've killed *us*."

"I need you to go home before they get here," Remy says.

The distant roar of engines speeding down the road draws the three of us to the open garage door. *Too late.*

"Shit. How'd they make it from Empire that fast?" Remy asks.

"Jiggy's been out this way a lot lately." Griff shrugs. "You want to ask him why, be my guest."

"Jigsaw threatened to cut off a customer's fingers for touching my leg last summer." I let out an awkward chuckle. "Imagine what he'll do to this guy."

Griff raises two eyebrows at my brother. "See. She's fine." He rests his hand on my shoulder and squeezes.

The roar becomes deafening as two Harleys pull into the parking lot.

I back farther into the garage.

The gunman stares up at me from the floor, the whites of his eyes bright in the surrounding darkness. He yells into the gag my brother stuffed in his mouth and thrusts his bound wrists at me.

"No can do." I shrug. "You should've listened to my boyfriend and beat it when you had the chance."

"Get away from him," Remy says.

The engines idle outside for a few seconds, then cut out.

I return to Griff's side. He quietly hands me his car keys. "I want you to take my car and go home after we give them a rundown of what happened, okay? Don't talk to anyone about this."

I pocket the keys and scowl at him. "How dumb do you think I am?" I gesture to the crowbar leaning against the back tire of my car. "I'm probably on the hook for some kind of felony assault myself. You had already subdued him when I attacked." Nerves keep forcing me to ramble and make up stuff to put Griff's mind at ease. "We're in this together."

He hooks his arm around my neck and pulls me against him. "I love you so much, baby," he murmurs. "I'm so fucking sorry this happened. I don't know what I would've done if you'd gotten hurt. I've never been so scared in my life."

I slide my arms around him and squeeze. "I couldn't tell you were scared. And I never doubted you were going to disarm him."

He pushes me back and cups my cheeks. "We need to work out some sort of plan or signal. I didn't know how else to tell you to get down on the floor and take cover."

"Duh. I figured when you tapped my hip, that's what you were trying to tell me to do." I point to the passenger side of my car. "I was planning to crouch down and hide behind the front corner."

A rush of harsh laughter bursts out of him and he hugs me again. "I hope it's the last time we ever have to worry about it."

Griff

The need to keep Molly close to reassure myself she's okay keeps warring with my need to keep her safe from the bloodshed that's about to happen.

I might have learned a long time ago how many shades of gray there are to life, but I'd rather have Molly stay innocent for as long as possible. Although her brutal use of the crowbar and rather quick acceptance that we're not calling the cops, suggests her innocence already slipped away.

Several pairs of boots scrape over the gravel outside. Remy leads Jigsaw and Wrath into the garage. *Fuck.* As enforcer, it's Wrath's job to take care of threats in his club's territory but I don't want him questioning Molly's ability to keep her mouth shut.

Wrath stops a few feet away from us and crosses his arms over his wide chest. "Stonewall, don't you have a fight you're supposed to be training for?" His disappointed dad tone and scowl hits me in an unexpected way.

I let out a harsh laugh. "Trust me, this isn't how I wanted to spend my afternoon."

He lifts his chin. "Nice car. Is it yours?"

"It's Molly's." I wrap my arm around her shoulders. "We were finishing up some work on it when that greasy little weasel over there showed up and pulled a gun on us."

Wrath's scary gaze settles on Molly. "You all right?"

She nods quickly.

"What'd he want?" Wrath asks.

A knot of embarrassment twists in my stomach but I meet Wrath's eyes and tell him the truth. "My mom's got...issues. She moved down to Jersey to start over a few months ago. I haven't been in contact with her since I got home. She left me some messages looking for money while I was on the show but..." I shrug. "I tried helping her out and taking care of her when she was here. And fuck knows she's drained a lot of money out of me over the years, but this is the first time someone's ever showed up to collect from *me*." I need to make it clear this isn't an on-going issue I've been hiding from the club.

"We don't know who he works for," Remy adds.

Jigsaw lifts a giant pair of bolt cutters, his eyes wide with wild, gleeful malice. "He's got ten chances to give up a name."

"Twenty if you start with his toes," Wrath suggests.

"This isn't my place." I hold out my arms, indicating the garage isn't the right location for the interrogation they're planning.

"That room in the bar's basement still available?" Wrath asks Remy.

Molly turns her wide-eyed stare my way. Until now, she'd been doing a great impression of a rock. Silent and completely still. She really doesn't need to be here for this conversation.

"You need to go home." I rest my hand on her lower back and give her a nudge.

"Not so fast, little girl." Wrath cocks his head and studies her. "What'd you see today?"

"Leave her out of it," Remy says.

Molly lets out a slow breath and flicks her eyes toward her brother. "I was *in it* when that guy pointed a gun at me. And even deeper in it when I smashed his leg with the crowbar."

Jigsaw reels back and cackles. "Guess that ruthless streak runs through your blood."

Remy sighs.

"Griff had him," Molly says. "But I already had the crowbar in my hands and I was afraid he'd try to run." She lifts her gaze and meets Wrath's stare head-on. "But if anyone outside of the four of you asks, all I saw was the inside of this garage while Griff and I were working on my car."

Wrath nods once, then turns his hard stare on me. "She's your girl."

He's not asking but I answer anyway. "Yes."

"She's *my* sister," Remy says. "She won't say anything."

"Okay," Wrath says.

Those two syllables land heavy. If Molly breathes a word of this, Remy and I will be punished for it.

Wrath pulls out his phone. "I don't think she should be at your house alone, though. I'm gonna ask Dex to stop by and watch your house until—"

"No," Remy says. "She can go over to Vapor and Juliet's place. She'll be safe with them and no one has a reason to look for her there."

Molly nods quickly. "I'd rather do that."

"All right."

I take Molly's hand and walk her over to the door leading out of the garage. "I'll have Remy bring me over there to pick you up later."

Outside we stop at my car and I open the door for her. "Be careful."

She lifts her chin. "What're you going to do with his truck?"

Shit, one of us should've moved it. "Don't worry about it."

"All right." She leans up and kisses my cheek. "I love you."

"Love you too." I watch her leave, then return to the garage.

The guys have our robber loaded sideways on a creeper. "Murphy's bringing a van," Wrath explains to me.

Wrath rips the guy's gag off.

"Are you talking, or are we snipping?" Jigsaw asks, showing the guy the bolt cutters.

In between sobs and sniveling over his broken wrist, black eyes, and shattered ankle, he gives up the name of his boss. I don't recognize it but Wrath's eyes light with interest.

Outside, tires crunch over the gravel. I grab the gag and shove it back into the guy's mouth.

"It's probably Murphy." Wrath jerks his head toward the door.

Remy opens one of the large, overhead garage doors and guides Murphy as he backs a plain, black van inside.

"What's up?" Murphy steps out of the van and pulls a black knit hat over his unruly dark red hair and slips on a pair of black leather gloves.

"I'll fill you in," Jigsaw says.

"Can we leave the bikes here?" Wrath asks me.

"Yeah. No problem." I lift my chin toward the parking lot. "I gotta get rid of his truck."

"Is that piece of shit out there his?" Wrath asks. "I thought it belonged to the shop."

"No, that's what he came in."

"Fuck, Griff. It's been sittin' out there all this time."

"You honestly think anyone's gonna come asking about this guy?" Remy asks.

"That's not the point," Wrath growls, his eyes narrowing. "You got a place you can get rid of it?"

"Yeah," I answer slowly. "There's a junkyard I have access to."

"All right. You two take care of that." Wrath slaps one hand on Remy's shoulder and the other on mine, his firm grip demanding no argument. "We'll take care of him."

My jaw tightens with determination. "This is my situation. I'll handle it."

"Ah, so strong and yet so wrong," Jigsaw rhymes, shaking his head at me.

It's probably the tension of the afternoon snapping, but I burst out laughing. "What?"

Wrath's stern expression doesn't waver. "We need you focused on training for that fight," he says. "Not gettin' distracted with a side quest. Dump the truck. That's all I need from you."

"You know I have no problem getting my hands dirty," I protest.

"We know," Murphy cuts in, his tone as forceful as Wrath's. "You also need to take care of that truck right now."

Arguing with him is pointless. "I'll get it done."

CHAPTER FORTY-NINE

Molly

AFTER THE ATTEMPTED ROBBERY, I NEVER HEAR ABOUT the guy again. I put it out of my mind and focus on school. Griff focuses on his training.

I can't be here to say goodbye when he leaves tomorrow morning. I'll be in class when his plane takes off. So he drove out to school to take me out to dinner tonight. Now that we're back at my dorm, I don't want to say goodbye.

I'm trying to stay strong, but I hate that Griff's leaving me again. At least this time there aren't as many unknowns. He has a schedule for fight camp that he's shared with me. We have plans to talk every day. The only filming that will go on at the camp is to gather footage to market the fight to pay-per-view audiences.

"In three weeks, you'll be in my arms again," he promises. "You're going to study hard and ace your finals for me, okay?"

I nod and swallow hard, trying to will any tears away.

"I'll try to scope out some good restaurants for us to try," he continues.

"No, don't do anything that distracts you from training for the fight. You need to make that guy eat every insult he's hurled your way the last couple of weeks."

His lips twitch. "You caught some of those interviews, huh?"

"Uh, yeah. My YouTube feed is full of them. *I* want to knock that guy out. Diane wasn't kidding about how obnoxious he is."

"Underhill *hates* him. I think training me is part of his personal vendetta against the guy."

"He's certainly worked you hard these last few weeks." I run my hands over his sturdy shoulders and granite-like arms.

"He and Wrath got along like vinegar and baking soda. It was a real joy." He scoffs. "Camp's going to be even more intense. Seven days a week. Coach has someone coming specifically to work on my takedown defense and strength work."

I don't have anything to add to that, so I reach up and wrap my arms around his neck. "You're going to be careful and watch your knee, right?" I ask.

"Yup." He lifts me off the ground and breathes deep, like he's inhaling as much of me as he can, then sets me down. "They've got a good recovery program there. I'll have access to cryotherapy and a physical therapist. Trust me, no one wants me to get injured before this fight."

"Good." It's getting harder to look at his handsome face. Every time I do, my heart squeezes with anguish.

"I'm going to call you every morning," he promises.

"And every night?"

"You know it." He settles his hands on my waist. "No more YouTube. No social media. Just concentrate on your last few weeks of classes. You can catch up on all that stuff on the plane when you fly out to meet me."

"Okay."

"Promise?" He teases his fingers under my sweatshirt, tickling my sides.

Laughing, I twist away. "Yes, I promise."

The RA on my floor brushes by us, then stops. "Hey, Molly. Are you coming to the ping-pong tournament? We're getting pizza and baking cookies after."

I can't play ping-pong when my boyfriend's leaving.

"You should go," Griff urges in a low voice.

"Uh, yeah. Sure," I say, giving her a weak smile.

"Third floor lounge," she says, then opens the door and slips inside.

"That sounds fun." Griff's forced upbeat tone doesn't work on me.

"It sounds silly."

"Please try to go and have a good time," he pleads. "I'll feel better if I know you're busy while I'm driving home."

"I hate that you're driving home all alone."

An affectionate smile curves his lips. "We talked about this. One of us was going to end up making the drive alone. I'd rather it's me."

"Fine." I pout and he leans down, drawing me into his arms again.

"You know when you make that face, I just want to kiss you." He presses his lips to mine and slides his tongue along the seam of my lips. I open for him and he kisses me soft and slow. He tastes like the coffee and chocolate cake we shared after dinner. His hand cups the back of my head as he deepens the kiss. I press closer, gripping his shoulders, never wanting this to end.

"My beautiful girl," he whispers, staring into my eyes. "I promise you, we're going to spend the whole summer together. Doing anything and everything you want. Drive-ins, road trips, you name it, I'll give it to you."

I just want you to come home with me from Vegas in one piece.

Along with all the interviews of Magic, I'd also watched videos of what his *opponents* looked like after going five rounds.

In my heart, I know Griff's the better fighter. He's going to win.

But it doesn't mean he won't get injured in the process.

CHAPTER FIFTY

Molly

ALMOST A YEAR AGO, I WAS AT THIS VERY AIRPORT TRYING to escape my life. Escape my broken heart and all my memories of Griff.

Now, I'm sitting in a plush leather seat next to my brother, while we wait for his friends to arrive and board the private jet that will fly across the country to meet Griff in Las Vegas. I'm too anxious to appreciate the luxurious interior of the jet that looks more like the living room of a fancy house than an airplane.

I survived my first year of college. I didn't get the straight A's Griff wanted, but I came close. In a few weeks, I'll find out if I'm awarded the same scholarship money for next year.

"What're you thinking about?" Remy nudges my arm with his elbow. "Nervous about flying?"

"No." I turn and study his face, hidden behind dark sunglasses. "I was thinking how different things are from the last time I was here." I gesture toward the window looking out on the runway. "I didn't make it this far."

He slips his arm around my shoulders and squeezes me to his side. "I'm glad you didn't. We had an okay time, right? You were a good helper."

My lips curve. "Better than *okay*. I liked working with you." I bump my shoulder into him. "Are *you* nervous about flying?"

"Not really." He glances over his shoulder and lowers his voice.

"More worried about using up all these favors. This fancy jet—it doesn't belong to the Lost Kings, it belongs to a friend of theirs."

"Not just 'a friend.' Dawson Roads," I remind him in a hushed voice. "If we meet him, I'm afraid I'll pass out and make a fool out of myself."

Remy chuckles. "Don't do that. The jet's stopping in Tennessee to pick him up."

"Seriously?" My eyes bug out. "Does Griff know all these people are coming to his fight?"

"He knows."

Just what Griff needs. More pressure. I kept my promise to him and didn't watch any of the pre-fight press coverage. But last night, after I moved all my stuff out of the dorm and was home in my own bed, I gorged myself on everything I could find.

The hype about the Magic v. Stonewall match has been non-stop. Dozens of YouTube videos have been dedicated to dissecting Griff's strengths and weaknesses. So many commentators have had the audacity to label him the underdog in this fight. Talking about him as if he's a child entering the big boy world and about to get his ass whipped.

I can't wait for Griff to prove them wrong.

"Mornin'!" a soft southern voice drawls.

I sit straighter and flash what I hope isn't a deranged smile at Shelby as she slides into one of the seats across from us. Her fiancé Rooster nods and shakes my brother's hand and sits next to Shelby.

Jigsaw takes a seat on the long couch on the other side of the plane. "You nervous, Molly?"

"A little," I squeak.

"*Psh*. All that trash everyone's talkin' is 'cause they know Griff's about to turn things upside down," Shelby says.

"I meant the flight, songbird," Jigsaw says to her. "Of course she knows her man's gonna win."

"Is it your first flight?" Shelby asks me.

I glance at Remy. "We went to Disney when I was little, but I don't remember much of it."

Remy snorts. "You fell asleep on me before we even took off. Mom asked me not to move and wake you. She was afraid you'd

freak when the plane was taking off. You drooled all over my arm."
An affectionate smile plays over his face as he shares the embarrassing story.

"Aww, if that isn't the sweetest," Shelby says. "You're so lucky, Molly. I always wanted a big brother." Her voice falters for a second and then her cheeks pull up in a full smile. She tilts her head toward Jigsaw. "And now I do."

Rooster chuckles. "More than one."

"Yeah, but I'm her favorite." Jigsaw grins.

"Yes, you are," Shelby agrees.

Apparently she hasn't seen him with a pair of bolt cutters.
Or maybe she has.

I tilt my head and study my brother. "He's not so bad. I think I'll keep him."

"Thanks." Remy reaches over and roughs his hand over my hair.

Eraser and Ella board quickly, their steps slowing as they approach. "Shit," Eraser says, "I thought we were late."

"Nope," Rooster answers.

I stand and hug Ella, so happy she's coming with us. "Are you nervous, McMuffin?" she asks, pulling away.

Why does everyone keep asking me that? "No, just excited to see Griff. We talk every night but it's not the same."

"Glad he's taking your calls," Eraser says.

"Bro, he ain't callin' me either," Remy says. "They give him thirty minutes in the morning and thirty at night." He points at me. "He's using them all to call her."

"Is it training camp or prison?" Jigsaw asks.

"There's a strict schedule," I explain. "But at least no one's listening in on our calls or monitoring what he says."

A voice too soft to understand murmurs something over the loudspeaker. Shelby cocks her head. "I think we're taking off soon."

Eraser freezes, staring at the couch, then the group of four seats behind us.

"Oh!" Shelby stands. "Sit anywhere. Except the bedroom and that little nook outside the bedroom. That's where Dawson always parks himself."

"Thanks." Eraser curls his hand around Ella's and leads her to one of the seats behind us.

I send Griff a selfie from my seat, then take a picture of Remy and send that too.

"Here, I can take one of the both of you," Shelby offers.

"Thanks." I hand over my phone. Remy puts an arm around me and I curl my fingers into a heart and hold them in front of me.

"Awww, so cute," Shelby says, handing my phone back.

I'm never going to get a better chance than this and I'll kick myself later if I don't ask. "Can we take a picture together, Shelby?"

"Sure!"

Rooster stands and offers me his seat. Shelby leans in and Remy takes a few pictures.

"Thank you." I return to my chair, but Remy and Rooster move into the seats behind us and Ella moves next to me.

Once we're all seated, a flight attendant takes drink orders and I settle in for the flight, pulling my tablet out of my bag. I quickly send one of the pictures of Shelby and me to Kyla, Darcy, Jenn, and Hayden.

The engines roar to life. A surge of excitement mixed with fear flows through me. We're really flying to Vegas. On a private jet.

In eight hours or so, I'll be in Griff's arms.

"You okay?" Ella asks, raising her voice to be heard above the engines.

"Yes."

Finally, we take off, hurtling down the runway. My stomach jumps as the jet soars into the sky.

I peer out of my window, watching the landscape get smaller and smaller.

CHAPTER FIFTY-ONE

Griff

FIGHT CAMP HAS BEEN A GRIND. EVERYTHING IS structured down to the minute. Unlike my time in the *Supreme Fighter* house, everyone at camp is serious about learning and preparing for battle. Nothing is dramatized for television ratings. There's a strict nutritional program we have to stick to. Thankfully, I don't have to cut weight like some of the other fighters.

My reward for all the hard work is finally seeing Molly when she arrives tonight.

For the couple days leading up to the fight, we've moved to the hotel next to the arena where the fight's being held. Training time's been reduced but not eliminated. It's supposed to give us time to recover and rest before the big day. But I have a long list of media events I'm supposed to attend. That shit stresses me out way more than the training. Underhill wants me to focus on meditation— sitting still, the one thing I'm not good at.

I'm in the hotel gym, finishing thirty minutes on the treadmill, when I sense someone standing to my left. Guys I trained with at the fight camp are spread throughout the gym. We usually try not to bother each other. Whoever this is on my side feels like an intruder.

I punch the speed down, grab my towel and jump off the machine.

A hotel employee scurries over and wipes down the treadmill and I step back to get out of her way. I haven't gotten used to that, yet.

I swipe my water bottle off the floor and take a deep sip.

A guy with blond hair and a way too eager expression sticks his hand out. "Sorry to interrupt your training."

I screw the cap back on my bottle and shake his hand. "You didn't."

"Jeb from *Skirmish Skeptic*." He introduces himself. Another guy stands behind him with a camera, but Jeb doesn't give him an introduction.

I recognize the name as one of the smaller YouTube channels. They spend more time roasting fighters than discussing anything meaningful.

Suspicious now, I raise an eyebrow and stare at him. "Who let you in here?"

"Uh, your coach said I could have a minute of your time. You mind if I film it?" He gestures to his buddy standing behind him.

I shrug and hold out my arms. "Yeah, whatever."

Underhill warned me that in the days leading up to the fight, I'd have to answer more and more questions. The hotel is crawling with bloggers, reporters, podcasters, YouTubers, photographers, and regular fight fans. No one's given me any training on talking to the media other than Underhill's warning not to insult any of the money guys paying for all of this. Since I don't know all the players involved, I've kept any complaints to myself and focused on only speaking about the fight and my training. I'm running out of creative ways to say I want to punch Magic's face into oblivion, though.

I stare at Jeb, waiting for whatever he wants to ask. "Well?"

"Oh! I wanted to know if you had any comment about what Magic said about you this morning on *The Warrior Force* podcast."

"I don't have time to keep up with all the stuff he says. I'm busy training for a fight." I shrug. "Maybe that's what he should be doing too."

Jeb holds out his phone and plays a clip of Magic's ugly face taking up half the screen. Some guy I don't recognize fills the other half. *"I want to change the arrangement of his actual fucking face."* Magic twists his hands in front of him like he's unscrewing a jar of pickles. *"Just rearrange that pretty boy smirk of his and give him a matching scar over his other eye. His little teenage girlfriend won't even recognize him when I'm finished."*

A hot flare of rage sparks in my chest. I don't give a fuck about what Magic wants to do to my face. Referencing Molly, even if he never uses her name, crosses a line. Keenly aware of the guy filming me, I grind my teeth and will my face to stay calm. *Give him nothing.* Otherwise Magic will know Molly's a soft spot he can poke whenever he wants a reaction.

"I'm busy prepping for war here." I roll my shoulders forward and back. "I'll be disappointed if after all this work, the only thing Magic brings to the cage is plastic surgery tips." Okay, not my finest comeback but fuck, I'm better at quick punches, not quippy lines.

Jeb snickers and pulls his phone away. "Nice one."

At least Jeb thinks I'm clever.

"Good luck, Griff."

"Thanks."

My watch buzzes and I check the incoming text. Underhill makes us lock up our phones when we're training but he didn't say anything about smart watches—a birthday gift from Molly that's made it easier to keep in touch with her.

Molly: We're here.

My skin tingles, knowing she's close. It can't be healthy to miss someone as much as I've missed her. The strict training schedule has been a blessing in more ways than one.

I'd given Molly our room number last night. And the front desk should have key cards for Remy, Eraser, and Jigsaw to get into the four-bedroom suite we're sharing.

Under the coach's watchful eye, I slip into the locker room and grab my phone out of my locker.

Me: In the hotel gym. I'll be here a lil' longer. You can come visit.

If Underhill is going to let random reporters in to ask me stupid questions, he damn well better let my girlfriend in.

Molly

"I'm ready." I step out of the bedroom I'll share with Griff and into the common area of our suite.

Remy's waiting on a long white couch, scowling at his phone.

"Everything okay?" I ask when he doesn't lift his head.

"Yeah." He stands and slips the phone into his pocket. "That fuckweasel Magic was talking more shit this morning," he growls.

"Oh, you mean the one where he said he wants to rearrange Griff's face, so his 'teenage girlfriend' won't recognize him? I heard."

"Stop looking at that stuff. I fucking hate them bringing you into it at all. That's just not cool."

"No, but like you said, he's a fuckweasel."

Remy snort-laughs.

"Whatever." I shrug it off like the comment didn't embarrass the hell out of me. "It's not a lie. I am nineteen."

He runs his gaze over my outfit. "Please put something over that."

"Duh." I roll my eyes.

"Are you planning to work out down there?" he asks. "Or are you just going to say hi?"

"I don't know. But I wanted to be prepared." I slip a cropped zip-up hoodie over my workout top. "Are you?" I nod to his shorts and tee.

"Griff asked if I'd help him work on some moves."

"Oh no. You two can't get into it—"

"Molly, we've worked together for years. Who do you think he was training with before he left?"

"Yeah, well. The last time you two stepped in a cage together—"

"That was different." He waves an impatient hand at me. "Let's go."

Eager to see Griff, I follow Remy into the hallway. The hotel is huge and has more than one gym. Of course, Griff's is the farthest away.

We navigate the long hallways and elevators down to a lower floor and finally find the gym. Outside the door, we're stopped by a security guy in a navy blue polo shirt with the hotel's logo stitched on the front.

"We're with Team Royal," Remy says. "Coach Underhill knows we're coming."

The guard runs his slow gaze over each of us. When his gaze lingers on my chest for too long, I'm grateful Remy reminded me to put on the jacket. Remy steps in front of me, shielding me from the guard's leering eyes. "Can we go in or not?"

"Yeah." He opens the glass door and a rush of cool air washes over us. "Go ahead."

Remy puts himself between the guard and me as we enter. The sleek, modern space sprawls in front of us, larger than I expected. A row of treadmills and ellipticals line the floor-to-ceiling windows overlooking the Vegas Strip. Several fighters pound away on the treadmills, their expressions focused and intense. None of them are Griff, though.

At the leg press, one guy lifts a heavy stack. Men and a few women are using free weights and kettlebells. Except for the hum of the machines, occasional grunts and the clanging of metal, it's quiet. The air is charged with focus and determination, not chatter.

Remy and I keep walking. To our right, there's another room off the main gym. The rapid, rhythmic beat of someone using a speed bag reaches us. Remy and I stop in the doorway. Griff's standing in front of the bag, his fists moving in small, precise circles. The movement's so fast it looks like he's barely making contact. That's what's creating the steady, hypnotic rhythm. Griff holds his shoulders and arms loose and relaxed, making it seem effortless.

As much as I want to run and hug Griff, to kiss him and have him hold me, I'm mesmerized by his skill and don't want to do anything to break his concentration.

"If I tried that, I'd probably get bopped in the face, wouldn't I?" I whisper to Remy.

His lips quirk, but he doesn't confirm my suspicion.

"How long can he do that for?" I ask.

"A while."

It's hot, almost humid in this part of the gym. I unzip my jacket and shrug it off. I recognize one of Griff's shirts draped over the bench next to us, so I drop my jacket there.

"Take ten," Underhill shouts.

Griff's shiny-headed coach nods to us.

The serious, focused expression on Griff's face morphs into happiness as he turns away from the speed bag and spots us.

"Go on." Remy nudges me forward. "Say hi first."

I sprint the short distance and jump into Griff's outstretched arms, not caring that he's hot and sweaty. "I'm so happy you're here," he says against my hair. "I missed you, Muffin."

"I missed you too."

Behind us, Remy's now talking to Underhill.

Griff still hasn't set me down. "You look really hot," I whisper into his ear. "Don't wear yourself out too much. Because I'm going to fuck you so hard later."

He pulls back, surprise sparkling in his eyes. "That a promise?"

"Oh yeah." I run my fingers over his sweaty chest and hesitate. "Sorry, was that too much?"

"Nope." He sets me on my feet and walks us to the bench. "I'm into this conversation." He drops down on the bench and pulls me onto his lap. "Tell me more."

I loop my arms around his neck and kiss his cheek. "I'm glad you told me to meet you here."

"Why's that?"

"So I could see you all sweaty and working hard." I ruffle my fingers through his hair. "Watching you drum that bag into submission did things to me."

He places his mouth against my ear and wraps my ponytail in his hand, gently tugging. "I've missed you terribly. I'm going to work you over hard tonight. I hope you're ready for me."

A rush of desire pulses through my veins. "I'm ready right now."

He glances down at my sage-green workout top that zips in front. His gaze travels lower to the matching high-waisted leggings.

"I like this color on you." He tugs lightly on my ponytail. "It looks pretty with your hair."

It's such a sweet, unexpected compliment from the man who'd been steadily pummeling a speed bag speed five minutes ago.

My cheeks warm with pleasure. I pepper kisses along his jaw. "Thank you."

"No, no, no," a deep voice announces behind us. "This is workout time. Make out on your own time."

Griff groans and nudges me out of his lap. We both stand straight as army recruits. "Coach, you remember Molly."

He gives me a dismissive once-over. "Yes. Hello. Training isn't over yet today."

"I know," I say quickly. "We just got in and I wanted to say hi."

"Five more minutes," he warns Griff, then walks into the other room.

Remy steps up and Griff embraces him like they're long-lost brothers.

"How was your flight?" Griff asks.

"Well, Molly didn't drool on me." Remy's lips quirk. "So that was good."

I cross my arms over my chest. "Ha, ha."

Griff shakes his head and shifts his attention to me. "I'm so sorry. I won't be finished for a couple more hours."

"That's okay. I knew that might be the case. Shelby asked me if I wanted to go shopping with her this afternoon." I didn't want to let Remy know how much Magic's dig at Griff about his "teenage girlfriend" bothered me. Finding something more mature to wear to the fight is my new number-one priority.

I run my gaze over Griff again. No, getting him alone in that giant king-sized bed in our room is my first priority, but finding a new dress is still high on the list.

Griff pulls me aside. "My wallet's in the safe in our room. Take my card and buy whatever you want."

I stand back and stare at him. "I have money."

He frowns in confusion. "Yeah, but you're out here because of me."

"Today, I'm just looking around. If I see anything I want, I'll go back and get it tomorrow."

He still seems conflicted. "Okay."

Griff

Remy returns to the gym with Eraser about half an hour later. After being surrounded by so many strangers the last few weeks, they're a welcome sight.

Eraser pulls me in for a big bear hug. "Jesus, you're huge."

"You say that every time you see me." I squeeze him extra hard. "How was the flight? Where's Ella?"

"She went shopping with Shelby and Molly."

I shift my gaze to Remy who holds up one hand. "Jigsaw and Rooster are with them," he explains.

My eyebrows shoot up. "Jigsaw went *shopping* with them?"

"I think he saw it as an opportunity to terrorize anyone who gives the girls a hard time." Remy shrugs. "So, really it's entertainment for him too."

Can't argue with that logic.

Underhill's thrilled to have not one, but two new people to put to work, helping me perfect some grappling skills. And since Remy knows my style, strengths, and weaknesses probably better than I do, we end up working on strategy together.

A couple hours later someone from the fight organization runs in and informs me I need to be downstairs in Conference Room A for a press meeting in fifteen minutes.

"Just go like this." He circles his hand in front of my face. "We want to show everyone how hard you're grinding in here."

As if I was going to run upstairs and change into a fucking suit.

"This wasn't on the schedule," Underhill snaps. "We have training to finish. And he needs to rest."

The guy gives Underhill a *tough shit* shrug and leaves.

"Assholes." Underhill pulls out his phone and starts checking his messages. "Go clean up and get ready," he mutters.

"We're going with you, right?" Remy asks.

"It'll probably be boring. They ask the same dumb questions over and over."

"Not this time," Underhill says, waving his phone in the air. "That pixie dick opponent of yours is finally coming off his high horse to do a joint Q & A."

"That's good, isn't it?" Eraser asks. "He's been doing all his interviews from whatever house he's staying at, right?"

"We'll see," Underhill grumbles. "He's gonna trash-talk your buddy, though. So behave."

"Whatever." I shake my head. "Let's see if he has the balls to say to my face all the shit he's been talking online."

Mike "Magic" Everson is every bit the asshole Diane warned me he would be. I already knew that from the videos I've watched but seeing it in person is a whole new experience.

I sit at a table next to Underhill on a stage. Someone handed me a microphone when we arrived, but I set it down. Magic never shuts the fuck up, so I haven't needed to use it much. He's on the other side of the stage at a different table answering questions about some shitty sneakers he's endorsing. A moderator stands at a podium between us. Several bouncers dressed in black standing shoulder-to-shoulder behind us in case Magic and I want to start the fight early.

"Next." The moderator recognizes a man in the third row with his hand in the air. The first five or six rows are only half full of press waiting to ask questions. The rest of the giant conference room is empty.

"Will from *Warrior Force* podcast. My question is for Magic. You lost to Captain Biscuit in your last fight. Griff is the same age. Similar skill set. Same wingspan. He put on an impressive performance week after week on *Supreme Underground Fighter*."

Why, thank you. About time some recognize that.

"So, after your recent loss, are you concerned at all?" Will asks.

"I'm eleven wins and *one* loss," Magic growls into the mic. "I ain't worried about no one." He waves his hand vaguely in my direction. "He's a nobody. Didn't even win that shit contest. I'm not even sure how we got here."

Oh, fuck that. I snatch the microphone off the table and switch it on. "You sure seemed to know who I was when your people were begging me to come out to Vegas and fight *you*. I didn't even know who the fuck *you* were."

Magic cackles into his mic. "You didn't know who I was? You didn't know? Are you serious right now?"

"Dead serious. But it doesn't matter. I'm here. I'm ready. I've got the skills and heart to win."

"Yeah. You're skilled all right. Skilled at bleeding," he grumbles.

I let out a loud yawn. "Please stop. I'm too young to die of boredom."

"You *are* young. I been at this fight game for years. You been here a minute."

I cock my head and shrug at the audience. "Imagine doing this for years and still acting this childish."

A low murmur of chuckles ripples through the room.

"You need to show some respect!" he shouts.

I slowly turn my head and stare at him. "Respect is earned, not given. I don't care who you are."

"Hard to respect someone who goes trolling for dates at the local high school," he mutters into the microphone.

Fury shoots through my chest. *Don't react.* I loosen my grip on the microphone and force out a harsh laugh. "You sure are obsessed with my love life. You tryin' to fight me or date me?"

"All right!" The moderator interrupts. "Let's take more questions."

"Griff!" A man in the first row raises his hand.

I point my microphone at him.

"Jeb from *Skirmish Skeptic*, we spoke earlier."

I nod quickly to acknowledge that I remember him.

"Speaking of your girlfriend. Will she be here for the fight?"

I open my mouth to answer but he continues. "After all, high school doesn't let out until mid-June in New York, right? Will she need a permission slip to fly to Las Vegas?" He smirks like he's really fucking proud of that one.

This prick. "What was your name again?" I ask.

The cocky tilt slips from his lips. "Jeb. *Skirmish Skeptic*. We met earlier," he repeats.

"Jeb with the blond hair and green shirt." I raise my hand and point to him. "Yo, Ruthless, that's him. Front row. Jeb with the goofy green polo."

Jeb's eyes widen and he turns around. "What—"

"You asked about my girlfriend. That was dumb, Jeb." I explain slowly enough for his little brain to process it. "My whole crew's here watching, including her brother. Don't worry. I'm sure he just wants to have a word with you, *Jeb*."

Laughter ripples through the room.

"We just want to talk, Jeb!" one of the guys screams from the back of the room. "Don't be scared!"

More laughter.

Two of the hotel security guys jump off the stage and storm through the aisles.

"All right. I think that wraps things up," the moderator says. "Thank you both."

I slam the mic on the table and push my chair out. Underhill follows me off the stage.

"Fuck this shit. I'm not doing this again," I say to him in a harsh whisper. "It's fucking pointless. I'd be better off spending the extra time in the gym."

"I know." He rests his hand on my shoulder. "Relax. You handled it fine. Kept it about the fight. Talked some shit but didn't cross any lines."

"No, *he* did by bringing up my girlfriend. *Again.* You don't see me talking trash about his wife's Only Fans account." I *almost* considered saying it, but it seemed like such a cheap shot. Poor woman's life is probably hard enough being married to such an asshole.

"That shit's beneath you, Griff," he says calmly. "That's why people like you." He shrugs. "It's also why some people will hate you."

Obviously.

"Look. You're done for the day. Take that ice bath. Rest. Meditate—"

"I told you, I can't."

He sighs. "You're making it more complicated than it needs to be. Just try."

I nod quickly.

"Good. I'll see you in the morning."

When he turns away, the last person I expect to see is standing in front of us.

"Diane!" Underhill smiles wide and sweeps the much smaller woman into an embrace.

"How's my favorite fighter doing?" she asks him.

"I'm standing right here," I say.

She chuckles but then looks to Underhill for an answer.

"Good. He's having a hard time with the slowdown in training this week."

I open my mouth to protest, then shut it.

"The rest and recovery time is important," Diane scolds, in the same tone you'd ask a kid to eat his veggies.

Underhill pats her arm and jogs up the aisle toward the exit. "Let's do dinner later," he calls over his shoulder.

She nods quickly, then moves in closer to me. "I warned you Magic was an asshole."

"You did." I shove my hands in my pockets and look her straight in the eye. "Why's he suddenly acting like he has no idea who I am?"

"Mind games. He's trying to make you feel like you don't belong here." She gestures toward the stage where Magic's still standing, surrounded by a bunch of reporters. "Trust me. He knows who you are. He's watched every piece of footage he could find on you. How else do you think he knew to poke you about Molly?"

I glare at her.

She points a finger at my face. "You did a better job concealing how much that bugs you up on stage."

"It wasn't easy."

"I know." She grins. "Calling on your homies to 'talk' to the reporter was brilliant. There will be dozens of that clip all over the place by the end of the night." She squeezes her fists together like she's trying to contain her excitement. "Damn, that was clever. I knew you were a natural."

"A natural at what? I have no fucking idea what I'm doing in all these interviews. I keep making an ass out of myself."

"No you don't." She frowns as if she's surprised that's how I see things. "You're well spoken. Polite but not afraid to trade a few barbs. Your dry sense of humor's very endearing. I haven't seen a bad video yet, kid."

I blow out a breath, annoyed her opinion actually matters to me. "Thanks."

I shift my gaze to the exit. I'm so tired of playing mind games with people. I just want to see Molly and relax tonight.

As if he read my mind, Eraser marches down the aisle to my rescue.

"Ready to go?" he asks without acknowledging Diane.

She shifts toward him. "You're not the brother, are you?"

"No." He drills her with a murderous stare. "But if you're who I think you are, I'm not a fan of what you did to Molly, either."

The corners of Diane's mouth turn down. "But I spoke to Molly at the reunion. I thought we were good."

"Molly forgives. I don't," Eraser says without so much as a twitch of his lips to indicate he's kidding. *He's not.*

I bite the inside of my cheek to hold in my laughter.

"Well." Diane squeezes my arm briefly. "You're doing good. And I have no doubt that you're going to win Saturday."

"Will you be there?" I ask.

"I'll be around all week."

Great.

Eraser's eyes narrow to slits as he watches her hurry away from us. "What's she doing here?"

"Honestly, I have no fucking idea. She said she's a fan of combat sports." I shrug. "Ready to go?"

He runs his hand over the back of his neck, suddenly seeming unsure of himself. "You looked good up there. Handled it well. I wanted to throw a chair at that punk."

"Same."

More neck rubbing.

"Bro, I love you, but I really want to get upstairs and see Molly," I say. "What's on your mind?"

"She's still with the girls." He runs his hand over his beard a few times. "I wanted to tell you I'm sorry."

That's a shift in conversation I didn't expect. "For?"

He cocks his head like he's annoyed he has to spell it out for me. "For giving you a hard time when you first came home."

"I remember you checking to make sure I wasn't dead several times."

He huffs. "Yeah, but you know what I mean."

"Ohhh," I draw out the sound to a dickish extreme. "You mean the part where you believed a bunch of lies and bullshit about me cheating on my girlfriend? Or where you were mad at me about the way they portrayed her when I had no control over it? Or, or, wait a minute, is it because you never warned me that your orange-haired troll doll of a cousin was taking advantage of the situation by trying to date my girlfriend?"

Now he plows both hands through his hair and gives me a sheepish look. "All of the above?" He holds his arms out wide. "I know you and Remy already had your come-to-Jesus match back home so if you need a sparring buddy this week, I'll volunteer."

I bark out a laugh. I had way more anger stored up for Remy. "Tell me the truth, were you mad because you care about Molly?"

"Yeah, she's my little McMuffin," he says, showing off the teddy bear living under his gruff exterior. "She tried being all brave and shit when the show said all that crap about her, but we all knew how much it was messing with her head." He closes his eyes. "And then *that* night. Holy shit. I hated seeing her so heartbroken. Then she fucked up her car." His lips twitch. "Although, I was a little proud of her for that one, honestly."

"Asshole. She could've gotten hurt."

"As for my cousin," he continues, "I had nothing to do with that. I didn't like it either, honestly. And I made that really clear to him *and* Remy when I found out about their *arrangement.*"

"You should've told *her.*"

He tilts his head. "Come on. I didn't want to be the one to tell her that. And I know you don't want to hear it, but he *does* like her."

"He's a fuckin' creep," I grumble.

"Anyway. When I watched that reunion show, Griff." He shakes his head in disgust. "Jesus Christ. I think it finally hit me how much lying and absolute bullshit you went through and I'm sorry if I made it worse by giving you a hard time."

I swallow hard, completely unprepared for this today. "Why you tryin' to get me all emotional during fight week?"

His head snaps up and his eyes widen. "Fuck, I'm sorry."

"I'm just messing with you." I open my arms and pull him in for a tight hug, thumping him on the back a few times. "Thanks."

"I'm really fuckin' proud of you, Griff." He holds out his hands.

"And you gave me all that shit for manifesting when we were locked up."

I snort, remembering his nightly ritual of wanting us to visualize our ideal lives or some shit. "No I didn't. I manifested the shit out of my Chevelle."

He snorts with laughter. "True. Did you think when we were fighting for our lives at Castle Correctional you'd end up here?"

"No, I figured I'd end up buried in a ditch in the woods."

"I think we all did." He cocks his head. "You ever think of looking up Ollie or any of those detention officers and paying them a visit?"

"Sometimes."

"Karma's been too slow for my taste."

We're wandering down a dark path I can't afford to travel this week. "So you're volunteering to spar with me, huh? Underwood's gonna love you."

His solemn eyes meet mine. "Whatever you need, brother."

CHAPTER FIFTY-TWO

Molly

WHEN I RETURN FROM SHOPPING WITH SHELBY AND ELLA, Griff's trying to conquer an ice bath Underhill wanted him to sit in for a few minutes tonight.

That didn't sound like anything I wanted a part of, so I stay in the bedroom and try on the dress I bought for Saturday night.

When Griff finally emerges from the bathroom with a towel wrapped around his hips, I turn away from the mirrored closet doors I'd been staring into, trying to decide how I feel about the dress.

"Does this make me look like a fighter's girlfriend?" I slide my hands over the smooth little pieces of silver sequins covering the dress. "Or a mob wife?"

Griff runs his heated gaze from my toes peeking out of my high silver sandals, to the short hem hugging my mid-thighs, to my hips, over my chest and finally to my face. "You look gorgeous." His gaze drops to my legs again. "So good, I'm not sure I want you going out in public like that."

I narrow my eyes. "You don't get to veto my outfits if they look *good*."

"I dunno. Gonna be a lot of horny fight fans in the crowd. Not to mention fighters from the earlier matches. One of them touches you, I'm gonna jump that cage and kill 'em."

"Aren't we sitting in the front row?" I tilt my head, trying to convey how silly he's being. "With our entourage in attendance, I'm sure I'll be fine."

His lips tilt to the side. "Will you be comfortable?"

"No. But focusing on breathing in this dress will help me keep my mind off of worrying about you."

"You don't have to worry about me. I know what I'm doing. I've trained hard. Feeling the best I've ever felt before a fight."

"Good, because I'm a wreck," I finally admit, tired of holding that in.

A furrow forms between his brows. "You don't have faith in me?"

"I have all the faith in the world in *you*. I still don't like you getting hurt. Even a little."

"I'll do my best not to," he promises. He runs his gaze over my dress again. "God damn, you look hot. Are you wearing the dress tonight?"

"No, it's for fight night." I bite my lip. "Although I bought a different dress. It's purple. Maybe I should wear that instead?"

"Show it to me later." He takes a step closer. "How easy is this to get off?"

"What?" I tiptoe backward, trying not to trip in the high heels.

"You heard me." He reaches for me again. "Turn around. Does it have a zipper?"

"I thought fighters had a no-sex rule before a fight?"

"Nah, that's a myth." A playful smile ripples over his lips. "You weren't worried about rules when you were promising to fuck me hard down in the gym earlier."

My cheeks heat. I did talk a good game. "Are you sure you want to risk it?"

"Well," he rubs his hand over his chin, still staring at me like I'm his next meal, "there's actual science that suggests the more times you climax, the bigger the boost to testosterone. So, it could be beneficial before a fight."

I can't help giggling. "So, sex for science?"

"Absolutely." He grins even wider, making him so damn irresistible. "My first professional-ish fight, I'd gone without, and I lost. So, yeah, let this be our scientific experiment."

"Ugh. You did *not* lose that fight as far as I'm concerned. You were *robbed*."

He captures me around the waist, pulling me closer but his expression's more serious. "Thank you."

"For stating the obvious? You heard how mad the audience was at the reunion show."

He's shaking his head before I finish my thought. "No, for even mentioning it. I know how much you hate the show."

"It's part of our story now, good or bad." It took some time to get to this point. "They tried to come between us and lost." I drape my arms over his shoulders. "You and me against the world, Griff."

"That's how it's always going to be." He stares at me for a few beats. "Thank you for being here with me," he says softly, pressing a kiss to my forehead.

"I go where you go." I rub the tips of my fingers through his hair and his eyes drift shut. "I'm sorry I wasn't here when you came back to the room."

"That's okay. I'm glad you went out. I think you'd be bored hanging in the gym." He opens his eyes and his mouth flattens into an annoyed line. "And that press conference was bullshit. I don't want you at any of them."

"I heard the high school crack about me. These dumbasses don't know how to count very well, do they?"

His angry scowl deepens. "Please don't listen to that bullshit."

"Griff, I don't care if they poke fun of my age. But I *do* care about them trying to imply bad things about *you* because of me." I step back, showing him my dress again. "I'm hoping this makes me look a little older?"

He studies my body with an appreciative spark in his eyes.

"I know you have more to worry about than my fashion choices," I say. "I'm just...nervous."

"Molly," he breathes out. "You always look...I don't know what word I'm looking for. Good isn't strong enough." He shakes his head, frustrated.

"Well," a nervous laugh spills out of me, "maybe I'm still a little traumatized from all the jailbait jokes they made on the show."

"I'm proud you're my girlfriend. Always. I like the way you dress.

Please don't change anything because of these assholes." He cocks his head. "Don't I always comment on how clever your outfits are?"

Yes, he does. Genuine, sweet compliments. Not gross "your boobs look good" comments. "Yes."

"I hope Magic is as bad in the cage as he is at trash talk. He sounded like an idiot in the clips I heard."

"He's a good fighter. He's only had one loss." His brow furrows with concern. "Are you sure you'll be okay at the fight? It's war inside the cage. Nothing glamorous or pretty."

"Will I be a distraction for you if I'm there?"

He pauses and seems to consider the question instead of giving an automatic no. "Once the ref sets us loose, I'm focused on getting the job done—taking down my opponent." He turns his head slightly as if he needs more time to consider my question. "I don't think you'll be a distraction."

Unease curls in my stomach. "If you think I'm going to distract you in any way, I'll watch from the locker room or something."

"No. I want you there," he says firmly. "Remy will be there. The other guys. I know you'll be safe. That's the only thing that would worry me."

I move over to the dresser with the lighted mirror and press my finger to the round dot in the corner of the glass. A bright, flattering light flares from the edge of the mirror.

Gathering my hair, I pile it on top of my head and stand sideways, studying my profile with the updo. "Should I wear my hair up for the fight?"

He steps behind me and presses his lips against my shoulder, then against the crook of my neck. "No. I won't be able to concentrate. All I'll be thinking about is doing this." He peppers more kisses against my neck.

His lips lightly brushing my skin tickles, and my shoulders jerk. He stands back and rests his hands on my waist.

I let my hair down and touch my chest. The dress has a simple round neckline that only shows a hint of cleavage, but my chest still feels bare.

"I didn't think to bring a necklace or anything other than my little diamond studs." I pinch my earlobe and wiggle the tiny round bezel-set earrings that had been my mother's. "The dress is so over-the-top sparkly, no one will notice, right?"

Griff's mouth twitches. He walks over to the nightstand by his side of the bed and slides the top drawer open, pulling out a white box. "Come here for a second."

I meet him and he pulls me to sit on the bed with him.

"Here." He hands me the box.

A pretty, gold logo embossed on top of the box is too elaborate to make out a name. "What is it?"

"Open it."

I hook my finger in a black silk loop of fabric and gently slide the bottom of the box out. A necklace of thin, glittering white gold with several small diamonds stationed at intervals along the chain rests inside.

"Wow," I breathe out. "It's so beautiful."

"You like it?"

"I *love* it." I lean in and press a quick kiss to his cheek. "You know me so well." The dainty strand of diamonds looks so elegant and pretty, I can't stop staring at it.

"I was going to give it to you after the fight, but I think it goes with your dress." He grazes my earlobe with his fingertip. "It kind of matches your earrings too."

I glance at the necklace again. "It does."

"Did you count the diamonds?" he asks.

"No." I carefully tap each small stone. "Fourteen?"

"One for each year I've known you."

My heart's ready to explode. "I love you so much. Thank you."

"As soon as I saw it, I knew I had to get it for you." Excitement quickens his words. "I think I owed you something extra nice since I gave you the same car for your birthday two years in a row."

"I love the car and if it's the only gift you give me for the rest of our lives, I'd still be happy." I hold out the necklace. "Will you please put this on for me?"

"Sure."

I turn and lift my hair. "When did you have time to even find it?"

"When we moved to the hotel, Underhill gave us a morning to go check out the Strip." His breath's warm on my neck as he works the clasp. "Got it," he finally says.

I press my palm against my chest, holding the chain in place while I hurry to the dresser to look in the mirror. "Oh, it's so pretty."

"You're pretty." He steps behind me and rests his hands on the dresser, caging me in.

In the mirror, I watch our reflection. Griff, so much taller and broader than me, staring at me with so much affection in his eyes as he runs his finger down my spine.

He bends at the knees lightly and slides his hands up my legs, pushing the dress with them, until it's bunched around my waist.

"What are you doing?" I move to turn around and he stops me with a hand on my back.

"Admiring your legs in those sexy silver heels."

I pull my hair up again. "There *is* a zipper back there."

He lets out an eager hum. His fingers graze my neck as he finds the zipper, sending a lovely shiver over my skin. Cooler air drifts over my back as he slowly drags the zipper down to my waist.

I carefully ease the dress down and step out of it, draping it over the end of the dresser. Griff sucks in a breath. "No underwear?"

"Well, I was only planning to try on the dress for a minute or two."

He rubs his hand over one cheek and gently squeezes. "I would've helped you take it off sooner."

"I'm sure you would have."

He works the clasp of my bra loose and I toss it near the dress. "Put your hands on the dresser."

Our eyes meet in the mirror, and I rest my palms on the flat surface. He skims his hands over my shoulders and down my sides.

"Missed you. I need to get reacquainted with your body." He glides over my hips, his thumb grazing my butt. "Fuck, these heels are just the right height."

I reach back and tug at the towel still knotted around his waist and encounter his erection. The towel drops to the floor with a soft *whoosh*. I curl my hand around him and stroke.

He hisses in a pleasure-mad breath. "Fuuuck. Thought I'd never get hard again after that fucking ice bath. And five seconds of looking at you and here we are."

"I knew you'd be okay."

One of his hands slides from my hip to between my legs, his palm scalding against my inner thigh. His fingers tease my opening, then slide higher, in torturously slow circles.

"You're hot now," I whisper.

He cups the back of my head and leans closer, crashing his lips against mine in a ravenous kiss that spins me into a vortex of need. He dips his fingers lower, pushing inside me.

I gasp and moan, inching my feet apart and pushing my hips against his hand, chasing my need for pleasure.

My legs tremble. "I need you."

"But I wanted to take my time." He kisses and sucks at my neck, increasing the ache at my center. I press my palms flat against the dresser again and arch my back. He slips his hand out, dragging my wetness along my stomach.

One of his hands tightens on my hip as he guides himself into me. "Is this what you want?" He nudges his cock against my opening, and I nod quickly. "So impatient," he teases.

I can barely keep my eyes open from the intense pressure and pleasure of him squeezing inside me. But I watch him in the mirror. A thrill runs through me at the pure concentration and satisfaction on his face as he pushes all the way inside. For a second, he seems to stop breathing.

From scalp to toes, my body tingles. Heat throbs through my body, slowly centering to where we're joined. He kisses and nips my neck. I push back against him and he lets out a tortured groan.

"Do that again," he whispers.

So I do.

In the mirror I meet his eyes. I place one hand over his and drag it from my hip to between my legs.

"Yes," he encourages. "Show me what you want."

"Touch me."

"You feel so good." He moves his fingers in the slow, circular motion that drives me crazy. Then he slides in and out with a slow, rocking thrust. Over and over. His whole body vibrates from maintaining the slow pace.

"More," I whisper.

"I'm afraid I'll hurt you," he rasps. "I want you so fucking much."

I meet his eyes in the mirror and clench around him. "I'll tell you if it's too much."

He moves faster, thrusting harder and harder. Relentless. His hands roam everywhere, sliding and squeezing. Sweat breaks out on my forehead.

The dresser starts to knock into the wall.

"Fuuuck!" He pulls out and captures me around the waist, hauling me to the bed.

"Griff!" I squeal and laugh as we fall onto it in a tangle.

He pushes up on his elbows, bringing himself into the center of the bed. "Come here. Get on top of me."

I eagerly swing my leg over his hips and promptly get my shoe tangled in the sheet.

"Fuck!" He works to unbuckle my shoe so I can take it off. "Get on my cock. I'll get your other shoe off."

I giggle at the absurdity of my shoes causing so many problems, then groan as I sink onto him.

"Yes," he sighs, squeezing his eyes shut. "That's my girl."

He finally works the other buckle loose and rips the shoe off, throwing it somewhere across the room.

"Please, I'm begging you, Muffin. Grind your hot little pussy down on my dick. Hard."

I find a perfect, pulsing rhythm—back and forth. "Touch me," I gasp.

He shifts his hand from my breast to my thigh, teasing his wicked thumb over my clit in time to my movements.

"Yes, yes, yes." Blood pulses through my ears. Electricity sparks over my skin. My body shakes. Pleasure shoots through me and I grind myself down harder.

His hands seize my hips and he holds me tight, snapping his hips up, extending and amplifying my orgasm.

His comes in a slow, agonizing release. He pulls me down over him, fusing our mouths together. He groans against my lips and holds tight.

I cling to him for the longest time. Until our hearts return to almost normal. He lifts me off him and I melt onto the bed, curling into a ball against him. He hugs me to his side and kisses my forehead.

"Coach keeps telling me to meditate," he rasps. "But I think I just reached a higher plane of awareness and absolute clarity with *you*."

Still buzzing with electricity, I kiss his cheek and nuzzle against his neck.

Griff

What planet am I on?

My body's just sort of floating on the bed. Molly's sweet, sweaty little body's clinging to me while she drops soft kisses on every inch of me she can reach.

The absolute clarity I reached—if I win Saturday, I want to ask her to marry me.

That probably wasn't what Coach was talking about.

"Griff?" Molly's voice holds a note of hesitation. "You've been doing *it* longer. Is it always like this? Amazing and explosive each time? Does it ever get...*boring*?"

"Boring?" How the fuck do I answer that? I need her to understand I'm dead fucking serious. "I don't remember *anything* before you. But nothing could ever be boring between us. No. Never."

"You'd tell me if there's a different way you want me to—" She bites her lip and frowns.

"Everything about you is perfect for me."

"But if—"

"Molly. I don't want anything different than who you are." I tickle my fingers over her ribs. "I love all those sexy fucking sounds you make right before you come."

Her cheeks redden but she grins at me.

I flex my arm, squeezing her to my side. "Anything different you want *me* to do?"

To my surprise, she tilts her head and actually seems to consider the question. Well, fuck. Wasn't expecting *that.*

I wait, curious what she's going to say. The corners of my mouth twitch into a smirk. Whatever improvement she suggests, I can't wait to start working on it right away. Like, immediately.

"You know when I'm on top of you?"

My cock twitches. Fuck yeah, having her ride me is one of my new favorite pastimes. "You mean, like you just did?"

She blushes an ever-brighter shade of pink. "Well, I like when you put your hands right here." She curls her fingers around my wrist and drags it to her hip and then lower to the crease of her thigh.

My thumb twitches over her soft skin and I grip her tighter. "Like this?"

"Yes," she whispers.

"Okay. I can do that." I wiggle my eyebrows. "Why don't you get on up there and let me give it a try?"

"You're not mad?"

I open my eyes comically wide. "Am I mad that you want me to put my hands on you?"

She sits up and shifts to her knees, her legs resting near my hip. "No, that I questioned your prowess."

I snort. "Question anything you want, Muffin." I clamp my hand over her hip. "I aim to please. Now, get your cute little ass up there and let's see if I can get this right."

She giggles and ducks her head. "You do everything *right.* I just asked for more of something in particular."

She glances at my spent cock, who is definitely perking up at this new development. "Well, we did say we have a science experiment to conduct."

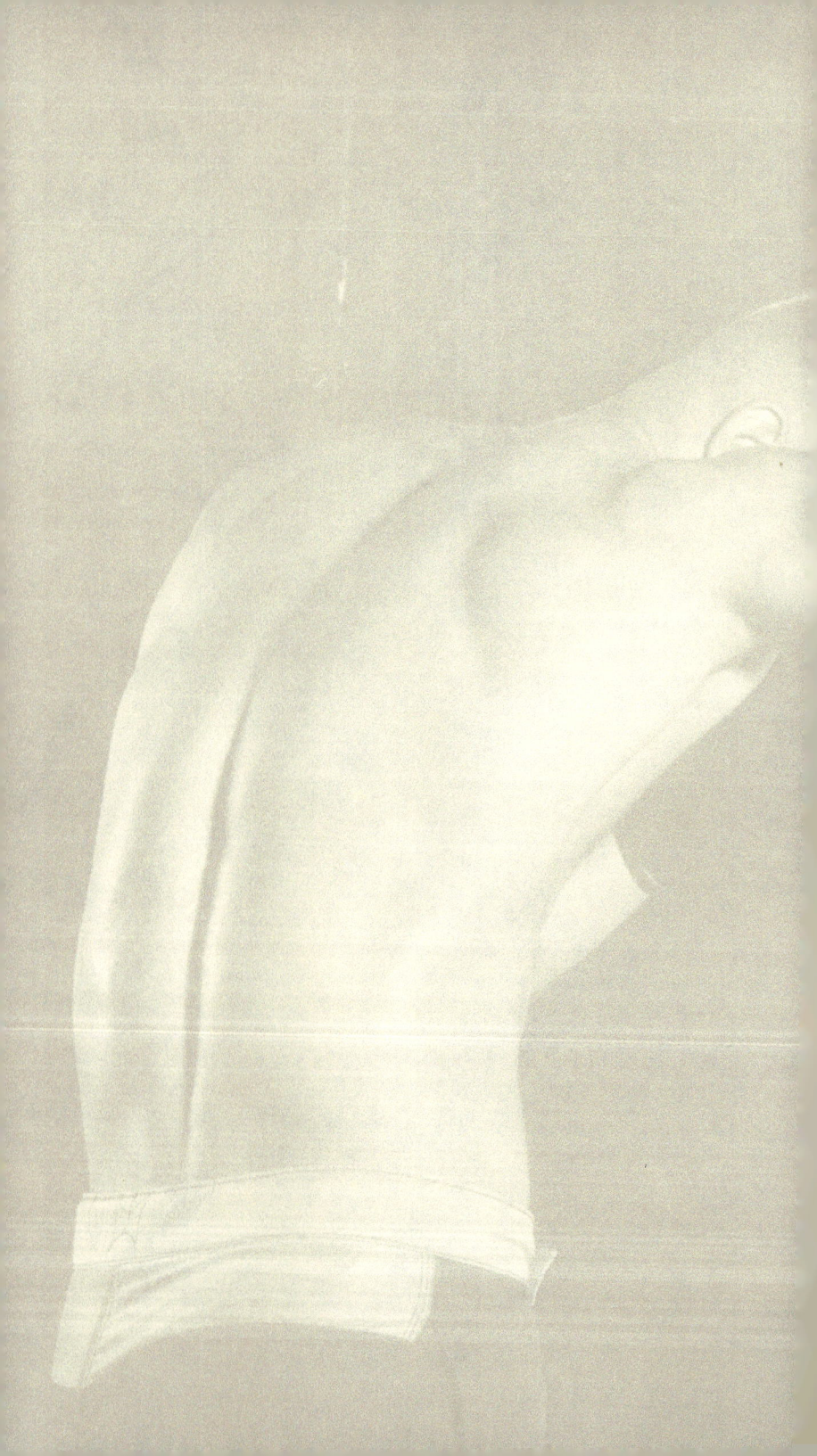

CHAPTER FIFTY-THREE

Griff

THIS IS A BATTLE.

I'm a warrior.

I have the strength.

I have the skills.

The power to win.

I repeat those five things to myself over and over while blasting Rage Against the Machine through my headphones backstage.

Molly's sitting next to me on the bench, her leg touching mine. Just her presence centers me.

After a few songs, I take my headphones off and open my eyes.

"Let's get those hands taped," Underhill snaps. He hadn't been thrilled I wanted Molly backstage with me. Or that she'd walk out with us. But I really don't care. He's a good coach and we clicked during training, but my personal life isn't open for commentary. You'd think he would've learned that during all the pressers.

Remy, Eraser, Underhill, and, weirdly, Dawson Roads, are also walking out with me into the area. Since he sponsored some of my training and flew my friends here on his private jet, he can walk with me anywhere he damn well pleases.

Molly holds up her phone. "Am I allowed to take pictures and video?"

"Baby, you can do anything you want." I lean in and kiss her cheek.

I stand and approach Underhill and the fight official who will sign the tape after my hands are wrapped. I hold my hands out palms-down. So much energy's coursing through me my legs won't stop moving, but I try to contain it and hold still while each knuckle and joint is carefully wrapped. Molly moves a few feet away and aims her phone at me. I throw her a cocky wink and she flashes a quick thumbs-up. Remy stands next to her, watching everything like a fuckin' hawk.

The hands take a while. Molly has time to do a 360 walk around me, filming every angle.

When the hands are done and signed, Underhill pulls out his black-and-purple focus pads. "Let's warm up."

He barks numbers for the combinations of punches, and I throw. He doesn't push into my punches as much as he did during training, this is just to get the blood flowing.

"Good, good. Keep moving. One, two, three. Right."

We repeat the sequence a few times.

"All right," Underhill says. "Break."

I grab a bottle of water from the fridge in the corner and take a few quick sips.

I pace the four corners of the mat laid in the center of the locker room, then up and down the middle.

The flat-screen television on the wall has a live feed from the fights out in the arena right now. Eraser's standing in front of it with his arms crossed over his chest, watching the men's featherweight match.

"Who's good?" I ask, stopping next to him.

"Both of them, really."

"Hey," I tap his arm, "after this, are you and Ella gonna take some time and do like a second honeymoon or something while you're here?"

"Yeah." A wide grin stretches across his face. "I booked a helicopter ride over the Strip to surprise her."

"She's going to love that."

"I know." His whole face scrunches up into a *pleased with himself* smile.

I clap him on the back and resume pacing, stopping in front of

Remy. "What'd you think?" I hold up my hands and pretend to throw some jabs.

He stares at me for a few seconds. "I'm really fuckin' proud of you. That's what I think, brother."

It'll go to his head if I let him know how much that means to me. "I'm happy you're here with me."

"Me too."

"This is the kinda shit we talked about in high school." Before my life took a few detours and Remy's did too.

"Ruling the fight world? Yeah, I remember," he says. "You're doing it."

I lean in, not wanting to be overheard. "I'm here. I'm ready to go." I throw my fists a few times. "I can collect my bag, no matter what. After I get in the ring, everything's gravy."

"You best believe I put some money on you to win," he says.

"You did?"

He stares at me like I'm crazy. "Fuck yeah."

People bet on me at The Castle all the time. It's nothing new. Just a different location. Bigger stakes. Large pool of gamblers.

No big deal.

We work through a few moves together. I pull him into a standing choke but don't apply pressure. Remy twists away and comes at me with a side kick grazing my leg.

Underhill supervises us and eyes Remy like a bull he wants to take to market.

"Magic is big." Remy runs his hand from the center of his chest to his shoulders. "Heavy. He'll be tough to take down. But I think once you do, you've got him."

"That's my plan."

He shrugs and gives me a sheepish look. "I know you have a plan."

"I always appreciate the advice." I slap his arm so he knows I'm not annoyed and return to the bench with Molly.

She's busy flipping through the pictures she took. I tap one of me with my head down, watching as my hands get taped. "You can post that to my Insta if you want."

"Yeah?" She pulls my phone out of her purse and hands it to me.

"You know the code." I have nothing to hide from her.

"But you're sitting right here."

I flash my taped hands at her.

She sends the photo to my phone and then loads it to Instagram. "How should I caption it?"

"No tricks tonight. Just fists of steel?" I suggest.

She squints. "I'll work on it."

Laughing, I watch her hands swiping over my phone, especially her bare ring fingers. "Hey, you have that selfie of us from the room?"

She flicks to the photo gallery and shows it to me.

"Post that too."

Her thumb hesitates over the image. "But tonight's about *you*."

"And *I* want you to post both pics."

She posts the pictures, then shuts off the screen and tucks my phone away.

"Would you rather hang with Shelby ringside?" I ask.

"I'm right where I want to be." She tugs on the sleeve of her oversized purple hoodie that's covering that smoking hot silver dress. "Thank you for this. I would've been freezing without it."

I drop my gaze to her bare legs, silky and gleaming with some kind of body oil she used after she got out of the shower. "Are your legs cold? I'll give you some sweats."

"I'm okay." She tilts her head. "How do you stand all this...anticipation?"

"It's only the second time I've had to do it. Last time was much worse. I really didn't know what to expect." I lower my voice. "I didn't have you."

"I'm here now. And I'll be here tomorrow and the next day."

I lean close to her ear, really not wanting anyone to overhear this. "Thank you for helping me add the new training session to my afternoons this week."

The corners of her mouth twitch and she slides a coy glance my way. "Oh, it was definitely my *pleasure*."

I pop a quick kiss on her cheek.

"Gloves on," Underhill calls out.

My stomach clenches. We're closer to showtime.

He helps me slide the regulation gloves over my taped hands. Another official comes into the locker room and wraps red tape around my wrists, then scribbles his signature across it in black Sharpie marker.

I glance at the television screen where Magic's walkout is about to start. "Is that the theme from *Halloween* he's using?"

Eraser shakes his head. "What a douche."

Arena security guys in black blazers line up outside the locker room door.

Molly grabs her high-heeled silver sandals and starts strapping them on her feet. I flash my gloved hands at her. "I'd help you, but..."

She laughs and shakes her head. "I got it."

Underhill rolls his eyes.

I tap my fist against his shoulder in warning.

Molly grabs her stuff and hurries to my side. I hold out my hand and she taps her fist against my palm.

"Mr. Royal, it's time," one of the security guards says.

Remy and Eraser enter the hallway first. I shake my shoulders and roll my head from side to side, then follow, with Molly right next to me.

Underhill and his assistant come out last.

Bright camera lights hit my face. I squint and slant my arm over my eyes, wishing I'd thought to bring sunglasses.

Molly taps something against my arm. I glance down.

Sunglasses.

"You're like a magic genie." I take them from her carefully and slip them on. "Thank you."

"I remembered how bad those lights were at the reunion and just in case..."

I put my arm around her quickly and pop a kiss on her cheek, not really caring if dozens of cameras film it and people mock me for the display tomorrow.

"What's the holdup?" Remy asks one of the security guys.

The big dude exhales a long, weary breath. "Magic takes a lap around the entire arena."

The security guards part ways and Dawson appears with his own security following behind him. Jesus Christ, I've got more men in black surrounding me than the president.

"How're ya feelin' tonight?" Dawson holds out his hand and I awkwardly wrap my gloved paw around it for a quick shake.

"Best I've ever felt." I dip my chin. "Thanks for doing this."

With all the trash talk this week and the massive odds against me, having a legit celebrity like Dawson show his support gave people something to gossip about besides how dumb I am for thinking I can take on an athlete like Magic so early in my career.

"Thanks for using my song for your walk out," he says.

It hadn't really felt like I *had* a choice. I like country music occasionally, but it really doesn't feel "skull punch-y" enough. Then Dawson played *Call Me The Underdog* for me, and I revised my opinion.

A big blond head appears above the crowd gathered in the hallway. People shift and step aside for Wrath to enter our circle.

"Hey, big guy." Dawson glances up and holds out his hand. "Been a minute."

"It has. We're sorry we missed the ride with you guys the other day." He turns toward me and runs his gaze over me. "You look strong."

That's high praise coming from Wrath.

"Feel it." I tap my fists together. "Thanks for coming."

"I wasn't missing this, although," he casts a pointed look at Eraser, Remy, Molly, and then me, "I'm insulted you don't have one of those snazzy purple hoodies in my size."

Dawson chokes on a laugh. "That's gonna be a special order."

"Next time," I promise him.

Wrath nods hello to Molly, then shifts his shrewd eyes my way again. "She walking out with us?"

Christ, is he going to tell me she shouldn't be part of this too?

"Yeah," I answer warily.

He nods quickly like he's revising his plan. "I'm gonna walk behind her and to the outside. Remy will be in front of her and Eraser in front of you and to your left. That work?"

No judgment. Thank you. I blow out a breath and nod.

Molly lifts her phone and takes a quick sideways selfie of us.

A low rumble from the arena vibrates through the halls. Security and the camera guys start moving.

This is it.

I flip my hood up over my head. The guys ahead of me start moving and I give them a few feet before following. I move to the center, throw a few fists, bend my knees, strike, and basically shadow box my way down the hallway.

Molly hurries to keep up, her face a mask of concentration.

We reach the final hallway leading into the arena.

I turn to Molly. "Your seats are by the cage door, right?"

"Yes." She holds up her phone. "Shelby and Trinity are there now."

"Stay with me through the pre-check, until I go in the cage, okay?"

She nods quickly and doesn't ask why.

The first notes of Dawson's song start. It's slow, rumbling—almost ominous—then it explodes into a powerful, grinding guitar riff.

I time my entrance into the corridor to the music, then march my way to the center of the arena.

With each step, my focus tunnels down to one thing—a trembling in my stomach, that spreads to my fists.

My blood runs hot with the need for victory.

CHAPTER FIFTY-FOUR

Molly

ENERGY COURSES THROUGH ME LIKE I'M ATTACHED TO A live wire. Every one of the twenty-thousand seats in the arena have been sold.

The bright lights disorient me, but I keep following the purple hood of Remy's sweatshirt.

Griff punches his fists in the air and bounces down the walkway, pumping himself up for the fight.

A few people scream "Stonewall!" as we pass.

Someone yells, "Fuck Naptime!" and I laugh.

A man pushes his way to the edge of the entourage but Remy's quick to shove him back.

He screams, "Marry me, Molly!" almost in my face.

Startled, I turn to see who he is, but Wrath's already at my side, blocking the crowd from even seeing me as we pass.

But as we draw closer to the center, fans hurl curses and insults at Griff. Most of them are the same trite, homophobic slurs that knuckle-draggers always seem to favor.

Griff's either too keyed up to hear what's being said or he's able to block out the noise.

I want to punch every single one of them.

We finally reach the mat outside the cage where Griff's supposed to stop for inspection. For a moment or two no one seems to know where to stand. No one seems to be in charge or offer any direction.

Everything's so much more chaotic than what gets shown on television.

The circle of people around us grows wider, but Wrath, Remy, Eraser, Dawson, and Remy's coach form a ring around Griff, the officials, and me.

Once he's on the mat, he has to strip down quickly. In front of twenty thousand people and probably as many cameras, he has zero privacy. He toes off his shoes and kicks them toward Eraser, then shimmies out of his track pants, unzips his hoodie and shrugs it off. Eraser ducks and collects the clothes, leaving Griff in nothing but his tight-fitting athletic shorts.

"Off." The official touches Griff's sunglasses.

He slips them off and passes them to me and I tuck them back in my purse.

While the official smears Vaseline on Griff's face, he stands with his eyes closed but his fingers keep restlessly wiggling.

Underhill hands Griff his mouth guard and he pops it in, working his jaw from side to side to put it in place.

In front of the entire arena, the official practically performs a full-body cavity search, running his rubber-gloved hands all over Griff's body. Griff stands straight, staring ahead, unfazed by the thorough pat down. Where on earth would he be able to hide a weapon—in between his toes?

I glance inside the cage. It's full of people. A ref, an announcer, camera crews, and a lot of other guys hanging out, like the canvas floor hasn't been soaked in blood all day long from the earlier matches. And might be again in the next few minutes.

My stomach churns. Maybe I should've watched from the locker room.

Then my gaze lands on Magic. That arrogant dickwad, with more muscles than brain cells, who's been taunting Griff with trashy insults all week. *And* poking fun at Griff for dating me. After he all but begged Griff to fight him. *Jackass.* I hope Griff really does punch a hole through his skull. He runs back and forth on his side of the cage, reminding me of a lion in a zoo. Nah, that's insulting to lions.

"All right." The official pats Griff's shoulder and steps aside. "You're all set."

"Show him how New York does it," Remy says, tapping his fist against Griff's glove.

"Get in there and crush him, bro!" Eraser pounds his fists together.

Griff turns toward me and tilts his head, silently asking for a kiss for luck. I reach up and brush my lips against his cheek. "Skull punch that wankhammer into next Tuesday," I say against his ear.

His eyes widen with amusement and surprise.

"I wuf ooo." The mouth guard gets in his way, but I get the message.

"I love you too."

My stomach ripples with unease as he skips up the steps like he's not stepping into a death cage.

"Come on." Remy presses his hand between my shoulder blades. "There'll be ten more minutes of yammering before it starts. Let's grab our seats. Show our support."

Eraser's staying with Griff's coaches in the corner. He stops and taps his knuckles against mine as we pass him.

Dawson flanks my left side as we cross the short distance from the cage to our front row seats. "I had the opportunity to watch some of his training earlier this week," he drawls. "You ain't got nothin' to worry about, darlin'."

I peer up at him and he gives me a friendly smile, his eyes crinkling at the corners. "I know." I press my hand to my chest, my diamond necklace cool against my skin. "It's still a lot."

"That it is." He dips his chin in agreement.

Shelby stands and hugs me as I approach our seats. "You sit here next to me, Molly. Logan's gonna sit with Dawson."

It doesn't matter. We're right in the front row.

In a daze, I give Ella a quick hug and say hi to Trinity. Wrath squeezes into the seat at the end of our row.

Backstage, I'd been freezing. Out here, it's hotter than a frying pan. I unzip the hoodie and shrug it off, a little self-conscious in the short, showy dress now. Why had this seemed like a good idea?

"Hot damn, that looks flockin' fabulous on you." Shelby smooths down pieces of sequins that were flipped the wrong way from my sweatshirt.

"Thanks." I lower myself into the short, uncomfortable metal seat. I nod to her sparkling purple jumpsuit. "I think fancy pants like yours would've been a smarter option, though."

She presses her hand to her stomach. "Already had some weasel ask me if I'm pregnant, so I'm thinkin' I chose poorly."

She's sitting so it's hard to tell what would've prompted someone to ask in the first place. She looks stunning, like she should be on a red carpet, not in the splatter zone of a cage fight. "You look beautiful. People are dumb."

"Thank ya." A wicked grin lights her eyes. "Logan scared the piss outta the guy, he won't be askin' me that again."

I bet he did.

"Hey, Molly," someone says from behind me, touching my shoulder.

I whip around and find Venom and Woolly in the seats behind us. "Oh my God!" I twist to say hi. "Does Griff know you're here?"

Venom pulls out his phone and nods. "I sent him a text earlier this week."

I introduce them to Remy, and we promise to catch up after Griff *wins.*

A man with a large professional video camera stops in front of us. Shelby leans in close and whispers in my ear, "Smile and look pretty for these little worms or they're gonna drag ya all over the Internet tomorrow."

Grateful for the reminder, I force a bright smile and tilt my head toward her. We both wave at the camera. Shelby adds an endearing shoulder wiggle. Another man, following the camera guy, shouts, "Who are you rooting for, Shelby?"

"Stonewall! Who else?"

"You think your boyfriend's going to win this fight, Molly?" he asks me.

Startled he knows my name, I blink a few times before answering, "Of course he will."

Satisfied, they move down the row and stop at Dawson. He stands to talk to them longer. I take a second to glance around the arena. I recognize a few people in the front sections. Actors, musicians, a whole row of broad-shouldered guys who could be football players, men in suits who could be politicians. Cameras are being shoved in all of their faces as well.

This is...so much bigger than I thought. All of these people are here to see Griff in his first professional match against a seasoned fighter.

"Molly? You all right?" Remy taps my arm.

I nod quickly. "It's...a lot."

"We're not in Johnsonville anymore, huh?" His voice holds a hint of amusement.

"Exactly."

He puts his arm around my shoulders. "Can you handle this? Be honest. I'll walk backstage with you right now. Griff won't be upset. If things get rough...he's worried about you."

Indignant anger sparks in my chest but fizzles fast. Remy's not trying to baby me or shut me out. He's genuinely concerned. He and Griff probably discussed this last night.

My gaze flits around the arena again. Several spectators have phones aimed at us. Anyone who watched that retched reunion show probably knows who I am. How will that look for Griff, if I walk out before the fight even starts?

"No, I'll be okay. I watched some other fights online. I know what to expect." *Bloodshed, broken bones, unconsciousness.*

Remy stares at me for a few seconds longer. "Okay. If you change your mind, just give me a tap." He pops his finger on my arm a few times to demonstrate.

"Are you asking me to literally *tap out* of watching?" I tease.

He snorts with laughter. "Yeah, I guess I am."

All the extra people file out of the cage. Griff and his opponent stop their restless warmups and stand in their respective corners.

Griff still seems to have extra energy buzzing through him. He keeps bouncing on his toes and shaking his arms. Underhill speaks to him through the fence and Griff nods every now and then.

The announcer's voice booms over the arena. "Ladies and gentlemen, welcome to the main event tonight! Reigning champion Mike 'Magic' Everson out of ME Army Gym right here in Las Vegas with an impressive record of eleven wins and one loss, versus the up-and-coming Supreme Underground Fighter Griffin 'Stonewall'

Royal out of Furious Fitness all the way in Empire, New York! You're here to witness history as Stonewall steps into the cage for his first professional fight tonight."

Griff raises his arms over his head and turns to face all sides of the arena.

A low, unfavorable-sounding roar moves through the crowd. We're on Magic's home turf. Good. A spiteful thrill runs through me. I can't *wait* for Griff to whoop this guy's ass in front of all his fans. But as he turns this way, our section bursts with chants in Griff's favor.

Unable to stop myself, I jump out of my seat. A scream rips out of my throat, and I clap wildly. Griff's eyes land on me and his cheeks push up. He points at me and tilts his chin.

The announcer keeps talking but it's impossible to hear him over the deafening roar of the crowd. I lower myself into my seat again.

My stomach flips as the announcer hurries out of the cage and the ref calls the fighters to the middle.

"Breathe." Shelby squeezes my hand. "He's got this."

"I know."

I take a breath and block out the noise from the audience and focus on Griff.

Magic seems calm, almost bored, as if he thinks this will be an easy fight.

Griff seems to have redirected all of his extra energy inward. He's impossibly stoic as he stands and stares Magic down. Magic bares his teeth and jerks his head forward, but Griff doesn't flinch.

Next to me, Remy's coiled tight, eyes fixed on the inside of the cage. Does he wish he was in there instead of Griff? Or does he want to pummel Magic the way I wish I could?

The ref says a few more words to the fighters. They tap their gloves together. The ref raises his hand and backs away quickly.

Griff crouches and puts his fists up. Magic tests him with a few probing jabs that Griff bats away. Griff responds with a low kick. Magic grunts and backs away.

"Shit," Remy mutters.

I turn and find him grinning.

"Slap him, Stonewall!" someone screams.

Magic throws a powerful right hook that Griff ducks. The missed punch throws Magic off-balance, giving Griff time to move in close and whack Magic across the face with an open palm. He grins as Magic's head snaps sideways and follows with a punch to Magic's chin.

Magic rocks backward, catching himself against the cage wall. He returns with a flying kick to Griff's midsection.

My heart hiccups with fear as Griff staggers backward. But he recovers fast and comes at Magic with several quick punches. Magic manages to pin him to the cage wall and they grapple, fighting to take each other down. Griff throws a sharp knee to Magic's midsection and they separate.

"Shit, Magic's already out of breath," Remy says. "Griff's still looking as fresh as a daisy."

I don't know about a *daisy*. Griff looks more like a highly trained K-9 focused on taking down a criminal with an anal cavity full of heroin.

Magic spins and lashes out with a wicked kick, aiming for Griff's temple. Griff dodges the foot and responds with a combination of punches.

"Jesus Christ." Remy shifts to the edge of his seat. "Magic's just standing there like a fuckin' zombie eating shot after shot."

Magic ducks and covers his head, but Griff's relentless, pouring on the punches.

The ref calls time. Griff calmly walks to his corner, hands on his hips, while Magic staggers over to his stool and falls onto it.

While I can't hear what Underhill and Eraser are saying to Griff in his corner, their animated gestures seem positive.

As the second round starts, Griff's confidence must be soaring. He's lighter on his feet, almost taunting Magic.

"Don't get cocky, bonehead," Remy mutters.

Magic lowers himself and rushes Griff, flipping him onto the mat. My stomach jumps as the hard thud of their bodies hitting the canvas reverberates.

"That was a mistake," Remy says. "Griff will finish him."

"Now who's cocky?"

Remy chuckles and hugs me to his side.

Our whole row's screaming as Griff and Magic grapple on the floor. The crowd starts chanting "Stonewall!" and I think it's almost over when the ref sends them to their corners again.

Heart pounding wildly, I jump to my feet, trying to see Griff better. The coaches and another person surround him in his corner. Did he get hurt?

The third round starts. Griff's just as bouncy and eager as he was in round one, while Magic seems to drag himself over the canvas.

Please finish this soon.

Magic ducks, like he's preparing to take Griff to the mat, at the same time Griff lifts his knee. Face and knee collide. Blood sprays from Magic's mouth and he staggers backward.

"Yikes, he gonna knock his own ass out!" Shelby yells.

The knee to the face was an accident, I think, but Griff uses Magic's disorientation to his advantage. He lands several body shots, steps back, then throws a punch straight to Magic's jaw.

Magic's arms fly out to his sides, he staggers backward, then crumples to the canvas.

"Done!" Remy jumps to his feet.

"Yes!" Shelby squeezes my hand. Everyone in our row explodes out of our seats.

I run over and hug Ella. "He did it! He did it!" she squeals in my ear.

Trinity gives me a big hug. "I couldn't breathe through the first half of that!"

Wrath's standing so close to his wife that I move from hugging Trinity to giving *him* a hug too. He freezes for a second, then pats my shoulder. "He did good," he bellows.

"He did! He did! Oh my God."

Remy's big hands curl over my shoulders and he steers me toward the cage. "He wants you in there!" he shouts.

I can't even see Griff with all the people blocking our path. "Get behind me." Remy takes my hand, pulling me along behind him while he muscles his way through the wall of people.

I scream at the top of my lungs with pure joy.

Rooster and Jigsaw meet us near the cage steps. Together with my brother, they form a protective semi-circle around me.

"You proud?" Jigsaw asks me.

"Damn right!"

Finally, I can actually see Griff. His dazed expression squeezes my heart. I raise my hand and wave wildly.

"Winner by knockout in the third round," the announcer shouts, "Griffin 'Stonewall' Royal!"

Griff raises his hands high.

Underhill's clapping and grinning like a proud papa.

The arena security guards who walked us down earlier notice me at the bottom of the steps and push some guys out of the way. "Let her through."

I run up the stairs but step carefully onto the canvas, so I don't trip. Griff's looking toward our seats. I open my mouth to shout his name, but I break into a run and end up squealing a bunch of nonsense. Underhill steps out of my way and I crash into Griff.

"There you are!" He grins down at me. "How'd I do?"

"Amazing." I study his face. He's red around his right eye but not bleeding at least.

"I feel like I could've gone ten more rounds with him."

"You looked like it."

He bends down and kisses my forehead. "Were you okay?"

"Yes."

Someone taps his shoulder and he swivels away but still keeps his arm loosely around my waist.

A man wearing a blue polo shirt, carrying a microphone, stops in front of me. Behind him another man holding a camera aims it at me. Nerves flutter in my stomach but I lift my chin and smile.

"You and Griffin have been together for a while, correct?" The man with the notepad asks. "This was a big fight for him. His debut. Now that he won, are you hoping for a marriage proposal this weekend?" The reporter shoves his microphone in my face.

Griff's still distracted with questions from a different reporter.

I rest my hand on his sweaty chest to capture Griff's attention, then answer the reporter. "Do you just assume every woman is waiting for a marriage proposal? Or am I special?"

"Well..." The guy works his jaw up and down but can't seem to answer.

"This is Griff's weekend." I glare at the reporter. "His victory. He trained hard for this fight. Everyone said he was the underdog this weekend, but he dominated this cage. Why don't you talk about *that*? I want him to enjoy every second of his win. That's the only thing I'm 'hoping for' this weekend."

He pulls his microphone back, ducks his head and scribbles something on a notepad, then turns and mutters something to his cameraman.

"Thank you, Miss Holt."

"Sure."

Griff wraps himself around me and lifts me so we're eye to eye. "Thank you, Muffin," he says in a low tone meant for my ears only. "You know I definitely plan to ask you that one day."

I tighten my arms around his neck and dust my lips against his sweaty cheek. "And I plan to say yes," I whisper in his ear.

Someone brushes a hand against my back and Griff carefully lowers me to the ground. I tug my dress into place.

Remy's standing behind me, glowering at Griff. "You lift her up any higher, she was gonna be flashing all these cameras."

"Good thing you were here to block them, then." I slap my brother's chest.

"Get over here." Remy pulls Griff in for a hug. "Fuckin' proud of you, brother. That was...incredible. You *owned* the ring."

"I'm really glad you're here."

"Me too."

Eraser joins us and pats Griff's back. "Team Royal for life."

"Castle Crew for life," Griff corrects, opening his arms wide and pulling them in.

Even though I'm sure dozens of cameras will capture the moment, I scoot back, pull out my phone and take a few pictures of my own.

CHAPTER FIFTY-FIVE

Molly

G RIFF HAD TIME TO TAKE A SHOWER, CHANGE, GET checked by a doctor, and then haul his butt down to the press conference about his win.

Shelby and I are in the front row. The rest of our crew's sitting in various spots around the conference room. We seem to have grown in numbers since leaving the arena. Woolly, Venom, Diane, and friends of Dawson's have all joined our group.

"Griffin, over here. Brett from Tridant True Media."

Griff turns his head, his eyes scanning the crowd until they land on the reporter. He picks up his microphone and nods.

"You were the underdog in this fight. This was a stunning victory—"

"I wasn't stunned," Griff says.

Everyone in the room chuckles.

Griff lazily points in our direction. "None of my crew was surprised that I won, either."

"Fuck yeah!" Jigsaw jumps out of his chair and throws both fists in the air. The rest of us whistle and shout in agreement.

Griff grins at the reporter and lifts his eyebrows. "Anything else?"

Clearly embarrassed, the guy ducks his head and taps his silver pen against his small white notebook. "Well, actually yes. Since you won, will you be proposing to your girlfriend this weekend?"

My heart stutters. Why would anyone ask that at a press

conference about Griff's monumental victory? It was dumb enough when the other reporter asked me outside the ring. The two so-called journalists must not have compared notes.

Griff blinks a few times as if he also doesn't see the connection. "My personal life is personal. Let's keep the questions fight-related."

"Why's everyone so nosy?" I grumble, crossing my arms over my chest.

"Their lil' pea brains can't come up with anything else." Shelby wiggles the fingers of her left hand at me, her pretty moonstone and diamond ring glittering under the sharp conference room lights. "Logan and I are engaged and I still get nosy reporters asking when we're tyin' the knot. As if I'd send one of 'em an invite," she scoffs.

At least that makes me feel better. "Thanks."

"You all right, chickadee?" Rooster towers above us, his gaze focused on Shelby.

"Just lettin' Molly know those dumb engagement questions will probably keep on comin'."

"I'm nineteen. Marriage really isn't on my radar." I lift my chin toward the table where one of the other fighters is answering questions. Griff nods at me. "They should be focused on Griff's win. All these people underestimated him. He should make them grovel before answering their questions."

Rooster rumbles with laughter. "Griff's lucky to have you, Molly."

I beam up at him. "I know." My smile flattens. "I'm lucky too, though."

After the press conference finally ends, Dawson takes the entire group out to dinner.

The longer the night goes on, the quieter Griff gets.

By the time we're finally able to go up to our room a few hours later, he can barely keep his eyes open. I have so many things I want to tell him, but we're surrounded by my brother and our friends in the elevator.

The ride seems to take forever, but finally dings on our floor. Everyone steps out of the elevator, but only Remy, Eraser, Ella, and Venom walk us to our door.

"You guys take this bodyguard thing seriously," I tease my brother.

"Magic's boys were pissed that he lost," Venom says. "We can't be too careful."

"That's so stupid," I scoff. "It's a fight. Someone's going to win and someone's going to lose."

"Yeah, but Griff made it look so fucking easy." Eraser chortles with laughter.

"And fast," Remy adds. "Damn, Griff."

We stop at the door to our suite and I produce the key card from my purse. Our whole group files into the common area. The large space shrinking fast.

"Please, we made it to round three," Griff says. "My plan was to submit him in round one."

Venom studies Griff's face. "I'm just happy it wasn't another bloodbath. God damn, he barely touched you."

"Stitches hurt. I wasn't doing that again," Griff jokes, then lightly rubs his hand over his abdomen. "He landed a few shots. I'll be feelin' it every time I take a breath for a few days." A wild grin stretches across his face. "Then I'll remember the shock in his eyes when I clocked him."

The guys explode with laughter and another round of rehashing the fight.

"You sure you don't want to come explore the Strip with us?" Eraser asks Griff again. "The club Dawson wants to take us to sounds like fun."

"I can't, bro, I'm wiped." Griff glances at our bedroom door longingly. "I want to sleep for like two days straight."

Now that all the excitement is over, that sounds like a perfect plan to me.

CHAPTER FIFTY-SIX

Molly

A SLOW, THROBBING PLEASURE WAKES ME THE MORNING after Griff's win.

Griff's hard body firm against my back.

One of his arms stretched over my head, the other draped over my hip, his fingers lazily drawing circles between my legs.

I gasp and stretch, shuddering.

"Morning, Muffin." His tone low and gravelly from sleep.

"Good morning," I whisper on a shaky exhale. "That feels so good."

His lips graze my shoulder, sending tingles of pleasure sparking over my skin. "I wanted to wake you with an orgasm."

"I...I think I am. Keep doing that. Please."

A little over twelve hours ago, I watched him beat another man unconscious in the ring. Witnessed the raw power his hands and body contain. The damage he can do to an opponent.

And this morning, those same rough fingers feather gentle and reverent strokes against my most sensitive skin.

My whole body shudders again.

"Lift your leg. I don't want to take my hand off you." Griff kisses behind my ear.

"Please don't. Don't stop." I raise my leg, bringing it forward, trying to present myself at the right angle to give him access.

He pushes his hips forward, his cock sliding against the slickness of my thighs.

"You're so wet." He groans and nips my earlobe.

His hips thrust again and again. Each slide of him pushing me higher but not giving us quite what we both need.

After several attempts, he groans in my ear. "Help your man out."

I lift my leg higher and reach down, guiding him inside me.

"Fuck." For a second, his fingers stop moving as he pushes in as far as he can go. "God, you feel so fucking good."

We stay like that for a while. Griff slides his free arm under my body, holding me close while his fingers lazily tease my clit and he leisurely thrusts into me. A slow, exquisite torture.

Waves of euphoria build and build, pulsing through my body in an endless loop.

He kneads my breasts, his rough fingers teasing my nipples. "You're squeezing me so fucking hard." He jerks his hips against me several times to punctuate his appreciation. "So fucking good."

I reach down, covering his hand with mine, pressing him against me. "I...I...it feels like I haven't stopped coming since you, ah..." I squeeze my eyes shut.

"Since I what?" He thrusts harder. "Buried my cock in you?" He half laughs, half groans.

"Yes."

He slips his hand from between my legs and slides his palm to my lower abdomen, gently pressing. His slow thrusting quickens, driving deeper each time.

A deep, shivery sensation builds as he presses on my lower belly and his cock continues, stroking the same spot inside me over and over.

"Griff," I whisper urgently. "I..." Pressure builds, my entire lower body on the verge of exploding. So intense a bit of fear hovers at the edge.

"Relax," he rasps. "Just let go. Let me have it."

The tension bursts, a wall of blinding pleasure showering over me.

"Yes, that's my good girl," he praises in a low, raspy hum. "You're drowning my cock." He kisses my temple. "Keeping coming for me."

"I..." My breath stutters.

When I'm limp and panting, he squeezes my hip and rolls to the side.

"No." I whimper at the loss of his warmth against my skin.

"Don't worry." He nudges me onto my back and hooks his arms behind my knees, spreading me wide and driving deep inside again.

I'm so wet, still trembling from my orgasm, that I let out a long, satisfied sigh as we reunite. Exquisite agony twists his handsome face as he thrusts harder. He lifts and tilts my hips, easily manipulating my body the way he wants, pleasuring me from every angle possible.

"You're gorgeous." His gaze slides from my face down to where we're joined.

We'd spent a lot of time in this bed in the days leading up to the fight. But this morning, he's wild, a man possessed, like he's determined to wring a lifetime of orgasms from my body or bury himself so deep inside me, we'll never be apart again.

"Fuck." His body jolts. His hands dig into my hips. "Molly." He gasps and drapes his body over mine, still slowly grinding his pelvis against me. His mouth finds mine, kissing deeply as he finds release.

Through panting breaths and pounding heartbeats, we kiss, rub noses, and finally he rests his sweaty forehead against mine. "Thank you."

He collapses on the mattress next to me and I rest my head on his stone-hard chest. So solid and firm everywhere after weeks and weeks of relentless training. My fingers absently trace ridges of muscle, stopping when I realize the faint reddish-purple marks on his skin aren't from our love session. I yank my hand away, afraid I'll cause him pain.

"Are you okay?"

He lifts his head, staring at where my hand's hovering over him. Slowly, he probes the bruise. He sucks in a sharp breath, then cups my cheek, drawing closer.

His lips find mine. "I feel like the luckiest man in the world."

"It wasn't luck, Griff. It was your skill."

"I'm not talking about the fight." He brushes a lock of hair off my cheek. "I'm talking about waking up with *you*. Not just the sex—

although, that was fucking amazing. And I definitely want to start every day like that."

"I don't know if I can handle it." I press one hand between my legs. "I'm still all tingly and fluttery down there."

He squeezes his eyes shut, pure satisfaction spreading over his expression. "That feels like a bigger achievement than winning any fight, you know that?"

I tickle my fingers over his pecs. "Do you want me to have a belt made up for you? We can call it the *World's Longest Orgasm Giver*, or WLOG belt for short."

He shakes with laughter for a few seconds, then wipes the smile off his face. "No, because I'd never let anyone challenge me for that title." He taps his finger against my nose. "We do have the results of our scientific experiment to discuss, though."

I press my lips tight and pretend to be serious. "It was successful."

He dips his chin in agreement. "That's how fighter superstitions are born." Griff teases his lips along my jaw and down to my neck. "We had lots of sex leading up to the fight and I *won*—won easily and with little damage, I might add."

Uncontrollable giggles shake my body. "I think I know where this is headed."

"Yes, so now it's been established, we have to have a lot of sex before every single one of my fights. Otherwise, I'll lose." He shrugs like he's completely helpless. "Those are the rules."

"Every single one of my fights."

Does that mean there will be more?

How many more?

Not now. Not today.

"I'll agree to those terms, Mr. Royal."

Thankfully, he's closed his eyes and laid back against his pillow, so he can't see the anxiety slowly chipping away at my joy.

I rest my head on his shoulder and kiss along his jaw.

"With little damage."

This time.

"Baby, I know I promised that if I won, I'd take you out so we could see Vegas." He yawns wide without opening his eyes. "But will you be mad if we just do *this* for a day or two? Laze around in bed? I'm exhausted. The training...the fight...all the stupid press stuff. My brain and body are completely fried."

Griff, who hates showing any sign of weakness, admitting that he needs rest, stuns me into silence for a moment.

"Anything you want." I rub my hand over his chest, but I think he's already fallen asleep again. "Today's your day."

CHAPTER FIFTY-SEVEN

Griff

It's late in the afternoon when I wake again.

Molly's sitting up in bed next to me, wearing one of my T-shirts and scowling at her phone like she wants to melt it with the power of her eyes.

"Why aren't you naked?" I rasp, reaching for the sleeve of her shirt.

She clicks the screen off and smiles at me. "Hey, champ. How do you feel?"

I sit up, groaning at the tightness in my abs. "Like I got punched in the gut a few times," I admit. I swing my legs over the side of the bed and sit there for a second. The heaviness in my head feels like I've got a skull full of wet towels.

Molly's hands, soft and comforting, gently massage along the lines of my neck down to my shoulders. I drop my head, enjoying her touch.

"Is this okay?" Her fingers slow.

"More than okay. It feels good."

She resumes the gentle probing and massaging, slowly working her way down and along my shoulder blades. I could almost fall back asleep like this.

I reach behind me, capturing one of her hands and bring it to my mouth, kissing her fingertips. "Let me run to the bathroom. I'll be right back."

"Okay."

When I return to the bedroom, she's standing by the dresser with her hand curled around the handle of my half-gallon water bottle.

Thirst slams into me and she holds out the bottle.

"You need to drink some water." Her tone's a mixture of stern and sweet.

"On it." I grab the bottle and flip the top. "Thank you."

The water's ice cold, the way I like it, soothing as it slides down my throat. I finish more than half, then set it on the dresser and stumble back to the bed.

"What were you reading when I woke up?" I glance at the nightstand. "Where's my phone?"

"Here." She picks my phone up off her nightstand and climbs into bed. Kneeling next to me, she holds it out for me.

Now that I have it, I don't *want* to look at anything.

"What's wrong?" I ask her.

"Nothing." She shrugs, then sighs. "Magic is a mega-douche. All the headlines are about your win. But he's already doing interviews about how he wants a rematch because he wasn't at 'his best' and he's still a better fighter than you."

Laughter bubbles and rushes out of me. "He can't even lose with dignity, huh? Fuck him. Everyone saw that KO."

A little smile twitches at the corners of her mouth. She scoops her phone off the bed and flicks it on. "This is one of the photos they're running with the story about his whining."

She turns the phone my way. The screen's filled with a stunning image of my fist smashing into Magic's jaw. His head tilted to the side, eyes already rolling back in his head, sweat flying. Pure, vicious fury stretching my face into something I barely recognize. "God damn. That's an impressive photo."

"There are dozens of them like it. But that's probably my favorite one of the fight." She wrinkles her nose. "There's one of you smashing your knee in his face, but it's a little bloody."

I definitely need to see that one.

I pat the bed next to me and, for the next hour or so, we scroll through all the different write-ups about the fight together. More than half of the articles also feature an image of me lifting Molly in the air in the middle of the cage.

The caption reads: *Biggest Night of His Life and Girlfriend is Still the Prize.* "This is my favorite." I turn the screen toward her.

She sighs and stares at the image. "Mine too."

"The caption's true, you know. Whoever this Brynn Banner is who wrote it, is a fucking genius."

She stares at the picture for a few more seconds, then rolls her eyes. "Remy's so mad about that one." She taps the screen where her dress got pulled up a little and my arms are the only thing stopping the camera from capturing a much racier picture.

"Tell him to unclench. I got you." I glance at the photo again. "You're hot as hell."

"A bunch of creeps in the comment section would agree. *That's* what Remy's annoyed about."

"What? Where?" I scroll farther down.

Molly's hand closes around my phone and she pulls it from my grasp. "That's enough."

I don't have the energy to argue. "Come here."

She squeezes in close, and I pull her against my side. She rests her head on my chest and one leg over mine.

"I love you, Muffin."

"I love you too." She carefully rests her arm over my chest and hugs me.

The thoughts that have been swirling around in my head since I arrived in Vegas spill out of my mouth. "Let's get married. This week. Before we go home."

Molly slowly lifts her head and blinks at me. Excitement and confusion play over her face. "But this week is supposed to be about *you*. You won your first professional fight."

I trace my finger over her cheek. "Marrying you would be the biggest win of my *life*."

She lets out a happy sigh and leans into my touch. "Mine too."

Then anxious Molly checks into the conversation. "But where would we live? I don't want to go back to New York and live in the dorms while you're all the way in Johnsonville. That's not how we should start our marriage."

"You *have* to finish school."

"I don't want to live in the dorms anymore, anyway."

I nod quickly. "I've been thinking about that a lot lately."

"You have?"

"When we get home, I want to look for an apartment or a house to rent near campus."

"What do you mean?" She frowns. "Why would we waste money on an apartment when we can live at home and I'll commute—"

"No." I cut her off quickly. "You need to be near school. And I want to be with you. It's not that long of a commute for *me*. There are all those nice houses with apartments for rent around the college. We'll look for one of those."

"You'd do that?"

"I'd do anything for you." I squeeze her leg.

"But then you'll be an hour away from everything important to you—The Castle, your job, the gym you work out at, all your friends..."

"*You're* the most important thing to me. The Castle isn't going anywhere. Jerry pretty much lets me come in when I want, I can find a new gym or just go there after work, and our friends can make the drive to visit us."

"You really have been thinking about this," she says.

"Yup. This way you can roll out of bed, walk to class, come home for lunch if you want, stay at the library as late as you need to. You can still have your full college experience. Without all the noise on the weekends."

"I can take classes online, you know," she insists.

Why is she being so stubborn when what I'm proposing is the best solution? "But you say you prefer going in person. It helps you learn better."

"Well, yeah," she admits.

"Good. Then when we get home, we'll start looking for a place."

"Can we afford it?"

"Uh, after this weekend, we can pretty much afford anything. Within reason." Fuck, how much money did our friends make from their bets last night? "And hopefully Remy's sitting pretty today and won't miss my rent money too much."

"Why?"

I glance over at her confused expression. "He bet on me to win." I flick my gaze to the door. "I'm pretty sure our entire entourage did. Since I was the underdog, the odds were very much in their favor."

She stares at me with a blank expression.

"It doesn't matter." I kiss her forehead. "We'll be fine."

"Griff?" Hesitation wobbles in her voice. "I want to marry you..."

My heart clenches at the *but* I sense coming. Is she going to ask me to give up fighting? After last night, I'm eager for another match. But not if it means losing her.

"This weekend's a little soon..." she says.

I blow out a breath.

"I'd like to at least be able to have champagne at my own wedding."

Relieved laughter bursts out of me. "Fair enough." I grin, so stupidly happy. "Two years. We'll come back and get married here? Or do you want your rose garden wedding back home?"

Her eyes widen. "You remember I wanted to get married in a rose garden? I said that when I was like ten."

I shrug. "I don't know. It just always stuck in my head."

"Awww." She sighs and nuzzles against my neck. "Vegas. Rose garden. Anywhere you want is fine with me."

I pick up her left hand. "You need a ring, though."

She tugs on her diamond chain. "You already gave me diamonds this week."

"That I did."

She still needs a ring.

CHAPTER FIFTY-EIGHT

Molly

"Would you please stop glaring at everyone?" I say to Remy in a harsh whisper. It's awkward enough that it's just the two of us holding down a long table set for twelve people. Remy throwing murderous looks at the two gym bros a few tables over, isn't making it any better.

"I'm not glaring at *everyone*. Just those guys who keep staring at you."

I raise my eyes, watching the front door to the restaurant for anyone in our party. "I'm sure it has more to do with being Griff's girlfriend than any interest in me."

"Yeah, that's even worse." He finally flicks his gaze down and stares at the restaurant's menu. "I thought Black Ball Cap looked like someone in Magic's crew."

"Ohhh, okay." I glance at the guy wearing the black cap, but he's poking his fork into his eggs and talking to the man across from him. Nothing about either of them looks familiar to me. "You could've just said that."

"I didn't want you to worry."

I reach over and rest my hand on his forearm. "Thanks for always looking out for me."

He slowly turns his head and stares at me. "Are you okay?"

"Well, I mean you're still a meddling, overprotective pain in my butt. But I love you."

"Love you too, kid."

"Griff and I made plans to get married here in two years," I blurt.

He chokes and sputters on his coffee. "I'm sorry, what?"

I grin at him. "He wanted to do it this weekend, but I said I'd rather wait until I can have champagne at my own wedding."

He takes several slow, deep breaths before calmly answering, "Sounds like a plan. Am I invited?"

"I hope you'll walk me down the aisle."

"Yeah." He reaches over and pats my hand. "Two years. Five years. Ten years. Whenever you want, I'm happy to do it."

"Ten years," I grumble, opening my menu. "I want to be done having kids by thirty-three."

More slow, deep-breathing exercises from Remy. "Uh-huh."

"Morning, kids," Wrath bellows. He settles his heavy frame across from me.

"Where's Griff?" Trinity asks me.

"Yes." Wrath reaches for a coffee cup, turning it up for our server to fill. "Where *is* our little golden goose this morning?"

The Lost Kings really did bet on Griff to win.

I guess it would've been stupid not to.

How much money did everyone win?

Now that we have company, I can't ask Remy about it. I should've done that instead of teasing him about my future wedding. But every time I think about Griff asking me to marry him, my heart flutters so hard it might fly out of my chest.

"He had some errands to run before our big goodbye breakfast," Remy says, staring at his menu. "I think Underhill wanted to meet with him."

"We saw Underhill early this morning," Trinity says. "He was checking out."

Remy tightens his hold on the menu, denting the edges of the thick cover. "He might have had a few other things to wrap up."

"Are you guys leaving today too?" Trinity asks me.

"No. Griff didn't get to see anything while he was training." My lips curve. "And he promised me if he won, he'd take me sightseeing."

"You should go to Red Rock Canyon," Trinity suggests, resting her hand on Wrath's wrist. "We went hiking there yesterday and it was beautiful."

"Trin got some nice pictures at sunset," Wrath says.

"Oh, that might be fun." I glance at Remy, silently asking if he wants to do that.

"I gotta head back tomorrow morning. Early." Remy snorts. "It'll be a shock, going from Dawson's luxury jet to flying commercial."

"Dawson's still around," Wrath says. "Offered a ride to anyone who wants it. I'm not sure when he's leaving, though."

Remy shrugs.

I lift my gaze from my menu and catch sight of Jigsaw stealthily crouching and inching closer to Wrath's back, silent determination written all over his face. His eyes meet mine and he presses a finger to his lips.

With careful precision, he extends one arm over Wrath's shoulder, aiming to loop it around Wrath's neck in a chokehold.

Seems suicidal to me.

Lightning-quick, Wrath seizes Jigsaw's wrist in his vise-like grip without ever taking his eyes off the menu.

"What'd I tell you would happen if you tried that again?" Wrath says.

Jigsaw squirms as Wrath applies more pressure. "You'd congratulate me for my fine, stealthy skills?"

"Wrong." Wrath releases him. "Sit the fuck down."

Trinity bites her lip and shakes with quiet laughter.

Remy stares at Jigsaw like he's lost his mind.

Jigsaw rubs his wrist, but he's grinning as he sits a few chairs away from Trinity and Wrath. "Violence is our love language," he says to me.

Wrath lets out a harsh laugh. "You could say that."

Rooster and Shelby approach our table, holding hands. Neither of them attempts to choke anyone.

"Is Jiggy still alive?" Shelby stops and taps Wrath's shoulder. "I warned him not to test you today."

"Nah, we're all good," Wrath says.

Rooster pulls out the chair next to me and Shelby drops into it, tucking her dress down around her legs. "Thank ya, Logan," she says to him.

"God, you two are nauseating." Jigsaw laughs.

"Don't act ugly on our last mornin' here," Shelby scolds.

"That ship sailed a long time ago," Wrath says. "Long, long ago."

"Morning, Molly," Shelby nudges my elbow. "You and Griff get to do any sightseeing yet?"

"Not yet." I can't stop my cheeks from warming. "He was worn out and just wanted to rest yesterday."

"That did *not* sound like resting coming from the room across from mine," Jigsaw says.

Remy shoots a scowl at him.

"What?" Jigsaw holds his hands up in the air. "They could've been playing tennis."

I sit there rigid as a flagpole, about to melt under the table.

"Jiggy, don't tease Molly," Shelby warns, patting my leg.

"Apologies, Molly," Jigsaw says in the most polite and formal tone I've ever heard from him. "I enjoy fucking with your brother. But it's rude of me to involve you."

"Oh, Lordy," Shelby mutters.

"Can you *not*," Rooster says.

Jigsaw winks at me.

Wrath flips a page of the menu. "Your own sister looked pretty cozy at Remy's bar, Jiggy. I wouldn't keep antagonizing him..."

Jigsaw's cheerful expression contorts into a scowl.

Remy chuckles. "Actually, she applied for a part-time job. Thinking of hiring her. She's got a lot of *experience*."

"And she makes a mean Paloma," Shelby adds.

"She doesn't *need* a job," Jiggy growls.

Wrath picks his head up, a wide *my work here is done* grin stretched across his face.

I side-eye my brother.

A server drops a basket of muffins and other breakfast pastries at each end of our table. "Will the rest of your party be joining us soon?" he asks.

"Yes," Remy says.

Behind the server, I notice Venom and Woolly strolling into the restaurant. Venom swivels his head, slowly scanning the tables. I lift my hand, waving for them to join us.

"Hey, Molly. Remy," Venom says. He nods to Remy and throws a glance around the table. "Where's Griff?"

"He'll be here soon," Remy says.

Wrath reaches over and shakes both their hands. "Sit anywhere."

"Since you're the elder of the table, Wrath," Jigsaw picks at a cinnamon roll, a devious smile twitching at the corners of his mouth, "will you be paying for breakfast this morning?"

"Spend all your money on strippers already?" Wrath deadpans.

"Where's Ella?" Shelby asks. "I finally found someone as short as me to hang with."

"Eraser took her on a helicopter ride over the desert," Remy answers. "Not sure how long it lasts."

"Nothing says romance like taking your wife on a helicopter ride with a crash rate higher than your chance of losing your keys," Jigsaw quips.

"Well, aren't you sunshine and unicorn farts this morning," Shelby drawls.

Griff passes through the front door of the restaurant, his gaze landing on me first. His tense expression softens.

Three teen boys run up to him, holding out papers for him to sign and bringing out phones for selfies.

He's patient while he talks to each kid and poses for pictures. When he finishes, he hurries to our table.

"Hey, Muffin." He drops a quick kiss on my cheek and slides into the chair between Remy and me. He glances around the table, saying hi to everyone.

"Get what you need?" Remy asks him.

Griff bobs his head quickly, then slides his arm around my shoulders and leans in to check out my menu. "What looks good?"

I point to the French Toast À La Crème Brûlée, with vanilla cream and maple syrup. "I also kind of want to try the Lobster Eggs Benedict, but I don't know if I like Hollandaise sauce."

"Ask them to skip it or put it on the side," Shelby suggests.

"Get both. If you don't like one, I'll eat it. I'm starving," Griff says, rubbing his hand over my back.

"What were you doing?"

"Ah, Underhill wanted to talk to me for a minute," he answers quickly, turning his head.

"Did Diane find you?" Venom asks. "She wants the three of us to return as mentors for season two."

"Fuuuuck that," Griff says.

Venom cracks up. "That was my answer."

Woolly shrugs. "I might do it. Help those poor little lost pups. Warn them about the perils of reality television."

"Are they paying in money or 'exposure'?" Rooster asks.

"She didn't get that far," Venom says.

"Betcha they ain't paying squat," Shelby says. "Wouldn't surprise me one bit."

"You'd be a good mentor, Woolly," Griff says. "But I don't think they deserve you."

Woolly shrugs. "I'll see what she says."

Across the table, I briefly meet Trinity's eyes. She flashes a quick smile.

She said Underhill left this morning. So if Griff wasn't talking to him, what was he doing?

CHAPTER FIFTY-NINE

Griff

IF SOMEONE TOLD ME A YEAR AGO THAT I'D BE IN VEGAS after winning my first professional fight, with a hefty bank account, about to propose to the only woman I'd ever loved, I would've asked them what they'd been smoking.

"Where are we going?" Molly asks as I lead her out of our hotel into a waiting limo. "Oh wow. This is nice." She slides her hands over the sleek, black leather seats.

I talked her into wearing the other dress she bought, a deep shade of purple with thin shoulder straps, a plunging neckline and flared skirt that reaches her knees. Very much her style.

As the limo moves, she slips a thin purple cardigan over her shoulders.

"Are you chilly?" I ask, pulling her closer.

"A little."

"I'll keep you warm." I thread my fingers into her hair, cupping the back of her head and dropping my mouth to hers.

She curls her hand against the back of my neck, eagerly returning the kiss. She sighs a happy, contented sound into my mouth as I deepen our kiss. I rest one hand on her knee over her dress. Dying to touch her soft legs but knowing once I do, I won't be able to stop. And I'd rather not give our driver a show.

She pulls away and stares up at me with love and trust shining in her blue eyes. "Where are we going?" she asks again.

"We'll be there soon." I'm so giddy, so close to cracking like an egg and spilling everything, but I want to surprise her.

I pull her closer and bury my face against her neck, tasting her skin and breathing in the cherry-vanilla scent of her hair.

"You know how much I love you?" I murmur against her neck.

She strokes her fingers against my cheek. "Not as much as I love you." Her lips brush my forehead over the now-healed scar. "I love being here with you. Discovering somewhere new together. I want to do so many things with you. Go everywhere. Do everything with you."

How is she stealing the words from my proposal? It doesn't matter. All it means is our hearts are on the same path. This is the perfect time.

The limo slows to a stop. A few seconds later, the back door opens. The desert air simmers against my skin as we step out. I take Molly's hand.

"Mr. Royal, welcome." We're greeted by the friendly, fatherly owner of the company. When I'd spoken to him earlier today, he promised to have everything ready and perfect for us.

"Hi, Mr. Roberts. This is my girlfriend, Molly."

"Welcome. Are you ready for the best view in Vegas?"

Molly's eyes widen as she takes in the hot-air balloon basket. She clutches my hand tighter. "What is this?"

"Sunset hot-air balloon ride." I lean down and whisper in her ear. "I'm feeling on top of the world right now and I want you to feel that too."

Her expression softens. "I already feel that way with you."

"Let's check out the view from up top, then."

The balloon's vibrant colors stand out against the late afternoon sky. I squeeze her hand.

Mr. Roberts shows us around the balloon and explains the safety procedures. A lot of it amounts to *don't be a dumbass*.

The one flaw in my plan is the stranger operating the balloon watching me propose. I'd rather do it without an audience. I *could* do it back at the hotel.

No. I'm doing it now. *Stick to the plan.*

My heart's racing with a mix of excitement and nerves. I love

Molly. There's no way this can go wrong. She's my peace, everything warm and beautiful in my life. I want to spend every last one of my days on this earth with her by my side.

The ground crew scurries around, checking ropes and the burner. The efficiency and attention to detail reassures me.

We step into the gondola of the hot-air balloon. Molly's eyes shine with excitement as she curls her fingers over the edge of the basket and stares out at the landscape. "We're really doing this?" Her voice barely above a whisper.

"Yup."

Mr. Roberts gives his crew a final nod. A powerful burst of flame shoots into the balloon's envelope and we slowly rise. The ground falls away slowly.

The sun's low in the sky. Lights twinkle below us, in contrast with the sprawling desert landscape. We drift higher and higher. The only sound an occasional burst from the burner and the gentle creak of the basket. It's peaceful. I pull Molly into my arms and we take in the view.

Now, I just need to time this right.

Molly

The serenity of floating above so much beauty steals my breath. Griff's quiet, holding me tight, but he seems lost in thought.

"It's beautiful, isn't it?" I whisper.

"It's incredible." He drops his gaze to my face. "Are you happy? Did I surprise you?"

"Yes, and yes. This is amazing. I can't believe how peaceful it is compared to how chaotic it was in the city."

The pilot shifts our direction, giving us a beautiful view of the desert sunset. The sinking sun casts a golden glow over the landscape. Vibrant shades of orange, pink, and deep purple slowly transform the sky. I peek up at Griff and he meets my eyes. The corners of his mouth curve, the warm smile he only gives to me. The one that makes my heart flutter faster.

"You're not watching the sunset," I say.

"I see it." He turns slightly toward the quickly setting sun, then back to me. "You're just prettier."

He kneels on one knee, the basket gently swaying.

My heart pounds with uncertainty. "Griff?"

There's a click from the pilot's direction, but I can't take my eyes off of Griff.

"What are you doing?" I ask.

"Give me a second." His eyes close and he reaches into his pocket, pulling out a small blue velvet box. "I need to ask you something."

"Griff?" My voice rises. Tears sting my eyes.

"You make everything so much brighter, more interesting. I want to go everywhere with you. See everything. Discover new things. Enjoy the familiar. I want to spend the rest of my life with you." His words die down to an emotional rasp. "Will you be my wife, Molly? Will you marry me?" His lips tilt into my favorite teasing grin and he meets my eyes. "Two years from now. Will you marry me?"

"Yes!" I want to jump into his arms, but I don't dare rock the basket. "Yes! You know I will."

He opens the box and pulls out a ring. Sleek white gold gleams under the fading light and the large stone in the center glitters like it's plugged into an electrical socket.

"Griff?" My voice is a hushed whisper. "What...oh my God. It's beautiful."

He slides the oval bezel-set solitaire onto my ring finger. It feels substantial, full of promises for our future.

Griff stands and pulls me into a kiss. The slide of his lips against mine feels both familiar and new.

"Congratulations!" the pilot says.

How'd I forget he was there?

Laughing, I pull away but keep my hand on Griff's chest. "Thank you."

Griff wraps his arms around my waist and turns, so we're facing the view. He leans down, kisses my neck, and whispers in my ear, "I want to make you happy every day."

"You already do."

Our balloon descends, the city lights becoming brighter before we veer toward the desert. The pilot lands smoothly and points out a small table with a bucket and container sitting on top.

"Thank you," Griff says to the pilot as we step out of the basket. The pilot hands him something and then Griff leads me to the table.

He picks up the chilled glass bottle. "It's sparkling cider," he assures me.

"Oh!" I lean in closer. "I wasn't going to tell anyone if it wasn't."

He chuckles and pops the top, pouring it into two champagne flutes and handing one to me. "To building a lifetime of memories just like this," I say.

"To building a life together," he adds.

We clink our glasses together and sip the sweet, bubbly cider.

It's still too dark to inspect my ring, but the weight of it on my finger reminds me of all it symbolizes.

"Oh, here." Griff picks up a square white box on the table and peels the lid back, revealing six plump strawberries drenched in dark and white chocolate.

My mouth waters. "They look so good." I pluck the smallest one out of the box and carefully take a bite. Strawberry juice runs down my chin and Griff swoops closer, kissing it away.

Laughing, I feed him the other half of the strawberry. My fingers curl in his T-shirt and I tug him closer to kiss me. The sparkling of my ring catches my eye. "It's so pretty. How'd you know I'd love it so much?"

"I was hoping I got it right." He takes my hand, admiring the symbol of his promise to me. "Did you see the little hidden halo of diamonds under the stone? I thought that was so cool."

"What? No! Is that why it's so extra sparkly?"

He nods, a pleased gleam in his eyes.

"Is this what you were doing this morning?" I ask, realization setting in.

He gives me a sheepish smile. "Yes. I'm shocked Remy didn't spill it."

My jaw drops. "You told him?"

He tilts his head. "Yeah, I did." He holds his hands up. "I didn't *ask* his permission. But yeah, I told him what I was planning."

My heart squeezes in the best way. "This morning, I told him we were planning to get married in two years and I thought he was going to have a heart attack at first. But he seemed to recover awfully fast. Now I know why."

Griff shakes his head like he's still processing tonight. "I'm going to be your husband," he says with the sweetest, goofiest grin on his face.

"Yes, you are." I loop my arms around his neck and pull him down for more kisses. "And I'm going to be your wife."

"I'll protect you and love you for the rest of my life, Muffin."

"I know you will. I love you so much." I trail my lips along his jaw. "I may not have your fists or muscles." I squeeze his bicep. "But I'll always have your back."

"That's all I need." He touches his lips to mine to seal our deal. "You and me against the world."

AFTERWORD

Thank you so much for reading Repairing the Wreckage! I hope you loved reading it as much as I enjoyed writing it.

Griff and Molly's story has been such a long time coming for me and now that it's finished, I find myself incredibly sad. So don't be surprised if I have something more for them in the future. Mr. Lake keeps reminding me that they'll be a large part of Remy's book, but you know me, I can't help revisiting the characters I absolutely adore. Griff and Molly are so young, you never know what trouble they'll get into in the future!

xo,

Autumn